PRAISE FOR PATRICIA WADDELL, FINALIST FOR *AFFAIRE DE COEUR*'S BEST UP-AND-COMING AUTHOR!

"Patricia Waddell and futuristic romance are a perfect, irresistible fit!"
—Mary Balogh, *USA Today* bestselling author

"A talented new author. Be prepared to step into another world!"
—Patricia Rice, *New York Times* bestselling author

"Patricia Waddell is a master storyteller. . . . Her characters are interesting; her tales intrigue and fascinate."
—*Affaire de Coeur*

"Don't miss this rising new author!"
—Heather Graham, *New York Times* bestselling author

"Patricia Waddell is quite a superb storyteller! She paints some fantastic word pictures that . . . capture your imagination immediately!"
—*The Belles and Beaux of Romance*

"MY BODY TO PLEASURE"

"There is an ancient saying that promises are made to be broken," Logan remarked nonchalantly.

"Not on Nubria," Zara replied. "A promise is a sacred pledge to us. To break it or dishonor it is unthinkable."

Despite the crush of people, Logan kept his voice pitched low so that only Zara heard his reply. "Then I can expect your wedding vows to be consummated with enthusiasm, my lady. I look forward to the night ahead. I have never had a female give a sacred vow to pleasure me."

Zara didn't blush this time. Her husband's arrogance was getting out of hand. She was after all a queen, and her royal duties had often included putting a prideful male in his place, especially one who had no understanding of Nubrian tradition.

"My vows said nothing of your pleasure, my lord. You should have listened more carefully." Her voice a bare whisper, Zara repeated what she had said standing by the sacred stone altar. "*My* body to pleasure, *my* heart to protect, *my* spirit to cherish."

Logan's laughter was not the response she expected. He put back his head and roared, reminding her of the wild animals that lived in the mountains to the north. When he finally spoke it was to best Zara at her own game. His voice was smooth, male velvet. "A command I will gladly obey, fair lady. Before Nubria's twin moons fade into a single sun, your body will know the pleasure only a man can give it."

Whispers
in the
Stars

PATRICIA
WADDELL

LOVE SPELL NEW YORK CITY

LOVE SPELL®

October 2002

Published by

Dorchester Publishing Co., Inc.
276 Fifth Avenue
New York, NY 10001

ISBN 0-505-52522-4

Printed in the United States of America.

Visit us on the web at www.dorchesterpub.com.

Whispers in the Stars

Chapter One

The Planet Nubria

Silence filled the room as Zara moved to the window and looked out at the soldiers gathering just beyond the castle gate. Her bridegroom was among the mass of black and red uniforms that identified the Galactic Guard, although she had no idea what he looked like. All she knew was that she was to marry before Nubria's twin moons graced the night sky.

"I will be by your side, my lady."

Zara turned to the gangly servant. Tolman was three times her age and countless times wiser in the way of things. His face was wrinkled, his eyes clear, seeing people for what they were rather than what they pretended to be. His hair was a gray wisp of soft down, growing thinner by the year, but his devotion and loyalty were beyond question.

"I will always have need of your friendship," Zara replied. Moving away from the window, she took Tolman's slender hand and gave it a hard squeeze. "Come," she

1

said. "We must prepare a royal greeting for my future husband. The waiting is finally over."

The waiting had been going on for three lunar cycles, ever since a rebel ship had crashed on Nubria and Zara had given its survivors medical aide and sanctuary. Located in the eastern quadrant and away from the fighting that had spread throughout most of the galaxy since the rebel uprising five years earlier, Nubria had been able to maintain a certain degree of neutrality during the conflict. Zara's actions in refusing to relinquish the rebels to the Unity Council had stripped her world of its impartiality, and now that the war was over, she would pay a price for her defiance. Nubria would have a male monarch for the first time in its history, and Zara would have a husband, whether she wanted one or not.

The servants waited in the grand hall. All eyes turned to their mistress as Zara entered the room, the hem of her purple gown lightly touching the white stone floor beneath her sandaled feet. The room was quiet except for the sound of people breathing and the occasional rub of clothing against skin as someone shifted his weight in the tense silence. The news of her marriage to the unnamed Guardian commander hung in the air like a dreaded prophecy.

Zara could sense the nervousness of her people. But then, she'd always been able to sense them, their needs, their dreams, their pain and their joy. Her unique insight was both a blessing and a curse. It was the reason she had inherited the throne. Nubria's crown was passed down from mother to daughter the same way the gift was passed down. Countless generations of women had sat on the dais of Nubria, each of them having the exceptional ability to sense unspoken things, to feel the past and the present as though it were happening at that very moment, to understand what others could barely comprehend.

The gift was as much a part of Zara as her violet-blue

eyes and silver hair. She couldn't recall a time when it didn't exist, nor could she imagine herself without it. It was a part of her soul, this sharing of invisible things, this link to the elements of the universe, the sensing of harmony and discord.

Most people accepted the physical world without question, but Zara knew there was another world, another dimension where physical met spiritual, a dimension that went beyond touch and sight and sound, a dimension where feelings were tangible things.

It was the faith of her people, an ancient faith that was older than recorded history. No one knew when the first believers had settled on Nubria. It didn't matter. The daughters of Nubria were as strong in their faith now as they had been then, and Zara was one of the strongest. As she walked into the grand hall, she prayed that her dedication would remain secure. Her people needed her now more than ever.

"A feast will be prepared," she announced. "See that the officers are properly housed and the men-at-arms well fed. I want no embarrassment suffered in Nubria's name. This is our home. We will display it proudly."

No one moved. It was as if they couldn't believe their ears. Their lady, their beloved queen, was welcoming the Galactic Guard with open arms. A soft murmur rippled through the room as the servants quietly voiced their surprise. Surely Lady Zara, couldn't be happy about the upcoming marriage? The man was an outsider, a non-believer; how could he possibly rule in their lady's place? It was unthinkable.

"Go, there is work to be done." A sharp clap of Tolman's hands sent the servants scurrying in all directions.

"They will come to understand," he said to Zara. "It will take time."

"Time," Zara mumbled. "If I only had more of it, perhaps I could think of a way to avoid the vows I will be forced to speak at evening tide."

"Perhaps your future husband will be weary of war and anxious to find the peace our world can offer him," Tolman suggested.

"Perhaps," Zara said, sounding skeptical. "I know nothing of the man, except that he is a warrior and has sworn allegiance to the Council. He will share my throne and my bed, but I fear he will never share my heart or the hearts of my people."

"Can you sense this about him?" Tolman asked.

Zara gave him a disgruntled look. "I can sense nothing about him," she admitted reluctantly. "You would think that I could feel his link already, knowing that he will be my husband, but it evades me."

"He is an outsider," Tolman reminded her. "War can hardened a man's heart. Time will soften it, and he will come to appreciate that which he has been given."

"I pray your words ring true," Zara replied, hiding her apprehension. If she was to keep the peace, she had to appear at peace with her husband. No one, not even Tolman, could know that inside she trembled with fear.

The military dispute that had turned into a planetary rebellion and then into a full-fledged revolution was secondary to her reasons for harboring the rebels. As long as there were men of ambition and government, there would be wars. As queen she had a responsibility to maintain the peace that had finally been reached after years of war. As a priestess of her people's faith, she had a responsibility to keep the harmony of their world intact. As a woman, she would carry the burden of a loveless marriage. The weight of that burden was already beginning to affect her. Zara could feel the elements straining against each other as her own personal harmony rippled with the shock of knowing that her first lover would be a total stranger, a man sent by the Unity Council to ferret out the whereabouts of the rebels she was still hiding.

Tucking her hopes and dreams away for the moment, Zara excused Tolman, then went to her chamber. The guards were gathering for a grand entrance through the castle gate and Zara knew she had only a few minutes to prepare herself. Content with her purple dress, embroidered with gold and silver thread at the cuffs and hem, Zara brushed her waist-length hair until it crackled with energy. She had refused the services of her chambermaid, wanting what little privacy she could find, knowing it would be her last.

"My lady?" The voice and a light tap on the door interrupted Zara's thoughts.

"Come," she replied, knowing that Nessa was even more anxious than Tolman. The old woman had been her teacher, a mentor of the ancient rites. Like Tolman, Nessa served the queen of Nubria with unwavering loyalty and devotion.

The door opened and Zara's unofficial adviser stepped inside, her shoulders bent with age, her face withered and wrinkled. Her robe was a dull gray and unadorned, but one only had to look into Nessa's eyes to know that this woman held more power in her mind than most warriors held in the muscles of their sword arm. Bright, pale eyes looked at the world with a clarity of purpose and a childlike sense of wonder that seemed contradictory at first glance.

"The bridegroom has arrived," Nessa said, smiling. "Can you sense him yet?"

"No," Zara confessed. "I feel nothing."

The old woman shook her head. "That's because you've forgotten the most important lesson. You can't force the link, my lady. You must let it come to you. His soul will find yours. All you have to do is open your mind. Relax and try again."

"There isn't time," Zara told her.

"There is always time for what must be done," Nessa said patiently. "Relax and try again. The bridegroom will wait for his bride."

Zara didn't need to be reminded that the day was

quickly passing and soon she would cease being a solitary queen and become the consort of a king, a partner to the throne, no longer alone but bound to a stranger.

Weeks of worry had exhausted her fears of the wedding night to come. There was so much more to contemplate than the loss of her virginity. That would take mere moments, while her future lay ahead of her, countless years married to a man who had accepted his commission from the Council. Or was it a reward? Had the warrior earned the kingship of Nubria by winning battles? What had lured him to accept the Council's petition? Or like she, was he bound by the unwritten laws of duty and obligation?

She had so many questions, and few answers.

Once again Zara walked to the window and looked outside. The soldiers had multiplied in number, making her wonder if the Council hadn't dispatched the entire army to subdue one female rebel. Closing her eyes, Zara drew in a long deep breath, willing her thoughts to calm and her body to relax.

She struggled through the emotions swirling around her; a castle full of confused servants, a courtyard filled with stiff-minded soldiers, a world of anxious souls, until she found her inner self. A sigh of relief passed her lips as she made the journey from the physical realm into the domain of the spirit, a world where images wavered like smoke on the horizon and sounds echoed like soft voices in a canyon. Gradually the smoke faded and the echoes died and there was only the peace of knowing she was home within herself. Trained in the ancient rituals since childhood, Zara instinctively focused all her concentration inward, sorting through her thoughts and fears one by one.

Like a circle, having no beginning and no end, Zara let the power of the sacred place move around her, engulfing her in an aura of invisible energy, absorbing her body and mind, her heart and her spirit, until there was nothing but her inner self and the gift, entwined so closely together that they ceased being separate things and became one.

The melting of her thoughts with the elements of the universe was so sweet, so uniquely peaceful that for a moment she feared she would lose herself completely. In that instant, in that minuscule second of time, Zara sensed the man waiting just beyond the castle gate. The merging of their minds was as brief as a heartbeat, but she felt it as keenly as a bolt of lightning slicing through her body.

Her eyes opened and her pulse raced. She looked at Nessa, unsure what to say.

"You found him." Nessa smiled.

Zara nodded. "His strength was overpowering," she replied shakily. "I felt as if I would be crushed under the weight of his spirit. Do all warriors have such strong thoughts?"

"Some," Nessa told her. "You speak nothing of evil."

"I felt no evil," Zara said, still trembling from the experience. Nothing in her spiritual journeys had prepared her for what she'd just sensed. It had been more physical than mental, a quickening of her body that still had strange sensations swirling inside her. "Only strength of purpose and . . ."

"And what?"

Zara shook her head. "I'm not sure. I've never felt it before, so I can't give it a name. It took my breath for a moment."

Nessa shrugged her shoulders. "Your spirit is as strong as his. Excellent."

Zara wanted to ask her teacher a thousand questions, but time wouldn't permit it. The bells in the prayer tower struck the hour. It was time to meet her warrior face-to-face.

* * *

Logan was talking to his second in command when the strange feeling assaulted him. For a scant second he felt as though someone had invaded his body. The tingling sensation vanished as quickly as it had arrived. He stopped in mid-sentence to look around him. The castle walls stood tall and straight before him, their white stones as smooth as the sunshine heating the meadow where his men waited impatiently to march inside the gates and get on with the reclaiming of Nubria. The wind carried only the sound of soldiers talking and the scent of wild-flowers.

"Is something amiss?" the officer standing next to Logan asked. Maddock was a big man, thick about the chest and shoulders, with chestnut hair and brooding dark eyes. Ten years Logan's senior, he was skilled with a sword and admittedly skeptical of anyone who didn't wear a Guardian uniform.

"Nothing I can name," Logan answered. "Just a feeling."

"I trust your instincts as much as I trust your sword arm," Maddock said. "Do you expect trouble once we're inside?"

"No more trouble than any man would expect from a woman."

Maddock laughed. "I hear that Lady Zara is as beautiful as she is rebellious."

"I care not what she looks like," Logan told him. "The Council wants the last of the rebels found and brought to justice."

"The Council petitioned more than a search party," Maddock reminded him. "What does it feel like to be king?"

"Ask me after I've met my queen," Logan retorted.

The sound of bells drew their attention. The tower had been set into the outer wall of the royal palace and the metallic melody that drifted on the wind sent another unexplainable shiver up and down Logan's spine. He couldn't explain it any more than he could explain the peculiar sensation that had invaded his senses a moment earlier.

"They have strange ways here," Maddock remarked. "There isn't a guard in sight and our scanners didn't pick up any weapons."

Logan had been briefed on Nubrian customs before leaving his home on Melya Four. Like Maddock, he found the ways of Nubria unsettling. The planet had maintained political neutrality for several thousand years. Its inhabitants were farmers and artisans, well known for their skills with stone and the soft metals that were mined in the mountains of the northern continent. Like the men under his command, Logan had stood on the observation deck of the transport ship and stared in awe at the purple clouds that shrouded the planet. Even now with the sun in full force, the clouds looked like amethyst puffs of smoke drifting against a pale sky. The land was full of color, as well. The trees hung heavy with lush green leaves and the meadow was dotted with brilliant blue and gold flowers. Sweeping hills and flourishing valleys were laced with crystal-clear streams and lakes that gleamed in the sunlight.

Nubria was a beautiful planet, ruled by a beautiful woman.

Lady Zara, his bride, was the only female sovereign in the galaxy. Nubria was a matriarchal society and had been since its foundation. The thought of a woman dictating laws and formulating government policy was as foreign to Logan's way of thinking as wings were to fish, but once the gates were opened and Logan claimed his bride, the matriarchal tradition would end. Nubria's new king would be a soldier, trained to fight and sworn to defend the Union.

Unlike the pilots of the Galactic Fleet, who fought in sleek star jets, Galactic Guards were true soldiers, trained to meet their enemies in hand-to-hand combat. They had never been defeated. Their skills were legendary and their reputation as fearless fighters well deserved. Logan's soul was a warrior's soul and his sword was stained with the blood of his enemies. Soon he would be a king and a husband.

He knew nothing about being a king and even less about being a husband, but the lack of knowledge didn't worry Logan. He was an honest man, fair in his judgment of others and patient with the truth. Ruling a planet wasn't that different from commanding a legion of men. He'd wed his bride, consummate the marriage, and assume the throne. Once he was in control, he'd find the rebels, turn them over to the Council, then begin building Nubria's first army.

The Council wanted the eastern borders enforced and the trade routes protected. They wanted to make their presence known to anyone outside the Union who thought their treasury drained and their army vulnerable. Watchtowers would be constructed and star cruisers dispatched to patrol the borders. Logan would command the regiment of men assigned to the east sector.

As he scanned the horizon for the possibility of opposition from the Nubrians, who disliked the idea of having their virgin queen wed to an outsider, Logan wondered what had prompted the Council to choose him. The war had gained him the rank of Commander, but he'd done nothing to earn a throne. He supposed his reputation with women might have something to do with his selection. Maddock had teasingly suggested that his commanding officer could persuade any female to give up her secrets.

The thought had merit, since he rarely had to do more than look at a woman to gain her favor. Still, Logan didn't like the idea of trickery. He hoped the punishment of forfeiting her throne would be enough to gain Lady Zara's cooperation. If not, Logan would do what he had to do. The rebellion was over. His job was to make sure its fire wasn't rekindled.

"Are the men in place?' Logan looked toward the castle gate. The structure was two stories high and made of sturdy dark wood. He couldn't read the exotic words engraved in the timber, but he assumed they were a welcome. Nubria had no enemies, or at least it hadn't had any enemies until its queen defied the Council and began harboring rebels.

"They're ready," his second in command replied. "Though I doubt they'll be needed. The planet's as docile as a well-fed garla."

Logan smiled. Garlas were known for their insatiable appetites and their preference for sleeping away the winter. They ate day and night as the colder season approached. With bellies that sagged like overstuffed pockets, they dug deep burrows, then crawled inside and slept for months on end, until the ground thawed and it was time to eat again.

"Docile or not, I want the men on guard," Logan replied. "The rebels haven't been found. Until they are, we stay on alert."

Maddock nodded in agreement, but his dark eyes gleamed with mischief. "If the lady is as tame as her planet, you're in for a boring wedding night."

"I doubt the lady is tame," Logan remarked. "It takes spirit to defy the Council."

"Spirit or stupidity," Maddock said, shrugging. "Time will tell."

Logan didn't reply. The sound of the castle gates being opened drew his attention.

The soldiers under Logan's command ceased their talking and assumed a battle stance, their hands resting on the hilts of their swords, their feet braced slightly apart, their eyes focused on the wide gates that were slowly opening to reveal the inner courtyard surrounding Lady Zara's private citadel. Overhead, mauve-colored clouds drifted across the face of a golden sun, casting a rainbow of colorful shadows on the white stones of the elaborate palace.

As the gates opened wide to allow them entry, Logan straightened to his full height, his obsidian eyes taking in the details of his new home. The interior courtyard was lined with flowers and neatly trimmed scrubs. Large urns, taller than most men and decorated with brightly colored depictions of the planet's exotic animal life, bordered a wide stone staircase that led to the main entry of the palace. Servants dressed in white and blue robes stood in front of the urns, marking the path to Logan's future wife.

The people of Nubria were as handsome as the planet they called home. Slight of build with varying hair color and pale eyes, their heads were held high as Logan marched into the courtyard. His men followed in rank behind him, their black and red uniforms alien attire in a world that had never found it necessary to form an army in its own defense. A thin man, wearing a loose-fitting blue robe adorned with silver thread about the hem, stepped forward.

"I am Tolman," he announced. "Our lady is waiting to greet you."

Logan appraised the elderly man with skeptical eyes. His gray hair had thinned to the point of being almost nonexistent, his hands twisted with age, but his voice was strong. Its respectful tone earned him a curt nod from Logan. "Take me to her."

Tolman turned and led the way into the palace. Logan noticed the anxious gazes he and his men drew from the servants, yet no words were spoken. Maddock followed with a small entourage of officers, while the bulk of Logan's men remained in the courtyard, silent but alert to any danger.

The interior of the palace was as pleasant as the outside. Wide corridors tiled in small blocks of white stone echoed the sharp click of Logan's military boots. The walls were adorned with colorful murals, paintings of the pastoral lifestyle of the planet's inhabitants. Baskets of flowers were suspended from the vaulted ceilings, their fragrant blossoms perfuming the air. It was a drastic change from the military barracks Logan had called home for most of his life.

When they reached a set of double doors, inlaid with gold, Tolman stopped and turned to look up at the large Galactic Guard who would become the king of Nubria before the prayer bells marked the end of the day. "Lady Zara is in the throne hall. The room is the ancient altar of our faith. I would ask that your weapons be left here."

"My sword is always at my side," Logan told him. "Open the door."

Chapter Two

Zara stood beside the stone altar that had once lain in an open field where ancient pilgrims had come to pray and offer sacrifices of dried herbs and fresh-picked flowers. Although her outward countenance didn't change as the doors opened to reveal a tall man wearing a Guard's uniform, on the inside Zara felt her heart race.

Tall, powerfully built, with wide shoulders and long limbs, the Commander of the Galactic Guard moved toward her. The throne room was long and narrow, with slender arched windows that allowed sunlight to fill the hall. As the man marched toward her, Zara forced herself to smile.

She looked into the face of a stranger who had but one purpose in life—winning whatever battles came his way. His eyes were as dark as a starless night, his face angular, his mouth drawn into a tight line that said he rarely smiled, if ever. His black hair was pulled back and secured with a leather thong at the base of his neck. His uniform boasted the gold braid of a high-ranking Galactic officer and a sword, sheathed in a black leather scabbard, hung from his waist.

A surety of power and confidence radiated from him like heat from a flame, and Zara knew now why the link she'd established a few moments ago had stopped her heart. Her future husband was a proud man, strong of purpose and disciplined by the harsh realities of war. His training showed in every movement of his body, in the hard angle of his jaw, and in the emotionless depth of his midnight eyes. He was a warrior, simple and true, and Zara found herself mesmerized by his strength the same way she was lured to the balcony just before a storm. The power of the universe was housed in this man's body, the same way it was housed in storm clouds moving inland from the sea.

The discovery surprised her, but only for a moment. She regained her composure, raising her chin as she looked up at the stranger who would soon be her husband.

"Welcome to Nubria, my lord," she said, still not knowing his name. "I am Lady Zara. May my home and my people serve you with honor."

Logan said nothing; he was too busy absorbing the beauty of the young woman standing before him. *By the stars, she's the most beautiful creature I've ever seen. Hair like spun moonlight and eyes like* . . . He'd never seen eyes that particular color, blue but not really blue. Then he realized that they matched the amethyst clouds that cloaked the planet. Violet eyes. Eyes that made a man think of pleasure and passion. Tempting eyes. Bewitching eyes.

His gaze dropped away from her face, taking in the feminine curves of her body. A deep purple dress molded her form, accentuating the soft swell of her breasts and the narrow width of her waist before the shimmering fabric flared out around her hips and fell to the floor. Her posture was regal, her back straight, her shoulders squared.

His future wife might be a rebel, but she was certainly the most beautiful one he'd ever encountered.

"I am Commander Logan," he said, his voice ringing with authority. His tone had its desired effect and he sensed Maddock's eyes, along with the gazes of the other officers, leaving Lady Zara's lovely face and seeking something else to focus upon. Like the throne of Nubria, its queen now belonged to their commanding officer.

Logan. Zara rolled the name around in her mind. It was a blunt name, like the man, but when she said it aloud, her voice softened its sound as the people of Nubria prayed their queen would soften his warrior heart.

"Welcome, Lord Logan," she said. "My people have prepared a feast. Would you and your men enjoy a glass of wine before the food is served?"

"My men will relax and enjoy themselves after the wedding ceremony," Logan said, surprised by his own impatience. After seeing his bride, he found himself eager to make her a wife. Too anxious. It was taking all his self-control to keep from showing just how much the sight and sound of her was affecting his body. "Where is the magistrate?"

Zara was tempted to chide him for insulting her hospitality, but she managed to leash her tongue before it could form the words. The man was an outsider. He knew nothing of their customs, so his rude behavior would have to be tolerated. For the moment. Once the formalities of their wedding were behind them, she would begin his education. The first lesson would be a reminder that she might have to share her throne, but she had no intentions of forfeiting it completely.

"Marriages are not legal contracts on Nubria," she informed him. "The joining of a man and a woman is a spiritual ritual, honored by our sacred rights and accepted by all believers."

Logan had dismissed the political tutor before he'd gotten around to Nubria's strange religious customs. He had little use for spiritual beliefs centered around invisible gods. He trusted his sword and his second in command, nothing else. "Then call the priest," he replied. "The Council demands our marriage before the last rays of sunlight fade from the sky."

Zara felt her temper bristling under the harshness of his words. She found apologies difficult, and she would owe this man and his officers several if she unleashed her displeasure and said what was on her mind. Logan's request for a priest hadn't been a request at all, but a blatant order, which he expected her to obey without hesitation. *The man has a lot to learn,* Zara thought. *And our marriage will give me a lifetime to teach him.*

"Tolman." She turned to the servant who had lived within the palace walls since her birth. "Summon Nessa; she will need to witness the rites."

"As you wish, my lady," Tolman replied, amazed by his lady's restraint. Commander Logan hadn't been treated to a dose of the queen's temper. Yet. When the warrior finally discovered his wife's true disposition, Tolman prayed he'd be far away.

The servants standing at the far end of the room shifted restlessly as Tolman went in search of the old woman called Nessa. The Galactic Commander had not impressed them or their queen with his attitude, and they were waiting for Nessa's sharp tongue to cut into his arrogance the way she frequently sliced away the rudeness of a servant who had forgotten his place. While the servants waited to present a meal to their new king, the queen allowed herself a moment to study the other men in the room.

Like their commander, the Galactic Guards stood strong and proud in the ancient hall where queens had ruled for generations. Zara looked at the man standing slightly to Logan's right and a few feet behind him. She sensed that the two men were friends, bound by mutual respect and honor.

"Do you have one among you who can stand in witness to your oath?" she asked Logan. "Our law requires the rite of marriage to be documented by friends and family."

"Maddock, my second in command, will stand at my side," Logan told her.

He was becoming intensely curious about the beautiful young woman he'd soon take as his wife. Her magnificent eyes told him nothing of her thoughts, yet logic told him that she had to be afraid. She was being forced to marry, to forsake her throne, yet she showed no signs of apprehension or regret. The afternoon sunlight, streaming through the tall windows, formed an aura about her, making her pale hair shimmer with life and her eyes sparkle like precious gems. When she moved, the soft fabric of her gown moved with her, making Logan think of the flowers in the meadows, moving in rhythm to the wind. The same way he wanted her body moving in rhythm to his, arching to meet him when he thrust deep inside her.

Zara felt her senses rebelling under the stress of waiting and watching the silent warrior. He was a big man, but his size didn't intimidate her. She wished she could say the same thing about his spirit. The small sampling she'd had when she'd linked with him earlier was still vibrating inside her mind—and her heart. She'd been linking with people all her life, sensing their moods, but she'd never encountered anyone like the man she would soon wed. The strange, unexplainable sensation she'd felt when she'd touched his thoughts was as fragile as a dream, yet she still felt it, lingering in her mind and her body.

Logan turned as the door opened and an old woman, dressed in a dull gray robe and leather sandals, entered the grand hall. She walked to where Zara was standing, not bothering to cast him or his men so much as a glance as she approached the stone altar.

18

"He is a nonbeliever," Nessa announced, looking at Zara but speaking to everyone in the room. "The rites cannot be performed until his body and mind are purified."

"You think to postpone the wedding," Logan said harshly.

The old woman turned to look at him. Logan met her unwavering gaze the same way he'd meet the fierce stare of an enemy. Warrior and withered old woman stared at each other for a long moment. The tension in the hall increased tenfold. The soldiers, who answered to no one but Logan, reached for their swords, while the servants, devoted to their mistress, sucked in their breath and held it. Tolman closed his eyes and mumbled an ancient prayer.

Zara stood unmoving, her eyes focused on the strange warrior who had suddenly become the center of her life. Logan had no idea what the marriage rites involved, but Zara did.

Before they left the hall, bound by ceremony, they would once again share what they had shared earlier in the day. They would link, mind to mind, thought to thought. Zara prayed that she could endure the contact without surrendering completely. If she allowed her husband to discover the pathway to her inner self, he could use it to find the rebels.

"Your weapons insult our queen," Nessa said, undaunted by the large man who would soon demand her allegiance. "There is no danger within these walls, and no vows of commitment can be spoken with sincerity while a sword dangles at your side. Remove it before you approach the altar."

Maddock took a step forward, but Logan stopped him with a glance. "Who are you?" he asked, hiding his amusement at the old woman's behavior. Whoever she was, she had lived long enough not to fear death. He would be within his rights to strike her down.

19

"I am called Nessa," she told him. "I serve Lady Zara, as I served her mother and her mother's mother."

The devotion in the old woman's voice was clear for all to hear. Logan's actions said he respected her loyalty. He unsheathed his sword and handed it to Maddock.

"Get the words said," Logan demanded impatiently. "My men are weary from travel."

Nessa laughed. The unexpected sound crackled like flames on a cold night. "Impatience can be a burden, my lord. Shed it before you speak the vows of commitment. The ceremony will demand all your concentration."

As she spoke, Nessa reached into a small wooden chest beside the altar and withdrew a blood red cloth. Like the queen's dress, it shimmered in the light. She draped it over the altar while Logan watched, unsure of what was expected of him but determined to get the religious ceremony behind him so he could get on with the more pleasing aspects of being married. His bride stood quietly, her gaze serene, her features more pleasing with each glance Logan cast in her direction.

Next came a tall silver goblet and a small dagger. The blade wasn't long enough to earn more than a moment of Logan's interest, but he was quickly becoming intrigued by the implements of the upcoming ceremony. The jeweled handle of the dagger gleamed like purple fire in the afternoon light and he realized the stones were the same color as Lady Zara's eyes.

Under the watchful eye of Maddock and his other officers, Nessa accepted a crystal decanter from Tolman. She lifted it toward the ceiling, mumbling words that none of the outsiders understood, before filling the goblet with water.

"Step closer," she instructed Logan. "Remove your jacket. The purification ritual requires the flesh over your heart to be exposed."

Logan moved toward the altar, shedding his uniform tunic with quick movements that said he was impatient to get things done. Tossing the garment to Maddock, he stood on the opposite side of the draped stone, facing his bride.

Zara saw the long scar that ran from his upper torso, slicing diagonally across his chest. She closed her eyes for a brief moment, trying to imagine the pain he must have felt when the wound was inflicted. Her husband was a beautiful man, with rippling muscles and a thick carpet of dark hair covering his upper chest, but she refused to let herself think of the physical joining that would take place later. Nessa had warned Logan that the ceremony would demand all his concentration. It would require even more of Zara. She would have to form the link, the connection that would allow her thoughts to merge with his. When the time came, she had to be ready.

Galactic Guards and servants alike watched as the old woman bathed Logan's upper body with water from the silver goblet. While Nessa's hands rubbed a soft cloth over his chest, Logan caught Lady Zara's gaze and held it. The lustrous glow of her violet eyes was more seductive than warm wine. Logan knew the old woman, standing so close she could see his response, was no doubt smiling to herself. Still, he couldn't control his body, not enough to conceal what Nubria's lovely queen called forth. He was hot and hard and more than ready for a wedding night, if he could survive the waiting.

"My lady will speak the words slowly, so that you can repeat them," Nessa told him, finally stepping back and dropping the cloth into a small basket at the base of the stone altar. "The joining will cause you no pain, although I am told it can be uncomfortable for a nonbeliever. Relax your body and open your mind to the power of the universe," she instructed him in a soft whisper. "All will be well."

Logan didn't reply, but his fierce glance spoke of his impatience with spiritual things. The old woman smiled

21

before leaving the altar. She stood beside Tolman and the other servants.

Zara closed her eyes, willing her strength of faith to return to her, the same strength that had allowed her to defy the Council, knowing the consequences. When she opened them, Logan was staring at her, his eyes shouting a dark warning that any trickery on her part would be rewarded swiftly and mercilessly.

Hands extended in front of her, palms up, Zara began repeating the ancient chant. The words would mean nothing to the man for whom they were spoken, but she said them with conviction, understanding their meaning, accepting the link they would form, the unbreakable bond between man and woman.

Logan listened to the soft cadence of Lady Zara's voice. With every word she spoke, he felt her presence more surely than he felt the beating of his own heart. His eyes narrowed in suspicion when she picked up the small jeweled dagger. Her slender fingers stroked the blade delicately, making his body tighten with desire. He longed to stroke her skin just as carefully, to tease her nipples with his fingertips and tongue until they hardened into tiny pink pearls.

Once again, Zara turned her mind inward, seeking the gift that would allow her to overcome the distracting sights and sounds around her. Although her eyes remained open, she began to lose sight of the warrior, bared to the waist, standing so proudly across the altar from her. Looking into her own heart, she called upon the powers of the ancient gods, asking them for the courage to face an uncertain future, needing their blessing, wanting it for herself and for her people. Holding the jeweled dagger in front of her, blade up, Zara pricked the index finger of her left hand. Blood oozed from the tiny wound.

Logan didn't move as she stepped around the altar and reached out her hand. When she placed her bloody fingertip on his bare chest, he remained as still as stone.

Once again Zara's voice lifted in a musical chant that filled the large room. Logan could feel the blood, her blood, warm and wet against his skin as she drew a circle on the left side of his chest, over his heart. She touched his naked skin as delicately as she'd touched the dagger's silver blade, yet Logan felt the caress as surely as he'd felt the lance that had left him scarred after a rebel attack. He looked down, away from the violet eyes that could easily capture a man in a female trap. The sleeve of Zara's gown had dropped to her elbow, revealing the slender form of her wrist and lower arm. The gold and silver threads that adorned the garment's cuffs gleamed in the sunlight streaming through the high, arched windows. She was a woman full grown, but dainty in build, with no more muscles than a sparrow perched on a tree limb, yet Logan could sense her strength. The strength of a woman who ruled an entire planet.

He'd be wise to put aside his sexual curiosity and focus on the lady's true purpose. She was still hiding the rebels, giving them sanctuary in spite of the Council's repeated demands that they be turned over for trial. Despite Maddock's earlier comparison, Logan knew his bride was far from docile. Nor was she stupid. She was as smart as the tiny dagger was sharp, and he'd be a fool to forget it for one moment. Still, her touch was soothing, her blood warm against his skin, and her scent intriguing. Wildflowers and herbs and woman, a tempting combination. As tempting as her unusual eyes and the womanly curves he would soon have the right to caress.

Zara felt more than sensed the change in Logan. His body stiffened slightly as her fingertip continued tracing the small red circle of blood on his chest. Dark, crisp hair absorbed the blood, matting under her touch, as she forced her sight to remain inward, her mind centered on the prayer she was offering to the ancient gods. Her future, the future of the world she ruled, the future of rebel lives, demanded her ability to use the gift the gods had given her to reach beyond this man's flesh and touch his heart. A warrior's heart, cold and distrusting, hardened by war and death.

Zara's voice changed, her tone turning into a whisper, as words as old as time itself floated toward the ceiling. Logan wondered if the words were meant to bewitch him. He found them strangely beautiful, or was it the woman's voice that teased his nerves and made his hands itch to reach out and touch her? Another circle was drawn on his chest before her fingertip left him. He looked into her eyes, unable to discern what she was thinking or feeling.

Most women wore their thoughts like bright garments for everyone to see. But this woman was different. Her eyes glowed with life, yet they told him nothing.

The chanting stopped as Zara lay her open palm against him, over the bloody circle she had drawn on his chest. Once again, Logan could feel her heat. It seemed to brand him, to sink beneath his skin like silky fire and touch him on the inside as well as the outside.

"I, Zara of Nubria, queen of the ancient order and priestess of the holy code, declare myself your wife," she said in a clear voice. "I give you the title of husband, and with the title I give you myself. My body to pleasure, my heart to protect, my spirit to cherish. I give you honor and respect. I take this vow willingly, knowing that from this moment on, I cease to exist without you."

The words surprised Logan as much as the conviction with which they were spoken. He'd never heard such vows. Most marriages were little more than the exchange of legal promises that protected a man and woman in a court of review. There was nothing said of loyalty or protecting one's heart. It was a strange custom, but one Logan found pleasing. Lady Zara had just promised him her body and her loyalty; what more could he ask?

Her hand dropped away and Logan waited. Zara nodded, silently instructing him to repeat the vows.

"I, Logan, give you the title of wife."

It was all he was willing to say.

Zara expected as much; the link she'd formed with him earlier had told her that he was a strong man, a stubborn man.

She turned and looked at Nessa. "Who here can witness the sincerity of my words?"

"I can." Nessa stepped forward. Her eyes sent a message to Zara not to be overly concerned about the outsider's unwillingness to commit more than his name. "You are Zara of Nubria, a royal daughter of the House of Queens, and true to your word. Let none doubt what you have spoken."

Logan looked at his second in command. "Who here can witness the sincerity of my words?"

Maddock raised his sword. "I can. You are Logan, a Galactic Guard, sworn to uphold the laws of Unity. Your words are as strong as your sword. Let none here doubt what you have spoken."

Logan mistakenly thought the ceremony complete. He was about to move away from the altar when Zara reached for the dagger a second time. He watched as she pricked the index finger of her right hand. Her blood shone red against the pale perfection of her skin. This time she reached out and touched Logan's forehead. Then her own.

There was a different rhythm to her prayer this time. The words were softer, as though she was afraid of bruising the air by speaking them. Her eyes were closed, hiding their rich color from Logan's sight, as she recited more mysterious words. He watched her, his gaze captured by her lovely face, his body aroused by her proximity, his thoughts racing with all the things he wanted to teach her once they were alone.

Zara drew on the strength of her faith, knowing her power lay within that faith, the same way Logan believed his sword honored his words. Slowly, carefully combing the outside world away one layer at a time, Zara reached the sacred place for the second time that day. The elements were strong there, the feel of the earth under her feet, the brush of air across her skin, the fire of her heartbeat, the gentle flow of blood in her veins. Earth, air, fire, and water. They combined to make the physical world, while mind, spirit, and soul formed the other dimension, the dimension that allowed one mind to blend with another.

Zara could feel the warrior's power. It was stronger, much stronger than she'd felt before, and she knew that the ancient ritual had opened the door. All she had to do was take the mental step, make the spiritual commitment that would merge her mind with the mind of the man she had just declared her husband.

Logan felt the sensation overtake his body. It was pain and pleasure combined, a sensual feeling that made his blood heat and his muscles tighten. It was stronger than before, more powerful, and he instinctively knew that Zara was causing it. Holding that thought, Logan tried to block the feeling, but it was too late. His mind exploded with images, bright colors and muted shadows that hid things he wanted to see. Sweat broke out on his body, and he sucked in a quick breath. He felt as if he'd been tossed into the sky, weightless, his body drifting with the clouds. The images were distorted, more color than shape, but he could see them, wavering on a distant horizon, beckoning him with a silent song.

The link only lasted a moment, but Zara staggered backward from the force of it. The power of her husband's thoughts were even stronger now that she had seen him, felt his heartbeat, touched his skin. She'd closed the link, but its strength remained, filling her mind until she felt as though one more thought would shatter it.

Her heart was racing, her limbs weak from the effort

26

it had taken to search out the sacred place and form the spiritual link that could never be broken once created.

Logan caught his wife, bringing her close to him, holding her limp body against his stronger one. She gazed up at him, and in that second, Logan felt the sensation again. Lighter, but still there.

He'd married a witch. A priestess who had invaded his mind as easily as the Galactic Guard had marched into Nubria's capital city.

"It is done," Nessa announced. "Let the union of Lady Zara, our beloved queen, and Lord Logan of the Galactic Guard, be recorded in the archives of Nubria."

Zara felt the warmth of her husband's arm as it held her at his side. She could feel his heartbeat again, his chest pressing against her arm, his breath caressing the top of her head. It was unnerving to feel his muscular strength the same way she'd felt his spiritual power. There was more to the man than a sword and a grim expression.

Who is this woman I call wife? Logan asked himself as he felt the light brush of Zara's breasts against his bare chest. He looked at Maddock. The soldier smiled, then raised Logan's sword in a silent salute. The officers who had witnessed the strange ceremony followed suit and a shout of jubilation filled the hall.

There were no joyous cheers from the Nubrians as Zara found her footing and stood on her own two feet. Her people had no call to celebrate the passing of an ancient tradition. A man now ruled Nubria, a stranger who wore a sword, an outsider, a nonbeliever who had avoided the ancient vows and declared his dominance instead.

Chapter Three

"My people gather to greet you," Zara said, stepping away from the altar.

Logan watched as she moved toward the gold inlaid doors that separated the throne hall from the main corridor of the palace. He reached for his tunic and slid his arms into the sleeves before buttoning it over his chest. His wife's blood had dried on his skin, and he wondered if she would wear the dot of blood on her forehead while his men feasted and celebrated their easy victory over the Nubrians.

If it was a victory. Something deep inside Logan warned him that conquering Nubria and its lovely queen would take more than a strong sword. Females were sly creatures and fierce protectors. He'd married a queen, a woman born and raised to guide her people. The warrior in Logan was challenged by the idea of turning his soft-spoken bride into a willing wife, but his more practical side, disciplined by battles won and lost, told him patience was the key to Lady Zara's secrets. She must know that his first order of business would be to find the rebels she'd hidden and bring them to justice. She was young, but she wasn't foolish.

"You've gained a throne and a lovely wife," Maddock congratulated him, then frowned. "That was the oddest wedding I've ever witnessed. For a moment, I thought you were in pain."

Logan shrugged his concern aside. "It was nothing. The deed is done; let's get on with the feast. I'm hungry."

"For more than food, I'll wager," Maddock teased. "I envy you, old friend. She's beautiful."

"And a rebel in her own right," Logan reminded him while he reminded himself. "See to the men."

Maddock did as he was told as Logan followed his wife from the hall. For the time being, he'd let her lead the way. The palace was unfamiliar to him, but come morning she'd realize her role as queen had been replaced by the duties of wife and lover.

Logan's dark eyes absorbed each and every detail of his wife's body as she moved gracefully down the corridor. The gossamer cloth of her gown clung to her body like a second skin, accentuating the gentle sway of her hips. Her hair was unbound, cascading down her back like a silver waterfall. She was delicately built but pleasing to a man's eye, and he felt a fresh rush of desire flood his body. The sun was setting, the night falling gently over the land. The night that would witness the consummation of their marriage.

Zara stopped at the base of a marble stairway. "Tradition demands that I show myself to my people," she told him. "You should be by my side."

"No," Logan told her, using the blunt tone that came as naturally as breathing. "You will stand by my side, lady wife. Nubria isn't the only world with traditions. You no longer rule alone. From this day forward, the people will know that I determine their fate."

Zara said nothing. Instead she motioned for Logan to walk in front of her. She knew that other worlds often held women in low esteem, thinking them subservient to men. The concept was alien to Zara. Her mother had ruled Nubria while her father stood as the queen's adviser. Their marriage had been a partnership, a sharing of minds and bodies. Love had dictated their behavior. Love of each other and love for the planet they called home.

But there was no love between Zara and the warrior she'd declared her husband. They were strangers, bound by the desire of the Unity Council. Taking a husband had been the only option offered to Nubria's queen. Had Zara refused, the Galactic Guards would have arrived on her world prepared for combat. She couldn't subject her people to violence. It went against everything they believed. Their faith was a gentle one, caring and generous. She was their queen. She'd made the decision to harbor the rebels. She alone would bear the consequences of her actions.

Logan climbed the stairs, knowing that the Queen of Nubria followed him. Maddock walked behind her, guarding her back the same way he'd guarded Logan's through five years of war.

The stairway led to a small corridor that opened onto a large balcony. Logan stepped outside, his sword sheathed at his side, his face devoid of emotion. To his left was the courtyard where his men gathered, to his right he could see the open meadow that surrounded the palace. The lush green plain was crowded with people, their faces raised in anticipation of seeing the man who would now rule at Lady Zara's side.

The gentle brush of purple cloth against his black uniform told Logan that Zara had come to stand by his side. Truth be known, he didn't need the soft abrasion of silk against leather to know that she had joined him. He could smell the light scent of her perfumed body. No, it was more than that, Logan realized. He could sense her presence the same way he could sense danger and death before a battle. The sensation vibrated through him just as her touch had moved through him during the wedding ceremony. He willed the peculiar feeling aside, focusing instead on the guards who waited for his signal of victory. With a deft hand, Logan unsheathed his sword and extended his arm into the air. The long blade caught the last rays of the sun, gleaming steel for all to see.

Below him, the men responded in kind. A hundred swords pointed toward the sky, while their voices raised in a deafening shout that made Zara long to cover her ears.

In the meadow beyond the castle walls, the people of Nubria waited to see what their queen would do. Logan knew the marriage vows he'd just spoken would satisfy the Council, yet nothing but their lady's blessing would calm the tension growing among her people. He had only to see his wife interact with those around her to know that she was revered by those she governed. Whatever words she spoke would pave the way for his acceptance or rejection. Logan and the soldiers who followed him were prepared for both.

Zara stepped forward. The crowd went silent. Anticipation hung in the air like the reluctant sun sinking slowly toward the horizon. Like the silk of her wedding dress, her hair moved as she moved, catching the fading light and holding it as though it were alive. Logan watched her with a guarded gaze, wondering if she would address her people in the ancient tongue that had sealed their marriage vows. When she finally spoke, her voice was as clear as the bells that had announced the opening of the castle gates.

"Welcome my husband," she called to the people gathered in the meadow. "Honor him as I honor him."

There was a loud shout from the back of the crowd, then everyone started cheering until the good wishes of the Nubrian people exploded in a crescendo of blessings for a long and fruitful marriage.

Logan watched and listened as Zara's name was repeated again and again, chanted by the people who called her queen. None spoke his name, but he wasn't offended. Logan didn't need adoration. In its place, he would demand loyalty and obedience, both from the people of Nubria and its queen.

Moving to his wife's side, Logan lay his hand on the small of her back. Zara felt the touch like the unexpected lick of a candle flame. The heat from her husband's hand passed through the thin fabric of her dress and into her skin.

The cheers went on as her people openly acknowledged the vows she had spoken in the throne room moments earlier. Logan recalled the sensation he'd felt when Zara had stood before him, eyes closed, her voice reciting ancient words that held no meaning to a nonbeliever's ear. The sensation was gone, but not the memory. His hand flexed, then relaxed, his fingers spreading to touch more of his royal wife.

Zara tried to ignore her husband's touch, but she failed. Like the loud voices of her people, it captured her senses, holding her hostage while she wondered if she could shield her mind from the physical joining that would come after the wedding feast. She had never been forced to close her mind before, to defend it against an outsider's intrusion, yet she had little choice. The promise she had given the rebel leader had been spoken with the same sincerity as her wedding vows. She couldn't defy her own words.

"Come," Logan said. "Your people's curiosity has been satisfied. Now it is time to satisfy my men's empty bellies. They have been without food since the morning meal."

"My apologies," Zara said, raising her hand in a gesture that brought immediate silence from the crowd gathered beyond the courtyard walls.

Logan smiled for the first time since arriving on Nubria. The expression turned his interesting face into a handsome one, and Zara felt her heart skip several beats. How in the name of all the ancient gods was she going to resist the power of her warrior? And he was hers.

Unlike her husband, Zara didn't need the physical consummation of their marriage to confirm her passage from bride to wife. The moment she had formed the link with Logan, she had become his and he had become hers. Two minds, two spirits, touching, merging, becoming one. The act was far more intimate than the physical one he would demand of her once the feast was over and they retired to the royal chamber above the throne room.

Maddock signaled for the men to form a line. Logan had been presented to the people of Nubria. It was now time for his wife to meet the Galactic Guard.

The presence of Logan's hand wasn't necessary to guide his wife across the balcony, but he didn't remove it. He wanted her to know that he wouldn't be relegated to the role of adviser. She belonged to him now and she needed to understand that his possession would be complete; her throne, her body, everything she owned and ruled, was now under his command.

Zara could sense Logan's tension and his intentions as she walked across the open porch and looked down into the courtyard. Her experience with men was limited and her exposure to outsiders was even less. The few she had met hadn't impressed her. The Commander of the Galactic Guard was different. Now that the link had been established, she was beginning to learn more and more about him.

"My wife," Logan announced to the soldiers. "Protect her."

Zara thought the command unnecessary, like the hot presence of Logan's hand at the base of her spine, but she forced a smile to her face and accepted the cheers of the guards, who saluted her with their swords held high. She told herself that her husband was a man of war and as such he had yet to accept the peace that was as much a part of her world as the gold and white lilies that bloomed in early spring. Time would ease his distrust.

Nessa announced that the feast was ready. Once again, Zara found herself walking between her husband and the soldier called Maddock. Sandwiched between the two giant men, she smiled for the first time since learning that a transport ship had landed. Her husband was acting as if danger lurked around every corner.

Logan stared at the large room lined with tables and lighted by torches. He'd been warned that Nubria had little use for the technology that allowed people to travel from one planet to another, but he hadn't expected to eat his wedding meal in semidarkness.

As Logan studied the room before him, Zara looked at the men stationed strategically around the banquet hall. Galactic Guards with swords and laser pistols were positioned in each corner and at the three entryways.

"The guards aren't necessary," she said, looking up at her new husband. "There is no threat here. My people are a peaceful race."

Logan's expression was cynical as he studied Zara's face. He was anxious to find the rebels and get on with the rest of his duties. He was also anxious to make sure his wife realized that by marrying him, she'd forsaken the right to rule her own life. He would be master of Nubria, the same way he was master of his brigade. To blatantly disobey him was to invite retribution. His men knew that already. His wife would soon learn.

"Life is full of threats," Logan replied. "There are still rebels about," he added, reminding her of the very reason she'd been forced to take a stranger as her mate. "Until they are captured, my men will remain on guard."

Zara struggled to keep at least a semblance of ladylike demeanor. It would not do to let her temper get the best of her. After a moment, she addressed her husband's unspoken concern, the one that had him wondering if he'd taken a step back in time. Although the link didn't give her the power to read his individual thoughts, the expression on his face told her that he wasn't used to quarters lit by torches and candles or food prepared by human hands.

"Do not let our lack of technology worry you, my lord. Our ways are uncluttered," she explained. "Our faith teaches us that simplicity is far more satisfying. The less we depend upon others the more we can depend upon ourselves."

"Is the food cooked over fire, as well?" Logan asked, realizing that his wife was well trained in the ways of diplomacy. She'd gracefully avoided the topic he most wanted to discuss.

Zara smiled at the unexpected question. She'd never eaten food prepared any other way; but then, she'd never been away from Nubria. "Yes. We don't eat the flesh of animals. Our faith forbids it. But the bread is warm and the fruit spiced. Come, the servants cannot feed your men until you take your place."

Logan's place was a tall chair, inlaid with gold on the back and arms, and big enough to seat four men. He stood in front of it. Zara took her place at his left side, the side closest to his heart, while Maddock stood on his right. She wondered if her husband realized the significance of her position, then pushed the thought aside. She couldn't expect him to think like a believer. He was an outsider, and thus ignorant of the small things that meant so much to her people.

The scent of hot bread and vegetables grown under the natural light of the sun filled Logan's nostrils. Military rations were synthesized. While they provided the nutrition his men needed to fight, they rarely pleased the palate. Nubrian food was just the opposite. The tables were covered with large silver platters brimming with exotic fruits and vegetables. Small loaves of bread, sliced and steaming from the ovens of the royal kitchen, lay within reach of the hungry men lined up and waiting for the slightest command to satisfy their appetites. Servants, male and female, dressed in blue robes, moved quietly about the room, filling glasses with red wine.

"What about your people?" Logan asked, expecting an entourage of courtly Nubrians to stroll into the room.

"They will eat after your men are served," Zara replied.

"No," Logan said. "Your advisers."

"My father advised me after my mother's death. But he is gone now, too. I have no other advisers," Zara said. "Only the people who willingly serve me."

"Am I to rule Nubria or Utopia?" Logan remarked. "No wars. No reason for wars. No political advisers cluttering up my court. It's beyond belief."

"Nubria isn't perfect, my lord," Zara retorted. "Though we strive for perfection, like so many things, it remains beyond our reach."

Zara said a silent prayer that love wasn't as unattainable as perfection. She wanted to share her heart the way her mother had shared hers with Zara's father. Like other women, queen or common born, Zara longed for the security of love, the knowledge that she was valued by her mate.

Logan was about to argue that perfection was indeed within his reach when he realized he'd be complimenting his new wife. He should, he supposed, but he was still wary of the simplicity she seemed to embrace. Life had taught him that nothing was as easy as a man might think it to be.

"Eat." Logan gave the blunt command that was immediately obeyed.

His men started reaching for the enticing food before they were seated in their chairs.

Maddock laughed. "They're a greedy lot."

"There is more than enough food to feed them," Zara said, surprised by the speed at which the bread and wine were already beginning to disappear. "Please, my lord, sit and enjoy yourself. Nessa's recipes have already pleased me. I hope you find the same pleasure in them."

"My pleasure will be found when I am finally alone with my bride," Logan said, his voice as smooth as the wine his second in command was tasting.

Zara tried not to blush but failed miserably. Heat burned her cheeks as she turned her attention to Tolman. The loyal servant gave her a reassuring smile and Zara blushed even more, knowing the old man had overheard her husband's remark.

Logan looked around the room, realizing that the elaborate chair was the only one suited for a queen. He'd come to Nubria with the intention of taking Lady Zara's throne, but not this literally. "Sit beside me," he commanded. "You will not be squeezed so tightly you can't enjoy the meal."

Zara sat down hesitantly. The thought of being so close to her husband that she could hear him chewing his food unsettled her already overtaxed nerve endings. She hoped that he would be patient enough to allow her a few minutes alone before he joined her in the bedchamber. She desperately needed the calming effects that the prayer garden beyond the great hall offered her whenever she felt the burden of her rank weighing upon her shoulders, and Zara had never felt it as heavily as she did now.

The link was growing stronger with each passing minute. Soon she would be able to discern her husband's moods without seeing his face or hearing his voice. Logan would be able to feel it, too, if he ever allowed his mind to clear of mistrust and opened his thoughts to things other than war and rebels who posed no threat to the Galactic Guards that outnumbered them ten to one.

Zara's next thought made her taut nerves tighten to the point of breaking. If Logan knew about the link, he could use it against her. She couldn't allow that. It was too soon to trust him, although her faith demanded she do just that. He was an outsider, linked to her, yes, but still a nonbeliever. Only time would show the true depths of his heart. Time and the patience Zara had thought she possessed until he'd touched her. Even now she was anxious to have the night behind them.

It would take all her power to keep her feelings from opening the link and allowing him to sense what she sensed—an attraction strong enough to shake her queenly composure to its very foundations. She knew little of the man she'd married, but her female instincts told her that he would continue to be a soldier first and a husband second. As a commander, he'd been trained in tactics and strategy. Giving him a weapon to use against her and the rebels she'd given refuge would be a tragic mistake.

Still, the attraction was there. She had felt it the moment he'd walked into the throne room. She could feel it now, growing more intense as she sat snugly wedged into the chair next to him.

Zara knew what was expected of her once they were alone, the door of their bedchamber sealed against the curious eyes and ears of both his soldiers and her servants. Nessa had prepared her for the wedding night, explaining what a husband would expect of his bride. She had no fear of the physical joining. It was the emotional joining that frightened her until her mouth felt dry and her bones brittle from the tension. Logan's ignorance of the spiritual link that existed between them would allow him the freedom to enjoy whatever a man felt when he experienced passion. Zara's knowledge of the link would force her to control her every thought, to shield her emotions while she tried to please the man she had taken as her husband. It was a confusing task, one that would test her powers and the gift that was an intricate part of her being.

Logan felt his wife's quick intake of breath and the tightening of her muscles as his body moved next to her. Logan felt the bittersweet pleasure of desire rushing through his veins once again. His wife was more tempting than the exotic fruit laying on his plate. Silver hair clung to the sleeve of his black tunic, while violet eyes avoided his gaze.

The Queen of Nubria was both beautiful and shy.

The combination intrigued Logan even more than the wine he was tasting. Spiced with herbs, it pleased his tongue and quenched his thirst. He began to eat, content to satisfy his physical appetite until the time came for him to appease his sexual hunger.

He'd never wooed a virgin before, although he was almost certain that Zara wouldn't fight him—not physically. She'd been too cooperative, too willing to please, to make him think that she'd turn into a shrew once they were alone. The women who had shared his bed in the past had quickly learned that he was a generous lover, taking his pleasure while he pleased them in return. His wife would learn the same thing. Pleasure could beget pleasure; all she had to do was surrender to his touch.

He noticed his wife's plate went untouched and frowned. "Are you ill?"

"No, my lord."

The link was growing faster than she'd expected. Whatever her husband thoughts, they were strong enough to make her body throb with sensation. It was the same sensation she'd felt when she'd touched his mind the first time. The same feeling that had made her legs too weak to support her when she stood by the altar and linked with him a second time.

Zara couldn't explain it, but she could feel it. It was the reason her stomach didn't want food and her mind longed for the silence of the prayer garden. She needed time to accept the feelings Logan aroused in her, time to control them, if she could.

"Where are you hiding the rebels?" Logan asked casually.

Zara laughed. The sound rippled through the air like

the song of a morning bird, heralding the new day's sun. The officers sitting at the table stopped talking long enough to look at their commander's new wife. Logan's fierce stare sent them back to eating.

"I can't tell you," she replied. She'd been right when she'd told Nessa that she sensed no evil in this man. Her husband was outspoken and direct, honest traits, not deceitful ones.

"You will tell me," Logan countered firmly. His impatience to have his wife to himself surfaced in his tone of voice. He rarely showed emotion. Soldiers lived longer if they didn't let feelings get in their way. But it wasn't anger firing his body to the point of sweet pain. It was his wife. A stubborn woman, he was discovering. "Where are they?"

"I cannot say, my lord," Zara said. "I gave my word and it will not be broken. On Nubria, a promise given is a promise kept."

"What of your promise to honor me?"

"One does not cancel the other," she told him politely. "I can honor both you and my promise to the rebels."

Logan's expression said he disagreed. It also said he wasn't accustomed to having a woman challenge his authority. His wife was seated in a room full of warriors, men pledged to uphold the laws of the Union, and yet she had the audacity to defy the most powerful man among them. Many would think it suicidal, yet Logan saw no fear in her eyes, nor did he hear any hesitation in her voice. He had to admire her courage at the same time he marveled at her foolishness.

Maddock had heard the blatant disobedience and Logan knew he was waiting for Lady Zara to have her first chastisement, one she wouldn't easily forget. Bracing himself against the mixture of emotions that were assaulting his senses, his wife's closeness, the soft scent of her perfume, the exotic taste of candied fruit and succulent wine, Logan told himself to be patient. There would be time enough to teach his wife what a warrior expected from his mate when they were alone. Until then, Logan would listen, and he hoped learn.

"There is an ancient saying that promises are made to be broken," he remarked nonchalantly.

"Not on Nubria," Zara replied. "A promise given is a sacred pledge to us; to break it or dishonor it is unthinkable."

Despite the crush of people, Logan kept his voice pitched low enough so that only Zara would hear his reply. "Then I can expect your wedding vows to be consummated with enthusiasm, my lady. I look forward to the night ahead. I have never had a female give a sacred vow to pleasure me."

Zara didn't blush this time. Her husband's arrogance was getting out of hand. She was after all a queen, and her royal duties had often included putting a prideful male in his place, especially one who had no understanding of Nubrian tradition.

"My vows said nothing of your pleasure, my lord. You should have listened more carefully." Her voice a bare whisper, Zara repeated what she had said standing by the sacred stone altar. "*My* body to pleasure, *my* heart to protect, *my* spirit to cherish."

Logan's laughter was not the response she expected. He put back his head and roared, reminding her of the wild animals that lived in the mountains to the north. When he finally spoke it was to best Zara at her own game. His voice was smooth male velvet. "A command I will gladly obey, fair lady. Before Nubria's twin moons fade into a single sun, your body will know the pleasure only a man can give it."

Chapter Four

Nubria's twin moons rose over the horizon, casting a silvery stream of light on the stone altar of the prayer garden. Seeking the cool texture of the ancient stone, hoping it would ease the anxiety boiling in her veins like a pot over an open fire, Zara knelt on the soft mound of grass at the base of the altar and laid her hands against the sacred rock.

Her nerves felt like kindling, ready to burst into flame at the slightest touch of a match. Pressing her hands more firmly against the polished stone, Zara closed her eyes and repeated the prayers that had soothed her for a lifetime. The words rolled easily off her tongue, recited so many times that they came as naturally to her as one breath following another. But no peace came with them. Her mind was a tangled web of thoughts, laced with apprehension and excitement.

The sensual hunger she'd felt when she'd sat next to Logan at dinner was still lingering in her spirit, resisting the serenity the prayer garden had always offered her. There was no escaping the memory of his touch, the way he'd looked at her, the velvety tone of his voice.

"My lady."

Nessa's voice was as gentle as the moonlight that washed over Zara like a spring rain. She raised her head, turning as the old woman stepped forward.

"I pray, but no peace comes to me," Zara said, knowing she couldn't hide her apprehension from Nessa. The old woman was too well trained in the ancient rites to be fooled by a perfunctory smile.

"Peace will come in time," Nessa replied. "Remember, you are as much a woman as you are a queen."

"A woman who is now a wife. Yet I know nothing about the man I have claimed to rule by my side. I sense him more with each passing moment, but the true quality of his heart evades me as surely as the falling sun evades the rising moons. Tell me, old friend, is my destiny to forever chase around the circle, never finding the beginning or the end?"

Nessa's smile was that of a caring mother. "Cease your worrying, my lady. Your destiny was foretold the day of your birth. You are a daughter of the House of Queens, blessed with a gift that will eventually bring you the peace you so diligently seek. Patience is the key."

"But not the answer," Zara said, too exhausted from the day's events to maintain the composure she had shown since the transport carrying the Galactic Guards had arrived. The prayer garden was her private sanctuary. No servants called upon her here. Only Tolman and Nessa dared to approach her when she sought the refuge of the small alcove. "Soon my husband will enter my bedchamber and I will be forced to feel his touch while I struggle to keep the link shielded. He can use it against me."

"I doubt that an outsider could find his way through the spiritual portal that easily," Nessa told her. "He will sense the link, but he will be unable to call it by its rightful name. It will be a feeling to him, nothing more. A vague dream unremembered."

"I felt his thoughts," Zara said in a strained voice. "They were strong. As strong as his body."

"Aye, his body is strong. But your heart is stronger," Nessa said calmly. "Your mind opens the link, but your heart is the source of its power. Never forget that, my lady. Lord Logan is a warrior, but you are a Nubrian priestess. If he chooses war rather than love, he will lose."

"Love." Zara shook her head. "I fear Nubria's new king values his sword more than he does the affections of a wife."

"Perhaps," Nessa replied teasingly. "A man finds it easier to love with his body than he does with his heart. But if a woman is patient, she can have both."

Zara blushed. She had meant the weapon hanging at Logan's side, not his manhood.

"Return to your prayers," Nessa told her. "Your husband is still meeting with his officers. You have time to refresh your mind before he visits your bed."

Zara reached out as though to stop her, then withdrew her hand.

As always, Nessa knew what Zara would have said even though the words hadn't been spoken. "Fear not. Your warrior is as fierce as any man I've ever seen, but his hands will be gentle tonight. Trust in yourself and all will be well."

For a moment Zara fought the unrest growing inside her. Nessa was right, as always. Logan was an outsider. He would have no knowledge of how the link worked. All she had to do was maintain her emotions and keep them from overflowing.

"Good night, my lady," Nessa said.

"Good night," Zara replied as she returned to her position in front of the altar.

She focused once again, forcing the doubts from her mind. She'd known when she'd defied the Council's

44

command that she would one day face their wrath. That day had come. She was married to a man of their choosing, one who was determined to rid the sector of the last nest of rebels. Warrior though he might be, Zara had glimpsed enough of her husband's mind to know that he wasn't an unreasonable man. If he looked for the rebels and didn't find them, he'd eventually give up the search. Time would win the battle for her.

Time and patience, according to old Nessa.

The softly chanted prayer gradually eased Zara's personal worries, but before she could reach the sacred place within her, the worries of her people intruded. Kneeling in the garden under the pale light of Nubria's moons, she often found their thoughts with her. It was as if they knew this was the time when she felt closest to them.

Nubrians were the most generous and open-minded of any race in the universe, but they clung to their ancient beliefs and feared anyone who might try to alter them. Zara's people loved their simple ways, the tranquillity of knowing that one day would be very much like the day before it and the day yet to come. The rebellion had touched their minds more than their bodies, since all Nubrians shared a small portion of the power that their queen possessed in abundance. Sensing the unrest had caused them great pain. Knowing that their beloved queen was caught between her honor as a Nubrian priestess and her obligation to the Unity Council had them worried.

Zara could sense their anxiety, and their adoration.

It always humbled her to know that her people truly cared for her. Millions of them, scattered about the planet, unknown faces and names, yet they were her family. She was linked to them as surely as she was now linked to the soldier called Logan.

Lord Logan, the first King of Nubria.

* * *

Patricia Waddell

"I want sentries posted at the palace entryways," Logan told Maddock. "Tomorrow we will begin sending out patrols."

The older soldier nodded, accepting the command. "I've yet to find a door with a lock upon it. Or a weapon. The palace guards are nothing but robed servants who greet everyone with a smile."

Logan frowned. He shared his second in command's confusion. He was beginning to think the only weapon Maddock would find was the small jewel-handled dagger Lady Zara had used to prick her finger. Remembering the way her delicate touch had effected him, Logan rubbed his chest, where her blood had dried. He would have to bathe before he called upon his wife's bedchamber.

Torn between trying to understand the emotions that had been assaulting him since he'd first seen his bride and the undefended hospitality of a planet whose people would rather celebrate the inconveniences of manual labor than the luxuries of technology, Logan looked around the room.

Tolman had called it the adviser's suite, which meant that Zara's father had once used the room as his private office. It was spacious, with a large fireplace and comfortable furnishings. The walls were lined with shelves, some holding written manuscripts, while others displayed pottery and small statues fashioned by the artisans who thrived on the planet. A cluster of candles, artfully arranged in a metal holder, burned on the corner of the desk, their flames teased by the breeze coming though the open windows.

The old servant had left Logan and Maddock to converse in private while he supervised the housing of the other officers. Although everyone's words had been gently spoken and filled with courtesy, Logan knew the people were curious about the outsider who had wed their queen so hastily.

"Do you think Lady Zara is hiding the rebels here in the capital city?' Maddock asked as he filled two crystal goblets with wine.

"No." Logan sat down his wine, untouched. "We know the rebel ship crashed in the mountains. Since our scanners couldn't find any debris, the ship was either buried or the planet's natural mineral deposits are shielding the site. If we can't detect it with our equipment, we'll have to find it with our eyes."

"That could take a long time," Maddock said. "The farther north we travel, the more mountains we'll have to search."

Logan walked to the open window and looked outside. The moonlight was bright enough for him to see the rim of mountains that formed the northern horizon. The capital city of Nubria was located on a narrow land bridge that connected the planet's two continents. The majority of Nubria's farms lay to the south in rich valleys naturally irrigated by tiny streams and meandering rivers that finally found their way to the sea. "If I was Keelan, I'd stay in the mountains. They're less populated than the valleys and harder to patrol."

"Then you think to find Keelan here, after all?"

"He wasn't among the rebels who surrendered," Logan said, keeping his back to the room while he stared at the twin moons suspended above the planet. "Rumors aren't as good as facts, but they frequently serve the same purpose. The war was going badly for them. Keelan was their leader. He was fleeing the war zone in hopes of finding a new base for his mutiny."

It had been a long time since Keelan had served as a Galactic Guard, but no one in the elite military unit could forget that the outlaw had once worn a black and red uniform. Keelan was more than a political rebel; he was a traitor. As long as the traitor was alive, the Guard had to bear the stain of his dishonor. The shame of that betrayal was the reason Logan refused to give up the search. He wouldn't stop looking until he'd seen Keelan's dead body with his own two eyes, or created the corpse himself.

"What about the Council?" Maddock asked, knowing his commanding officer well enough to feel a small quiver of sympathy for the rebel Keelan. Logan hadn't gained the rank of Commander by patiently waiting for the fight to come to him. He was an aggressive predator, determined to capture his quarry.

The candlelight accented the decorative gold braid on Logan's uniform as he turned to look at Maddock. Although his hands were folded behind his back in the customary stance of a soldier at ease, Logan's features were taut with tension. "The Council has what it wants," Logan replied grimly. "Lady Zara is wed to a trustworthy Guardian. The last nest of rebels will be found and brought to justice. The watchtower will be built and the eastern borders protected."

Maddock lifted the goblet to his mouth, cautiously studying his friend over the rim of the crystal glass. He savored the sweet wine for a moment before speaking. "And you will have the revenge you seek, along with a beautiful wife to keep the winter chill away."

"A beautiful dissident who hopes to turn me into a farmer." Logan voiced his suspicions aloud.

Maddock chuckled. "I'd like to hear the ancient prayer that could make you put down your sword and pick up a plow. It would have to be a lengthy one."

For an instant, Logan thought of the words his lovely wife had spoken when she'd touched him for the first time. He hadn't understood a single syllable, but he'd felt her power. He told himself it was the natural power of a woman to arouse a man's desire, to make him want what was within reach, to tease his senses and make his mind swirl with sensual possibilities.

He didn't like being susceptible to a woman's charms. The last thing he needed was a female boggling his mind, yet he couldn't shake the image of Zara standing before him, her pale hair unbound, her eyes shining like gemstones. Those enticing eyes had somehow touched him, and in spite of himself, Logan couldn't brush the intangible caress away. He was curious about the woman he'd claimed as his wife. What was it about her that fired his blood so forcefully? She was beautiful, but he'd seen beautiful women before. Her status as a queen didn't impress him. She was a woman, nothing more, a female favored by rank and privilege, and yet . . .

She was more.

A challenge, to be sure. The very thought of taming her spirit, of teaching her the pleasures of being a wife, had his body clamoring for release.

"Where is my queen?" Logan asked irritably, trying to control the yearning that was heating his blood and hardening his manhood.

"Praying," Maddock told him. "In a small garden just beyond the throne hall where you were wed. I have men nearby, watching over her."

Logan picked up the wineglass he'd ignored until now. He drained it dry, wondering if his virgin bride was praying for the power to please him or deceive him.

Chapter Five

Incense perfumed the bedchamber as Zara walked inside the room she would now share with her husband. Candlelight flickered and danced on the tiled floor, while moonlight glowed outside and a mild breeze ruffled the silk draperies at the open windows.

Three servants moved about the room, one turning down the bed, another readying the sleeping gown that would adorn their lady's body when she greeted her husband, while yet another made sure the wine was warm and a tray of fresh fruit within easy reach should the royal couple find themselves hungry after a night of lovemaking.

Zara's eyes followed the servants, unsure how to dismiss them without revealing her nervousness. Despite her stately manner, she was still feeling the strain of the day's events. The prayer garden had calmed her, but its relief was only temporary. Soon she would be expected to accept a stranger's kiss, to permit his touch, to surrender her body to his pleasure.

No man had ever kissed her. There had been no suitors to seek her hand, no men arriving at court to pay homage to her beauty. Until the Union had demanded a marriage, she'd had no thoughts of a husband, trusting in the ancient gods to provide her a mate when the time arrived.

The time had come.

Tonight.

"What else do you require of us, my lady?"

Zara flinched at the sound of the servant's voice. She'd been too preoccupied with thoughts of her husband to notice that the three women were standing in front of her, awaiting her instructions. The oldest one smiled, and Zara realized that her fears were no different than the fears of any new bride. All women who married came to know this moment. Of course, most women knew more about the men they married than their name and military rank.

"I have no further needs," she told them.

There was silence for a short time, as if the servants wanted to linger, to give Zara their emotional support. Wind whistled outside, puffing up the sheer curtains and sending them into the room like silken arms reaching for someone to embrace.

"May you be blessed, our lady," the servants finally said, taking their leave.

Once they were gone, Zara removed her purple dress and put on the white gown. The sheer material clung to her body in a suggestive manner, hugging her breasts and hips before flaring to the floor in folds of shimmering silk. She brushed her hair, then poured herself a glass of wine, thinking the mild elixir might help to calm her nerves.

Praying hadn't helped.

It was ironic that the one night she needed her faith more than ever was the night it seemed to elude her. No matter how hard she tried to relax her mind and allow the inner peace of the sacred place to fill her, all she

51

could think about was the warrior named Logan.

Zara was raising the wineglass to her lips when the door opened and her husband marched into the room. The steely hilt of his sword gleamed in the dim light. Clothed in a black uniform with red and gold trim, his face half in shadow, half in light, his appearance did little to ease Zara's virginal fears. His greeting intensified them.

He said nothing.

Not one word passed his lips as he shut the door, then walked to the table where the servant had left the wine. Once he'd poured himself a glass, he turned and looked at her. Silence filled the room as he lifted his goblet in a mock salute to his new bride before emptying it in one long swallow.

In that moment, Zara knew that her husband's beliefs were as deeply rooted in his mind as her faith was entrenched in her own heart and soul. This was a man who would give no quarter, show no mercy. When he moved, it was a forward motion, without a glance over his shoulder to view what he was leaving behind. He'd come to Nubria to rule. His path had been set, his goal clearly named. He was a man who used life to his advantage, rarely enjoying it the way she and her people believed it was to be enjoyed.

Inwardly, she wanted to weep for him and for the twist of fate that had brought him to a planet that had no wars to fight and no enemies to conquer.

Logan saw a gleam of disapproval in her eyes. His wife thought he was consuming too much wine. He'd been raised on Carsenean ale and Bervian whiskey. Nubrian wine was nothing but fermented fruit and water. It would take gallons of the sweet liquid to effect his control. Did she think him weak? A pliable man to be twisted around her finger like a strand of hair?

Zara could sense her husband's displeasure. The cause of it escaped her, but the results were real enough. She could see it in the cold glare of his ebony eyes and the grim set of his mouth as he sat the empty goblet on the table. His movements were precise, curt, as if he wanted to be anywhere but where he was.

For the first time, Zara realized that like her, marriage had been forced upon Logan. His remarks in the dining hall had been blatantly seductive, yet now, looking at him, she had to wonder if he needed the benefit of wine to bring himself to consummate their vows. Had he left a woman behind, one he preferred to the virgin Queen of Nubria? Like her, did he resent the Unity Council dictating his life, demanding passion where none existed? Or was he a man of duty, bound by his oath to the Galactic Guard, obligated to do whatever was requested of him?

Could a man join with a woman and feel nothing? Could his body perform while his mind remained detached, his thoughts elsewhere, his emotions hidden?

Could a woman?

Zara knew she could not. Her mind was already linked to Logan's. There was no separating her body from her thoughts. Her faith taught her that they were one. She belonged to this man, emotionally and physically.

"Do you pray every evening?" Logan demanded. It had been over an hour since he'd dismissed Maddock from the adviser's suite. His impatience spurred his temper as much as his wife's beauty spurred his desire.

Zara was taken aback by the harshly spoken inquiry. She wasn't used to having anyone question her actions. "It is a habit I have acquired since becoming Nubria's queen. Yes, my lord. I pray every evening. It clears my head of the day's confusion and brings peace to my thoughts before I retire for the night."

She wanted to suggest that a few minutes of prayer might rid her Guardian of his surly attitude, but Zara held her tongue. Logan was her husband. She would have to accommodate herself to his personality the same

53

way he would eventually have to adjust to hers. Beginning their marriage with an argument would serve no purpose.

"Drink your wine," Logan said, forcing his hands to remain at his side when what he wanted to do was reach for his wife.

No.

His bride.

There was much to be done before he could legally call Zara his wife. And he was anxious to get about it. The mere sight of her was making his body throb until he dared do nothing too quickly, least she discover the power she already held over him. The white gown she wore was little more than transparent cloth. He could see the soft curves of her body, the dark circles of her nipples, and the long graceful line of her legs. He wanted to strip the gown away and feel the woman. He wanted to comb his hands through her silver hair, cover her mouth with his and absorb her cries of passion. He wanted to feel her slender legs wrapped around his hips, her body arching up to meet his, her female heat bathing him as he entered her, ending her virginity and beginning her womanhood.

Zara tasted the wine. While the sweet flavor pleased her palate, her eyes remained on her husband. He was moving about the room, inspecting his new domain. Zara's heart skipped several beats when he stopped at the side of the bed. She watched as he unstrapped his sword and lay it on the table, within reach, as if he expected the rebels to storm their bedchamber.

Once Logan's weapon was set aside, his hands went to the front of his uniform. Strong fingers undid the metal clasps holding his tunic together. Although she'd seen him bared to the waist only a few short hours ago, the sight of his muscular chest made Zara's heart start racing again. She forced the sip of wine past the lump in her throat, then set the glass down next to her husband's empty one.

Logan tossed his tunic aside, then sat on the edge of the bed and began removing his boots. He knew Zara was watching him. He could feel her eyes the same way he'd felt them every time she glanced in his direction. Their unusual color seemed to have the power to see beneath his skin. He was already at a disadvantage, being on a strange world with strange customs and assuming the leadership of a people he knew nothing about. Being at the mercy of his wife's incandescent gaze added to that disadvantage. Logan didn't like it.

"Maddock asked if our morning patrols would stumble over rebels," he said casually.

Zara gave him a brief smile before countering his words with ease. "Your men will find no rebels hiding among the citizens of our capital city. Nor is there a need to have your soldiers march up and down the streets. They will find no discontent among my people."

"What will they find?" Logan asked.

"A peaceful city with parks to amuse our children and witty merchants to sell them goods."

Her confident response made Logan frown. "I ask again, do I rule Nubria or Utopia?"

Zara knew he was testing her, trying to discover if her pride was a weak point. "And I tell you again that my people are a peaceful people, my lord. The war you fought so valiantly has no place here. It was not our ambition that caused it. I pray you remember that."

"I remember five years of bloodletting," Logan replied harshly. "Death caused by the personal greed of men who called themselves soldiers, men who thought nothing of destroying whole cities to gain what they called freedom. They were free," Logan told her. "Free to infest their people with lies and distrust until those who followed them reached for laser pistols instead of common sense. The Union had every right to defend itself."

Patricia Waddell

Zara felt his anger. And his pain.

"The freedom the rebels sought evaded them," she said, keeping her voice calm. "The Union was the victor. Its unity has been maintained. The Galactic Guard was the weapon of their justice. Perhaps it is time to put the past behind us and think of the future."

"Only after the last rebel is brought to justice," Logan stated. The draperies fluttered again, catching his attention. When he turned back to Zara, she could see the shadow of distrust in his eyes.

"What justice is there in adding more death?" she replied. "War is wasted energy. The universe is lucky to have survived men's folly up to now."

Logan pierced her with his dark gaze. "Men's folly or not, the rebels will be found and judged of their crimes. I have sworn an oath to see no other end."

Zara almost asked him about the oath he'd assumed by becoming Nubria's king, but she sensed it was the wrong time to remind him that ruling by her side didn't require a sword. She withheld her remark, remembering that Nessa had told her patience was the key.

Muscles rippled and bronzed skin gleamed in the amber candlelight as Zara watched her husband strip out of his warrior trappings, until he was wearing nothing but black trousers. Zara could see the bloodstain on his chest, where she'd touched him during their wedding ceremony. Her eyes followed the path of crisp dark hair covering his body, thicker where it covered his upper chest, thinning as it approached his navel, disappearing completely when it reached the waistband of his pants.

Her hands itched to touch him once again, to feel the power of his masculine body, to surrender to the storm of emotions she'd glimpsed on two occasions. While her eyes absorbed the sight of him, Zara's mind sought to close the link, to keep her thoughts private.

It was a battle of wills. Body against mind—desire against determination.

56

"I will summon Tolman and have him prepare the bathing pool for you," she said.

"No."

The one-word command hung in the night air like Nubria's moons.

"You stained my skin." He looked intently at her. "You can clean it."

Logan had meant to bathe before coming to his new wife, but speaking with Maddock and sorting out his own thoughts had taken more time than he'd realized. Perhaps the delay was worth it. Having his wife's hands wash away the blood on his chest would be an interesting form of foreplay. One he intended to enjoy.

"Very well," Zara replied. She walked to a long table at the opposite end of the suite and poured water into a basin. Once she'd retrieved a soft cloth from the shelf below the table, she turned to confront her husband.

When he didn't move to sit down in one of the chairs, Zara carried the basin of water to the table, soaked the cloth, and raised it to his chest. She told herself that he was just a man, just a vessel of flesh and blood, who needed to have his chest washed. Zara told herself that with every stroke of the soft cloth over his muscle-hardened chest, but she didn't believe it. Touching him, as casually as she was, was like touching the sun. She could feel his power as his chest rose and fell under her hand. Her senses were being bombarded, assaulted by his strength, his closeness, even his scent.

He smelled like a man. Musky and warm, like freshly plowed earth after a long rain.

Logan watched his bride watching him, her violet eyes wide with curiosity. He wasn't a vain man, but he found himself hoping she liked what she saw. The lady was delicately made and he had no wish to frighten her unnecessarily. Their joining would be almost painless if he could control his desire long enough to arouse her.

If he could control his desire? His body was growing harder with each passing moment. The light caress of his bride's hand was making him burn.

"There, you are clean again," Zara said, dropping the cloth into the basin and stepping back. Her husband frightened her in ways she'd never experienced before. Just as she had sensed that he would fight without mercy, she sensed that he could give without limits. Her future, and the future of her people, depended upon how he used those qualities.

"Has the wound healed?" Logan asked, reaching for her hand.

Zara put her hands behind her back, fearful that if he touched her, she would evaporate like mist under the power of the morning sun. "It is nothing, my lord. A prick of the skin. Do not concern yourself."

"But I am concerned," he said. His eyes searched her face. "You are my wife now. Everything you do concerns me."

Zara longed to tell him that everything he did concerned her, as well, but she kept the words inside. Along with the feelings that were growing stronger by the minute.

As raw desire radiated through Logan's body, he forced himself to move slowly, to take a deep breath laced with incense and the perfume of night-blooming flowers. He wasn't a boy to reach and grab without thought, or an animal to mount and mate without caring if his bride received the satisfaction that was her due. He was a man, a soldier, who knew his strength could bring pain as well as pleasure. Calling upon the discipline the military had taught him, Logan held out his hand.

"Come to me," he said in a husky tone. "We can debate the rights and wrongs of the universe some other time."

Zara felt her muscles tighten with apprehension. Her husband's voice was deep, full of authority. His expression said he expected her to obey him. She wondered if he meant to begin their marriage like a military campaign, to conquer her by force, if necessary.

After a moment, Zara calmed her racing heart and took the steps to close the distance between herself and the man who now ruled by her side. She offered him a smile. "Where were you born?"

Taken back by the question, Logan gave her a skeptical look. "On Melya Four. Why?"

"I'm curious," she replied candidly. "I know nothing about you."

He watched her with eyes that were as dark as the night.

"Melya Four is a military colony," she commented, thinking she'd come upon an explanation for her husband's behavior. If all he'd ever known was the Galactic Guard, she couldn't chastise him for his gruff manner. Soldiers were gruff men. Their existence was for war, and they led their lives as if a battle waited on every horizon.

Logan considered her curiosity, wondering if she thought to discover something to use against him, a weakness that would make him vulnerable to her rebel friends. Deciding a few personal facts might lessen the tension in the room, he told her what most of his men already knew. "The men of my family have always been soldiers. I was fostered on Melya Four by a brigade of Guards."

"Fostered?" She'd never encountered the word before.

"Adopted," he explained with a grudging tone. "My father was killed during the riot on Sarcaus, in the western sector."

"What about your mother?" Zara asked. The more she knew about her husband, the better prepared she'd be to make a life with him.

"What does my mother have to do with calming your virgin fears?" he asked.

His bluntness embarrassed Zara at the same time as it infuriated her. "I'm trying to have a conservation," she said, unable to control her temper. Nessa had always said

59

it was quick to spark. "Is that so unthinkable?"

Logan smiled, a lopsided, boyish smile that softened his stern features and made him totally irresistible. "I don't usually talk to women."

Zara didn't need to ask what he did *do* with women. She was standing a scant few inches from him and could sense his power. It was vibrating through her body, joining the storm of sensations she was doing her best to quench. If she didn't get herself under control, all would be lost. The moment Logan discovered she was vulnerable, he'd start probing her mind, seeking the location of the hidden rebels. Although Nessa didn't believe an outsider could use the link, Zara wasn't so sure. The Commander of the Galactic Guard was like no outsider she'd ever met before. There was a raw, untamed energy about him. A power that could easily match her own, if it were properly channeled.

It was said that when a daughter of the House of Queens met her true mate, she would be able to link with him so strongly that she would indeed be able to know his thoughts as surely as she knew her own. Not telepathy, but a unique bonding of minds that would offer her and her husband an emotional satisfaction that would parallel their physical pleasure when they made love.

Sensing Logan the way she did now, Zara could believe the legend.

Logan examined his bride. She was standing a breath away, her pale skin glowing in the candlelight, her eyes clear and true, her body tempting his resolve. Beneath his outward control, his body throbbed with need. He didn't like wanting Zara of Nubria so much that he had to calm his desire by remembering that she was harboring rebels. Rebels who would willingly rekindle a galactic war if given the opportunity.

He'd been telling the truth when he'd said that he rarely talked to women. The females he'd known in the

60

past were for pleasure, not conversation. Yet, he realized that this female was different. She was his wife. His mate for life, according to Nubrian custom. It would benefit him, and his plans for the future, if he didn't forgot that fact, and in his haste to have her, close a door that would serve him better if it remained open.

"The female who gave me birth was a vessel," he finally told her.

Zara had heard of planets where children were carried in the womb of women who had been paid for the service of gestating a child. The technology of their time had done away with the concept of a true family. If a man wanted a child, he simply hired a woman to receive his seed, planted it, and paid the female for the infant once it was born.

Zara thought the practice heartless. The idea of Logan being conceived in such an unfeeling, mechanical manner made her blood run cold.

There was no point in questioning him further. Any man born from such a union knew little about true affection, especially a man who had been raised by a garrison of soldiers.

"Any more questions?" Logan asked in a low voice.

Zara shook her head.

Logan held his breath as a mixture of moonlight and candlelight caught in his bride's pale hair, making it shine as if it were on fire. For a few moments, he allowed himself the pure pleasure of looking at her, knowing that she belonged to him.

Zara tried to maintain a calm facade, although her mind raced in time with her heartbeat. She thought of the stone in the prayer garden, of the gentle song of the nocturnal birds that visited the alcove after sunset, of the pleasant coolness of the spring breeze. None of the images soothed her.

"What is it like to be a queen?" Logan asked her unexpectedly. The proximity of his beautiful bride was making it difficult to control himself. He wanted to seek the warmth of her body, to feel the texture of her skin, to taste the wine that had just moistened her lips.

"Frightful at times," she admitted candidly. Then, recalling the love and affection that her people gave so freely, she added, "Humbling. Wonderful. A responsibility of the heart, as well as the mind."

The breath came out of Zara as Logan reached out and lifted her chin with the tip of a callused finger. The simple touch flashed through her like a bolt of unexpected lightning, setting her senses ablaze.

Logan felt the slight tremor that went through Zara at his touch. He realized that she was afraid of him, or what he planned to do to her. He didn't want her afraid. He wanted her warm and willing, desperate for his caress, clinging to him until her body was damp with sweat and her eyes were glazed with desire.

"You speak as if each of the people you rule is a personal friend."

"My people are more than friends, my lord. They are a part of me."

Logan didn't understand the jealousy that sprouted inside him. It was simply there, nourished by a desire too long held in check. His hand moved from the edge of Zara's chin until it wrapped around the back of her neck. He pulled her close, forcing her to stand on her tiptoes to meet his descending mouth. Before their lips touched, he growled. "I hope they forgive me for not inviting them into our bedchamber. Tonight, their queen belongs only to her husband."

The thoughts that had been bouncing around in Zara's head vanished the moment Logan's mouth came crushing down on hers. For the first time in her life, she couldn't think of anything.

Logan fought the urge to rip away the sheer fabric that was shielding his wife's body from his touch. For the time being, he simply kissed her, tasting the warm wine-spiced texture of her lips, capturing her soft gasp of surprise as his mouth molded to fit hers. The scent of burning incense mixed with the fragrance of a woman, filling his nostrils, floating up from her warm skin as he allowed his hands to come to rest on her bare arms. Her skin was as soft as the cloth that covered her body, reminding him of the harsh life he'd led and how easily he could bruise her if he tightened his hold.

Having never been kissed before, Zara had no way of knowing if Logan was an expert at the craft, but she suspected he was. His mouth was hot and hard on hers, his tongue probing gently, teasing her until she felt her body weaken and go limp. Her brain was able to register the impossibility of keeping her emotions caged as he pulled her even closer. There was no way she could keep her mind separate from her body when he was pressing so intimately against her. There was no way she could pretend not to feel the powerful arms that held her so easily, or the strength of his warrior's body. Her only redemption was knowing that her mind was too boggled by Logan's touch to form any rational path he might be able to follow.

"My lord," she gasped softly as he ended the kiss.

"My name is Logan. Say it." His breath was a brush of warm air over her thoroughly kissed mouth.

"Logan."

"We are man and wife," he told her before his mouth sought hers a second time.

Logan wasn't sure why he'd verbally reaffirmed the vows they'd spoken earlier in the day. Perhaps it was because he wanted to reassure his virgin bride that nothing that passed between them was wrong, or perhaps it was because he needed the reassurance that she was his. Either way, he'd said the words. They were the last ones he intended to speak for a long time.

Keeping his passion in check, Logan lay siege to Zara's senses with the skill of a well-trained general. While his mouth possessed her completely, his hands began to move, slowly edging their way up her arms, pausing briefly at her shoulders, then retracing the path. She trembled under the restrained touch, but it wasn't a shudder caused by fright. It was a woman's response and it made Logan want to shout in triumph.

His hands moved once again, but this time he didn't stop at her shoulders. His fingertips found her collarbone beneath the silky cloth, then the soft hollow of her throat. Inch by slow inch, he discovered her. And inch by slow inch, Zara was unraveled by his touch.

Her skin tingled at the gliding heat of his caresses on her exposed flesh. Her pulse quickened and her blood heated until it was flowing like a spring flood through her veins. Never had she imagined a man's caress frightening her and exciting her at the same time. Never had she wanted to hold on to another human being until their flesh melted together and they were no longer separate, but one person. The thought would have been staggering if she'd been able to hold on to it long enough, but it raced out of her mind as quickly as it came.

"You feel good," Logan said. He wasn't a man of fancy words and he'd done an excellent job of saying those three. He was kissing her, touching her, but it wasn't enough. If he believed in his wife's ancient gods, he'd offer a prayer for patience. His was gone.

While Logan looked at her, his hands continued their gentle attack, weakening her defenses. "Don't be afraid," he said. "I'm a soldier, but I've no war with you, lady wife."

Zara wasn't sure if she should be reassured or alarmed at his words. What she could sense about Logan said he was a man who knew little of affection or compassion, yet his touch was as light as sunshine, and just as warm. Zara looked into his eyes. They were still as dark as night, but the angry gleam that had heated them when he'd

marched into their bedchamber had been replaced by a
midnight softness. She felt dizzy from the whirlwind of
emotions that he aroused in her—fear, excitement, anticipation, things she was too inexperienced to understand. Mysterious things that were just beyond reach.

Logan saw the confusion in her eyes and smiled. His
hands stroked gingerly up and down her back, feeling
the outline of her spine, savoring the texture of silk and
warm skin under his fingertips. His bride was delicate,
but her power as a woman was strong. He was a man,
hard and ready, but he didn't want to rush her.

"Relax," he whispered as his tongue teased the side of
her neck.

Zara almost laughed. There was no relaxing the seeth-
ing sensations assaulting her body. They wouldn't go
away, not as long as Logan's hands caressed her so gently.
When he gathered her hair up in his hand and released
it to fall back against her, Zara caught a shaky breath.
When he reached for the laces holding her gown in
place, she stiffened.

"I want to see you," he said matter-of-factly. "Don't be
embarrassed."

When Logan was kissing her, touching her, she could
forget that he was a stranger. Having him stare at her,
appraising her worth as a female specimen, was something else altogether. She started to protest, but he
stopped the words with a dark stare that said he would
have what she'd pledged to him in front of her people
and his soldiers.

He gave the laces of her gown a quick tug. The garment loosened, but it didn't fall. The sheer silk clung to
her breasts, accentuating the hard nipples his kisses had
aroused. Realizing his determination, Zara closed her
eyes and yielded to what she couldn't prevent.

Slowly, Logan peeled the silk away from her skin. His
eyes narrowed as he saw the creamy color of her breasts
revealed. Desire curled through him, around him, mak-

ing it more difficult to control his impatience. He wanted
to take the pink crowns into his mouth. He wanted to
suckle her until she was moaning, begging him to end
the sweet pain and fulfill the promise he'd given her in
the dining hall—to pleasure her the way only a man
could pleasure a woman.

Zara opened her eyes to find Logan staring at her. The
feelings she could sense coming from him ebbed and
flowed through her, currents of emotion so strong that
they threatened the ability of her legs to hold her upright. His gaze seemed to burn her skin, yet she could
feel the cool breeze blowing through the window. The
combination of night wind and imagined heat made her
tingle all over.

Logan wanted to tell her that she was beautiful. As
beautiful as anything he'd ever seen, more beautiful than
the women he'd paid to ease the physical needs of a
soldier returned from battle, but he didn't say the words.
Instead, he continued to look at her.

After what seemed like an eternity of slow-moving seconds, he reached for her. Zara found herself pressed
against his chest, bare skin to bare skin, heartbeat to
heartbeat, woman to man. His mouth was more urgent,
his hands more demanding. His kiss stole what few
thoughts she'd been able to gather while his touch made
the small fire inside her burst into an uncontrollable
blaze of need.

The kiss ended and their eyes met and held. Zara resisted the urge to stand on her tiptoes and claim Logan's
mouth again. The lack of affection between them should
have been enough to make her wary of his touch, but it
wasn't. Like the power of his thoughts, the male strength
of his body beckoned her, calling to female needs as old
as the universe.

Another tug from Logan's war-callused hands and the
white gown fell to the floor. Zara flinched, but she didn't
retreat. Like the link she had formed with him earlier,

there was no stopping the course of events their marriage had set into motion.

There was a trace of amusement and satisfaction in his eyes as he reached out and lifted her off her feet. Before Zara could protest, she was being placed in the center of the mattress. He stood next to the bed, casting a shadow over her body, while his eyes consumed her. She held back a gasp of surprise when he undid his trousers and slid them down his legs, stepping out of the constricting pants.

She'd seen statues of naked men—the artisans of the north delighted in displaying the physical form—but she'd never seen a real man, a flesh-and-blood man, stripped down to nothing but his skin. Her husband was the same golden color all over. His long, lean muscles were stretched over a tall frame. She could see several small circular scars, caused by the pinpoint heat of a laser pistol, but the imperfections only enhanced the primitive quality of his well-toned body.

All thoughts of rebels and watchtowers left Logan's mind as he looked down at his beautiful bride. She was female perfection. And she was his for the taking.

Chapter Six

Zara's embarrassment increased as Logan stood staring at her. A tangle of emotions began to grow, coiling inside her. Fear, anticipation, desire. Although she'd never physically wanted a man before, she recognized passion for what it was. Strong, pulling, a magnet reaching out for what attracted it.

Logan sat on the side of the bed. His eyes never left her face as his hand began to caress her. He rubbed a hand up her bare arm, feeling the silkiness of her skin. Slowly, his hand continued upward, until it was stroking the long strands of silver blond hair. His bride was a peculiar kind of witch, he decided. A witch who could cast a spell with nothing but her jeweled eyes.

While his hand gently brushed her hair, a small smile curved the line of his hard mouth. "Did you inherit your beauty from your mother?" Before Zara could answer, he bent his head and kissed her, sealing off her reply.

Her hands went to his upper arms, then gradually to his shoulders, clinging to him as his mouth demanded more and more of her attention. The kiss was long and surprisingly gentle. His tongue teased her lips and they parted, allowing the slow penetration of his own.

Somewhere deep inside her, the fire leaped again, burning away everything but the heat of her husband's body as he pressed against her. Her warrior might not understand love, but he wasn't a cruel man, his touch was firm but controlled, and Zara knew he meant her no harm.

Lifting his mouth just a bit, he whispered, "Trust me. Give yourself to me."

His dark eyes studied her as he continued caressing her arm, moving to her collarbone, then slowly downward. Although she didn't speak, she knew he could see the answer in her gaze. There was no fighting what was happening between them. It was an inevitable attraction, one they both felt.

When his hand covered her breast, Zara closed her eyes for a moment to contain the spark of surprise that spiraled through her. His hand was large, his palm hot and callused, and it felt wonderful. She laced her arms around his neck and kissed him fervently, lost in the storm of sensations he'd unleashed.

The candles continued to flicker and dance as the evening breeze turned into a warm summer wind, but all Zara could feel was the intensity of his touch. She was getting drunk on his kisses. They were thoroughly intoxicating and oh, so wonderful.

Logan fought the urge to mount her and bury himself in her feminine warmth. He'd promised her pleasure and he would give it to her, as much as she could handle, until she cried out for him to take her. He watched her eyes widen as he unlaced her arms from around his neck and stretched them out to the sides, exposing her breasts for his full attention. He could feel the tension in her body and the apprehension in her gaze. He had her naked and at his mercy, and she both wanted and feared what he would do. Lovemaking was still a mystery to her,

this queen who ruled a world. But not for long. Logan
meant to teach her as much as one night would allow.

The rasp of his fingertips made her aroused breasts
grow even tighter. The pearly crowns begged for his
mouth and he answered. Lowering his head, he licked
each rosy tip. A small gasp escaped her mouth, and he
smiled to himself. His bride had passion, but did she
have enough to equal the desire of a man who had gone
months without a woman?

Knowing the strength of his need, Logan banked the
fires heating his blood and continued his slow seduction.
The warm womanly smell of her enticed him, and he
circled her hard nipples with his tongue, teasing them
until she arched upward, silently demanding more.

When his mouth closed over her right nipple, Zara bit
back a whimper. He suckled her gently at first, his tongue
laving her nipple, his hand caressing the slope of her
breast. She squirmed, unconsciously trying to get closer
to the unbelievable pleasure. She'd never imagined anything feeling like this. The harder he sucked, the more
the sensations swirled through her body, warming her all
the way to the bottom of her feet.

His mouth moved to the other breast, treating it to the
same care. His hands moved up and down her rib cage,
stopping to knead her breasts as he continued teasing
them with his tongue, then his teeth. The small nibbling
of her flesh started an uncontrollable ache in the center
of her.

Suddenly Zara wanted to touch him, too. Her hands
went to his shoulders, then hesitantly they began to move
downward, exploring the thick mat of dark hair that covered his upper chest. Flat male nipples were as hard as
hers, and she wondered what he would feel if she put
her mouth on them.

Logan shuddered as her nails raked over his chest. His
need was fierce, but he was determined to make their
wedding night more than a physical joining. He wanted

his bride to surrender more than her body. For some unknown, inexplicable reason, he wanted her to accept him as her real husband, not just a bedmate she had to tolerate in order to keep her throne from being completely taken away from her. He wanted her to know that she belonged to him.

Logan didn't analyze the reasons why he wanted so much from his bride. Like so many things in life, he accepted them. The universe was full of unanswered questions.

His hand swept down her thigh, caressing all of her that he could reach. His touch made the soft skin of her stomach tighten, then relax, as she gradually learned the feel of him, and he of her. His lips left the sweet flesh of her breasts and returned to her mouth, tasting her more fully this time. When his fingers combed through the silvery curls that shielded the most female part of her, Zara tried to pull away from him.

Logan wouldn't let her. "Trust me," he told her in a low, husky voice. "Relax and enjoy what I can give you."

Zara tried to relax her body at the same time she tried to control her mind. It was like sitting still and walking at the same time—an impossible task. The more Logan assaulted her physical senses, the wider her mind opened to absorb the exotic sensations he was creating within her. Her thoughts were a riot of confusion. She couldn't stop them from dashing around in her head, bouncing off one another, as his mouth and hands taught her all the wonderful things Nessa's explanation had only hinted at. Her worry about forming a link vanished as she realized it was impossible to think clearly and feel so intensely at the same time.

"Touch me," Logan said, making the request sound like an order.

Zara ignored his gruff tone and did as he asked, wanting to know his body as thoroughly as he was learning hers. Her hands moved from the hair on his chest to the

71

hard muscles of his upper arms and shoulders, then around to his back. Her husband was pure male strength. She could feel his power, touch it, and it pleased her.

Zara could also feel more scars, reminders of battles fought on faraway worlds, worlds where distrust and greed and ambition were commonplace.

She longed to teach him the other side of life, the wonderful, blissful pleasures that came from knowing the contentment of your own soul, but she didn't dare speak of such things now. If she could speak. The ability to say anything was quickly leaving her, being replaced by a need that only Logan could satisfy.

His fingers teased the female curls he'd discovered, then slowly penetrated them, touching her gently, probing to discover if she was ready for more. Zara trembled under the intimate caress and moaned his name.

The sound of it made Logan's impatience grow tenfold. He was wild to have her, and he knew he couldn't contain his need much longer. Still, he fought the primal urge to mate for the pure physical release of easing his loins. Insistently, gently, thoroughly, he touched the sensitive flesh between her legs until Zara opened them wider, giving him access to her entire body. Logan took what she offered, his caress growing bolder, while he rained kisses over her mouth, her neck, her breasts, and then the soft, pale skin of her stomach. He couldn't touch her enough, taste her enough, nor could he stop watching her, reveling in the soft sounds she made as he taught her that passion could be pain and pleasure combined.

Logan kept touching his bride, exploring her body, assaulting her senses, until she went stiff for a moment, then began writhing and arching up against his hand. His mouth covered hers, drinking in her female cry of surprise and pleasure. She was beautiful in her passion, and he relished the fact that he'd kept his promise.

Zara lay limply on the sheets, blinded by the unexpected upheaval of the universe. Nothing had prepared her for what she'd just felt. She drew in a deep breath, fighting to regain her composure.

Logan didn't want her composed; he wanted her wild. He wanted to take her to the point of being mindless again, to entice her beyond her limits, to feel her shiver under him as he joined her this time.

His eyes glittered with raw desire as he grasped her legs and spread them wide, then braced himself over her and slowly lowered himself until his aroused flesh was resting against the natural cradle of her body. Zara opened her eyes and looked up at him, and in that moment, in that twinkling of a second, he *felt* her pleasure as if it had been his own. His hands clenched in the silken sheets as the thought exploded in his mind the way the pleasure had exploded in his wife's body. It took Logan's breath.

Zara felt the pulsing internal energy of the link and knew that in her moment of mindless surrender, she'd allowed her thoughts to be totally exposed. Logan's touch had stolen her control. Before he could realize what had happened, she closed the link and called back the images that were little more than swirling colors and an intense burst of energy inside his mind.

Her husband's big body shuddered, then went still. He looked down at her and Zara smiled, letting the expression tell him how wonderful he had made her feel.

Logan saw the tears glittering in her violet eyes and something inside him clenched as tight as a fist. Whatever he'd felt was gone, but not forgotten. "You are a witch," he said, his voice raw with desire. "But know this, lady wife. From this moment on, you're *my* witch."

Supporting his weight on his arms, Logan slowly began to enter her.

Zara bit her bottom lip to keep from crying out as his hard flesh pushed into her. She felt stretched and full and strangely impatient.

Logan eased into her, claiming her body slowly. The hot, sleek feel of her was enough to make him grit his teeth. He was close to the edge already, but he refused to be pushed over by the silky clenching of her inner muscles as her female heat surrounded him. Holding on to the last of his self-control, he began to move in slow, patient strokes until she became accustomed to having him inside her.

Zara kept her eyes closed, afraid that if she opened them, she'd open her mind, as well. The magnificence of their physical joining was more than she could control. It was robbing her of her senses, slowly, erotically stealing her willpower from her, leaving her vulnerable. As Logan continued moving within her, she clutched at his shoulders, holding on to the only thing in the universe that she could—her husband.

Logan felt her body begin to respond again as he brought her to the brink of pleasure for the second time. He buried his face in the hollow of her throat and kissed her, then let his tongue tease the sensitive place. Zara whimpered softly, and he repeated the caress, using his teeth the second time. He could feel his control slipping away with each tormenting stroke inside her. There was no stopping it, no calling it back, and Logan started moving more forcefully, driving deeper and deeper into her, wanting more and more of her.

The sensations built inside Zara until she thought she would die of the wanting, the excruciating need and wonder of it all. She moved with him, lifting and arching and digging her nails into the sweat-dampened skin of his back. Logan's body responded to her female urgency, moving more powerfully, giving her all she demanded, demanding all she had to give.

When he felt her tighten around him, felt the tiny pulses of her body that increased with each thrust of his hips, heard the tiny cry of her satisfaction, he buried himself in her velvet sheath and relinquished himself to the same passion. There was no sense of time or place, only a hot rush of pleasure that left him feeling weakly content and strangely vulnerable.

The second sweet explosion overwhelmed Zara even more than the first, transforming her. Hot shimmers of exotic pleasure streamed through her body, taking her breath, stealing her thoughts once again. She squeezed her eyes shut, unaware that tears dampened her lashes, and rode out the rapturous storm.

Logan felt the rippling currents that were consuming his wife. They consumed him as well, bringing him another kind of satisfaction—the satisfaction of knowing that he'd found an equal partner for his desire, a woman who gave as blissfully as she received.

In the aftermath of the sensual storm, they lay together. Logan was reluctant to leave the warm nest of his wife's body. He shifted his weight to the side and, wrapping his arm around her, held her close.

Zara savored the closeness, the silent intimacy that existed between them now that the storm had passed. Her fingers stroked his shoulders. She found the leather tie that secured his hair and untied it, tossing it aside so she could run her fingers through the thick black mane. Logan made a deep purring sound as she massaged his neck and scalp.

Zara smiled.

"You look pleased," Logan said smugly.

"And you," she whispered.

Her answer was a long, deep kiss that said she knew she hadn't disappointed her husband. Their bodies were still joined, and Zara felt the kiss in more ways than one. Logan pressed against her, letting her feel his presence, telling her in his own way that the possession was still in progress.

Zara knew their joining didn't hold the same meaning for her warrior as it did for her. Intuitively, she under-

Patricia Waddell

stood that his ability to understand and receive love was limited by his lifestyle. He had been born to be a Galactic Guard, to give his loyalty and his life completely and courageously to the cause. He was extremely cautious, hardened by war and the things he'd seen. He guarded his heart as carefully as he guarded the borders of the Union, suspicious of anyone or anything that came too close.

"Do you want some wine?" Logan asked, caressing her again as he withdrew from her.

Zara shook her head, sending a shimmering wave of pale hair around her shoulders. She watched as he got up from the bed and walked to the serving table a few feet away. Instead of refilling his glass with wine, he poured some water from the crystal pitcher sitting next to a plate of succulent fruit. Unable to resist, she looked at him again, her eyes absorbing the masculine planes of his body.

"Are you hungry?" he asked.

Once again Zara shook her head. She couldn't find the words she wanted to say to him, so she remained silent.

Logan returned to the bed. Zara moved over to make room for the large man who would sleep with her from this night forward. As she did so, she reached for the coverlet, feeling embarrassed again.

"Don't cover yourself," he said. "I like looking at you."

He caressed her again, bringing her close. He was a solitary person, but Logan found he couldn't detach himself from this woman by merely leaving her body. He liked the sight and sound and scent of her too much to deny himself the pleasure of holding her. It was puzzling to think that a few hours of marriage and one intimate encounter could effect him so strongly. He wasn't a man given to sentiment or emotion. He'd married Zara because he'd been ordered to marry her. He'd made love to her because she'd aroused his body, and he was hold-

76

ing her now because she felt too good to let go.

She was his, by law and by mating, and he could accept that. She'd come to accept it as well. And with that acceptance, she'd eventually tell him what he wanted to know—where she'd hidden the rebels.

Zara was pleasantly exhausted and close to sleep, but the change in Logan's mood brought her eyes open. She could sense the direction his thoughts were taking and prepared herself for an arrogant demand that she reveal the rebel's hiding place before they both slept.

What she got was Logan's hands lifting her, until she was lying on top of him. She shifted, trying to get comfortable, and his hands positioned her legs on either side of his muscular thighs so that she was straddling his body. She could feel him pressing intimately against her and his readiness surprised her.

"You belong to me," he said. He wrapped his hand around the nape of her neck. His grip tightened as his mouth closed over hers. The kiss was long and hard and possessive.

The heat of Logan's hands unraveled Zara's anger at being addressed like one of his soldiers. She returned the kiss as he teased her breasts, bringing her nipples to an aching alertness that said she too wanted more of what he had to offer her. She pressed helplessly into his warm palms, loving the feel of his hands and the tingling sensations that went up and down her spine.

Logan ended the kiss, his eyes glowing with renewed passion, his body throbbing as he felt the center of her pressing against his need. "There will be no secrets between us," he insisted as he lifted her gently, then entered inside her so deeply that she gasped. "No secrets and no lies. Do you understand?"

His demand pushed aside the pleasure long enough for her temper to flare. Clutching his shoulders, feeling the intimacy of his body inside her, she glared at him. "I understand that you know nothing about me."

77

"I know all I need to know," Logan said in a low growl as he pushed his hips upward and probed the depths of her tight silken sheath. "You are my wife. My queen."

Zara had never wanted to strike another person before, but she desperately wanted to slap the smug look off her husband's face. Fighting the urge to slide back down on him, to feel his blunt flesh stretching her again, to enjoy the shimmering sensations it created, she pierced him with a violet stare and shook her head. Silver hair fanned out around her. "There is more to me than my body," she said. "I have thoughts and hopes and dreams. A husband should care for these things."

Logan moved again, returning and retreating in slow, smooth strokes that made Zara's anger a thing of the past. He watched her face as the ecstasy began to build with each thrust of his hips. Seeing her passion excited him. His hands fisted in her pale hair as he kissed her again. "Take me with you," he murmured against her lips. "Let me feel your pleasure."

Zara tried to control the sensual storm stealing her senses, but it was useless. Her body filled with heat, making her skin damp and her breathing labored as the tempest built and built inside her. The storm couldn't be stopped or restrained. When Logan arched upward, his hands on her hips, holding her in place as he claimed more and more of her, Zara tossed her head back and cried out his name.

A short time later, Zara slept in his arms. Moonlight filled the room, outlining the simple furnishings. The candles had burnt out. Logan thought to ease himself from the bed, but Zara's head was resting on his chest, her breath fluttering softly over his bare skin. He found himself smiling as he watched her.

The temptation to wake her was overwhelming, but he fought it. He had years to make love to her, to feel her passion, to watch her eyes glaze with need and then satisfaction as he poured himself into her.

He lifted his hand and carefully brushed a strand of silver hair away from her face. He'd never known a woman to give herself so completely, holding nothing back. He'd told her there would be no lies between them and there hadn't been, at least not in the bed they shared as husband and wife. But their marriage wouldn't be confined to a single room of the palace.

In the coming days he would stand by Zara's side as an equal ruler. Nubria's first king. The responsibility deserved thought and attention. He had much to learn about the planet and its people.

The old woman, Nessa, came to mind, and Logan decided to seek her counsel. Her loyalty to his wife was unquestionable, but he'd sensed her wisdom would be given freely if asked, and he wanted no surprises while the watchtower was being constructed. Once the tower was in place, he'd have the ability to survey the entire planet within minutes, as well as the surrounding expanse of space that separated Nubria from its closest neighbor.

Unaccustomed to sleeping with a large man in her bed, Zara moved restlessly, opening her eyes. "Is something wrong?" she asked lazily, still drifting between the dreamy world she'd left behind and the darkness of the room where she lay curled up at her husband's side.

"Sleep," Logan said, knowing that if she awoke completely, he'd take her again, and he didn't want to abuse her delicate body.

Zara yawned and sat up slowly. Although the bedchamber candles had gone out the moons drenched her husband's body in soft light. She looked at the dark hair covering his chest and arms and legs. He was a powerful man and it showed even though he was lying relaxed at her side. His masculine beauty took her breath for a moment and she was amazed at how gentle he'd been with her.

"I'm not sleepy," she said, stretching her arms over her

head, unaware that in doing so she was making Logan's mouth water to taste her breasts again. "I'm hungry."

He laughed and got out of bed, totally at ease with his nakedness, while Zara reached for the coverlet. He selected some fruit from the tray and carried it to her. "Do you always eat in the middle of the night?" he asked, as she reached for the plate in his hands.

"No," she told him. "I usually sleep until dawn without any interruptions."

He laughed again, a deep rumbling sound that pleased Zara's ears. "Am I an interruption, then?"

In spite of her maturity as queen Zara blushed. "No. I'm not used to sharing my bed with a husband."

"You'll get used to it," Logan said as he poured Zara a glass of water and himself the last of the wine. "Just like you'll get used to sharing your throne with me."

Zara nibbled on a wedge of red melon. The fruit was one of her favorites, but its short growing season would be coming to an end soon and she'd have to wait another year to taste its delicate flavor again. "Nubria's throne may not be what you expect, my lord."

"How so?"

Zara shrugged. Her husband was a complex man, but not so complicated that she wouldn't be able to sort out his moods. Eventually.

"Our government is more spiritual than political," she told him. "Nubria is divided into provinces. As queen I rule the Assembly meetings, but each province governs itself. The province is overseen by a panel of councillors. They collect taxes and distribute surpluses for various needs. The citizens elect them to serve, and they are held accountable for the offices that bear their name. Of course, every Nubrian citizen has the right to appeal to the throne for consideration if he believes the provincial council is not addressing the issue properly. But my duties as high priestess outweigh my political responsibilities."

The political tutor had explained the functions of pro-vincial rule to Logan, so he wasn't surprised to find out that Zara didn't rule supreme. What did surprise him was the intermingling of religion and government. On most worlds, religion was considered a private matter, not one to be endorsed and encouraged by its leaders.

"I have no wish to interfere in your spiritual duties," he told her.

"Then you have no wish to share my throne," Zara replied calmly. "You cannot have one without the other, my lord."

Logan gave her a fierce look. "Don't mock me, lady wife."

Zara let out a frustrated sigh. "I am not mocking you, my lord. I am trying to tell you the ways of things here on Nubria. You are mistaken if you think you can rule with a sword. My people have no need of an iron hand. A compassionate heart will serve them much better."

"Is that why you defied the Council and gave the rebels sanctuary?" he asked her. "Compassion?"

Zara nodded. She could sense Logan's anger, and more; something stronger than anger was making the fragile link between them vibrate. The dark emotion was beyond her reach, but it was there, hidden within the warrior. Whatever his motives, she knew they had to be satisfied before he could open his heart to the life her world offered him, a life she would share.

"Nubria does not condone violence in any form, my lord. Nor do we shelter those who harm others. You will find no threat here," she told him, knowing he wouldn't believe her.

"I'm not looking for threats," Logan said. "I'm looking for Keelan, the leader of a rebellion." He looked at her with eyes the color of death, black and unforgiving. "And I will find him, lady wife. With or without your assis-tance."

Her husband might be a gentle lover, but he was a

dangerous man when he was on a mission, and he'd come to Nubria to find the rebels. Knowing one night couldn't undo what a lifetime of military training had instilled in him, Zara kept her voice light and her expression calm. "Whatever you find on Nubria, my lord, I hope it brings you contentment."

Chapter Seven

Logan's contentment lasted only as long as he slept with Zara in his arms. The morning after their marriage, he awoke to find his lovely wife gone. Angry with her because she would vacate their bed so quickly, and angry at himself because his soldier instincts had been so soundly asleep that he hadn't felt her leaving his side, Logan reached for the black trousers he'd discarded in his haste to consummate their marriage. When he was once again dressed in the uniform of a Galactic Guardian, his sword at his side, he walked to the door and bellowed out Tolman's name.

The servant came running, the folds of his blue robe flapping about his skinny legs.

"Yes, my lord. How may I serve you?"

"You can find my wife," Logan said with a grunt.

Tolman smiled. "Our lady is in her private garden, attending to her morning prayers."

"More prayers!" Logan gave the bed a quick glance. He'd awoken ready to teach his beautiful queen another lesson in the exotic art of lovemaking only to find her gone. His body was as hard as his mood. "Is that all the woman does?"

Tolman was wise enough not to laugh. "Lieutenant Maddock is having the first meal with the other officers. Does my lord care to join them or have his meal privately?"

"Your lord wants to know where this private garden is," Logan said none too politely.

Thinking the ways of outsiders were indeed strange, Tolman nodded respectfully and motioned his new king toward the door. The sharp sound of Logan's boots filled the empty labyrinthlike corridors until they reached a portico at the back of the palace. Tolman nodded that they'd reached their destination, then made himself scarce.

Logan stepped outside. He blinked as the bright sunlight hit his face. Then stared as he realized the light was more pink than gold. Looking up at the sky, he quickly realized that the rays of Nubria's golden sun were being defused by billowy purple clouds. *Pink sunlight.* It was the strangest thing he'd ever seen.

His amazement lasted until Logan saw his wife. The Queen of Nubria was kneeling on a small mat in front of an oblong white stone. The unmarred rock was smaller than the one in the throne hall where they had taken their vows. Her back was to him, her luminous hair flowing to her hips, her feet bare in reverence to what she considered a holy altar. Her arms were raised high, as if she were embracing the morning sun, palms held up, fingers spread wide.

Like the soldier he was, Logan surveyed his surroundings, absorbing the details of the queen's private retreat. Like the unusual sunlight, the garden was filled with plants and flowers unknown to other worlds. Thick vines, heavy with white and gold blossoms, covered the stone walls that gave the garden its privacy. Trees with wide green leaves and small red berries clustered at the tips of their branches offered shade from the sun's warmth. Unseen birds, hidden in the thick boughs of the trees, chattered and sang. Their natural song blended with the lyrical words of his wife as she offered a prayer to gods Logan had no desire to know.

"What do you pray for?"

Zara had felt her husband's presence the moment he'd stepped into her sanctuary. Hearing his voice made her heart leap with anticipation. When she turned to look upon his face, would his eyes hold the tenderness of a lover or the displeasure of a warrior? She closed her eyes and reached for his thoughts. *Displeasure.* She shouldn't be surprised. He'd gone to sleep with images of rebels and revenge in his mind.

Slowly, gracefully, Zara stood and turned to Logan. She saw the hard curve of his lips, the dark expression in his eyes, and knew that his displeasure was directed at her rather than the rebels he planned to seek.

"I hope the morning finds you well, my lord," she greeted him, then remembered that he had asked her a question, and as a commander of the Guard he would expect an immediate answer. "I was praying for the wisdom of a new day."

"I would think that a new wife would be more concerned about her husband than wisdom," Logan said, unappeased by her response. "I woke expecting to find my wife by my side, yet I am forced to call upon the services of a stoop-shouldered servant to ferret out her hiding place."

Zara longed to tell him that her prayers for wisdom had indeed been centered around him, but she wasn't ready to admit how much power this man held over her, so soon and so easily. Just looking at him made her heart beat oddly and her skin tingle in anticipation of his next kiss. It was unnerving and just a little frightening to find her female passion so quickly kindled. He was still very much a stranger to her. But not so much a stranger that

85

she couldn't recognize his displeasure for what it was. He had planned on making love to her again this morning and she had upset his plans by not being within reach. Did the man really think he could control her mind and her heart by conquering her body? Yes. Zara realized that was exactly what her proud warrior believed. She smiled to herself. Nubria's new king had a lot to learn.

"I have prayed in this garden every morning since I was a child," she told him. "My position as queen obligates me to seek spiritual guidance for my people. As your wife, I am required to attend to your needs as well. It may take time for me to find a proper balance between the two."

Logan laughed. "You are a well-versed diplomat, lady wife."

Zara smiled. "Another requirement of my rank."

Logan's laughter ceased as he looked down at her. The pinkish sunlight made her eyes glow like jeweled fire and her skin appear as soft as the clouds that shrouded Nubria's sun. His heart pounded with renewed desire and he buried his big hand in the thick mane of her silver hair, pulling her close. All thoughts of prayers and diplomatic words were forgotten as his lips met hers with an urgency that transformed his anger into need.

Zara felt his hard chest against her breasts, the steely strength of his thighs and the power of his arms, and reveled in the differences between them. She clung to him, instinctively moving her body closer, wanting what he wanted.

Knowing his men were watching, even though no hint of black and red uniforms could be seen, Logan ended the kiss. Zara leaned against him, her breasts heaving, her mouth damp from his kiss. "Come," he said, his voice gentled by his wife's willingness. "There is much to be done this day."

"What is so urgent that it forces us to leave the peace of my private garden?" Zara asked, still wrapped in his warm embrace. "It is a lovely day. Can you not spare a few moments for the sunlight and flowers?"

Logan was sorely tempted to give in to her. The scent of her, mingled with the natural perfume of the flowers blooming in the garden, made him want much more than a few moments with his new wife, but he dared not give them. He couldn't let Zara's bewitching qualities make him forget his mission.

"The engineers will arrive by week's end," he told her, reluctantly loosening his hold so she could step back from him. "I have to select a location for the watchtower."

"Watchtower! The Council said nothing to me of a watchtower." Her mood changed in the blink of a violet eye. "I will not allow it."

"The decision is not yours to allow or disallow," Logan told her candidly. How like the Council to leave it up to him to reveal the rest of their demands. His disgust for anything political increased as his wife fisted her hands on her hips and glared up at him. "I rule Nubria, now, lady wife. There will be no sharing in its protection."

"Nubria doesn't need protection," she argued, letting her temper rule for the first time in days. "Its neutrality is its protection. Its generosity and compassion for others have kept it safe for thousands of years. A watchtower will do nothing but announce distrust to the universe. It will make us liars in the eyes of those who once thought us a peaceful people."

Logan wasn't in the habit of debating military theories with women any more than he was used to having them flee his bed. To show compromise now would be to forever weaken his position with his unpredictable queen. Zara had to learn what becoming his wife really meant. He didn't expect her loyalty; he demanded it. "Nubria forfeited its neutrality when its queen gave sanctuary to the enemies of the Union."

"So this is to be the justice of the Council," Zara hissed.

"My people are to be punished for the sins of their queen."

"Building a watchtower is necessary, not punitive," Logan said, feeling his temper surfacing. "You've been too long sheltered," he told her. "The galaxy is full of greedy governments that covet what the Union has built. The tower will dissuade them from thinking that they can take what they haven't earned."

The look he gave Zara almost frightened her, but she didn't cease her argument against the military installation that would forever change her planet. "A watchtower is an abomination to my people," she told him. "It shames our faith."

"It will protect the Union's eastern border, nothing more," Logan said, his expression colder than any Nubrian winter.

A shudder went through Zara. The gentle lover who had sought her trust on their wedding night was not the fierce soldier who stood before her now. She was seeing Commander Logan, the Galactic Guardian, who had been sent by the Unity Council to make sure a wayward queen with strange beliefs caused no more trouble. Her eyes dropped to the sword, sheathed at his side, and she remembered that it had been within his reach even while he was making love to her. She could feel the dark emotion again; it radiated from him like heat from the sun.

"We can talk after you've eaten," she suggested, searching for a way to end the argument without giving in to it.

"There will be no talk about the watchtower," Logan said, knowing she thought to change his mind. "The tower will be built. There are no words that can change what has been done or will be done."

Zara couldn't believe that. She wouldn't allow herself to think that there was no solution to the problem that had risen with the morning sun. Accepting her husband's mandate for the moment, she returned to the prayer mat and retreived her sandals. She put them on, then walked into the palace, ignoring the Galactic Guardian who watched her with cautious eyes.

"Have you selected a location for the watchtower?" Maddock asked as he joined Logan in the adviser's suite after the morning meal.

"Not yet," Logan admitted, turning away from the topography maps of Nubria he'd been furnished before leaving Melya Four. "I'll make my decision before the engineering crew arrives."

Maddock peered at the maps, displaying the rough terrain of Nubria's northern continent. "The mountains would seem better suited to the tower's capabilities," he remarked. "If we build to the south, we'll be tripping over farmers."

Logan neither agreed nor disagreed. His mind was on his wife. The confrontation in the garden had shown him another side of Nubria's beautiful queen. She was a stubborn woman.

"Find the old woman," he told Maddock, "and bring her to me."

His second in command arched a bushy brow. "The one they call Nessa?"

"Yes. I have questions that need answers."

Maddock left, wondering what the old woman could answer that the young queen could not. A short time later he returned with Nessa at his side.

"You seek my attention, Lord Logan," Nessa remarked as she entered the room where Zara's father had often consulted with her in the past.

"I wish to know more about this religion you seem to think controls your lives," Logan replied, getting right to the point. "Does it have a name?"

Nessa pondered his question for a moment before answering. "None that is remembered, my lord. To believers it is simply the faith we hold in our hearts."

89

"What does it demand of you?" He posed the question as he helped himself to a glass of water. He found he liked the taste, although water was supposed to have none. When he'd asked Tolman about it earlier, the old man had remarked that the city's drinking water came from the mountains to the north, where it was naturally filtered through the rocky passages that guided the river downstream and purified without adding modern-day chemicals.

This time Nessa didn't mull the question over. She answered immediately. "Our faith demands nothing but that, my lord. Faith."

"Your answer is nothing but a riddle, old woman," Logan shot back. "If I am to rule Nubria and its people, I need to understand them."

This time Nessa smiled. "I think you seek to understand one woman, my lord, not a populace of millions."

Maddock made an uncomfortable sound.

Logan gritted his teeth.

Nessa continued to smile.

Moving with the determination of a soldier, Logan put his hands on the table and leaned over it, glaring at the elderly female standing on the other side. Nessa's smile didn't waver. Finally, Logan's expression softened. "If your queen's faith is that of this planet, then understanding one will give me guidance for the other, will it not?"

"Perhaps," Nessa told him. "Our lady's faith is her strength. She is our High Priestess. To know her is to know what we hold dear to our hearts."

Logan was more concerned about Zara's stubbornness than her heart. She hadn't spoken a word to him since leaving the garden. It pricked at his temper more than any weapon had ever pierced his flesh. "Get on with it," he said impatiently.

"I will need to sit down," Nessa said. "The telling could take hours."

Logan rolled his eyes toward the ceiling as if he were

seeking patience from the gods he knew nothing about. Maddock stifled a laugh.

Once Nessa was seated comfortably in a chair beside the window, she folded her wrinkled hands in her lap and looked at Logan. "Our faith represents the eternal things," she began. "Once it was the faith of many worlds, but time and progress robbed peoples' hearts of what they believed, hardening them to the truth, turning their attentions inward instead of outward, blinding their eyes to the harmony of the universe.

"Nothing exists by itself," she continued. "No element is solitary, no person totally independent, no mind completely separated from the thoughts of another. It is in this truth that our faith achieves its purest form."

"If you believe that every person is dependent upon another, then why separate yourselves from other worlds, denying your people the luxuries that would make their daily burdens easier to bear?" Logan asked, truly curious.

"Other worlds celebrate the creators of luxury, not the creation of life," she told him. "You have seen but a small part of Nubria's natural beauty, my lord. Our trees grow strong, our flowers perfume the air, our children laugh and play in the sunlight. We carry no weapons because we do not fear one another. The food you have tasted was grown in a field furrowed by man and animal, not mechanical robots. Did you find its flavor a burden?"

Logan didn't need to answer. The appetite of his men at the two meals they'd eaten in the palace spoke for him. "You seek simplicity, or so my wife tells me."

Nessa nodded. "Simplicity of heart and mind and body is the practice of our faith. We believe in the everlasting qualities of the soul, my lord. To us, the universe and the soul are one and the same. A soul exists in the granite peaks of a mountain as surely as it exists in the beating of our own hearts. To dishonor the plants and animals that make up our world is to dishonor ourselves. To take without replenishing is to steal; to destroy that which we

91

do not have the power to replace is the greatest of all sins."

Logan frowned. "A watchtower would destroy nothing."

Nessa's pale eyes widened, then narrowed, as she realized why Nubria's new king had summoned her. "You think to build a watchtower."

"I *will* build a watchtower," Logan told her. "The rebellion has led others to think our union weak from the inside. Nubria will defend our eastern border."

"You have told our lady of this."

Logan nodded. "She isn't pleased."

The old woman's laughter was a crackling sound that made the hair on the back of Logan's neck stand up. "Lady Zara will never be pleased with a watchtower," she told him. "It will defile our world and shame our faith. She will never allow it."

"She can't stop it," Logan said with authority. "I rule Nubria now."

Nessa shook her head. "You may call yourself Nubria's king, but the people will follow their faith and the woman who manifests it."

"You speak treason, old woman," Maddock said bluntly.

Logan raised his hand, silencing his second in command. "Do you threaten me with another rebellion?" he asked Nessa.

"No, my lord. There is no threat in what I say, only truth."

"Explain yourself."

Nessa came to her feet. "Do not underestimate that which you do not understand," she cautioned him. "Your wife may not carry a sword, but her strength is the strength of a heart and mind true to the faith. For thousands of years the daughters of the House of Queens have maintained that which other worlds have coveted. The power of faith can be stronger than any sword."

"You give me another riddle," he fumed at her.

Nessa spread her arms wide. "I give you the answer to all you seek, my lord. It is up to you to open your heart and mind and see the truth that lies within your reach."

After several long, tense moments, Logan waved the old woman toward the door. Nessa went, bowing respectfully before she left her new king and his second in command staring after her.

"The foolish old woman," Maddock mumbled.

"Perhaps," Logan mused. Like his wife, Nessa had spoken with conviction. She believed, and that belief made her as strong of heart as any soldier under Logan's command.

Before Logan could return to his study of the maps and a location for the watchtower his wife so obstinately opposed, a knock on the door interrupted him.

Maddock walked to the closed door. He opened it to find a guard standing outside. "What is it?" he asked neutrally.

"The commander's wife," the soldier told him. "She plans to leave the palace."

Logan let out a curse he'd learned on Rysor, a mining planet at the center of the galaxy. The single word stung the ears of the two men close enough to hear it. "Where is she going?"

The soldier shook his head. "I'm not certain, Commander. I overheard her telling Tolman that she would be in the city for several hours."

Logan marched through the palace corridors, oblivious to the brightly colored murals that decorated the wide hallways. Maddock followed him. The new king had but one intent, to discover what his lovely queen was about to do, and where she was going to do it.

Did she think to hurry to the city to warn a rebel spy of the Council's intentions, or did she think to sulk in the marketplace because he would not bow to her wishes and forsake his mission?

Patricia Waddell

Tolman exited one of the rooms, and upon seeing his lord's face, gathered up the hem of his robe and hurried alongside Logan. "Can I serve you, my lord?"

"Where is my wife?" Logan asked, realizing it was the second time in the course of a single day he'd been forced to ask the ridiculous question.

"She is preparing to visit the city, my lord," Tolman replied, looking over his shoulder to see that Maddock wore the same grim expression as his commander. "She left only a few moments ago."

Logan's strides became longer. He marched into the courtyard, expecting to find his wife and a royal escort of servants. What he found brought him to an abrupt halt.

His wife was standing beside a beast that was half the size of a galactic scout ship. The animal was tall and bulky, with long ears that nearly reached the ground and legs as thick as a man. Tufts of course black and brown hair covered the beast's shoulders and forelegs, growing thicker near the animal's feet, which were wide and flat. Small black horns, adorned with gold paint, jutted out from the sides of the animal's elongated head. Its wide back and fleshy flanks were covered with a red blanket trimmed in gold fringe, and atop that was a saddle of sorts, with a high back to support the rider. A wide leather harness curled around the animal's huge belly and thick neck, keeping the chairlike saddle in place.

Zara was affectionately stroking the beast's wide snout while a small boy held what Logan assumed was a leash. The boy was outfitted as colorfully as the animal. He worn a red and gold vest and loose-fitting white trousers that tied just above the ankle. A pointed hat covered his dark hair, and in his right hand he carried a flimsy whip made of white and gold rope.

"By the stars," Maddock muttered. "I've never seen the like."

"Nor I," Logan agreed. He walked toward his wife. "Is this the way you plan to get to the city?"

"This is a *malaro,*" Zara said without turning around. "They're friendly animals and very loyal to a good master."

"I'd hate to see an unfriendly one," Maddock said under his breath.

Logan gave the officer a hard glare, then turned his attention back to the huge beast and the delicate woman who was stroking it like a pet kitten. Small amber eyes, partially hidden by baggy brown flesh, blinked lazily as Logan reached out to touch it.

"Put your hand under his nose so he can get your scent," Zara told him. "His name is Cyrel. He's been my transport since I was a small girl."

Cyrel's nose was large and dark and wet. Logan held his hand, palm up, while the prodigious beast sniffed and snorted. When a wide red tongue lashed out and licked Logan from fingertip to wrist, he pulled back.

Zara laughed as her husband wiped his hand on his pants. "He only licks people he likes. It's a compliment."

"One I can do without," Logan told her. He surveyed the *malaro* with cautious eyes, silently wondering how his wife thought to gain the saddle when her head didn't reach the animal's furry shoulder. The boy answered the question for him.

A short command brought the *malaro* to his knees, leaving its sizeable hind quarters sticking up in the air. The boy put one foot on the animal's flexed leg, then fisted his hand in the shaggy hair hanging off the *malaro*'s ear and climbed onto its back. Once he was sitting astride the beast's thick neck, he reached behind him and unlatched a rope ladder attached to the saddle.

Zara looked at him. "I have duties in the city. Would you care to accompany me?"

Logan wasn't so sure he wanted to ride a beast that

weighed more than twenty men, but he wasn't about to let a woman know that.

"What duties?"

"I meet with the governor of the city on this day every month," she explained.

"Very well," Logan said. "I will escort you." He turned to Maddock. The officer gave him a skeptical look, then shrugged as if to say riding the *malaro* couldn't be any more dangerous than fighting rebels. "We will return before the evening meal," Logan told him. "In the meantime, find someplace for the men to practice. I don't want them growing fat and complacent."

The cloth of Zara's blue gown swirled about her ankles as she moved toward the ladder lying against the *malaro*'s thick middle. "I'll go first. Cyrel won't forget his manners once he knows I'm on his back."

Logan silently hoped not. He could envision what would be left of a man if he got caught under the animal's huge feet. Grateful that his wife wasn't sulking over his decision to build the watchtower, and curious as to what he'd find in the capital city that bore the same name as the planet he now ruled, Logan waited while Zara climbed up the rope ladder and seated herself gracefully in the saddle.

He followed, and soon he was sitting atop the huge beast, looking down at Maddock and Tolman. Zara was seated in front of him, her legs draped over the *malaro*'s back. Logan wrapped his left arm around her waist, enjoying the feel of her soft body. His right hand clutched a small handle on the saddle that he assumed was fashioned for just that purpose, to keep the rider from toppling off the animal's back when it began to move.

"This is Leal," Zara introduced him to the young boy straddling the *malaro*'s neck. "Leal, this is Lord Logan."

The boy gave him a wide smile before he slapped the flimsy whip against the animal's front leg and shouted another curt command. Cyrel began to walk toward the open gate. Actually, it was more waddle than walk. Logan held on to the saddle railing while his wife laughed.

"It takes some getting used to," she said over her shoulder.

Logan gritted his teeth as the animal's heavy steps jarred every bone in his body. "Does everyone on Nubria travel this way?"

"It's faster than walking," Zara told him.

Logan wasn't so sure. At the pace Cyrel was moving, they'd be lucky to reach the capital city before dark. At least the ride offered one pleasantry—Zara was in his arms. He tightened his hold slightly, easing her weight back until she was resting against his chest. In the bright sunlight, her hair gleamed like spun silver. He brushed his lips lightly across her hair. "I'm glad to see that you're not angry," he whispered as he placed another kiss on the edge of her ear.

"Anger is an unproductive emotion," Zara said, trying to pretend that the light caress didn't effect her. It did. The warmth of Logan's arms sent pleasure coursing through her body. But she couldn't let down her guard. Not this time. "I apologize for losing my temper."

Everything had changed since she'd discovered that the Council wanted a watchtower built. Somehow she had to convince her husband that building the tower would destroy rather than protect. Somehow she had to make him realize that Nubria wasn't strange. It was unique. A uniqueness that required preservation, not alteration. That was the reason she'd invited him to join her in the city. She hoped the more he learned about the world he now ruled, the more quickly he'd realize that the watchtower wasn't needed.

"Does your apology extend to forbidding the construction of a watchtower?" Logan asked.

"No," Zara replied candidly. "I will continue to disagree with you on that matter, my lord."

Logan pondered his wife's words for a moment. The

longer he was married to Nubria's queen, the more she perplexed him. He hadn't thought marriage would be so complicated. But then, he hadn't planned on being wed to a beautiful witch who could disarm a man's anger with a simple smile. "Then we will continue to disagree," he said as he brushed her hair away from her neck and nibbled the soft skin just below her ear.

At the unexpected kiss Zara squirmed against him just as Logan had hoped she would. No matter how different their philosophies, they shared a common passion for each other. His second well-placed kiss was meant to remind Zara of this fact.

"You distract me."

"I certainly hope so." Logan chuckled lightly. "If you hadn't fled so early this morning, we would still be in the chamber, pleasing one another. When tomorrow's sun lifts over the horizon, I expect to wake and find you by my side."

Zara stiffened in spite of her husband's enticing lips. "Is everything on Nubria to change according to your wishes, my lord?"

Logan knew they were on the verge of another argument, but he'd fought too many battles to be lured into an ambush by his tempting wife. Instead of answering her, he turned her until she was resting against his arm instead of his chest, then kissed her.

The hard pressure of his mouth took Zara by surprise. Like everything else about him, Logan kissed with a commanding presence. His tongue probed gently, teasing her lips apart until he could deepen the kiss. Zara fought to keep her mind closed while her body absorbed the titillating sensations that raced up and down her spine. It was no easy task, but she managed. This time.

When Logan finally ended the embrace, she was trembling in his arms. She opened her eyes to find him staring down at her, his dark eyes softened by their shared passion. "What I wish," he whispered huskily, "is that we were abed instead of astride a beast the size of an asteroid."

Zara's laughter made Cyrel turn his head. The *malaro* gave Logan a suspicious look, if such a thing were possible, then snorted indignantly.

Chapter Eight

Nubria's capital city was as beautiful as its queen. Although Logan had seen its panorama from the transport ship during landing, his orders to marry the planet's queen had kept him from exploring the maze of buildings that housed government offices and political dignitaries.

Like the palace, the city's buildings were constructed of smooth pallid stones with balconies on the second and third floors. Some windows were shuttered, but most were not. Brightly colored banners fluttered in the warm wind and flowers were everywhere, sprouting out of window boxes and hedgerows along the streets. Large trees with fingerlike boughs shaded the thoroughfare, while people dressed in loose robes and casual-fitting trousers and tunics mingled about the open market where merchants and farmers sold their wares.

As the *malaro* approached with Nubria's king and queen riding on its back, people smiled and waved as if greeting neighbors. Zara waved back, addressing several residents by name.

Logan noted that the people regarded him with shielded curiosity, while they eyed the sword at his side with blatant skepticism. The patrols, four men to a unit, were strolling along the streets, fully armed, and he wondered if they were as surprised by the splendors of the city as he was. It had been a long time since Logan had been in a place that didn't bear the scars and degradation of war.

The path Cyrel took toward the governor's office seemed dubious and uncertain to Logan. "Does nothing in this world travel in a straight line?" he asked, sliding to the left and then the right as Leal maneuvered the massive *malaro* through the narrow streets and around corners that led from one alleyway to another. The only thing that kept its passengers from toppling off the beast's wide back was the riding rail, which Logan clung to with one hand while he kept his wife in place with the other. "I've orbited planets without going in this many circles."

Zara laughed. "The circle is symbolic of our faith," she explained. "The capital city is a series of circular streets connected like the spokes of a wheel."

Logan rolled his eyes and hung on tight as the *malaro* wedged its way around another corner. A few minutes later Leal shouted a command, slapped Cyrel on the front flank with the stringed whip, and the animal stopped. Almost. It took several moments for the saddle to cease moving. Logan cursed, then let out a sigh of relief.

In front of them was a spacious city park, laid out in the form of a circle with gravel walkways joining in the center. The paths were bordered with high hedges and slender trees dotted with bright red flowers. Decorative stone pillars and statues were nestled among the greenery. Beyond the park was a large building with a flat roof, protected by stone parapets. A large canopy covered the building's entrance. Two government greeters, robed in

101

blue and white, stood under the fabric awning, directing citizens to the appropriate offices inside the governor's complex.

Logan unfastened the ladder and climbed off Cyrel's back. Zara followed, clearly more accustomed to dismounting than her husband, and clearly upset by the presence of Galactic Guards in the city she loved. Logan ignored her frown.

They walked across the park toward the governor's office. Once inside, they were greeted by a tall man with brown hair. He was wearing loose trousers and a hand-painted tunic. Underneath a cloth hat his features were pleasant, his blue eyes alert, his nose long and narrow. His mouth curved into a smile of greeting.

Zara introduced him. "Lord Logan, may I present Solon, the governor of the City of Nubria, and my brother."

Logan extended his hand in the customary greeting. No one had told him there was more than one royal sibling.

"I am honored," Solon said, releasing Logan's hand to bow at the waist with his arms spread wide. "May life on Nubria bring you contentment and prosperity."

"I'll be content when the last of the rebels are purged," Logan said stiffly. He didn't like surprises, and discovering Zara had a brother was surprising. What other secrets was she hiding, along with the location of Keelan and his gang of cutthroats?

"You're being rude," Zara hissed in a low whisper.

"No. I'm being honest," Logan countered.

Zara's brother ignored the exchange and ushered them into a spacious office with large windows overlooking the park. After a short toast to the wedded bliss of the new couple, he sat down behind his desk and opened a ledger. "We have a lot to discuss," Solon said, looking at his sister.

"Whatever needs to be discussed will be discussed with me," Logan interrupted before Zara got too comfortable.

It was time everyone realized that he intended to play an active role in the rule of Nubria.

"Of course," Solon replied, forcing a smile. "Forgive my rudeness. I meant no exclusion."

"My brother is used—" Zara began.

"Let your brother speak for himself," Logan said. "He doesn't need a woman putting words in his mouth."

Zara blanched at the curtness of her husband's words. She was about to give him a few in return when her brother laughed. She turned her scathing look from Logan to her one and only sibling. "He's rude."

"He's an outsider," Solon remarked. "And he's right. I may not sit on the throne of Nubria, but I do have vocal cords."

Zara's eyes went wide, then began to sparkle with anger. She didn't know which man needed yelling at the most, her arrogant husband or her turncoat brother.

"Sit down," Solon told her. "Your husband is curious about the world he inherited as a wedding present. I don't blame him. It isn't every day that a man finds himself king."

Zara sat down, but she wasn't happy about Solon scolding her so openly. He was her older brother, and they had always disregarded formality in each other's presence, but she hadn't expected him to side with her husband. She'd come into the city today not just to discuss business but to seek her brother's advice. Since her father's death, Solon had become her unofficial adviser. Being a man, he should know how to deal with one. It was apparent that Logan thought her female opinions frivolous and illogical.

Logan watched the family exchange with amusement. At last, he'd met a Nubrian with common sense. "Your sister is upset because I've been commissioned by the Council to build a watchtower."

Solon folded his hands on top of the open ledger, remaining quiet for a few moments before responding to

Logan's statement. When he did, he addressed his remarks to his sister. "It's only logical that the Council would want to fortify its borders now that the war is over. A watchtower would not be my choice of how to do it, but the decision doesn't surprise me."

"You can't agree with him," Zara said, coming to her feet. "It's against everything we stand for."

Logan was content to listen and learn while Zara and Solon debated the issue.

"Our faith has survived for over three thousand years," Solon replied calmly. "It will survive another three thousand with or without a watchtower."

Zara couldn't believe her ears. Solon, of all people, a man who cherished Nubrian customs like a mother cherished her firstborn child, should recognize the threat a watchtower posed.

"Why don't you go and see old Goldwren," her brother suggested. "You can get your temper under control while he bores you with stories you've already heard a hundred times."

Logan didn't ask who Goldwren was for the simple reason that Solon had described him as old.

"Are you dismissing me?" Zara asked with a sting to her voice. After all, she was queen.

"No," Solon said, standing up and coming around the desk to give her a brotherly hug. "I'm asking you to give your new husband and your brother a few moments of privacy. Men get acquainted better when there isn't a woman around to intimidate them."

Zara didn't think a herd of *malaros* could intimidate her spouse, and she said so. Solon laughed. Logan's mouth twitched, but he didn't comment one way or the other.

When the door closed behind the Queen of Nubria, her brother turned to Logan. "You have to forgive my sister her enthusiasm. From the day she was born, she's been taught that the people of Nubria come first. If she thinks them in danger, her claws begin to show."

"I understand loyalty," Logan replied.

Solon gave him a thorough looking-over. "Yes. I'm sure you do."

"What I don't understand is your sister's stubborn resistance to a watchtower. Surely she knows that the Pharmon Empire is eyeing everything within its reach with greed."

The Pharmon Empire was more like a flock of vultures than a government. The loose-knit nomadic tribes had been content to remain on the edge of the galaxy for the last thousand years, but they had no one to steal from but themselves, and they were gradually becoming united. Since the rebellion had turned the Union's attention inward, the Pharmons had become more daring in their raids. Nubria would be a banquet lain at their feet.

Solon released a weary sigh. "Zara has never left our planet," he explained. "Unlike most rulers, she cares little for politics. When my father was alive he received the envoys from the outer worlds. Since his death, I have been Zara's unofficial adviser. She's seen nothing beyond Nubria's purple clouds."

"Yet she gave sanctuary to Keelan and his mob of rebels."

"She gave sanctuary to the survivors of a crashed space transport," Solon said. "It was the only thing she could do."

Logan didn't agree. "When the Council requested their deportation, she refused."

"It was her right as queen."

"And you agreed with her decision?" Logan asked sardonically.

"I agreed with her right to make the decision," Solon retorted. "And her reasons."

The two men stared at each other for a long, tense moment. One a warrior, the other a diplomat, both caught in the web woven by a beautiful woman. The standoff was broken as Solon walked to the serving table and poured two more cups of wine. He offered one to Logan. "To Zara," he said, lifting his cup high. "Your greatest challenge will be to understand her."

Logan wasn't sure if his brother-in-law's words were a salute or a warning. He drank the wine, then sat down across from the governor's desk, bidding Solon to take his seat. "Nessa tried to explain your faith to me," he said. "She called it simple. I call it complicated."

Solon smiled. "It's both, my lord. But it is our faith, and we hold it inside our hearts with gladness and joy."

"No weapons, no fears," Logan mumbled.

"Our only fear is that we will allow ourselves to be compromised by the technology the rest of the galaxy embraces so willingly. That is why we prefer to be separate. Our faith is our identity. If we lose it, we lose ourselves."

Logan could understand what Solon was saying. As a Galactic Guard, he had the same pride in his own identity. It set him apart from others. It gave him purpose.

"You're not entirely opposed to a watchtower?" Logan queried him.

"I'm not opposed to protecting our traditions and our lifestyle," the governor answered. "Like you, I'm aware of the Pharmon threat. It's not an immediate one, but it does exist. Zara may not want to admit it, but she does understand that the universe isn't always fair and equitable to its inhabitants. My mother signed an alliance with the Unity Council because my father advised her that one day a danger might exist and without the Council we would be helpless to deter it. The watchtower would be a deterrent."

"Why aren't you Nubria's ruler?" Logan mused, then held up his hand. "I know. You don't have breasts."

Solon laughed. "Nor the gift."

"What gift?" Logan arched a dark brow.

"I forget that you've only been among us for a day or

so," Solon replied. "My sister's path to the throne wasn't totally dependent upon her female endowments. Nubria's queens serve two functions. They are the figureheads of our government and they are the high priestesses of our faith. The gift of faith is passed only to the females of our race. Only they can inherit the insight and mental powers that enable them to sense what the gods wants us to know."

The more Logan learned, the less he understood. "Explain this gift."

"I'm not sure I can," Solon replied. "At least not the way Zara could explain it. She feels it every day of her life."

"Ancient rites, a gift of mental powers, feelings," Logan scoffed. "None of them will protect Nubria if a fleet of Pharmon warships decide to land."

"Perhaps not," Solon agreed. "But understanding them may help you persuade my sister to be more cooperative."

"I'm listening."

"When I was a young boy I went on a pilgrimage to the mountains. It's a solitary rite of passage most young men on Nubria take before they leave home and begin their own lives. There was a storm and I was pinned under the branch of a fallen tree. There was no one to help me. No one for miles. By the second day, I was unconscious. Zara sensed my distress and led my father and Nessa to where I lay dying."

"Telepathy," Logan said.

Solon shook his head. "Telepathy requires two receptive minds. I was unconscious."

Logan's silence said he wanted more of an explanation.

"The gift is more than telepathy. It's an awareness of one's surroundings. People, plants, animals, storms, everything. Zara has the power to sense things about her environment. Not only from people, but from nature.

She can lay her hand on the stomach of a pregnant woman and tell you if the child is going to be male or female. I've seen her do it hundreds of times, and she's never been wrong. *Never.*"

Logan thought about the time in the courtyard before he entered the palace, and the two times since then that he'd *felt* something. "Are you saying my wife can read my mind?"

"Not exactly." Solon shrugged. "It's different. She can sense your emotions, feel your moods. She knows when you're angry or happy."

"That isn't difficult," Logan grunted. "My men are experts at it. All they have to do is see me and they know when to scatter."

"Zara doesn't have to see you," Solon explained. "You could be miles away, and if she focused in on you, she could feel what you were feeling."

"That's impossible."

"With Zara it's very possible."

The conviction of Solon's words convinced Logan that Zara's brother believed what he was saying. Logan wasn't so sure he did. "Why didn't the old woman tell me this?"

"Nessa has powers of her own, although they aren't as refined as my sister's. And she's very protective of Zara. So is Tolman."

"I noticed." Logan frowned. He wouldn't be surprised to discover that the two old servants had slept outside their queen's bedroom the previous night, ready to come to her rescue if she called out.

He thought about what Solon had just told him, frowning as he realized the ramifications of having a wife with a gift that left him few secrets. If she could sense him, he wouldn't be able to catch her unaware. It was an advantage he wouldn't mind having himself.

"You said Zara has never been away from Nubria," Logan remarked, formatting a quick plan.

"The last Nubrian queen to leave the planet was my

great-grandmother," Solon told him. "She visited several outer worlds, declared them unfit for civilized habitation, and came home all in the span of a lunar cycle."

"Then perhaps it's time for your sister to see what lies beyond her limited horizons," Logan said, coming to his feet. "My second in command is Lieutenant Maddock. He will be in charge of my men while we're gone. I'll rely on you to keep Nubria intact until my wife and I return."

"Return from where?"

"Rysor," Logan announced. "It's only a day's star travel from here and holds a variety of interests."

Solon had heard of Rysor. It was a mining colony that served as a port of call for merchant ships in the eastern sector. Before he could comment on Logan's decision, there was a light tap on the door.

"Come in."

Zara opened the door and walked into the office, avoiding Logan's eyes. His wife was followed by an elderly man. Goldwren, Logan assumed. His assumption proved correct as Solon made the introduction.

"Goldwren is our royal jeweler," he told Logan.

The old man had a narrow face and bright brown eyes. He bowed to Logan, then held out a small pouch. "A wedding amulet," he said. "I have already gifted our lady with a smaller one."

Logan opened the cloth pouch and found a solid gold chain with a circular pendant attached. The amulet was crystal. Its slated edges refracted the sunlight like a rainbow. The craftsmanship of the stone was superb. Logan had never seen anything like it. Two circular bands of gold were embedded in the crystal, intertwined, one resting horizontally, the other vertically. He rubbed the edges, trying to feel the seam where the two layers of crystal had been joined to encase the gold rings. All Logan could feel was the hard, cool surface of the crystalline stone. How Goldwren had gotten the rings inside was a mystery. Even the finest technology couldn't transfuse gold through another solid object.

"May your life on Nubria bring you contentment and prosperity," Goldwren said, bowing at the waist and spreading his arms wide the same way Solon had done earlier.

Logan put the gold chain over his head. He looked at his wife and saw a smaller, identical pendant resting between the valley of her breasts. Breasts he intended to bare and suckle at the earliest opportunity.

"Thank you," he said to Goldwren. "You are indeed a talented artisan."

"Did you and my brother get acquainted?" Zara asked after Goldwren left the governor's office.

"We discussed several topics," Logan said, avoiding a direct answer. He didn't want Zara to know that he'd discovered a few of her secrets. As an experiment, he concentrated on his wife's tempting body, forming a detailed picture in his mind of what he wanted to do to her the next time they were behind closed doors. If she could sense his moods, she'd be able to tell that he was becoming aroused.

She stared at him for a moment, then moved to where her brother was standing. Her face seemed slightly flushed, but Logan couldn't be sure if he was the cause. She could still be angry because she'd been dismissed so the two men could talk.

Solon pulled her close for a quick brotherly hug. "Don't worry, I haven't deserted our faith and become a nonbeliever."

"Did you convert my husband?"

"That is something only you can do, my queen."

Zara wasn't so sure. Logan seemed determined to demote her to the role of a subservient lover. She didn't like it and she didn't like the images flashing in her mind. She knew they were coming from him. Her body was starting to tingle the way he'd made it tingle last night. It was very distracting.

"At least try to convince him that we don't need armed patrols strolling up and down the streets," she said to Solon. "It isn't good for the children."

"The patrols aren't a topic open for discussion," Logan informed her.

"You won't find any rebels lurking in the city," she said, her voice tight.

"My soldiers are here to stay," Logan stated firmly, giving her more of an explanation than he'd offer anyone else. "You and your people will have to get used to them."

"Why?" she argued. "There's no reason for them to use their weapons. The only troublemakers they're going to encounter are mischievous children doing what all children do, playing and learning about life."

"Are you telling me that there are no rebels on Nubria?"

She looked at him. The dark glint of his eyes made her wish that she hadn't brought up the subject of armed guards and playful children. Testing her husband's resolve in front of her brother was the best way to ensure Logan didn't budge an inch. She should have known better. A man's pride was as easily bruised as a flower's petals.

The midday prayer bell chimed. Solon excused himself, leaving his sister and her new husband squared off against each other.

"You're wasting your time," Zara finally told him. "Your soldiers will walk themselves into the ground before they find any reason to use their weapons."

"That's my concern, not yours."

"Everything that happens on Nubria is my concern," she corrected him. "I won't be relegated to the position of walking two steps behind you with my head bowed."

If possible, her husband's dark eyes grew even darker. Zara knew she'd gone too far, too fast.

Logan liked spirited women, but only to a point. Zara was too used to being a queen and too new at being a wife to realize that she had overstepped her bounds. It was time she learned, the same way the men under his command had learned. If Logan valued anything, it was discipline. His expression grew stern while his eyes turned to black ice.

"Don't ever question my authority again."

Zara also knew she'd gone too far to back down now. "Don't threaten me. I'm not one of your soldiers to be stripped of his rank. This is my planet and these are my people."

"Wrong. Nubria belongs to me now. All of it, including its queen."

Zara wasn't fast enough to keep herself from being caught by one of Logan's deft hands. She went still, her eyes searching his face, her mind too full of her own thoughts to make room for those of her enraged husband. His hand relaxed and she thought herself soon free, only to be fooled. Logan pulled her close. So close she could feel the pounding of his heart.

He lowered his head and kissed her. Not the strong, domineering kiss Zara had expected, but a lingering, sweet kiss that made her knees go weak and her hands cling to his shoulders. His caging arms folded her even closer, until there was nothing between their bodies but the heat of passion and a wanting Zara could no more deny than she could deny her own name. The kiss was a lesson. It hurt her pride to accept its teaching, but her body was more than willing to accept its pleasure.

She became aware of his hands, pressed to her bottom, holding her in place at the same time they lifted her against him, forcing her to feel the power of his desire, making her keenly aware of her own aching need. Was passion always this strong? she asked herself. Did it always wash away a woman's reason?

The kiss changed into a series of kisses, warm moist

caresses that teased her mouth and the sensitive skin of her neck. His hands touched lightly, his fingertips kneading the base of her spine and the soft mounds of her bottom as his lips licked and taunted and tasted until she was melting against him.

When he knew she was mindless to anything but his touch, Logan raised his head and stepped away from her. "For the next five days, you will be nothing but my wife."

Zara blinked, clearly confused to find herself being held so intimately one moment and set aside the next. "What?"

Logan towered over her. "For the next five days, you will be nothing but my wife," he repeated. "We leave for Rysor as quickly as my transport ship can be readied. Until we return, you will be no more than a wife, and I will be no more than your husband."

Zara shook her head to clear it of the sensual fog clouding her thoughts. Pale hair shimmered in the sunlight as she shook it more vigorously once Logan's words registered. "I can't leave Nubria."

"You will," he told her.

"But . . . I've never left Nubria. I have no reason to leave," she said, so taken aback by his remarks that all she could do was stammer like a child just learning to speak.

"I'm your reason," he replied. "You need no other."

Zara's rational mind returned in a rush. Her head lifted and her chin took on a stubborn tilt. "If you have duties on Rysor, then by all means go there."

"That isn't the way it works, my clever little queen," Logan said, taking her by the arm and hauling her toward the door. "Nubria doesn't rule the universe, although you would like to think it does. The rest of the galaxy follows one simple rule: A wife goes where her husband chooses for her to go. And this husband is taking you to Rysor with him."

Zara pulled back, but it was useless. Logan's grasp was

inescapable. "I won't go," she told him. "You can't take me away."

Logan stopped just short of the door. The look he gave her clearly said he could, and would, take her wherever he pleased.

Chapter Nine

"He's taking me away," Zara told Nessa.

Candles flickered, their small amber torches bowing and sputtering, as Zara walked past them. Her husband had left her side as soon as they'd returned to the palace courtyard. At this very moment, he was confined in the adviser's suite giving his second in command a list of orders while a crew prepared the transport ship for launching. A soft rain prevented the two women from meeting in the prayer garden as was their custom. Instead Zara was pacing the length of the throne room, empty but for the ever-faithful Nessa and her sympathetic smile.

"Other queens have left Nubria and returned without catastrophic results," Nessa said patiently. "Quiet yourself, my lady. All will be as you wish it to be."

Surprised by her mentor's complacent attitude, Zara swirled around. "How can you say that? He's taking me away. This very day! What will the people think? What will happen if one of his men stumbles upon Keelan?"

Understanding shone brightly in Nessa's old eyes.

"Keelan is safe. Fear not. Go with your husband and experience what the outer world has to offer you. Not all wisdom is held on Nubria."

Once again Zara couldn't believe her faithful teacher was acting as if Logan merely meant to take her on a leisurely stroll. A part of Zara knew she was overreacting to her husband's mandate. It warred with the part of her that was afraid. Terribly afraid that if she left Nubria, she'd be . . . Zara wasn't entirely sure what had her so frightened, the thought of being away from the people she trusted and loved, or the thought of being at the mercy of a man who had no mercy.

"What you fear the most is the least likely to happen," her mentor said reassuringly. "The mountains will keep your secret safe while you take time to acquaint yourself with a husband and customs that must be learned in order to keep peace between you."

"What of *our* customs?" Zara beseeched her. "My husband shows no hesitation in pushing them aside as if they don't exist. Yet you talk of compromise. Must it all be on my part?"

"Would you see one rebellion quenched only to have one of a different kind erupt on Nubria?" Nessa answered a question with a question.

Zara's exasperation increased. "How can there be accord between myself and my husband if he refuses to accept that he rules a people of peace, not war? He's determined to find the rebels and build a watchtower. The very thought makes my blood run cold."

Even as she spoke, Zara knew she had no one to blame but herself for the dark cloud of circumstances looming over her. She had made the decision to shelter the rebels and now she was facing the consequences. She'd told herself she could handle whatever the Council sent her way, but she was quickly discovering that she'd underestimated them. They'd sent a man like none she'd ever met before. But how could they have known that the warrior called Logan would touch her heart as strongly as he'd touched her mind? If fate had selected her husband, it had turned against her. Even Zara's mental powers weren't enough to dissuade the warrior from his course of action.

"He's taking me to Rysor," Zara said, her tone admitting that she had little choice but to go. "Do you know of this world?"

Nessa shook her head. "Very little. It is outside our faith, but that doesn't mean you have to fear it."

Nessa opened her arms.

Zara rushed into them, hugging the old woman like the mother she had become. Nessa soothed her with some ancient words, then gave her a stern look. "Whatever Rysor has to teach you will be worth the learning. Go. Spend time with the man you have claimed as your husband, learn his ways, listen to his words. He is a part of you now. Do not deny yourself the completion only he can give you."

"I'm afraid," Zara whispered softly.

Nessa arched a thin brow and waited. "What has the link brought you?"

"Dark feelings," Zara said, although the words were inadequate to describe what she sensed. "Black emotions. I don't understand them yet. The link hasn't matured enough, but I can feel them."

"When?"

"Whenever the rebels are mentioned," Zara told her. "I think Logan knew Keelan personally. Maybe they faced each other in battle. I'm not sure. But I am sure that the feelings are there. They turn Logan's mind dark with hatred."

"Do you see no light in his thoughts?"

Zara remembered her wedding night and the array of emotions she'd experienced. Their memory was alive in her mind, making her body wish for another such night.

Not wanting to discuss such personal details with Nessa, Zara simply smiled. "At times."

Nessa laughed. "There is little about his appearance to make me think he will ever be lukewarm about anything. Hot or cold. Love or hate. A strong heart feels strongly."

"What about compassion and compromise?" Zara asked. "A man needs them, too."

"I suspect our new king is capable of both. Don't forget he's a trained warrior. Soldiers have little use for compassion, and they can't afford compromise. Either one could be the weapon that strikes a fatal blow."

"He feels strongly about finding the rebels," Zara said. "I fear what may happen if he discovers Keelan too soon."

"Keelan is safe, along with the others," Nessa reassured her. "Now, you must prepare for your journey to Rysor. I will pray that you return with a smile on your face and hope in your heart."

"You leave so soon," Maddock remarked, watching his commanding officer with a wary eye. Something had happened. He could always tell when Logan was preoccupied. He had a distant expression in his eyes, showing that his thoughts were elsewhere.

Logan reached for one of the figurines on the shelf. He studied the miniature likeness of a young Nubrian woman. The small statuette's details were magnificent. The soft marbled stone, brown swirled with streaks of amber and white, was cool to the touch. Logan rubbed his callused fingertips over the figurine, caressing it the way he'd caressed his wife's body during the night. The intricate carving of the girl's face and the dedication to detail was very impressive. Logan wondered if the artisan was Goldwren. If it was, the old man's talent was awe-inspiring.

"My wife is the key to everything," Logan said, returning the tiny statue to the shelf. "I want her undivided attention for the next several days."

"Rysor isn't what I'd call a honeymoon planet," Maddock said after a few moments. "It's as rugged and uncivilized as any place in the Union. More so."

"Exactly," Logan told him. "It's time the Queen of Nubria realizes there is more to life than purple clouds and smiling servants."

"The lady isn't coming to heel as easily as you thought, then?"

Logan grunted. The sound was noncommittal, but Maddock suspected it meant his commanding officer had finally found a woman who wasn't intimidated by the aura of a Galactic Guard. It would be amusing to watch the two people come to terms with the marriage the Council had demanded of them.

"The city's governor is Zara's brother," Logan said. "His name is Solon, and he seems to have a backbone about him. I've commissioned him with seeing that the citizens of Nubria remain peaceful while you oversee the men and their patrols."

Maddock frowned. "If things get any more peaceful than they are now, the men will be falling asleep at their posts."

"I'll not have them complacent," Logan said. "We don't know how many rebels survived the crash, or where they're hiding. I want the men drilled every day, no matter how bored they become with Nubria's passive citizens."

Maddock nodded. "What about the watchtower?"

"I'll be back from Rysor before the engineers arrive. In the meantime, concentrate your efforts on learning as much as you can from Tolman and the old woman, Nessa. They know what their queen knows. I'm sure of it."

Logan looked at the maps Maddock had been studying when he'd come into the room. "I want a meeting of Nubria's Assembly called as soon as I return from Rysor. We will announce the location of the watchtower then."

"Where?"

"Here," Logan said, placing his finger on the map. The location he'd selected was in the heart of the Oberlin Mountains that lay north of the capital city. "Once the Assembly members have been notified, we'll take a patrol of Guards and engineers and begin our survey."

"Why notify anyone?" Maddock asked him. "You're the ultimate authority here now."

"I'm a king, not a dictator," Logan said. "Besides, I can't catch the prey if they don't come to the trap."

His second in command laughed. "You think Keelan will attack us."

"I think once a rebel, always a rebel," Logan replied. "Why waste our time combing the mountains when I can bring Keelan to me."

Prayer bells chimed, marking the hour and the approach of the last meal of the day.

"Is the transport ready?" Logan asked. He was anxious to have his wife to himself with no governmental duties to divert her attention. By the time he and his queen returned to Nubria, Zara would know just how dangerous the Pharmon threat really was. Rysor was known to be a haven for the nomadic raiders who enjoyed its raw, untamed lifestyle.

"I'll rally six Guards to be your escort," Maddock said, preparing to leave the room.

"No." Logan's curt voice stopped him. "I can fly the shuttle once the transport is in orbit around Rysor. I have no need of an escort."

Maddock's expression said otherwise, but he didn't argue. There wasn't any doubt of Logan's ability to pilot the shuttle or protect his wife. The older officer simply didn't like the idea of a single Galactic Guard being surrounded by the riffraff that frequented Rysor's ale houses and brothels. One of the first rules of military survival was that there was safety in numbers. Although Logan's skills as a warrior made him the equal of ten men, it didn't set well with Maddock to let him go unescorted into a world of Rysor's sordid reputation.

"See to the preparations," Logan told him, noting Maddock's reluctance.

Maddock left the room while his commanding officer walked to the window. Nubria's sun was sinking toward the horizon. Golden rays of light sliced through a mauve-tinted sky while servants rushed about the kitchen and dining hall, preparing to feed three dozen Galactic Guards. After the meal, Logan and Zara would depart for Rysor.

His decision to take his wife away had come upon him suddenly, but Logan didn't regret having made it. Taking measure of his motives, Logan had to admit that one of them was the need to know more about the woman he called wife, as well as her complicated religion. He hadn't been overstating his convictions when he'd told Maddock that Lady Zara was the key to his success.

Now that the rebellion was all but quenched and the Union was turning its attention to expanding its trade routes and recovering from five years of debilitating war, it was time for him to sort out his own future. He'd accepted the commission to wed the Queen of Nubria for several reasons, the least of them being the Council's demand. As much as he wanted to wrap his hands around the throat of the rebel leader Keelan, Logan wanted to make a place for himself in the galaxy, as well. He was in his mid-thirties, and everything he called his own actually belonged to the Guard. Even the uniform he wore was his by military issue.

As much as he enjoyed the victories of war, he hated the knowledge that one day he would be too old to go into battle. He knew it was time to take a more pragmatic view of the future. Assuming the kingship of Nubria and commanding the defense forces that would be assigned to the watchtower brigade was one way of keeping his hand in the proverbial fight, but he wanted more. He wanted . . .

By the stars, what did he want? A wife, children, a family? He'd never taken the time to give his inner longings a name. He simply knew they were there, and along with them the knowledge that above all else he'd never procure a child by fee the way his father had.

The transport ship looked like a huge metallic insect sitting on the launch platform. Zara gave it a disapproving glance. It was a big, ugly thing, this craft that would take her away from Nubria and all she knew. Big and ugly and foreign to the world she loved so dearly. Yet board it she would, and in obeying her husband make it clear to both him and those who watched that she was now at his command.

The subservience of the act fueled her anger, which she held just barely in check as she walked beside Logan. Their meal had been a silent one, broken only by a few words of polite conversation while his men gobbled down food and her servants hovered nearby to make sure their new lord's plate was properly filled and his wineglass never empty of drink.

"Welcome aboard, sir," a uniformed guard said in greeting. He was a tall man with gray hair at his temples and a long jagged scar that ran from his left cheekbone to the tip of his lower jaw. "Lady Zara," he added, nodding his head. "The ship is ready for launching."

Zara grimanced as she reached out to grab the metal balustrade that ran the length of the boarding platform. It felt cold under her hand.

"Go aboard," Logan told her. "Lieutenant Barjum will see you to our quarters. I need to speak with Maddock before we leave."

The officer motioned Zara inside and she went, leaving her husband to instruct his second in command. The inside of the ship was as ugly as the outside. There was nothing hospitable about the transport, designed for efficiency and speed. Zara had taken only a few steps when she felt as if she was walking into the belly of a mechanical beast, being slowly ingested by its metallic walls and the grated flooring under her feet. A heavy door slid open, and Zara saw two men wearing gray uniforms. These men weren't Guardians and she instinctively knew that they were responsible for piloting the transport ship to Rysor. Beyond them was a large room, filled with the technological wonders that had made space travel possible. Zara was curious about what made the ship defy gravity so easily, but she kept her questions to herself. She had a lifetime to absorb the wonders of her husband's world. For now, she needed to concentrate on each day as it came.

At Nessa's suggestion, Zara was wearing modest clothing; loose-fitting blue trousers and a long white tunic that laced up the front. The gold strings tied just above her breasts and the intricate stitching on the cuffs and collar displayed the talent of her seamstress. The wedding pendant that Goldwren had given her lay under her tunic, against her skin. Its presence was reassuring, although she couldn't say why.

Lieutenant Barjum didn't speak until they reached another set of double doors. He punched a command into a small lighted panel and the door opened. "Your quarters."

Zara stepped inside. The room was spacious, considering the size of the transport. The floor was neither carpeted nor covered, but a slate-gray metal too dull to reflect anything but the sound of her sandaled feet as she moved about the room. There was a table and chairs for meals and a long sofa covered in dark fabric. The artificial lighting was adequate, but it lacked the ambience that came with candles and flickering torches. Zara frowned as she noticed the absence of color. Everything was gray or black or a dull silver shade that was no color at all.

How drab, she thought. She was still on Nubria, but she felt the loss of her brightly colored world already.

The door closed behind her and Zara turned to find herself alone. Had her husband given the command that his men were to remain aloof, or was it just their military nature that made them speak in abrupt sentences, then disappear from sight?

Venturing around her new living quarters, Zara discovered that another room lay just beyond a single sliding door that moved when she stepped into range of its sensors. A large bed was built into the wall like a bunk. There was a clothing closet with a mirror and a bathing stall. Her belongings, along with her husband's military bag, had been delivered and were lying in the center of the bed, waiting to be unpacked.

Zara stared at the strange, unadorned mattress, wondering if she and her husband would find the same pleasure on it as they had in the royal suite at the palace. It was unsettling to know that a man could make her feel such outrageous sensations, and perplexing to realize that she wanted to feel them again. Passion was confusing, she decided. Confusing and wonderful and distracting.

"Are you tired?"

Zara jumped. She hadn't heard her husband enter the room. She swirled around, sending a mane of silver hair fanning out in all directions. "You startled me."

A smile creased Logan's face, then vanished. "I'm your husband. These are our quarters. I enter and leave as I wish."

"You are overly sensitive to insult, my lord. None was intended, I assure you. I was startled because I did not hear you come in. Nothing more."

Logan stared at her for a moment, then stepped closer. He wasn't overly sensitive, he was aching with need, but his naive little wife didn't seem to understand that. He reminded himself that she was new to the art of lovemaking and therefore required patience. His was running short, but he'd manage to control himself until the transport was launched. After that he was free to relax and enjoy his new wife, and that was exactly what Logan intended to do. For the next five days, Nubria's queen belonged exclusively to him.

Zara didn't step back, although it was her first instinct. Instead, she stood firm while her husband walked toward her. She could sense some of his feelings, but like so many of her perceptions of late, it was muddled by her own emotions.

Logan wrapped his hand around her neck and drew her close for a long, lazy kiss that made Zara's mind swirl even faster and her body hum in anticipation of what the embrace promised but did not deliver—at least not yet.

"Come," Logan said, once he'd freed her mouth. "We can watch the launch from the viewing port. You should find it interesting."

Zara was more interested in sorting out her feelings than leaving her world behind, but she didn't voice her opinion. It was plain that her husband wanted her to view the launch, so she followed him out of the sterile living quarters and down a hallway that looked like all the other corridors in the transport. The viewing port was a large window in the rear of the ship, over the cargo bays. Once they were inside the rectangular room, lined with benches that were welded into the walls, Logan shut the door. Zara didn't see him enter the locking code that would keep intruders outside.

The engines began to hum and the large body of the transport began to shudder as the pilots began the launch sequence. Logan was standing so close to her that Zara could feel his breath on her hair. Although his hands were at his sides, she could imagine them touching her, and her pulse quickened to match the escalating force of the ship's massive engines.

In a silence that was intensified by her husband's proximity, Zara watched as the large ship lifted slowly away from the launch platform. It seemed to hover like a pollen bee over a freshly opened flower before rising high into the sky. She watched as the trees became smaller and smaller and the world she loved moved away, leaving nothing outside but amethyst clouds. For a few short moments, the ship was engulfed in the billowy layers of mauve-colored moisture that blanketed Nubria.

Unaware, Zara made a small sound of alarm as the clouds gave way to the blackness of space. She stared down at her world, feeling more alone in that moment than she'd ever felt in her entire life. Set amid the blinking of distant stars and the midnight shroud of space, Nubria looked beautiful. It was a haven in a galaxy of discontentment, yet Zara knew that her husband saw only the peculiar color of the clouds. Tears dampened her eyes, but she wiped them away.

"We will only be gone for a few days," Logan said, seeing her distress. He wrapped an arm around her waist and pulled her to his side.

It was the gesture of a husband offering comfort, and Zara reveled in it, knowing that Nessa was right. It would take time and patience to reach Logan's warrior heart, but it could be done.

"It's so beautiful," she whispered. "And so fragile-looking. It grieves me to leave it behind."

"Grieve not," Logan said, kissing her lightly. "We will return. In the meantime, you will see things you have never seen before. And feel things you have never felt."

The first thing Zara felt was her husband's mouth nipping lightly at the lobe of her ear. His breath was warm against her skin and tiny shivers of excitement rushed through her. Before she could form the sound of his name, Logan's hands moved to the lacings of her tunic.

It came undone slowly as his fingers unfastened the golden cord. Each movement was a delicate caress, and Zara sucked in her breath as she felt the heat of his hands and the first tremors of desire overtaking her body. She had never known anything to equal the powerful emotions this man could evoke in her and she was defenseless to stop them.

The sight of Zara's soft skin and the wedding amulet nestled in the valley of her breasts was Logan's undoing. His breathing increased as he brushed a finger across her pink nipples and watched them harden in response.

"It has been too many hours since you fled our bed," he said in a gruff whisper. "I find myself impatient to touch you again."

Zara felt the same impatience. With trembling hands, she reached for the fasteners that kept her husband's body shielded from her touch. One by one, the metal buttons gave way, and she touched his hard, hair-covered chest. Beyond the viewing screen, the midnight void of space went unnoticed, as her hands explored and learned him anew. She could feel his heart pounding under her palm and she smiled.

Logan's breath held in his chest as he watched Zara's violet eyes. Could she sense how hungry he was for her? Just how many of his thoughts were private? And if she could tell what he wanted, did she want it too? Logan knew he could arouse her body. But what about her spirit? What about her heart? And why did he wonder? He had never given pause to think about a woman's feelings before, not beyond the ones that gave her pleasure. He justified his thoughts about Zara by telling himself that she was his wife, and having that status, it made her different than the other women he'd coupled with in the past. When Zara's tongue darted out to moisten her lips, he caught it in a long, hard kiss that left her clinging to him.

Patricia Waddell

"Too many clothes," he mumbled, wanting to touch her all over.

The sensual promise in his voice made Zara's heart leap. Whether she wanted it or not, this man, her husband, had the power to make her body rebel against her common sense. There was no controlling her thoughts or emotions when his hands roamed over her, stroking and caressing until she was squirming against him, trying to get closer to what his body was promising hers.

Logan's hands shifted from her bared breasts to the drawstring holding her silk trousers. With a quick tug they were loose. He put his hands inside, caressing the smooth skin of her stomach, then her hips. Zara moaned as he cupped her bottom in his callused palms and pulled her tight against him. His mouth demanded more and more from hers, his tongue probing, his teeth gently biting then releasing her bottom lip.

The intensity of their embrace was making Zara shake. Her clothing lay on the floor, pooled around her feet in a mingling of blue and white silk. Logan smiled to himself as his mouth moved in a sensual journey from her neck to her breasts. He lifted her without preamble and walked to one of the benches. Holding her snugly with one arm wrapped around her waist, he unfastened his trousers and shoved them out of the way. Before Zara could draw a fresh breath, she was sitting astride his lap, her legs dangling over his muscular thighs.

"I want you," Logan said roughly. He moved her until she was covering him, letting the warm center of her body tempt his hard flesh. He lowered his head and licked at her nipples, tempting her as well.

Zara closed her eyes, clinging to his shoulders for support. Heat rushed through her, a hot, frightening heat that made her bones melt and her blood boil. Logan suckled her like a greedy infant, stopping to let the tip of his tongue tease and torment, before shifting his attention to her other breast.

128

"I'm . . . I'm burning up inside," Zara mumbled, unable to find any other way to describe what she was feeling.

"Then let me feel the fire," Logan said, lifting her until the blunt end of his flesh was poised against her moist opening. "Let me burn with you," he whispered, then took her mouth in another kiss as his body slowly began to penetrate her.

His hands guided Zara, holding her still until he too could feel the heat of her arousal. He watched her with a dark gaze, made even darker by passion, as her body accepted his, stretching and opening around him. Slowly, gently, he entered her, until there was nothing between them but the heat of desire and a fire that burned brighter with each measured push of his hips.

His hands held her still while his mouth devoured her breasts once again. His tongue circled, his teeth nipped, and his mouth suckled her until Zara thought she would explode like one of the stars outside the viewing port. With each insistent, gentle probing of his body into hers, she felt the flames burn higher. Her legs shifted wider, bringing them closer, bringing more of Logan's hard flesh into contact with her soft, sleek womanhood.

Desire splintered throughout Logan's body. This was what he'd wanted since waking up that morning. To be inside Zara again, to feel her hot response flowing over him, around him. The sterile air of the viewing room took on the scent of their bodies as Logan closed his eyes, savoring the luxurious feeling of being tightly sheathed by his wife's warmth. He inhaled the smell of her skin and the womanly essence of her aroused body. It was a natural aphrodisiac and he surged deep inside her, no longer content to be patient and let passion come like a slowly earned reward.

"Logan." His name was a question and an urging from Zara's lips as she wrapped her arms more tightly around his neck. She couldn't breath for the fire consuming her, scorching her all the way to her soul.

"Burn for me, wife," he said, lifting her as his hips rose off the bench. "Forget yourself as you make me forget myself. Burn."

The cool air of the temperature-controlled room seemed like steam to Zara. She was already burning, so hotly, so deeply, that she feared she would dissolve like mist washed away by the sun's heat. Logan's breathing was strong, urgent, as he pushed deeper and deeper inside her. Zara's body responded by opening more for him, unable to refuse what he was demanding of her—everything she had to give and more.

Logan fisted one hand in her silken hair as his body threatened to explode. Not yet, he told himself. The enjoyment was too great to forfeit this soon. But control was something Logan discovered he'd left outside the viewing room. Zara began to move with him. The gentle, female undulations of her hips brought a sharp curse to mind, but Logan didn't speak it. All his energy was focused on gaining the pleasure of the moment, of feeling the tiny convulsions that were making his wife's tight sheath throb around him.

Her release came in a soft moan as her nails dug into the damp skin of his shoulders. Logan's came in a wild rush that left him depleted and satisfied at the same time.

Chapter Ten

The cold void of space engulfed the transport ship as it
sped toward Rysor, but Zara was unaware of the passing
of time. There was no sunrise to mark the beginning of
the day or moonlight to gentle the darkness of a night
sky. There was only Logan, taking her thoughts and her
body as he pleased.

The hours of their journey were consumed by Logan's
sensual campaign to overwhelm Zara's willpower, to
make her totally his. She recognized his intent even as
she surrendered to his assault. The body she had once
claimed as her own belonged to her no longer. It responded to Logan's touch, not the commands of her
own mind. His simplest caress sent her heart racing. His
lightest kiss made her senses hum with an erotic excitement that kept Zara from thinking about Nubria and the
responsibilities of being its queen.

On board the transport, she was only Logan's wife, a
woman discovering herself and the mysterious depths of
passion. They made love, slept, ate, and made love again.
Her Galactic Guard taught her things no gentle queen

should know. Never had Zara imagined a man worshiping a woman's body with his mouth, his hands, his eyes. Yet she felt worshiped, cherished, as he brought her to pleasure time and time again.

"I'm too weak to move," she complained as Logan looked at her, his eyes still glazed with passion from their most recent session of lovemaking.

His laugh was soft and male and arrogantly satisfied. "The fault is your own, lady wife. Every time I think I've had enough of you, my body tells me otherwise."

They were lying on the bed in their private quarters, although Zara had learned that a bed wasn't necessary for the pleasure Logan gave her. He'd taken her sitting down, standing up, leaning over the table in the outer room. There were no restrictions to where or how his desire manifested itself.

Even as Zara lay exhausted at his side, she knew she'd only managed to keep the link a secret because Logan's touch confused her senses so completely, she couldn't think at all whenever he was near. But the link was growing stronger. She could feel it now, as they lay quietly by each other's side, their breathing the only sound in the room. He was looking at her and she could sense that he felt it, too. It was binding them even more closely together than the pleasure that stole her breath when it exploded in moments of sheer ecstasy.

"Are you hungry?" Logan asked, reaching for the tray he'd brought into the room earlier. Zara hadn't left the privacy of their quarters since they'd returned from the viewing room.

"No," she mumbled, then closed her eyes.

Logan helped himself to some of the fruit that had been brought aboard before leaving Nubria. Like his wife, its taste was sweet and pleasing to the tongue. He was a man who enjoyed sex, but the last few days had been more than a sexual marathon. He'd wanted Zara in the viewing room when they first boarded the ship, and he wanted her now. Time increased his need, rather than decreasing it, and Logan knew he'd become a victim of the sensual trap he'd set for his wife.

Every time he was inside her, he felt something inside himself quicken. But it wasn't desire. This feeling, this emotion went deeper than physical need, and Logan wondered if his wife's mental witchery was weaving a spell around him. The more he touched her, felt her soft skin and the gentle shivering of her body, the more he wanted to understand her.

At times, he thought he could. When she found satisfaction, when she was quivering in his arms, her eyes closed, her head arched back, her body totally at his mercy. It was a confusing moment, that instant when she seemed to become a part of him, yet Logan felt their connection as surely as he had felt the burning pain of a well-aimed laser pistol and the cutting edge of an opponent's sword. He lifted a strand of silver hair and twisted it around his finger. With an unspoken curse tainting his thoughts, Logan stared down at the woman who was his wife.

Who was this female, this defiant queen, he had wed? She was young, but she had the courage to stand up for what she believed to be right. He admired that trait, yet he'd found it rare in women. Zara perplexed him at the same time she enticed him. He'd conquered her body, making her moan his name, but Logan knew he was far from conquering her mind. She submitted to him because she'd vowed to do so. Finding pleasure at his touch made the submitting more enjoyable, but he knew that she was holding something back.

It was more than the whereabouts of the rebels. He'd find them eventually, with or without her help. No. It was more than the secret that had forced her to wed at the command of the Unity Council or lose her throne. Whatever his lovely wife was hiding, she did it well, and that was what enticed Logan more than anything. He'd never met a woman who could shield herself so thoroughly that a man knew less about her after having had her than he'd known before he'd stripped away her clothing and seen her naked beauty.

He got up from the bed and walked into the bathing stall. Hot water pounded his body, washing away his wife's scent. Unfortunately there was no washing away the doubts that teetered on the edge of his mind. He'd decided on the hasty trip to Rysor because he wanted his Zara to see that Nubria wasn't the center of the universe. She had to understand that her world was a part of the Union pledged by her mother's signature on the Unity documents. She needed to realize that the Union was vulnerable now, and that her world was a part of that vulnerability. It would take twenty years to replace what five years of war had destroyed.

If the Pharmons used time to their advantage, they could deplete the Union's resources and gain control of the galaxy with little effort. The Guards would fight to the death to keep that from happening, but they were men who needed food and supplies and weapons to win a war. The Union needed time to heal and replenish itself before it could withstand another siege of rebellion.

Curse Keelan and his ambition, Logan thought, as he lathered his body, then rinsed it clean. They'd been friends once, this man who had turned his talents as a soldier into a quest for a political throne. But that friendship had ended when Logan realized Keelan was recruiting Guards for his own army, traitors bent on destroying the very government Keelan had once pledged to uphold.

Zara had given Keelan sanctuary. She defended her decision by cloaking it with religious ideas and theories that mattered little to Logan. Right was right and wrong was wrong, no matter what label people put on it, and Keelan was as wrong as a man could be.

Logan stepped out of the bathing stall, determined to

find the rebel and put an end to the five-year hunt that had consumed his life. Then, and only then, could he allow himself to think beyond the pleasure Zara could bring him—in and out of bed.

Once he was dressed, Logan looked at his sleeping wife. She was lying on her stomach with her hands folded under the pillow. Her platinum-colored hair was her only covering, and Logan felt his body quicken as though it hadn't been sated in weeks. Knowing if he touched her, they'd still be making love when the transport assumed an orbit around Rysor, he called out her name to wake her.

It took three times before his gruff voice penetrated the dreams that held Zara captive. She opened her eyes and looked up at him.

"It's time," he told her. "We will arrive at Rysor within the hour. You need to bathe and dress."

Zara blinked, surprised by his curt command. Where was the man who had soothed her with gentle words and encouraged her with erotic phrases only a few moments earlier? Gone, she realized, as her husband turned and left the room without a backward glance.

Before traveling to Rysor, Zara had never been in a bathing stall, and although she should shun the technology that made it possible, Zara savored the delicious feeling of the hot water running over her body. She pampered herself by taking twice as long to shower as she should have, knowing Logan expected her to be ready to leave the moment the transport ship was in a stable orbit around Rysor. When she was dressed in another pair of trousers with a floor-length purple tunic that buttoned to her waist before flaring out like a robe, Zara braided her hair in a sedate style and slipped her feet into soft leather boots.

As expected, Logan was waiting for her in the viewing room. His dark eyes swept over her and Zara smiled.

"This is Rysor," he said, pointing toward the planet below them.

Zara stepped to the window. Her smile turned into a frown as she saw their destination. There was nothing majestic or beautiful about Rysor. It looked like a big brown ball floating in the black ocean of space.

"Come," Logan said, seeing her disapproval of the planet he'd chosen for their honeymoon. "I'll shuttle us down."

Zara wasn't in a big hurry to make the acquaintance of the ugly planet, but she followed her husband out of the viewing room and down the corridor that led to the discharge bay. The shuttle was a smaller version of the transport ship. Its metallic hull bore the insignia of the Union, a black eagle displayed on a red background. Her attention was diverted from the small space coach when Lieutenant Barjum joined him. The junior officer handed Logan a laser pistol and an ammunition belt that held small metal pellets. Zara watched as her husband slipped the belt over his head, letting it rest on his left shoulder and across his chest. The laser pistol was housed in a small holster next to his sword.

"Aren't Rysorians hospitable?" Zara asked.

"It isn't the Rysorians I'm worried about," Logan said matter-of-factly. "Rysor is a port of call for more than mining freighters."

Zara wasn't sure what Logan meant. She looked at the lethal weapons he wore as casually as she wore shoes and prayed that he'd come to no harm.

A short time later, Zara was sitting next to Logan as he piloted the shuttle toward one of Rysor's largest cities. Desalken was on the northern continent near the mining center that was the planet's main source of income.

"When we reach the surface, stay close to me," Logan cautioned Zara.

"You expect trouble, don't you?"

"Rysor is known for trouble."

"Then why did you bring me here?"

Logan glanced away from the controls to look at her. "You'll see soon enough."

Her husband turned his attention to the communication module and asked for clearance to land. A gruff voice replied, giving him landing instructions and welcoming them to Rysor.

Zara looked out the narrow side portals as the shuttle passed through dullish brown clouds to slip into the planet's lower atmosphere. Desalken lay beneath them, bordered by reddish brown mountains to the north and a dirty waterway to the south that flowed sluggishly toward the sea. Zara knew immediately that she wasn't going to like the planet Logan had brought her to see. The world lay under them like a vast wasteland, dotted with factories belching black smoke from their refineries as they turned Rysorian ore into the metal used to build Union star cruisers.

"Where will we stay?" Zara asked, curious in spite of her instinctive dislike of the world that seemed to have forgotten anything but mechanical wonders.

"With a friend," Logan told her.

Moments later the shuttle landed faultlessly on a small triangular pad and Logan shut down the engine. He unstrapped himself from the pilot seat and reached for the small bag of personal items Zara had brought from Nubria. Among her possessions were the prayer stones she used in meditation.

Once outside, Zara took a deep breath and started coughing. The planet's air purifiers weren't able to filter out all the rock dust the mining lasers sprayed into the atmosphere.

Logan slapped her gently on the back, then laughed. "Rysor's air takes some getting used to."

Zara looked around her. The sun was shining, but the wind was cold. She shivered. To her left was a large mass of buildings that seemed to mushroom out of the brown earth. Although artificial light gleamed in the windows, there was nothing to hold her gaze for long. Like the transport, Rysor lacked color.

Logan started walking, keeping his hand wrapped around Zara's upper arm to keep her close. A squat structure sat on a small rise above the landing platform and he moved toward it, telling her that he had to register the shuttle before they could go into the city.

A fat Rysorian sat behind a metallic desk lined with viewing monitors. His bald head gleamed in the light coming from a fixture over his head. Zara noticed that his hands were as dirty as the floor under his feet. The man's gaze settled on her the moment she walked into the room, and she tried to push his offending thoughts out of her mind. She'd never encountered a Rysorian before and if this man was like the rest of the planet's population, she didn't care to meet any more.

She stepped as close to Logan as she could without crawling into his pocket while he negotiated a fee to have the shuttle stored for three days. The overweight clerk didn't seem impressed to be conducting business with a Galactic Guard, so Zara assumed he dealt with the intimidating soldiers all the time.

"Come for a few days of fun, have you?" he asked, looking at Zara again.

"My reasons for being on Rysor are no one's but my own, old man," Logan answered, his voice as cold as the wind rattling the shutters on the windows.

The Rysorian clerk didn't need to be told twice. His eyes dropped to the nearest viewing screen as his thick fingers plucked up Logan's coins and put them in the cash drawer. "Three days, then. Do you need the shuttle refueled?"

"No," Logan said, taking Zara's arm once again. "I've set the alarm system. If anyone touches that shuttle, they'll answer to me."

The clerk's quick nod said he understood the threat

in Logan's statement. He mumbled something about enjoying what Rysor had to offer as Zara was hurried out of the building.

"Is everyone on Rysor like him?"

"How so?" Logan asked, turning toward the center of the city.

"Unpleasant and unclean," Zara replied candidly.

Her husband laughed. "Not everyone."

Zara hoped not. She walked alongside Logan for a short distance, trying to smile as they passed more dingy buildings with dusty windows. When they reached a metal gate with a bright red sign, Logan stopped.

"This is the shuttle path," her husband said. "It will take us into the city."

The path wasn't a path at all, but a conveyor belt that allowed pedestrians to input their street destination into a computer and be sent on their way like raw ore to a smelting pot. Logan punched in the address he wanted, inserted several coins into the vending slot, and told Zara to hold on to the railing. When the mechanical walkway began to move, she gasped and wrapped her right hand around the balustrade. The shuttle path was fenced on either side with small gates along the way where passengers got on or off. It stopped several times. Within a few minutes, Zara was surrounded by Rysorians.

Most were miners, covered in dust and wearing air purifiers strapped on their backs, the others were Rysorians moving about the city in their normal course of business. None of them said a word of welcome or offered the slightest hint of a smile. They were a stern-faced lot with blotchy skin and a distant look in their eyes, as if they didn't care about anything or anyone.

The normal attire for Rysorian men seemed to be leather trousers, knee-high boots laced up the side, and a hip-length coat with large pockets and metal buttons. The majority of the men who boarded the shuttle path had short-clipped brown hair and brown eyes. They were of average height with more bulk than muscle, except for the miners. Everyone who got on the shuttle path gave Logan's uniform an anxious glance before they took up a position as far away from the Galactic Guard as possible.

"Where are the women?" Zara asked, keeping her voice low so only her husband could hear her.

Logan smiled. "You won't see any females in this part of the city. The landing platform is too close to the mines."

"Where are we going?" she asked, anxious to get off the moving sidewalk and inside, out of the pungent air.

"You'll know when we get there," he said, as if answering her question was more of an inconvenience than a courtesy.

Her temper bristled at his curt tone, but she managed to bite her tongue. This wasn't the time or place to give her husband a lesson in manners. Fearful that the time would never come when she could speak her mind freely with the man, Zara concentrated on prayers instead. She recited the ancient words in her mind, holding on to the promise they gave to the faithful.

The stubborn thread of hope that she might eventually reach Logan's well-guarded heart kept Zara's thoughts occupied until the pedestrian walkway stopped and her husband opened the gate.

The unpainted metal gave way with a metallic creak. He motioned her to step off the mechanical platform and out into a mud-drenched street. Bleak shadows covered the buildings she discovered once they were free from the transport system that served Desalken.

The city was dark and dingy and far from the welcoming metropolis Zara had hoped to find waiting at the end of their journey. The midday sun didn't reach the cluster of shops and factories nestled in the center of the city. Like the world to which it belonged, Desalken was little more than a clump of gray and black images, swathed by dusty clouds and bathed in thick brown mud.

A silent cry of regret echoed in Zara's mind, but no words formed to reveal the dismal thoughts in her head. When Logan spoke her name, she looked up at him.

"We have some walking to do before we reach Sherard's home. Stay close to me," he cautioned her again. "Don't look anyone in the eye. Especially the men."

Zara nodded that she understood, although she didn't understand anything about the cold, barren world around her. Didn't people speak to one another on Rysor? Or was it forbidden for a woman to speak until she was spoken to? If so, she disliked the place even more. She wasn't accustomed to being told that she couldn't look someone in the eye if they addressed her.

She walked by Logan's side, noticing the inhospitable glances he drew from the Rysorians they passed as they made their way through narrow streets lined with square buildings that all looked alike. Every window was grime-streaked, testifying to the fact that the rain did little to wash away the dinginess of the city, just as Zara suspected little alleviated the despair that seemed to engulf Rysor's people.

Zara could feel the desolation around her. Her heart ached with the plight her eyes could clearly see. The people of Rysor moved like robots, walking up and down the streets, immune to what they were missing in life. They breathed the dusty air, but they were dead inside, frozen and unfeeling. Their hearts were as heavy laden as the conveyor belts that carried the ore from deep inside the planet's belly to the factories that turned it into useable metal.

By the time they reached a shabbily painted doorway, Zara longed for a bath. The air was thick with dust, and it covered her face and hands. She looked up at her husband, while the sound of metal carts and factory wheels disturbed the silence she was used to having this time of day. How she longed for the peace of her prayer

141

garden and the surety that the melodious sounds of birds singing and wind whispering always gave her heart.

"This house belongs to Sherard," Logan told her. "He was once a Galactic Guard, like myself. An injury keeps him from serving the Union as fiercely as he once did, but he is still my friend."

"Then he will be mine," she replied, wondering if fighting and dying with a sword in his hand were the only things her husband could appreciate.

Logan knocked on the door, demanding entry, while Zara stood by his side.

It opened to reveal a humped-shouldered old woman with unkempt hair and round bleak eyes that reflected nothing more than indifference to the people waiting on her threshold.

"I seek Sherard," Logan told the old woman.

"Then seek him inside," she replied in a raspy voice. "He is in the game room."

They stepped inside the house, and Zara was relieved to discover that it was clean. The walls and floors were bare but neatly scrubbed, and the furnishings modest but comfortable.

Logan dismissed the servant once the door was closed and took Zara by the arm. He led her down a dimly lit corridor and into a large room. The artificial light gleamed off a metallic table where a man was seated, looking into a monitor while he grumbled under his breath.

"Stay here," Logan whispered before leaving her side.

As he approached the man with his back to them, Zara sensed that her husband was amused while the man, who she assumed to be Sherard, was angry. Their host raised his hand and pounded on the table, uttering words that didn't need interpretation for Zara to know they were profane.

"You never did have patience," Logan stated, reaching over the man's shoulder and punching a button on the

142

monitor's control panel. "You set yourself up for an ambush."

Sherard exploded from his chair with a shout of joy and a string of insults that were heaped upon Logan's broad shoulders while he slapped his friend on the back. "Logan, you son of a Sybanian slug. What are you doing here?"

"I've come to see a friend," Logan told him with a smile. "How are you?"

Sherard turned, and for the first time since entering the room Zara was able to see that he had only one arm. A short stump, barely more than an inch or two of flesh, protruded from his left shoulder. Instinctively, she knew that his arm had been severed in battle. The sleeve of his tunic had been cut and sewn shut, capping the stump that had once been a useful arm.

"Who is this?" Sherard asked, arching a pale brow as his gaze moved from Logan to the woman standing in the doorway.

"Zara. My wife," Logan announced.

"*Wife!* You've got a wife!"

"What's so unusual about that?" Logan asked calmly. "Lots of men have wives."

"Not you." Sherard laughed, although Zara wondered how he could make a joyful sound when his mind was filled with such pain and hatred.

She could sense the emotions swirling inside him, blackening his mind until it matched the color of Rysor's sky, dark and forbidding. Like his body, Sherard's heart was scarred by battles won and lost.

Logan motioned Zara into the room.

She put a smile on her face and stepped forward. "Sherard." She said his name because she didn't know his title or rank, or if he possessed either one.

"This is Zara," Logan repeated himself. "My wife."

The man with one arm stared at her for a long time before his face softened with a smile of welcome. He looked from Zara to Logan as his smile widened and finally reached his eyes. "She's beautiful. Tell me, old friend, how did a seasoned, unsavory soldier like you talk a lovely lady into marriage?"

"That isn't important," Logan said. "I've a few days to spare, so I thought I'd see if you can still cheat at rumbol."

"I never cheat," Sherard chuckled good-naturedly. "Like it or not, the game is the only thing you've ever been bested at."

"What game?" Zara asked, resenting the fact that her husband had said *he* had a few days to spare. Did the man think he'd walked into the room alone?

"Rumbol is a game that requires skill and patience," Sherard announced, moving to a nearby table where a tall bottle filled with amber liquid sat next to a row of empty glasses. He poured the liquor, filling only two tumblers, then handed one to Logan. "It's a game of warriors. I'm the only man who has ever beaten your husband at the rumbol board. It doesn't set well with his ego. Which is of considerable size, in case you haven't noticed."

"I've noticed," Zara replied, smiling in earnest this time.

"Intelligent and beautiful," Sherard mused with a smile. "You've done well, Logan."

"Enough," her husband said, lifting his glass high. "To Medash."

"To Medash," Sherard echoed the toast.

Zara watched as the two men downed the amber liquor. Medash was the name of the planet where the last battle of the war had been fought and won. She wondered if Sherard had served under Logan's command when Keelan's rebels had finally been driven to surrender. Or had the man's injury retired him before the war had ceased, leaving him bitter because he'd been denied the ultimate victory?

144

"Welcome to my home," Sherard said, pouring himself another drink.

"Thank you," Zara replied, not sure if she liked the man or not.

Sherard emanated conflicting emotions, some sad, some almost happy now that Logan had arrived. She sensed a deep friendship between the two men. For a moment she felt jealousy—within herself. The emotion surprised her. Why should she mind if Logan cared for the man with one arm? Sherard was an injured friend, a veteran soldier. She was Logan's wife.

"Do you have a room to spare?" Logan asked, waving off his friend's offer of a second drink.

"I have a whole house," Sherard told him. "Take whatever room you like. Stay as long as you like."

"Thank you," Logan said. He moved to Zara's side and wrapped his arm around her waist. She could sense that he was wearing a mask for his friend's sake, a smile that hid the anguish he felt because Sherard could no longer hold a sword in his hand and fight for the preservation of the Union.

They made their way to a room on the second floor of the house. Like the downstairs chamber, it was clean and comfortable. A bed stood against one wall, two chairs and a rectangular table against the other. Light fixtures made from smoky-colored glass and silver metal were suspended from the ceiling.

"It isn't a queen's bedchamber, but the mattress looks comfortable," Logan announced, shedding the laser belt as he spoke. "Do you want another bath?"

"Yes, please," Zara said, hating the gritty layer of dust that covered every part of her body not protected by clothing. "I hate feeling unclean."

Logan smiled. "The bathing stall should be beyond that door." He pointed across the room. "Don't take too long. I'm hungry."

Zara nodded, then opened the small pouch of clothing

Nessa had packed for her journey. She withdrew a long gown of dark blue fabric and draped it over one arm.

Logan watched her, wondering what she thought of his friend. Anxious to hear her reaction, he waited until she was removing the dusty sandals from her feet before putting the question to her. "What do you think of Sherard?"

"He's a sad man," she replied honestly. "Is that why he lives here? Does the desolation of Rysor suit him better than a place where the sunlight isn't as brown as mud?"

"That's one way to describe this place," Logan said, thinking it a good description. "Sherard lives here because it's the only place he can afford to live. His military pension isn't as much as it should be."

"It would seem that a man's arm is worth more than a square house on a dirty planet," Zara remarked. "I didn't realize the Union only honored soldiers who could still fight and die."

Her words hit closer to the truth than Logan liked to admit. The war had cost more lives than he wanted to remember. Sherard wasn't the only Galactic Guard forced to retire because he was missing a limb. "Hurry and change," he said impatiently. "Sherard will expect us to take the evening meal with him."

Sensing that her husband didn't want to discuss the victims of war, Zara took a quick bath in the water stall, then donned the blue gown. It clung to her slender body like bark to a tree, bringing a frown to her husband's face once she returned to the sleeping room they would share as long as they remained on Rysor.

"Have you nothing else to wear?"

Zara looked down at the dress. As Logan had requested, Nessa had packed only sensible clothes. None of her garments displayed her rank as queen. None of them glittered with gold and silver thread or gleamed with the tiny jewels that were frequently stitched into the collars and cuffs of her more regal gowns. Having no

146

vanity, she wasn't aware that the dress enticed a man to think about the womanly body it covered.

"I have another pair of leggings and a green tunic," she told him. "Don't you like blue?"

"The color isn't important," Logan grunted, then shook his head. His wife would be beautiful wearing anything, so why bother ordering her to change? "Leave the dress on. Sherard is my friend. If his eyes wander, I won't mind. As long as his hand doesn't follow."

It took Zara a moment to realize that Logan had paid her a compliment. She smiled as she walked toward him, the fabric of the dress clinging in all the right places as his eyes followed her every movement. "Tell me about Sherard. How did he lose his arm?"

"On Medash," he said, confirming her original suspicion. "We were fighting a rebel force that was as keen as it was elusive. By the time we had them cornered between us and a river that was too swift to swim, we had our swords drawn. Sherard fought like a madman against three of them. He killed two before the third severed his arm."

Zara's heart ached for the man who had offered them the hospitality of his home. "And now he thinks he has nothing to offer. Neither his sword nor his soul."

Logan looked at her as if she'd taken the words out of his own mouth. Compassion wasn't an emotion he'd encountered often during his lifetime, yet it seemed to be the core of his wife's existence. The only thing that seemed to offend her was his plan for a watchtower.

"Don't let Sherard see the pity in those lovely eyes," he warned her. "He's a proud man."

"What man isn't?" she said. "And it isn't pity you see, my lord. There's no reason to pity a man because he's too blind to see that life is more than having two hands and two feet. Life is precious, no matter what form it takes. I pray that one day he will come to realize that his mind is just as important as his body."

Logan didn't say anything. He turned toward the door. "Come. If I remember correctly, Sherard likes his food served on time. The hour grows near."

She followed him downstairs into a small room with windows that were covered with heavy fabric. Zara wondered if the dark green curtains were used to keep the drab world outside hidden from view or to keep Sherard's drab life hidden from outsiders. The old woman who had greeted them at the door was placing trays of food on a table, her wrinkled hands hard at work.

"Sit down," Sherard announced as he joined them. "Dominia isn't very pretty to look at, but she's a good cook."

Zara looked at the food being served and felt her stomach churn. A platter of meat sat in the center of the table. The thick slices of animal flesh were covered in a heavy sauce. The idea of actually putting the food into her mouth made her feel faint. She looked at Logan, willing him to see her distress. When he glanced down at her, she grimaced. "I can't eat that," she whispered, pointing at the main dish while Sherard selected a bottle of wine to go with the meal.

"There are vegetables and bread," he said, unconcerned that she might offend their host. "Eat whatever pleases you."

Relieved that she wasn't expected to taste everything on the table, Zara sat down. Logan sat beside her, while Sherard took a chair on the opposite side of the table. For a man with only one hand, he was agile and well coordinated. Once he'd poured the wine, offering her the first glass, he turned his attention to Logan.

"What brings you to Rysor? And don't waste your breath telling me that you fancy an hour or two at the rumbol board. I don't like having my intelligence insulted."

Logan smiled. "My reasons aren't important. Can't I visit an old friend without an interrogation?"

"You never do anything without a reason," Sherard replied. "And why bring a wife with you? Rysor isn't where I'd take a beautiful woman."

"A wife goes wherever her husband wishes her to," Logan replied, reminding Zara of her obligation. "Enough questions. I plan on beating you at rumbol later this evening, so eat your dinner. You're going to need your strength."

Sherard laughed, and Zara was surprised to sense that the laughter actually came from his heart. Scarred and bitter though he was, he truly considered Logan a friend. Holding on to the hope that one day she might be able to laugh with her husband as well, she reached for a bowl of vegetables and began filling her plate.

The meal wasn't the best she'd ever eaten, but Zara managed to satisfy her appetite for food while her husband and Sherard discussed politics and the Unity Council's plans to enforce the borders that separated them from the Pharmon Empire.

"They're thieves and murderers. All of them," Sherard said as he stabbed a slice of meat with a metal fork. "Lazy, thieving murderers who would rather kill a man for his food than plant their own. The sooner the Union sends forces against them, the better."

"We've no forces to send," Logan said after a moment. "The rebellion took its toll."

"That it did," his friend agreed. "But sooner or later we have to face them in battle. They're as greedy as they are ruthless."

"When we do fight them, we have to win," Logan announced. "Until then, we have to strengthen our defenses and wait them out. The Pharmons might be greedy, but they're not stupid. They don't have the technology to get by our watchtowers. That weakness will buy us the time we need to strengthen our army and plan a strategy that will force them to come to us. I'm in no hurry to attack the asteroids where they hide after raiding our borders."

Sherard shivered and shook his shoulders. "Cold, dead places. And the Pharmons feel right at home."

Zara ate slowly, trying to absorb the discussion around her. She knew nothing about soldiers and war except that they were useless on Nubria, but she could sense the value both her husband and Sherard put on defending the Union. Being the queen of a Unity planet, she didn't deny that the government alliance to which Nubria belonged was important. What she didn't understand was the underlying pleasure each man felt when he spoke of going into battle. What was pleasant about facing death? What possible pleasure could a man get from fighting, knowing that he might be killed?

When the meal came to an end, Logan stood. "Bring your wine," he told his friend. "The rumbol board is waiting."

Zara wondered if her husband had forgotten that she was sitting beside him. He'd barely spoken to her since coming downstairs. She stood up, thanking Sherard for the meal.

"I'll join you later," Logan said, looking down at her. "Can you find your way back to our room?"

"I could if that was where I was going," she said smoothly. "I've never seen a rumbol board."

Sherard stifled a laugh while Logan frowned at his wife.

"Rumbol is a soldier's game."

"Then more the reason for me to learn the rules of play," Zara told him in her most polite voice. "I'm married to a soldier. If you grow bored with me, we can play rumbol."

Sherard couldn't contain his amusement any longer. Logan knew it was the thought of any man becoming bored with a woman as beautiful as Zara that made the injured soldier shake with laughter. A man would have

150

to be stone-cold dead not to prefer Nubria's queen over a game played with metal soldiers and pieces of crystal.

"Let her watch," Sherard said. "She can console you after I win."

"We'll see about that," Logan grunted, taking Zara by the arm and leading her out of the room.

Chapter Eleven

"Why did you let Sherard win last night?" Zara asked in a sleepy voice.

It was already midday, but she and her husband were still in bed. Logan had refused to quit the rumbol board until dawn was streaking over the city. She'd watched from a neighboring chair, fascinated more by the players than the large board patterned in black and white squares and the intricately carved figurines that were moved with a military strategy.

"I didn't *let* him win," Logan insisted, then grimaced. He'd forgotten how much Bervian whiskey Sherard could consume in one night, and he'd matched his friend drink for drink. His head felt as if it had been run through one of Rysor's ore smashers.

Zara smiled. "Yes, you did." She yawned, then snuggled closer to her husband's warm body. Rysor's temperature wasn't as hospitable as her homeworld's and the room was cold. "You let him win."

Logan frowned. He suspected Zara's gift was responsible for her knowing that he'd intentionally allowed

Join the Love Spell Romance Book Club
and **GET 2 FREE* BOOKS NOW–**
An $11.98 value!
Mail the Free* Book Certificate
Today!

Yes! I want to subscribe to the Love Spell Romance Book Club.

Please send me my **2 FREE* BOOKS**. I have enclosed $2.00 for shipping/handling. Every other month I'll receive the four newest Love Spell Romance selections to preview for 10 days. If I decide to keep them, I will pay the Special Members Only discounted price of just $4.49 each, a total of $17.96, plus $2.00 shipping/handling ($23.55 US in Canada). This is a **SAVINGS OF $6.00** off the bookstore price. There is no minimum number of books I must buy and I may cancel the program at any time. In any case, the **2 FREE* BOOKS** are mine to keep.

*In Canada, add $5.00 shipping and handling per order
for the first shipment. For all future shipments to Canada,
the cost of membership is $23.55 US, which
includes shipping and handling.
(All payments must be made in US dollars.)

ᏚᏚᏚ

NAME: _____

ADDRESS: _____

CITY: _____ **STATE:** _____

COUNTRY: _____ **ZIP:** _____

TELEPHONE: _____

E-MAIL: _____

SIGNATURE: _____

Sherard to capture enough rumbol pieces to win the lengthy game that had lasted all night. He was too good a player to make losing look easy.

"Sherard saved my life once," he confessed in a gruff voice. "If letting him win at rumbol is all I can do to repay him, then so be it." He turned on his side, wrapping his arm around Zara's waist and pulling her closer. He hadn't made love to her last night because he'd been too drunk and too tired to do it properly. Instead, he'd stripped her out of the clingy blue gown and tucked her next to him in bed. "He doesn't know I could have ended the game an hour sooner by capturing his sentry."

"He's proud."

"That goes with being a man," Logan told her.

"And a Galactic Guard," Zara said, looking through her lashes at the man she'd married. Logan wanted to deny the fact that he had a heart, but he hadn't been able to hide it from her last night. Every time he'd looked at his friend the link had vibrated with his feelings. Her husband's reaction to the life Sherard was now leading was a spark of hope to Zara's heart.

If Logan could feel compassion, he could feel love.

The link between them as husband and wife was growing each time they touched, but the spiritual joining that could follow was even more important if their marriage was to be successful. When she'd declared Logan her husband it had been with the hope that one day the link between them would be an open door, an avenue of thought and feeling that would resonate with respect and admiration and eventually love.

She'd learned a lot about her husband the previous night. She'd realized that his world was straight lines, roads that led from one military objective to another. Her world didn't have any direct route; it flowed like a river, weaving its way from day to day in a natural pattern that had nothing to do with gaining objectives and everything to do with enjoying life.

Patricia Waddell

Logan's world was precise. Orders given and obeyed. On Nubria life was less structured, allowing people to follow their hearts.

"Being a Guard is more than wearing a uniform," Logan said, then hesitated, as if he wasn't sure how to express himself. "It's . . . hard to explain to a woman."

Zara pulled the thick hair on his chest and got her bottom swatted for the effort. But it didn't stop her from pursuing the topic that was uppermost in her mind. "If you mean that women have a hard time understanding military games and watchtowers, you're right."

"Sherard has nothing to do with the watchtower. You heard his opinion of the Pharmons at dinner. He agrees with me." He opened one of the eyes his pounding headache had forced him to close and peered down at his wife. "I will build the watchtower. It isn't a subject open for debate."

"I'm not debating your right to build it," she said diplomatically. "All I'm asking you to do is delay the construction. At least until you have time to get to know my people. Your people."

"I'm not Nubrian."

"You're a Nubrian king," Zara said, raising her voice just enough to get her husband's undivided attention. She arched above him, her silver hair draping over his chest like a silk curtain. "Is being a soldier in the Galactic Guard more important than being a Nubrian king? Does your sword mean more to you than the hearts and lives of millions of people? People who are depending upon you to honor their faith and preserve their lifestyle."

"Enough lectures," Logan said, untangling himself from his wife's arms and getting out of bed. His eyes narrowed into splinters of dark ice as he stared down at her. "I will build the watchtower," he repeated for the last time. "You're the priestess of your people's faith. I'll leave their hearts up to you."

Zara looked from her husband's face to the drab draperies covering the windows. She could sense that once Logan's mind was made up, there was no way to change it. But then, she wasn't trying to change his mind. She was trying to open his heart. An impossible task if he refused to admit that he had one.

"I'll be downstairs with Sherard. Don't disturb me."

Zara didn't say a word while Logan dressed, then left the room. She knew better than to waste her breath on an argument she had no chance of winning as long as her husband was suffering from an excess of drink and an overdose of male pride.

A short time later, Zara was up and dressed. Wearing green leggings and a long tunic that brushed at her calves when she walked, she went downstairs. On her way she met Dominia. The old woman looked tired, but Zara sensed that it was an exhausted spirit, not a weak body, that kept the housekeeper from smiling when she mumbled a greeting.

Zara was feeling the effects of Rysor, as well. Unlike her own world, where flowers bloomed and animals nestled in the forest, Rysor was a world of ore-filled mountains and contaminated lakes. A world of taking, not giving. Her mind was reverberating with the despair of Rysor's inhabitants. She could feel the bleakness of their existence.

"Is there someplace I can be alone?" she asked Dominia. "A garden perhaps, or a room with lots of windows?"

"I don't know what you want to look at," the old woman replied. "But there's a gathering room in the back of the house. You're welcome to it."

Following the suggestion, Zara made her way toward the rear of the square building Sherard called home. The room was larger than the others she'd seen, but less comfortable.

It was void of furnishings. The windows were bare and streaked with dust. The rain that had fallen the previous night had added to the visual distress, splattering dirt and mud on the lower half of the windows that ran from floor to ceiling.

Reminding herself that faith didn't require a temple, Zara moved to the center of the room and opened the small pouch that held her prayer stones. The smooth white stones had been handed down from the first Queen of Nubria. Legend had it that the stones had once been part of a holy altar in the Oberlin Mountains, and that Nubria's first queen had brought them back with her to the royal city to remind her that faith wasn't a stationary thing. It moved with the heart, traveling from place to place with the believer.

Desperately needing to replenish the energy Rysor was draining from her, Zara laid the stones in a circle in the center of the room, then stepped inside. She stood with her eyes closed and her hands held high as she began to recite the ancient words that belonged to another world.

"Are you sure you know what you're doing?" Sherard asked as he poured two cups of steaming liquid. After passing one to Logan, he sank into a chair, then frowned. He'd just learned that Zara was the Queen of Nubria, and his best friend the planet's new king. "Building a watchtower is one thing. Ruling a planet like Nubria is another."

"I don't have a choice," Logan replied, hoping whatever he was drinking eased the pain in his temples. It tasted terrible. His head was still pounding, and having Zara bring up the watchtower only added to his aggravation. He wasn't used to having his decisions questioned. "The Council ordered me to Nubria."

"And into marriage with a beautiful woman," Sherard said, half smiling. "My luck should be so good."

"She's as naive as she is beautiful," Logan said. "She thinks all you have to do is smile and the universe will smile with you. You should see Nubria. The people don't have any idea what lies beyond their purple clouds. Maddock couldn't find a single weapon to confiscate. There's no army. No defense against Pharmons or anyone else who wants to march in and take control. They pray every time a bell rings."

"Is that why you brought her to Rysor? To show her the ugly side of life?"

Logan finished the last of the awful brew Sherard's housekeeper had prepared, frowning as he put the cup on the table beside him. "She needs to see a Pharmon or two. If that doesn't open her eyes, nothing will."

"They're ugly enough to make her want to shut her eyes," Sherard remarked teasingly "But something tells me that a woman who had the courage to defy the Unity Council isn't going to be dissuaded by a few hideous Pharmons."

"It's more than that," Logan said with a grunt.

In a silence that vibrated with Logan's frustration at trying to understand a planet that didn't realize the threat of a Pharmon invasion, Sherard studied his friend. Outside the weather was blustery, blowing brownish-red dust around the city streets. Inside the coldness was leaving the room with the help of a mechanical heater built into the wall.

Realizing that Logan had never come across this particular set of problems, Sherard smiled and offered him what advice he could. "Whether your wife recognizes the Pharmon threat or not, I agree that a watchtower is necessary. But it's not the watchtower that has you frowning."

"Keelan," Logan admitted. "I know he's on Nubria. When I find him—"

"Your wife is going to realize what it means to be married to a Galactic Guard." Sherard shrugged his shoulders, making the stub of his left arm shake slightly. "Perhaps that's for the best. You can be a soldier and a husband, but you can't be two men, Logan, any more than you can serve two commanders. Sooner or later, you have to choose the role and follow your destiny—king or soldier. You can't have both. That's what turned Keelan into a rebel. He got greedy."

The two friends continued to talk, discussing the battles they had fought, the carnage of war. When Logan's head had finally cleared enough to think straight, he went in search of his wife. His boots clicked rhythmically on the wooden stairs that led to the bedroom they had shared. He took the last set of steps two at a time, anxious to have Zara to himself again, anxious to spend a few hours cloistered behind closed doors with the passionate woman who was his wife.

When he discovered the room empty, Logan turned on his heel and marched back downstairs. It didn't take him long to find Zara. He stood in the doorway staring at her, listening to the musical cadence of the words she was reciting in a hushed whisper.

Zara sensed him immediately. Facing the dingy windows with her eyes closed and her back to the door, she could feel his presence. It made the link vibrate with dark shadows, stripping away the peace of mind she had gained after an hour of prayer.

She didn't acknowledge him with movement or words. Instead she kept her eyes closed and her mind focused on that spiritual place that existed within every person, that small pinpoint of light that linked every creature with its Creator. The words continued to flow from her mouth, softly spoken, recited with feeling and a deep, heartfelt knowledge that what she believed was real. More real than the wars her husband had fought. More real than the physical union that pleased them both. As real as the love she was beginning to acknowledge for a man who didn't care about love.

Logan tried not to be mesmerized by Zara's beautiful voice, but he couldn't keep from being enticed by the words that held no meaning for him. They rolled off her tongue like the sound of a waterfall rolling off a rocky knoll. Something inside him quickened, and for a brief moment he felt the same pleasure he experienced when she was lying beneath him, holding his body inside hers. The sensual sensation caught him off guard and he cursed out loud, breaking the fragile spell that had engulfed him.

"What are you doing?" he demanded, entering the room. He stopped just short of the prayer stones circling his wife.

"Refreshing my spirit," Zara replied in a voice as gentle as a lover's caress.

Slowly she reached for the reality that would bury the swirling colors and patterns of her faith back inside herself. The celestial peace that had surrounded her vanished as she blinked her eyes and closed the link. Logan had the ability to reopen it, but the power had to come from his own heart and mind. Until then, he would never be able to feel the gentle spirit that lightened Zara's soul even on a world as desolate as Rysor. She had no choice but to safeguard the link until her husband was ready to accept the power and faith that lay dormant within him. The love she knew was there.

Logan wasn't sure what had him angry. Maybe it wasn't finding Zara in their room where he'd left her, or perhaps it was finding her praying to some unknown gods. Gods he didn't understand. Either way, he didn't like the jealousy rising within him. Soldiers couldn't afford to be jealous. They had to be focused to be effective.

"It's time to go into the city," he said in a curt voice.

Zara looked at him, her colorful eyes revealing nothing of her inner thoughts. The dim light that was able to penetrate the dirty windows made her skin look pale, but the paleness only added to her beauty. Her tunic swirled about her legs as she knelt to gather the prayer stones, returning them to the embroidered pouch with a delicate touch that made Logan's skin burn to feel the caress of her hands.

His body reacted to his thoughts, and he felt his loins

tighten with a rush of desire. Damn the woman for making him forget who and what he was at the most inopportune times. If she'd been upstairs where he'd left her, he could have made use of the bed before they ventured into Desalken.

"Where are we going?" Zara asked as she closed the cloth pouch.

"I have business in the city," Logan said, holding on to his temper and his passion with an effort that was twice what it would be with any other woman. His wife was the most distracting female he'd ever met.

"I'll get my cloak," Zara said, moving toward the door.

Logan stepped aside so she could pass through the entryway and into the long corridor that acted as a trunk for the rooms that branched off to the left and right. He followed her up the stairs, watching the graceful sway of her hips as she went to fetch the only garment that could shield her beauty from the probing eyes of lustful men. And Rysorian men were lustful. Sex was the planet's main distraction and attraction.

Across the city, brothels were as common as the men who visited them. The women were brought in from all over the galaxy. Beauties on their own worlds, they were bought and sold on Rysor like the ore that kept the planet from being a lifeless lump of rock.

It wasn't uncommon for women to be shipped to the planet against their will, especially by Pharmon raiders who stripped the planets they robbed bare of anything of value, and on Rysor, a beautiful woman had twice the value she might bring elsewhere.

Logan wondered if Zara was ready for what he was determined to show her. He wasn't worried about her safety, not with Sherard at his side. The disabled soldier was a better man with one arm than most men were with two.

"Where are we going?" Zara asked again, taking her cloak out of the storage stall where it had been hanging since she'd unpacked. She didn't like the idea of Logan arranging her life to suit his personal agenda.

"I want to show you something."

Zara could sense that something wasn't going to be pleasant, but she held her tongue as they returned to the first floor of the house where Sherard was waiting for them. She'd never seen an artificial limb. The mechanical arm looked awkward, but she knew that Sherard was wearing it because of his pride, not because it made him feel whole. Once the prosthetic limb and his good arm were covered by a thick tunic, Logan handed his friend a laser pistol.

Under normal circumstances Zara would protest the weapons, but Rysor wasn't the world she normally lived on, and what little she'd seen of its capital city hadn't impressed her. Still, she resented the pistols and swords that her husband and Sherard were carrying.

When they arrived at their destination, Zara understood why her husband and his friend were armed. The *kaefe* was large and filled with people. People who hadn't bathed in several days. Zara wiggled her nose at the unpleasant smell and the dusty air that didn't seem to effect her husband or Sherard. The moment the two men walked into the room she felt the tension begin to ripple like wind across the surface of the sea.

The occupants of the *kaefe* moved aside, giving the visitors a wide path, as the two Guards and their companion made their way to one of the corner tables. Although it wasn't uncommon for Galactic Guards to be seen on Rysor, they were avoided whenever possible.

Logan insisted that she keep the hood of her cloak up, shielding her face from anyone who wasn't staring directly into her eyes. Zara tried not to look at her surroundings. She had sensed the building long before they had entered it, but now that she was inside she couldn't ignore the dark feelings that engulfed her. She'd never felt the link vibrate so negatively.

161

Logan led her to a table in the far corner, opposite the doorway, and told her to sit down. Zara grimaced at the dust that covered the furnishings, but she didn't argue. Even though the link was crowded with negative power, she could sense that her cooperation was necessary. And she didn't want to distract Logan. Sherard sat down beside her, effectively sandwiching her between his larger body and her husband's strength. Although she hated to admit it, Zara felt much safer with Logan at her side.

"Don't be afraid," Logan whispered, leaning his head down so no one else could hear his words. "We won't be here long."

Fear wasn't something Zara was used to feeling, but she couldn't deny the uncomfortable sensation that inched its way through her body as a stained curtain opened to reveal a pavilion built a few feet above the surface of the *kaefe*'s grimy floor.

The men in the room, mostly miners dressed in grubby clothing, turned their attention to the stage as several musicians, sitting cross-legged on the floor, started playing stringed instruments. There was no harmony to the music, no beauty. It was raw and unadorned, like the ore the men shoveled out of the Rysorian underground.

A drum joined the stringed instruments as a man stepped onto the raised platform. He was tall, but the torso of his body seemed out of proportion to the length of his arms and legs. His head was bald, his round eyes gleaming amber holes in a leathery face. His mouth curved into a demonic grin as he motioned for the drummer to increase the rhythm of the music.

"For your entertainment," he called out to the crowd. His voice was thick and raspy from breathing too much Rysorian air.

Zara flinched against the invasion his presence created in the natural linkage that existed in the room. She'd never felt true evil before, but she knew she was feeling

162

it now. If a soulless creature existed in the universe, it was the man standing on the stage.

"Is he a Pharmon?" Zara asked, keeping her voice as low as she could and still be heard over the furious beating of the drums.

"One of many," Logan replied matter-of-factly.

Knowing now that her husband had brought her to this place so she could see the Pharmons for herself, Zara was ready to tell him that she'd seen enough. The longer she looked at the oddly proportioned man, the more she wanted to leave. She searched the link for something positive about him, something that would give him and his species a redeeming quality, but she sensed nothing. Looking into the man's mind was like staring into the darkest night she could imagine; his thoughts were black and shapeless.

The music reached a feverish pitch, then stopped without warning. Once again the Pharmon moved to the center of the stage and held his lanky arms wide. "One bid should do the trick," he said to the miners guzzling down liquor as fast as two overweight Rysorian females could pour it. "Make it worth my time."

The music started again, but this time it was slow. Another curtain opened, revealing a smaller platform built atop the first. The artificial light shone down on a young woman. She was about Zara's age, but taller. Her hair was dark, her skin slightly bronze in color. Dressed in a flimsy gown that was little more than scraps of cloth stitched together, she turned in time with the music. Her body performed a flow of intoxicating movements as she danced around the stage. Her feet were bare, but the gold chains and tiny bells adorning her ankles accentuated her every step.

Zara wasn't interested in the woman's enticing movements or the way her stomach and hips twitched and surged to the beat of the drum. She stared at the young woman's face. Her eyes were blank, their brown depths as lifeless as the Pharmon's heart.

"They drug their women," Sherard explained, seeing her concern. "It keeps them obedient."

Zara started to get up. She wanted to run away, but Logan held her fast.

"Look and learn," he said. "This isn't an abstract world. It's real."

Zara gritted her teeth as she was forced to watch the men watching the young dancer. When the music stopped again, the girl sucked in her breath, making her breasts rise against the sheer fabric that kept them just enough of a mystery for the miners to start calling out their bids.

It was disgusting.

It was inhuman.

But most of all, it was real.

Logan was right. If she hadn't been forced to see it, she wouldn't have believed that anyone could be that cruel or that greedy. The Pharmon was auctioning off the woman like a market vendor selling vegetables.

"I've seen enough," Zara said, coming to her feet before Logan could stop her. "Get me out of here."

Neither man objected. They moved toward the door, Logan leading the way while Sherard, with his good hand on the lever of his laser pistol, protected Zara from behind.

When she was finally outside the crudely painted building, she leaned against it and took a deep breath. Even the dusty air of Rysor was better than the stench of the room they'd left behind.

"That was a little extreme." Sherard reprimanded Logan for his action. "You could have picked a less colorful display of Pharmon manners."

Logan didn't say anything. He didn't have to. Zara said it for him.

"He wanted me to see the threat the Pharmons represent. He thinks I'm being stubborn about the watchtower."

"Are you?" Sherard asked.

"Probably," Zara admitted. She wrapped her cloak more snugly around her, then looked at her husband. "I want to go home."

"Not yet," Logan said, taking her by the arm. "But soon."

"What more is there to see?" She dreaded the thought of being exposed to any more Pharmon activities.

"Nothing," he replied, then added, "I want you to convince Sherard to come with us."

"Have you asked him?"

"No."

"Why not?" she asked, skirting a large puddle that was more mud than water.

"Because he'll say no. I don't have your powers of persuasion."

Zara stopped walking. Her husband was smiling. Before now it was an expression she had only seen when they were alone, so it took her a moment to understand that he was teasing her. "You want *me* to ask *your* friend to leave a dirty, contaminated planet and return to my beautiful Nubria?"

"Something like that," Logan said.

Sherard muffled his laughter with a curt cough while Logan regarded his wife with dark eyes that gleamed with emotions he rarely showed to anyone.

Zara looked from her husband's handsome face to the tortured eyes of the soldier who had lost his arm defending the Union. "Come to Nubria with us."

Sherard shook his head. "Rysor suits me," he said in a mocking tone. "It's as useless as I am."

"Don't be absurd," Zara retorted as her hands went to her hips. It wasn't a regal pose, but it delivered the message well enough. "You aren't useless, and Logan needs all the friends he can get. He isn't the most cordial of monarchs."

Sherard laughed at the unflattering description of the Galactic commander. "Are all the ladies on Nubria as beautiful as their queen?"

"I'm not beautiful," Zara argued. "I'm stubborn, and it's going to take more than one Galactic Guard and a single heartless Pharmon to convince me that a watchtower is necessary."

"Then I guess I've got no choice," Sherard said, smiling as they started walking in the direction of his house.

Logan smiled back.

The exchange went unnoticed by Zara, since both men were a great deal taller than she. But under the rim of her hood, she smiled, too. Not because she was finally going to leave Rysor and its tainted air behind her, or because Sherard was returning with them. She was smiling because she'd felt the happiness in her husband's heart. The sentiment had only been a flash of feeling, but it had been there. It was the first time she'd felt that particular emotion from him, and it made her own body sing with joy.

Chapter Twelve

Logan stood on the balcony overlooking his wife's private prayer garden as the soft pink rays of sunrise were replaced with the clearer light of another Nubrian day. Everywhere he looked, flowers bloomed, dotting the green landscape with flashes of color.

As he watched Zara's morning ritual of kneeling in front of the rock altar to pray, he wondered if he would ever understand the woman who brought as many complications into his life as she did pleasure. Since their return from Rysor, Zara had taken to spending more and more of her time in the garden. She rarely went into the capital city to converse with her brother, since Solon and Maddock had taken up the habit of meeting every few days to discuss local matters, thereby eliminating the need for political visits by the queen.

Sherard had become Logan's third in command, after a strong recommendation from Nubria's new king to the Unity Council had restored his previous rank in the Galactic Guard. With Maddock overseeing local matters, including security for the royal couple and their residence,

167

and Sherard supervising the engineering crew that had arrived shortly after their return from Rysor, Logan was free to manage his own agenda. The item at the top of his list was finding the rebel leader, Keelan. Unfortunately, his progress was being delayed by his wife's total lack of cooperation.

"Brooding so early in the day?" Maddock asked as he entered the room to find his friend staring down into the lush garden. "I take it your queen is still trying to postpone the inevitable."

"She's the most stubborn female on this world or any other," Logan complained as he moved away from the balcony railing and into the room where Maddock was spreading a map on the desk. "She insists that every location I've selected for the watchtower is a sacred and holy place to her people." Logan ran his fingers through his hair, still damp from a morning bath, and frowned. "At first I thought she was stalling. Then Nessa told me that Nubria has thousands of 'holy' altars. It seems every rock that has ever been overturned on this planet has some sacred significance. It's the most ludicrous thing I've ever heard."

"Ludicrous or not, it's got a team of engineers eating and sleeping their time away," Maddock commented, thinking Logan might have finally met his match. "Why don't you have your wife select the spot?"

"I tried that," Logan grumbled. "She insists that choosing a location for the watchtower is the same as condoning its construction. She refuses to have anything to do with it."

"What about Nessa?"

"My wife learned how to be stubborn from the old woman," Logan said with disgust. "Solon's smart enough to admit that we need a watchtower, but he also admits he wouldn't know a holy place if he stumbled over it. Tolman is too loyal to his mistress to do anything more than shake his head, and everyone else just looks at me and smiles."

Maddock laughed. "Remind me never to go to war with your wife."

"I'm not at war, I'm married," Logan said as he looked at the map. He studied one of the peaks in the northern mountains, wondering just how many "holy" places there actually were on Nubria. Common sense told him that he was being played for a fool, but every time he looked into his wife's lovely violet eyes all he could see was the truth shining back at him.

In addition to his wife's innate honesty, a by-product of the blessed gift, or so old Nessa had told him, was her uncanny ability to make him lose his train of thought whenever he enjoyed her company alone. Every evening since returning from Rysor, he'd been determined to engage her in a conversation that would end only when he'd impressed upon her the importance of the watchtower and she'd relented regarding its construction. That had been three weeks ago and he was still trying to get the conservation started. Every time they were alone, he ended up touching her, and every time he touched her, he forgot everything but pleasure.

Their lovemaking was becoming an addiction.

Last night had been no exception. After the evening meal, they had retired to the privacy of their bedchamber. He'd watched as Zara groomed her hair, thinking it the most beautiful of her features, with the exception of her violet eyes, of course. He'd encountered enchanting women in his life, but none of them had effected him the way his wife did. When she'd finally put down the brush and turned to him, he had opened his arms, and the need to talk to her had been replaced with the need to touch her.

He was beginning to think her more witch than priestess.

It was more than the physical pleasure she gave him.

Whenever he was touching her, he felt an inner peace, something that pushed the rest of the world aside, as if it didn't exist. His mind was centered on her, and he couldn't seem to hold a coherent thought. And when the pleasure took him it was the most remarkable thing he'd ever felt. The more he made love to Zara, the more satisfying it became. His whole body seemed to come alive in those brief moments when he was emptying himself into her womb.

"What about here?" Maddock suggested, stabbing the map with a thick finger. "There's nothing for miles in any direction."

Logan shook himself out of his mental musings and marked the point. "Where's Sherard?"

Maddock chuckled. "In the kitchen arguing with the cooks. He keeps insisting that the men need meat, and they keep insisting that it's impossible."

Logan smiled for that first time that morning. "I will have a rebellion on my hands if I let Sherard butcher a *malaro*."

Maddock shuddered at the thought of eating one of the huge, furry animals. He refused to ride one, although several of his men had tried and were now patrolling the city from the swaying saddles that straddled the beasts' backs.

By the time Logan and Maddock had selected another site for the watchtower, Zara was finishing her morning prayers. She sat in the garden, content to listen to the harmony of the wind blowing through the trees and the occasional song of a morning bird calling to its mate. The more Zara kept to herself, the more she yearned to find a way to reach her husband's heart. Considering the short time that they had been married, she was amazed that the link between them had grown so quickly. Even now, she could sense him in the room above the garden. His thoughts were on her, and it pleased her to know that she was more than an object of passion to the man she had married. Yet she worried. Their physical union was so intense, it allowed her the freedom to enjoy the pleasure they shared without leaving her vulnerable to his probing thoughts. But for how long?

How much longer could she keep the link closed? Sooner or later, he was going to realize that her gift was a dual channel, a passageway that had both an entrance and an exit. When that time came, he would use it against her, and Keelan's whereabouts would be as easy to discover as the mountain peaks that loomed over the valleys of the northern continent.

Afraid that even now Logan might be able to discern her thoughts, Zara guarded against thinking about the rebels and the chain of events their crash on Nubria had triggered. She refused to discuss the rebels with her husband, convinced that every word she spoke gave credence to his belief that Keelan was nestled in a mountain retreat fostering another burst of defiance against the Unity Council. Nothing could be farther from the truth, but Logan refused to believe it.

She had asked Sherard about her husband's obsession with Keelan only to be told that the rebel had once been a Galactic Guard. Using the few facts she did know and a bit of logic, Zara assumed that Keelan and her husband had encountered one another before the rebellion. Perhaps they had even been friends. Knowing her husband's pride and the nature of the Guard, she could understand Logan wanting to erase the plight of rebellion from their honored record and correct what he saw as a betrayal. It might be a coincidence that she sensed a personal hatred for Keelan, but it didn't seem likely. Her husband's mind filled with blackness whenever the rebel's name was mentioned.

The only satisfaction she could gain from the situation was knowing that none of Logan's men had found anything suspicious to report. She hoped her husband would cease the daily patrols and come to realize that no one on Nubria presented any danger to the Union.

She held out hope for such an eventuality, but knew it was unlikely.

Her husband was the most stubborn man to ever grace the galaxy.

"Good morning, my lady," Nessa said, strolling into the garden to enjoy the warmth of the sun.

"Good morning," Zara replied, then belied her words by frowning.

"Has our king found another mountain upon which to build a watchtower?" Nessa asked, knowing there had been little talk of anything else since the couple's return from Rysor.

"He studies the map on a daily basis," Zara told her. "Soon he'll find a peak that has no altar, and I won't be able to stop him from sending Sherard and his engineers."

"You told me you looked into a Pharmon's mind. If they are the evil race you sense them to be, why not point the way for our king and be done with it?"

Zara let out a long sigh, then shrugged. "Because I want him to understand what he's protecting before he protects it."

Nessa's smile made her age-ridden face appear years younger. "When he understands that, he'll understand all he needs to know to be a husband and a king."

"Exactly." Zara sighed again, looking toward the sky as if the amethyst clouds overhead held the solution to all her problems. "But how can I make him understand without opening the link, and how can I open the link without betraying myself and the promises I have made?"

"You can't," Nessa told her. "Only Logan can."

"I don't need another riddle," Zara scoffed. "My husband is more than enough to keep me going in circles."

"It's not a riddle," Nessa told her. "Trust your heart. You'll know when the time is right, and when that time comes you must trust your faith to pave the way for his.

Logan himself will discover what you cannot tell him, what your sacred vow commands your voice to leave unspoken. After you have touched his mind, his heart will open, and all will be as it should be."

Zara's eyes closed for a moment. The sun bathed her in its warmth as the power of her faith once again became centered in the wisdom of her ancestors. The peace of the sacred spirit that was the beginning and end of all things lightened her heart. It spiraled through her, passing from the sun to the earth, using her as the vessel by which it traveled. Slowly the tension eased from her body. "You're right," she said as her violet eyes once again looked at the amethyst sky. "I will concentrate on the present and trust the future to my faith."

By the end of the day, the future was looking bleak.

Zara stood outside the closed door of her husband's private chamber, sensing that he seemed very pleased with himself about something. Wondering what that something was, and dreading to discover that he'd finally located a site for the ghastly watchtower, she tapped on the door and waited.

When Maddock opened it, she could see that the elation she'd sensed belonged to more than Logan. Sherard was in the room, smiling from ear to ear.

"You sent for me," Zara said.

Logan motioned her inside, but not before he gave her a fiery glance that said he wished they were alone. Feeling the energy of his gaze flow into her own body, Zara averted her eyes and walked to the table where a large map of the northern continent was spread across the wooden surface, its corners weighed down with empty drinking goblets. She'd seen the map at least a dozen times in the last few weeks, and each time she and Logan had disagreed upon the spot he had marked with a tiny red flag.

Under Sherard's supervision the engineering crew was

getting anxious to begin the task the Unity Council had sent them to Nubria to perform. Freighters were waiting to be signaled that the goods in their cargo bays were needed to begin the mammoth project that would take several years to complete. But most of all, her husband was getting restless. Zara could sense the restlessness along with the other emotions that were making the link between them vibrate.

As she looked down at the map another emotion joined the mental chain that tied her to her husband. Logan was fiercely satisfied about something. A second glance at the map told Zara what had him smiling on the inside. The tiny red flag had been moved. Now it sat atop another mountain in the Oberlin range to the north.

Zara's heart sank as she recognized the spot. Unlike the others Logan had selected, this mountain had no holy places and no altars of stone. It was located in the very center of the Oberlin's highest peaks, a mountain surrounded by mountains. There were no villages nearby and no pilgrim paths. There was nothing but miles and miles of rugged terrain and thick forest.

"Tell me there's an ancient altar there," Logan challenged her.

"None that I know of." Zara was forced to admit.

She studied the map more carefully, hoping against hope that her husband had overlooked some small speck of ink that would tell her the watchtower would interfere with her people's pastoral existence, but she could find nothing. Not the tiniest hamlet existed in the rocky summits that were tipped with ice caps during the winter season and covered by storm clouds in the spring.

Logan had chosen well. The building of the watchtower would not be an easy task, but it could be built. Not by Nubrian methods, but by technology. Instead of deterring her husband, Zara's stubbornness had opened the door for the very thing she had hoped to keep outside her world. Space cruisers and gravity cranes. Laser drills and noisy generators. The watchtower would be more than an atrocity to the peaceful philosophy of her people, it would be an engineering wonder that would make their simple hammers a thing of the past.

Logan had won. His single-minded intensity to do what he believed to be right had forced him to select a mountain that no Nubrian holy woman had ever set foot upon.

His watchtower would be built. The commission given him by the Unity Council would be satisfied, just as he'd satisfied the first order—to marry Nubria's queen. There was nothing left for him to do now but find the missing rebels.

Zara's heart felt empty as she realized that the world she loved was about to be forever changed. Tiny, splintering increments of pain swelled until there was nothing but a deep aching inside her chest.

She looked from her husband's face to those of his second and third in command, soldiers all. None felt what she was feeling; but then, none of them knew the true beauty of what they were about to destroy.

"Can you argue with my selection?" Logan asked, seeing the somber look in his wife's eyes and knowing he had won without her saying a word. But still he had to ask, to know that the silent battle between them was finally over.

A flash of guilt darted across his mind, but he pushed it away. He had been ordered to build a watchtower at any cost. Zara had to understand that his duty to her as a husband couldn't compete with his duty to the Union. Without the watchtower the Pharmons would eventually come. Another war would be the end of everything—the Union, Nubria, everything that was civilized and honorable in the galaxy. What Zara had seen on Rysor was a teardrop in the ocean compared to what she'd see if the Pharmon Empire wasn't stopped at the eastern border.

"Build your watchtower," Zara said, feeling as if the

very fibers of the universe were straining to contain her grief. The weight of the loss brought tears to her eyes, but she turned away before the three men could see them. "You will find no holy altar on the peak you have chosen."

The truth was more painful than any falsehood she could have told, if she was capable of speaking one.

"Leave us," Logan said.

Maddock and Sherard vacated the room with a nod of their heads. Neither man spoke to Nubria's queen as they closed the door behind them.

"I told you I would build the tower," Logan said, keeping his voice neutral. He had no wish to argue with Zara. His only wish was that she would accept what could not be changed.

"Yes, you told me," she replied. Her voice was dull, lifeless.

How could she reach Logan without opening the link? Nessa had told her not to try, that only Logan himself could open the passageway that led to his heart. Still, a part of her longed to expose what she had been able to keep hidden for these many weeks, to show the man she loved what only love could reveal.

For the first time in her life, Zara felt truly trapped by her faith, rather than set free by its giving nature.

Logan saw her distress. It showed in the single tear that escaped her eye and in the grim set of her pink mouth. He was torn between being satisfied that construction on the watchtower could finally begin and the guilt of causing Zara pain.

He walked to where she was standing with her back to the room, her eyes fixed on the open window that overlooked the courtyard. "It must be done," he said. "If anyone is to blame for your distress it's the Pharmons. Their greed and ambition force the Union to defend itself."

"I know that," she said, remembering the soulless Pharmon who had auctioned off the dancing girl. "I weep for the entire galaxy, not just Nubria."

She turned to look at him, her eyes sparkling with unshed tears. "Is there no way I can make you understand? Are there no words that can open your ears to hear what I'm really saying?"

"I hear your words," Logan told her. "Do you think I want to shove a watchtower down Nubria's throat? Do you think I want another war?"

"I don't think you know what you want."

A rush of anger went through Logan, but he held his temper. "I'm a soldier."

Zara nodded. "And a Nubrian king, and a husband, and one day you'll be a father."

The thought of having a child sent a shock wave of emotion through him, but Logan dared not let his wife see the effect of it. He wasn't used to justifying his orders, especially to a woman, but then again, he wasn't used to having a woman question them.

Any other time, Zara would have given in to the authority of her husband, but not this time. There was too much at stake for her to ignore what needed to be said between them. "You said you don't want another war, and I believe you. But this isn't about the war that the Pharmon Empire may or may not bring to our borders. It's about Nubria. What it is, what it represents. It's about people and a culture that can't be replaced once it's tainted by outside poisons. It's about us, our marriage, our future as man and wife."

"The watchtower won't change our wedding vows," Logan retorted. "It won't change what holds us together."

"What holds us together?" Zara asked daringly.

"This."

Logan's hands tightened on her shoulders, then pulled her close. His eyes gleamed with desire and determination as he lowered his head to kiss her, to demonstrate in the only way he knew how that they were husband wife.

Zara turned her head aside, causing her husband's mouth to fall against her temple. It was the first time she'd ever denied him. "There is more to marriage than reaching for a wife," she said. "If passion and your pleasure is the only thing that holds us together, then we are as far apart as Nubria and the asteroids the Pharmons call home."

Logan's hands tightened, then relaxed. Silently he questioned his motives in trying to kiss Zara when she was clearly upset about the watchtower. As a soldier, he should know that a fortress was defended to its fullest when the threat was nearby. He glanced at the map on the table, then stepped back, leaving tension to fill the space between their bodies.

"You say I don't understand, yet you give me riddles instead of reasons."

"I have never spoken anything but the truth to you," she defended herself. "What reason would you accept? Do I plead for my faith? A faith you mock behind my back. Do I beg for my people? A people you think hopelessly ignorant."

It was one of the few times Logan had seen his wife's temper, and she hit her target accurately. Inwardly he flinched at her words. On the outside, his mouth hardened into a thin line that said his own temper was getting harder and harder to control.

"Give me logic, not religion," he replied in a clipped voice. "I'm building the watchtower the last place my engineers want to build it. Why? Because you insist it can't be built anywhere else. My men eat bread and cheese and vegetables, not the meat they need to keep their bodies strong. Why? Because it would offend your cooks to prepare the flesh of an animal. What more do you want from me, lady wife?"

Love, Zara wanted to shout. Instead, she took a calming breath and tried to find something logical in the way she felt. But love wasn't logical. Neither was the faith that sustained her and her people.

"Tell me what you want," Logan demanded.

His voice was rough, but Zara could sense his frustration as much as she could feel his anger. Choosing her words carefully, she tried once again to make him understand. She walked to the doors that opened onto the balcony. "What do you see when you stand here?" she asked. Not expecting an answer, she went on. "Nubria is more than fertile fields and mountaintops. You've been its king for weeks now, but the only people you've met are the ones who work in the palace. Until you know my people, you can't understand me. Until you understand me, you can't understand what the watchtower will defend. Is the riddle so complicated?"

For a long moment, Logan simply looked at his wife with the unwavering gaze of a warrior assessing an enemy. She said nothing more as his mind raced from one thing to another, one argument to the next. He didn't like the bitter taste of disappointing her, but he couldn't serve two masters. Sherard had told him as much. The frustration he was feeling affirmed it.

"What would you have me do? Pray in the garden every morning for enlightenment?"

Once again, his voice had a harsh ring.

"The Feast of Oberlin draws near," she said as an idea came to mind. "It is a pilgrimage as old as our faith. Come with me to the sacred mountains. Get to know the people who accepted you as their king."

"The watchtower will still be built," Logan stated. "No amount of camaraderie with the good people of Nubria will change my mind."

"I'm not asking you to change your mind," she said, hoping it would change itself. "I'm asking you to do what every monarch of Nubria has done. I'm asking you to walk among the people."

"When does this feast take place?"

"As soon as I have blessed the Altar of Oberlin. The people will celebrate for three days before I arrive and for another three days after the blessing."

"Six days," he said, wondering if he was making a mistake. If he gave in to Zara now, she would be forever testing his tolerance. Still, six days was not too long to wait. Once Sherard sent word that construction would begin, it would take twice that long before the first freighter arrived to orbit Nubria.

"Very well," he finally answered her. "I will attend the feast with you." He gave her a fierce glance that said it would be the last compromise he offered. "We will leave in the morning."

"Thank you," Zara replied, wondering if her husband knew what he'd committed himself to do. She hadn't lied to him. But the few things she'd intentionally omitted might be her undoing once he discovered what the pilgrimage entailed.

"Is that all I get?" he asked, standing his ground between Zara and the main exit of the room. "Two simple words?"

Zara didn't need the link to know that she'd bruised her husband's pride. She'd denied him a kiss. He'd given in to her request to attend the celebration. It was her turn to compromise.

She closed the distance between them, stepping softly until the toes of her simple shoes touched the black leather of his military boots. "You are a stubborn man, Lord Logan."

"I am that," he replied, looking down at her.

It took a keen eye to see the humor in his gaze, but Zara saw it, gleaming like a distant star in the night. "Would a simple kiss do instead?"

"There's nothing simple about kissing you," Logan mumbled as he wrapped his arms around her.

It was the last thing either one of them said for a long time.

Chapter Thirteen

"What do you mean, my wife's in retreat?" Logan demanded rather than asked.

"My lady is in retreat. It is her custom to seclude herself before beginning a pilgrimage," Nessa informed him.

Logan relieved a frustrated sigh that would have told any of his men that his patience was close to being exhausted. Nessa simply gave him a brief smile, then waited patiently with her hands folded in front of her. His first impulse was to sidestep the old woman and fling open the closed door that separated him from the throne room where his wife had taken sanctuary, but he decided against it. It wouldn't do to let either of Nubria's holy women know that he'd grown accustomed to having his wife by his side.

He and Zara had been interrupted earlier in the day, before he'd had a chance to do more than kiss her. He'd been waiting impatiently since then, anxious for the night to fall so he could have his wife all to himself. Learning that she'd retreated to the altar in the throne room, where she intended to spend the night on her knees, purifying her spirit for the pilgrimage she would begin the next morning, only added to his frustration.

Knowing anything he said would only add to Nessa's amusement, Logan turned on his heel and walked back to his private chamber, trying to control his anger at being bested again by his lovely little wife. He told himself it didn't matter if he slept without her for one night. He'd slept alone all his life. It wasn't his wife's seclusion that made him angry, it was the realization that he didn't want to sleep alone.

When he opened the door of his private chamber to find Maddock and Sherard studying the map, Logan gritted his teeth. He wasn't in the mood for company, unless that company was a sassy Nubrian queen with violet eyes and silver hair. If the weather wasn't so blustery and rain wasn't soaking the courtyard and gardens, he'd march out the front door of the palace and threaten anyone who came within a hundred yards of him.

Recognizing his anger for what it was, childish jealousy because his wife was spending the night with a lump of rock instead of her husband, Logan walked to the serving table and poured himself a drink. By the time he joined his friends, his temper was under control. "So tell me, Sherard, can you build a watchtower on that mountain or can't you?"

Sherard gave him an amused look. "I didn't expect it to be easy."

"What is easy on this simplified world?" Logan mumbled, setting his drink aside.

It was Maddock's turn to smile. "You're in a strange mood this evening."

"There's nothing strange about wanting to find Keelan," Logan replied, turning the topic away from Nubria's eccentric ways and onto a subject he could understand.

"You still think he's in the mountains to the north?"

"I'm sure of it," Logan said with conviction. "The patrols haven't turned up so much as a footprint that isn't Nubrian here in the valleys. The mountains are the best place to hide, and to stay hidden. If I were Keelan, that's where I'd be."

Sherard nodded his agreement. "Is that why you agreed to go on a pilgrimage with your wife? Do you expect to stumble over rebels along the way?"

"I'm not sure what I expect," Logan admitted. "Call it instinct."

Since both Maddock and Sherard trusted Logan's instincts better than they trusted their own, they began studying the map again.

Maddock traced the route Zara had told Logan they would be taking. The opportunities for ambush were too numerous to count. "How many men will go with us?"

"No more than a dozen, including Sherard and yourself," Logan told him. "I don't want my wife getting suspicious. If I march a legion of men into the mountains, she'll know I'm looking for rebels."

"Too many men will keep Keelan at a distance, too few will endanger you and those you lead," Sherard said candidly. "A dozen is too few by half. You don't know how many men escaped with Keelan. What if he's convinced some Nubrians to join him?"

Logan shook his head. "I doubt it. In fact, I doubt anyone could convince a Nubrian to take up arms. They're as stubborn as the stone walls of this palace."

"Do you have a plan?"

Again, Logan shook his head. "We will have to keep our eyes open and our senses as sharp as our swords. Remember, Keelan was once one of us. We don't have any secrets from him. He knows what we're capable of, how we think and how we fight. He'll use that against us if he can. The trick is to act as if we're doing nothing more than escorting Nubria's queen to a sacred festival. Once we're in the mountains, I'm sure Keelan won't be able to resist the temptation. He's as anxious to be rid of me as I am to be rid of him."

Sherard looked at Maddock. Both men knew that the rivalry between Logan and the rebel leader went much deeper than the simple fact that Keelan had turned traitor. There had been a time when the two soldiers had been the best of friends. Betrayal cut deep when it cut that close to the heart.

Logan entered the courtyard at dawn, expecting to find a herd of *malaros* saddled and ready to ride. What he saw didn't please him anymore than the large shaggy beasts that were used for transportation. Instead of cumbersome animals, he found his wife, clad in a wispy white dress. The hem was stitched with gold and blue designs and stopped midway along her slender legs. Her feet were bare and her hair hung down her back like a silver waterfall.

Nubria's queen looked like a forest nymph, dressed and ready to frolic in the grass. Logan's expression went from slightly sleepy to completely disapproving in the blink of an eye. He wanted to scoop Zara up in his arms and march back into the palace. He hadn't slept more than an hour all night.

The morning prayer bells pealed from the tower at the far end of the courtyard, calling those who were not already up and about to open their eyes. Logan's gaze swept to the right and then to the left. The courtyard was empty except for the servants and guards who had been chosen to serve the king and queen on their journey to the Oberlin altar of stone.

Nessa was standing with her lady, holding a basket woven from reeds that grew along the banks of almost every stream in the valley. Tolman stood on Zara's other side with a pouch tossed over one shoulder. Both were wearing their customary tunics and wooden sandals laced with ginger-colored hemp that tied around their ankles.

Logan looked from the servants to the ten Galactic Guards lined up just behind them. The men were wearing their field uniforms. Black and red, like their dress attire, the casual uniforms fit more loosely, offering fewer restrictions than the braided garments that designated their rank. Each man was carrying a laser pistol and a sword. Both Maddock and Sherard had an extra belt of ammunition crisscrossing their chests. All of the men, including Logan, had six-inch, freshly sharpened knifes sheathed in the narrow scabbards that were part of their boots.

The two groups of travelers presented a sharp contrast. Zara and her servants looked as if they were ready to take a simple stroll. Maddock and his men looked ready to go to war.

"Good morning, my lord," Zara greeted him with a smile. Her eyes gleamed like two perfectly polished gems as she met him midway through the courtyard. "Are you ready to begin our pilgrimage?"

"Where are your shoes?" Logan demanded, his voice uncharacteristically sharp for that time of the morning.

Zara looked at her bare feet, then wiggled her toes. She'd sensed her husband most of the night. His sleep had been restless, as if he'd found their bed big and empty without her. Pleased that he might have missed her, Zara continued to smile. "I won't wear shoes until our return trip. It's a custom as old—"

"As old as your faith," Logan finished for her. He glanced at his men again. His scowl made the mischievous grin that was playing across Maddock's face disappear. Once his second in commander remembered his place, Logan's gaze moved around the courtyard. "Where are the *malaros?*"

"In the stables," Zara told him. "Pilgrims don't ride. They walk."

"Walk!" Logan looked over her head toward the purplish-gray summit of the Oberlin Mountains. The sun

185

was inching its way over the ragged peaks, outlining them against the softer shades of the morning sky. A soldier might make the march in twenty days' time, but he'd arrive lean and exhausted. "Do you know how far away those mountains are?"

"One year I counted the footsteps it took me to reach the altar. It's a long journey, but not an unpleasant one."

Logan looked from his wife's sunwashed face to the weathered expression of her teacher. Nessa flashed him a girlish smile, then adjusted the basket on her arm, as if to say it was time they got on their way.

The King of Nubria realized he'd been bested again. His scheming little wife had gotten him to agree to postpone the construction of the watchtower until they returned from the holy pilgrimage she made every year. Quickly judging the distance, then adding an additional week to allow for the slower pace they'd be forced to maintain in order for Nessa and Tolman to keep up with them, Logan realized his engineering crew would be idle for another six to eight weeks.

"You're as sly as you are beautiful," he said as his dark eyes focused on her eyes, which glittered with mysteries but offered no clue as to what Zara was thinking. He could see the pleasure in her expression, but he wasn't sure if it came from her subtle victory or the sheer joy of wiggling her bare toes in the thick grass that carpeted the courtyard.

"What about supplies? Food and bedding?" he inquired as he nodded for his men to take their position among the other pilgrims.

"The people will supply whatever we need," Zara told him. "We won't go hungry or sleep without a blanket to keep us warm."

She wondered if her husband had ever trusted anyone to provide for his needs. She doubted it. Logan had been trained from childhood to depend upon no one but himself. The next few weeks would be interesting. The purpose of the pilgrimage was to emphasize both the physical and the emotional link that existed between Nubria's monarch and its people. She hoped by the time they reached the altar nestled among the peaks of the Oberlin Mountains, Nubria's king would have a different opinion of the people he now ruled.

Logan signaled Maddock to begin the lengthy trek. Tolman and Nessa took up a place behind Logan and their queen, followed by Sherard and ten armed guards. The second in command unsheathed his sword and raised it high over his head. The gate bell tolled at his silent order and the massive wooden doors began to open, slowly revealing the meadow that fronted the royal palace.

It had rained most of the night and the sun hadn't yet burned the moisture from the foliage. The ground smelled rich and sweet as the royal procession walked through the palace gates. Logan was surprised to find a large group of Nubrian citizens in the meadow, kneeling in prayer and seeking to bless their queen. Logan wasn't naive enough to think Zara's people gave a damn about him. He watched as the women closed their eyes and chanted words like the ones his wife recited in her private garden at the beginning and end of every day.

Around the citizens offering their blessing, a symphony of insects and birds swelled with song, chirping and chittering as naturally as they did every morning. A Nubrian owl hooted, its long, soft voice muffled by the thick boughs that would be its shelter while the sun shone.

"It's a beautiful day," Zara said as her bare feet crushed the delicate grass growing along the path that split to the north and south where the meadow ended. The most well-worn trail led south into the capital city. The other, not as frequently burdened by the weight of people and *malaros,* turned north, through a thick forest that hugged the gradually rising foothills of the Oberlin Mountains.

Logan knew where they were going, even if he hadn't been aware of how they'd get there. He'd studied the maps of the northern continent, but he knew little about the creatures that called the large rainforest home. In the morning light, the thick foliage sparkled as though the raindrops had been turned into precious jewels by the miraculous rays of the sun. Brawny limbs and stubby shrubbery mixed and mingled to form a green wall around the flat, flowerdotted meadow. Fragile ferns, growing at the perimeter of the field, waved and flitted in the brisk breeze.

Zara could sense the tension in her husband as his dark eyes scanned the landscape, searching for danger. It would take every day she'd conspired to postpone the building of the watchtower to gain his trust. The wall he'd erected around his heart was as thick as the palace gates.

"Postponing the watchtower is only temporary," Logan told her, keeping his voice as soft as the wind teasing the thick blades of grass growing around them. "It won't change anything."

I pray that it does, Zara thought to herself as she lifted her face to the man who now held Nubria's fate in the palms of his war-callused hands. "May I ask a favor of you, lord husband?"

"What?" Logan answered as his eyes darkened to show his skepticism.

"From this footstep forward until we reach the holy altar, put thoughts of the watchtower and war away from your mind. Enjoy the day," she said, spreading her arms wide as if she could embrace the warmth and beauty of the land. "Enjoy every day that we walk among our people. It is a blessing, not a curse."

Logan suspected that his wife was trying to convert him to the simple ways of her world by asking him to forget his allegiance to the Union and the reason he'd been sent to Nubria.

Then he realized that this was the first time she'd asked him for anything. From the moment he'd stepped into the throne room to claim her as his wife, she had argued, debated, and lectured him, but she'd never asked him for anything.

"I will try," he said, doubting that he could cleanse his mind of the responsibilities and burdens he'd taken upon his shoulders when he'd accepted the Union's commission. "But I make you no promises. I am a soldier. My mind is a soldier's mind."

The smile Zara gave him made his body clench with desire. She was as radiant as the silver-white light that surrounded her. "That's all I can ask."

Logan almost said it wasn't all she could ask of him. If she but gave him the slightest hint that she wanted his touch, he'd willingly sweep her into his arms and march into the forest to find a secluded glen where he could make love to her until neither one of them could think of anything but the pleasure that came when their bodies were entwined.

"For you, my lady."

Logan stopped walking as a young Nubrian girl with waist-length brown hair and pale blue eyes handed Zara a flower. The petals were large, a delicate pink brushed with white powdery pollen.

"May the blessing of our faith be upon you and your husband," the girl said, bowing her head before she stepped back.

"Thank you," Zara said in return. She held the flower close to her nose, inhaling its gentle fragrance.

When she passed it to Logan, he hesitated. Her eyes told him that he would offend the girl if he didn't smell the flower, so he took it. The blossom's fragile scent lifted into his nostrils as he inhaled deeply. Soldiers didn't smell flowers, but the delicate fragrance pleased him almost as much as the smile on his wife's face. Realizing that his men were watching, he quickly handed

189

the pink blossom back to Zara. "We'll never get to the mountains if we don't start walking," he said gruffly.

"It's not the destination that matters. It's the journey."

Logan flashed her a disgruntled look, then started putting one foot in front of the other. He couldn't let his wife's beguiling glances distract him from his mission. Keelan and his rebels were hiding in the Oberlins, he was sure of it.

A great shout went up from the meadow behind them as they reached the rim of the forest. Zara laughed when Logan's hand went to the hilt of his sword. "They're only celebrating the beginning of our pilgrimage," she told him. Turning, she waved at the faithful who had gathered to wish her a pleasant journey, bestowing her dazzling smile on every man, woman, and child cheering for them.

"They're not the ones walking," Logan grumbled under his breath.

Zara ignored his complaint as she faced the thick forest ahead of them. As they stepped out of the warmth of the sunlight and into the dim shadows of the woodland, she sensed Logan's mind becoming more alert. Once again, his eyes surveyed the thick trunks of the trees and the branches overhead as if he expected to find treachery lurking behind each one. Zara prayed for patience. It was going to take more than a fragrant flower to relax her husband's vigilant ways.

There were few places where something wasn't growing on the dense forest floor. Moss and grayish-white mushrooms grew side by side with creeping vines and a variety of wildflowers. Some of the blossoms were pear-shaped, in shades of white and pink and yellow, some were bell-shaped with long, thin purple petals that dangled downward instead of reaching for the dappled sunlight that dusted the ground.

Zara refused to be rushed. She stopped whenever something caught her eyes, reaching out to touch the petals of a flower, or stroke the sleek green vines that wrapped their tiny arms around the towering trunks of trees that were too old to be recorded in the ancient archives of Nubria. The forest had existed from the beginning of time and it still stood proud and tall, untouched by the people who called Nubria home. The wildness of the forest had always fascinated her. She stopped a few minutes into their journey to pick the dark, wild berries that grew in thick clumps at the bases of the hardwood trees. When she offered one to her husband, he accepted it hesitantly, then popped it into his mouth.

"They're sweeter than I thought," he admitted grudgingly.

"Nessa gathers them sometimes," Zara told him. "She crushes the fruit and collects the juice to flavor cakes. I'm sure she'll bake some along the way. She knows I'm partial to them."

The thought of kissing his wife while her soft mouth was flavored by the sweet fruit sent a surge of desire through Logan that was so intense that he had to look away to keep from dragging her into his arms. They had a lot of walking to do before the day ended. It wouldn't do to let her get to him so easily. He was already painfully aroused, and they'd traveled barely more than a mile from the palace.

Remembering that he was a disciplined soldier, Logan continued to watch the forest as they moved north. He'd never seen anything as lush as the foliage around him. Everywhere he looked, something was growing. Trees, flowers, vines, shrubs, all competed for the sunlight streaming through the thick forest ceiling, yet they all prospered. He stopped trying to count the different flowers and plants. Glancing at Maddock and Sherard, Logan knew his men were just as enthralled by the dense woodland as he was. It had been a very long time since they'd enjoyed anything but war zones and battle sounds.

The forest was as quiet as it was beautiful, but the silence wasn't total. Logan could hear the crunch of his boots on the undergrowth that was mostly thick grass and tiny vines so closely woven together that they formed a green and brown carpet that sprang back to life the moment a pilgrim's foot was lifted. The hum of insects floated in the air, but their gentle buzz was more like music than noise. In the distance, the shriek of a bird sliced through the air, but it complemented rather than distracted from the peacefulness.

"Stay alert," he ordered Sherard at midday when they approached a break in the thick woodlands.

Nessa mumbled something under her breath, but Logan ignored it. Let the old woman think him a fool if she wished. He had more important things on his mind.

The forest opened into a small glade where a pool shimmered in the sunlight that came pouring through the breach in the leaf-laden canopy above them. Maddock stepped into the ring formed by the surrounding trees, his laser pistol drawn and ready.

Zara watched as the seasoned soldier scanned every green bit of foliage, his eyes absorbing the woods around the pool. When he lowered his hand and motioned that it was all right for them to enter, Zara walked forward. "There is nothing to fear," she said, losing count of the number of times she'd repeated that phrase since the guards had arrived on her world.

Logan followed her, his steps cautious, his gaze skeptical as they moved toward the glistening water that poured out of a large group of boulders. The rock formation was the first they'd encountered since entering the forest. It loomed over them like a giant statue with moss-covered arms. Pure, clean water trickled out from the stones, running smoothly down their cool surfaces until it pooled at the feet of the large boulders, filling a crystal-clear trench in the otherwise smooth earth.

Zara knelt at the pool's edge and studied her reflection. She could see the watery image of her husband standing behind her, his hand near the hilt of his sword, his eyes wary as they guarded her. Behind her husband, Nessa and Tolman began to prepare the midday meal, while Logan's guards searched the area around the pool, peering behind trees and into the thick shrubbery as if they might find more than birds nesting on the ground.

Logan watched as Nessa began to pluck fruit from a nearby tree with branches that sagged almost to the ground. Tolman was pulling long stalks from the damp earth, then shaking them to loosen the dirt from their roots.

"More roots and berries," Maddock mumbled as he joined his commander. "I keep telling myself they don't provide the energy I need, but I've never felt better. In fact, I'm beginning to like the taste of whatever it is the Nubrian cooks put on the table every day."

"We don't have much choice," Logan said dryly. "We eat what's available or we starve."

Zara smiled to herself. Her husband was doing his best to find something to grumble about. Well, let him. By the time they reached the altar, he would find himself enjoying more than the simple foods upon which the Nubrian people dined. He would have to be heartless and soulless not to see what she was trying to show him, and his compassion for Sherard had proved he was neither. Time and patience were on her side. Eventually, she'd be free to open her mind and heart the way she longed to do, and then she'd beckon her husband inside. Remembering what old Nessa had told her, Zara knew she couldn't force Logan to take the first step, but if the door was open, his curiosity would bring him inside.

Until then, she was going to enjoy teaching her handsome warrior that their life together was destined to be more than passionate nights and doubt-filled days.

* * *

"Does the food meet with your approval, my lord?" Nessa asked when Logan reached for the last of the broiled roots Tolman had washed in the small pool then wrapped in thick leaves before cooking them over a small fire.

"It serves its purpose," the new king admitted, licking his fingers. "Food is food."

"And men are men," Nessa retorted before strolling to the far side of the forest pool to wash her hands.

"She needs to learn some respect," Logan said, looking at his wife. Zara was sitting beside him. Her dress was flared out around her, hiding her slender legs from anyone's view, including that of her husband. He looked at her bare feet instead, holding back a smile when he saw the dirt that smudged her dainty toes.

"If Nessa didn't respect you, she wouldn't bother teasing you," his wife explained. "It's her way."

Logan continued chewing, wondering how Tolman had gotten a lumpy vegetable to taste like Schellean beef. The roots almost melted in a man's mouth, and their flavor was certainly pleasing enough to satisfy his appetite. But Logan's real problem wasn't with the food. Every time he glanced at his wife, his body started to throb. He wished he could send his men and the servants on their way with an edict that Nubria's king and queen wanted to be alone, but his pride wouldn't let him. Maddock and Sherard were already dangerously close to realizing just how enthralled Logan was with his new queen, and he suspected Nessa and Tolman weren't far behind in recognizing the importance Zara had assumed in her husband's life.

Logan was willing to confess that he was sexually captivated by his wife, but he was far from admitting that what he felt for Zara was more than a sensual need that increased daily.

The second half of the day was very much like its beginning. The small band of pilgrims picked their way through the forest, using their hands to push back the soft, ferny branches that blocked their path. The sun was sinking low on the horizon when Maddock finally called a halt to the trek that was taking them continuously northward. The older soldier suggested that they might want to rest for the night, and Logan agreed. Not that he and his men were tired. Far from it. Galactic Guards were trained to go extended periods without food or sleep. He looked at Nessa. The old woman might be as tough as synthetic metal, but she wasn't invincible. Both she and Zara needed rest.

"We'll camp here for the night," Logan announced.

"Not yet," Zara said, running the sleeve of her dress across her forehead to wipe away the sweat that had gathered from their long walk. "There's another glade not far from here. The ground is smooth and the water is sweet. We can rest there for the night."

Logan didn't like having one of the few orders he'd issued that day countermanded, but the forest was thick and their path was growing more uneven the farther north they traveled. Instead of a smooth carpet of undergrowth and thick vines, small rocks shot up from the forest floor, crowned by rich moss and making it increasingly difficult for the men guarding Nubria's queen to look anywhere but at the ground they walked upon.

"Very well," he relented.

Zara smiled, then motioned for Nessa and Tolman to move in front of them. The servants continued along the overgrown path, seemingly content to keep walking as long as their queen decreed it. Logan might not understand the strange religion that prompted them toward some ancient altar, but he did admire the servants' loyalty. He sincerely doubted whether any monarch, male or female, had ever been more faithfully served.

A few minutes later, the trail gave way to another glade, different from the one where they had rested earlier in the day. Tolman let the pack fall from his shoulder as he moved ahead of Nessa. Maddock once again scanned the surrounding forest, his eyes ever diligent to a danger that had not yet materialized.

Logan looked at the tear-shaped pond in the center of the clearing, its source hidden from the human eye as the water slowly seeped to the surface from deep within Nubria's fertile belly. The surface of the pond was as flawless as his wife's lovely face. It shimmered under the fading light, offering the pilgrimage a much-needed drink of its cool, sweet water. Through the gaps in the thick branches around them, Logan could see the last rays of daylight completely fade from the evening sky. If they were at the palace, this would be the time when Zara entered her private garden to pray.

As the twin moons rose in the night sky, the servants began preparing a meal of vegetables and berries gathered from the forest around them. Tolman tended the fire while he instructed Sherard on how to keep the flames from licking at the large plump roots suspended in vine baskets from a wooden tripod. Nessa began to harvest tall reed plants from the edges of the pond. After a quick nod from Logan, several of his guards stepped forward to aid the old woman in her task.

"We're not going to eat those, are we?" Maddock asked, frowning at the thin reeds clutched in Nessa's wrinkled hands.

"No," the old woman told him. "Sit down and I'll show you how to weave them into sleeping mats that will keep the dampness of the ground from seeping into your discontented bones."

Maddock flashed a scowl, but he didn't lessen his pace as he followed her to the east side of the pond, where flat rocks provided a place for them to sit while they went about their work.

With everyone busy preparing either their meal or their bedding, Logan sought out his wife. He walked to where she was sitting at the northern tip of the forest pool. Pale fingers of slender moonlight spiraled down from the night sky, shimmering and twisting their way around her as she lifted her face to the heavens.

Logan sucked in his breath at the image he saw. A beautiful woman perfectly at peace with her surroundings. The sincerity of her expression touched him the way it had touched him that day in the throne room, when they'd become man and wife, and he wondered if he'd ever be comfortable with the feelings she created within him.

"You'll sleep next to your husband tonight," he said in a firm voice.

"If you wish," Zara replied, opening her eyes and looking up at him. She could sense that he was angry about something, but the anger was tempered by other emotions that brought a smile to her face. "Are you sorry that we haven't been attacked by rebels, my lord?"

"You mock me."

Zara slanted a violet glance in his direction, then laughed out loud. "No, my lord. I'm teasing you. There is a difference."

Unable to resist the temptation any longer, Logan reached down and grabbed his wife by the hand. He didn't look over his shoulder to see if anyone noticed them making their way from the pool to the dark shadows of the forest. Instead his steps were determined, making sure the path was clear for the barefooted woman who was being led by a firm grasp on her wrist. When he was certain they couldn't be seen by either the light of Nubria's twin moons or the flickering illumination of the camp fire, Logan pulled his wife into his arms.

Zara went willingly, savoring the hard pressure of his mouth over hers the way she'd savored the cool water of the forest pond. After half a dozen kisses that didn't come anywhere close to satisfying her greedy husband, Zara slumped against his chest. "We're not alone," she reminded him.

Logan didn't like being reminded that he didn't have the freedom to rip the soft dress from his wife's body and make love to her under the blanched light that seeped through the tree branches. "When will we be alone?" he asked, dreading the answer as his hands molded themselves to Zara's curves, enjoying the sheer pleasure of touching her again.

"Not for a long while," she said breathlessly. "You must be patient."

"Curse patience," Logan said, picking Zara up as if she weighed no more than the fragile moonlight that guided his steps. He knew Maddock and Sherard had watched him lead his wife from the camp, and he knew they wouldn't interfere with what was about to happen. Neither would Nessa and Tolman, if they knew what was good for them.

Logan didn't stop weaving through the forest until he found a place where nothing existed but diffused moonlight and sturdy trees. The sultry scent of forest flowers mingled with the dew-kissed fragrance of moss and ferns as he moved through the darkness. Slowly, he lowered Zara's feet to the forest floor and pressed her up against one of the trees. His body covered hers as he captured her between the cool bark of the tree and the heat of his hungry body, giving his hands free rein to unbutton and tug the wispy dress from her body. All the while, Zara clung to him.

A bolt of desire lanced through Logan as his hands freed his wife from her clothing. Shaking with impatience, he freed himself from the restrictions of his uniform. "Wrap your legs around me," he ordered in a husky whisper.

Zara did as he asked, her cry of pleasure and surprise muffled by her husband's mouth. Her breath came in short, soft gasps as he entered her body as smoothly as the night had overtaken the forest.

Logan drank every soft moan that came from his wife's

throat as he moved inside her, gliding and retreating, then returning, until the night turned into a blackness where ecstasy ruled supreme. When he couldn't endure the sweet pleasure a moment longer, he surged deep inside her silky sheath and held himself there while his body trembled and his soul seemed to explode.

When he finally spoke, his voice was as soft as the gentle kiss of the wind upon Zara's bare legs. "We have to go back," he said, the regret evident in his voice.

"Yes," she agreed breathlessly, wishing that she could feel the same contentment in her husband's heart in the heat of the day as she felt now, masked by moonlight and shadows.

When the King and Queen of Nubria returned to the camp no one seemed to notice that they had been missing. Logan smiled at Zara, delighting in the slight flush that colored her cheeks. "My men are too disciplined to embarrass you, and Nessa and Tolman are too smart."

Saying nothing, Zara left his side and walked to where a thin mat of woven reeds covered the ground. Logan joined her, reluctant to let any distance gather between himself and his wife now that they had stopped walking for the day. A short time later, Nessa appeared in front of them with two wooden plates. She handed the first to Zara. "Eat, my lady. The morning sun will bring another day. You will need your strength."

Logan caught the mischievous gleam in the old woman's eyes as she handed him the second plate. Being both king and soldier, he allowed himself the luxury of smiling at her, then giving her a wicked wink that said *her* lady was really *his* lady now.

His contentment lasted for another hour, until Nessa collected the plates and walked to the pond to wash them. Zara stood up. "It is time for my prayers."

The simple words washed away the sensual peace that had lingered between them since returning to the small camp. Logan frowned as he watched her retrieve her prayer stones from a small pouch inside the larger one Tolman had carried into the forest. As the night grew darker around them, he continued watching and listening to the musical words that flowed from his wife's mouth, words that separated them as surely as they joined them.

Logan didn't care to feel like an alien in a world he now ruled, but the ancient prayers caused a strange jealousy to rise within him, and there didn't seem to be anything he could do to stop it. When Zara was praying, she belonged to her invisible gods, not to him. When she was draped in the sacred shroud of her prayers, she was untouchable by the man who had caressed her body only a short time ago.

An uneasiness ran in Zara's blood as she slowly surrendered the peace of the evening prayers to the reality of her husband's thoughts. Like the darkness of the forest, his emotions could be frightening, but she felt no fear as she packed the small prayer stones away and handed the pouch to Tolman. Logan was battling within his own mind, which meant the confidence of the warrior was fighting with the happiness of the man. It wasn't a pleasant thing to endure, but Zara knew her husband had to experience the battle before he could enjoy the peace. Nubria's new king had to earn the peace of mind his role demanded of him. There was no other way.

"Come. It grows late," Logan said as she joined him.

Her husband had moved their sleeping mat to the far end of the glen, away from the soldiers and servants who would be their constant companions for several weeks.

Wordlessly, Zara accepted his outstretched hand and followed him to the place where they would sleep under the silent stars. Once she was tucked into his embrace, his arm around her waist to keep her nestled into the natural cradle of his bent legs, she smiled.

"Good night, my lord," she whispered softly.

"Good night," Logan replied, kissing the nape of her neck.

Within minutes, they were both sound asleep.

Across the glen, old Nessa sat in front of the fire, warming her tired bones and smiling as she thought about the first steps in the very long journey Nubria's new king had yet to make.

Chapter Fourteen

Morning arrived in the forest with a swirling white mist that floated inches above the foliage, washing the ferns and smaller plants in a moist cloud that made the glen seem almost mystical. Logan awoke to find his wife sleeping contently by his side. Tolman was already up and about, his agile hands tending the fire.

Logan sat up and stretched, then looked around him. Long, curling strands of fog wove their way through the surrounding trees as birds, nesting in the upper canopy of branches, chirped hello to the wakening world. He edged off the mat, careful not to wake his sleeping wife, and stood erect. A faint wave of fragrance came with a deep intake of breath, and Logan searched the thick underbrush for the familiar scent. There growing among the lush fern was a cluster of pink flowers. The petals opened like tiny sails, capturing the morning light, as small winged insects fluttered just above them.

He was tempted to pluck one of the blossoms and use it to tickle Zara's nose until she blinked sleepy violet eyes at him, but the impulse passed as Logan realized old

Nessa was awake and watching him. He broke his gaze free from the fragile pink flowers and fixed it on the surrounding forest. Except for the sound of songbirds and chirping insects, all was quiet.

Dawn was only a few minutes old when Maddock and Sherard joined Logan next to the crystal-clear pond situated in the center of the grassy glen. "Nothing strange happened during the night," Maddock said. "I had men on watch at every hour."

"We haven't reached the mountains yet," Logan reminded him. He glanced at the tranquil forest, then back to Maddock. "I don't want the serenity of the pilgrimage to make them complacent. We don't want to get caught with our pants down."

"You should have thought of that before you went venturing off into the forest last evening." Sherard reminded his commanding officer with a grin. He held up his hand when Logan's temper turned his face as intimidating as the mountain peaks. "Don't worry. I was close enough to keep watch without seeing anything private."

Logan's temper subsided when he realized neither Maddock nor Sherard would ever do anything to embarrass Zara. But they wouldn't forget their duty, either, which meant he'd have to be careful the next time he wanted to spend time alone with his wife.

"Tolman said there's a village at the end of today's walk," Maddock told Logan. "He also said that Lady Zara always stops there to visit with the local magistrate and supervise a prayer circle, whatever that is."

"Who knows." Logan shifted his gaze to the sky, laced with pink streaks of sunlight. The Nubrian religion wasn't obstructive, but it was difficult for an outsider to understand. He had yet to hear the name of the god or gods the people worshiped. Their altars were naked stones where they knelt and recited prayers he couldn't understand, yet he sensed that their faith was as real to them as the hard metal of a sword was to a soldier like himself.

It was puzzling, yet Logan found himself feeling grateful that he wasn't married to a woman who cared more about jewels and clothing than she did the people she ruled.

By midafternoon, the group had reached the village. The small hamlet of rectangular houses was situated on a large knoll that rose gradually from the forest floor. The settlers gathered in front of the largest building to greet their king and queen. Logan hid a smile as the women eyed him and his soldiers with open curiosity. As in Nubria's capital city, the buildings were painted with colorful shutters over the windows and trimmed on the bottom by wide wooden boxes where flowers grew as abundantly as they did in the fertile forest. At the edge of the village, bricks were mortared together to protect the well that supplied their drinking water.

Long wooden tables had been carried outside, where a feast was to be served in the queen's honor. Young women carried serving bowls filled with fresh fruit and vegetables, while Zara introduced the village magistrate to Nubria's new king.

"My lord, this is Kamilin. He oversees the village and reports to the Assembly."

"Lord Logan," Kamilin said, bowing from the waist as he spread his hands wide at his sides. "Welcome to our humble village. May our faith bless you and our beloved queen."

"Thank you," Logan said as formally as he could. The magistrate was a plump man with round cheeks and dark eyes. His hair was cut short and the beard that covered his lower face was neatly trimmed. After greeting his new king, Kamilin introduced his wife, a robust woman with a large bosom and a bright smile.

Within minutes of arriving in the small community, Logan and Zara were surrounded by swirling currents of people. Men and women alike, dressed in loose-fitting tunics and leggings. Maddock positioned his ten soldiers around the perimeter. It was easy to see that his orders confused the occupants of the village. When Logan explained that his men were there to guard the queen, Kamilin looked as confused as his people.

"There is no danger here," he said, glancing around him. "The animals of the forest are easily tamed by our lady's hand."

"What animals?" Logan asked. The only animals he'd seen so far were the colorful birds that perched in the thick boughs and sang from sunrise to sunset.

"He's talking about the *juna,*" Zara explained.

"What exactly is a *juna?*" Logan asked, following his wife's glance as it moved to the thick woods that rimmed the village.

"It's a big cat," she told him. "Once we reach the mountains, you'll be able to hear them calling for their mates at sunset. They're one of Nubria's most beautiful creatures. Wild and as free as the wind."

"I've seen our lady tame them with nothing but a touch of her hand," Kamilin said proudly. "It's the gift of a holy priestess."

Logan didn't like the idea of Zara taming anything that was as wild as the wind, and his expression said as much. He continued frowning when she linked her arm through his. "Don't worry. *Junas* don't like humans. We might hear them, but I doubt that we will see them. They're very elusive."

"As elusive as rebels," Logan replied, keeping his voice low so only his wife heard the retort.

Zara stiffened at his side, but she didn't release his arm. Instead she drew him away from the magistrate and toward the eastern edge of the village, where young children were playing a game that consisted of spinning brightly painted hoops into the air, then tossing a ball through them before the hoops fell back to the ground.

"There are no rebels on Nubria," Zara whispered tightly. She reached inside the front of her tunic and withdrew the marriage amulet she had worn since old Goldwren had given it to her. "This means I cannot lie to you. Nor would I, even if I could."

"Withholding the truth and lying are two different things," Logan replied softly. "Look me in the eye and tell me everything that happened the day Keelan's ship crashed in these mountains. Tell me where you've got the survivors hidden."

Silver tears brimmed against Zara's eyelashes. "A promise given is a promise kept."

As soon as the words left her mouth, she sensed the distance between herself and her husband increase to mammoth proportions. It was like watching a ship set sail, powered by the wind, drifting away on the ocean tide, elements not even a high priestess could control.

Logan pulled his arm away. His hand went to the front of his uniform to unfasten the top two buttons. His fingers wrapped around the marriage amulet that matched the one his wife was wearing. "The day will come when you have to choose," he said. "Sherard once told me that I could not be two men. I would pass his advice on to you. You cannot be two women, my beautiful Zara. Soon you will have to choose between being my wife and Nubria's queen." His eyes were as cold as the timeless void of space as he looked down at her. "Think carefully before you decide which promise you will keep."

With those words, he left her.

While she watched him walk away, Zara felt the hope of reaching Logan's heart fade like the sun setting behind granite mountains. Her husband was a man with only one purpose. He'd come with her to find rebels. Logan had no real interest in understanding her or the ways of her people. Embracing their faith was the furthest thing from his mind. And she had to touch his mind before she could touch his heart; it was the way of her faith. The same faith that now had her trapped between promises, the one she'd given to a rebel named Keelan and the one she'd given to a Galactic Guard the day she'd become his wife.

"What bothers you?" Nessa asked as she joined her lady.

"What has bothered me since the day a ship crashed into these peaks," Zara replied sadly. "I am a woman of faith who is caught between the Unity Council and a war that should have ended months ago but hasn't."

For a moment there was only the sound of children playing, laughing and calling out to one another, enjoying life. Nessa's eyes narrowed as she looked from her queen to where Nubria's new king stood talking to his second in command.

"Our king's heart won't be easily won," Nessa said. "Do not fight what comes naturally to you. There can be no peace in a victory that gains nothing but more discontentment."

Zara gave her teacher a cool glance. "I haven't had real peace in my heart for so long, I'm not sure I can recognize it any more. I pray and pray, but the problems outweigh my words."

Nessa's smile was the same reassuring one she'd given Zara on the day she'd discovered that the Unity Council had demanded her marriage to a man whose face and name she didn't know. It warmed Zara's heart in the same way, making her worries seem overstated.

"Go," Nessa instructed her. "Take some time to prepare yourself for the prayer circle that awaits you once the sun has set. Concentrate on the things you can change, not the things that are beyond your control."

Zara stole a glance toward the table where half of Logan's men were about to be served. The other half stood guard, watching for a danger that existed only in their commander's heart. Logan was still talking to Maddock. Sherard had joined them. The three men had their backs to her, but Zara didn't need to see their faces or hear their voices to know they were plotting a way to find the rebels. Her heart clenched with pain as she realized her husband would never find what he was seeking so diligently. Nor would she, if his words were to be believed.

There could be no compromise for her. No forsaking of one promise in order to keep another. Her faith demanded that she keep both the vows she'd spoken. Individually and equally. It wouldn't be an easy task; but then, her faith didn't require an effortless devotion, it required a diligence of spirit that her husband couldn't comprehend.

Sensing that by trying to bring Logan closer to her, she might actually drive him away, Zara walked into the forest.

Logan ceased talking as his wife moved toward the thick trees that shielded the village from winter winds. His eyes followed her graceful figure as it disappeared into the cool forest.

"Stay with her," he said to Sherard. "Don't let her out of your sight."

The one-armed soldier left his commander's side without question or hesitation. Whatever was brewing between Logan and his lovely wife wasn't any of his business. He was a soldier, doing what he was told. If he thought his superior a fool, it was an opinion he'd wisely keep to himself.

Sherard followed Zara easily enough. The queen had only walked a short distance into the woods. She was sitting on a flat rock, her hands folded in her lap, her face lifted toward the sky, her eyes closed. The seasoned warrior slowed his pace as he caught sight of her, stepping carefully to keep from making any unnecessary noise. He leaned his good arm against a tree and watched as Nubria's queen sat silently, as unmoving as the rock that was her chair.

"Come closer, Sherard," Zara called out unexpectedly.

Knowing he hadn't been heard or seen, Sherard stepped out from the natural cover of the forest and stood before Logan's wife. "He sent me to guard you."

"I know," Zara replied. "What he doesn't understand, refuses to understand, is that there is nothing here that can harm me."

"Are you sure?"

"Yes," she told him. "But that is a matter to be sorted out between myself and my husband. Come. Sit beside me. You have weighed heavy on my heart for some time. I want to speak to you."

Sherard looked around himself, as if he expected to see Logan watching them. Zara smiled at his hesitation. The one-armed soldier's loyalty to her husband was as unwavering as Nessa's loyalty to their faith or Tolman's loyalty to the noble house he served. Knowing her husband needed his friends more than he was willing to admit, she motioned Sherard to join her.

He moved toward a fallen tree, its trunk still sturdy even though its roots had been upended by a spring storm. Sherard shifted his sword as he sat down, making sure the handle could be easily gained with his one good hand.

Zara gathered her thoughts and words carefully. Sherard was a proud man. As proud as her husband. "How did you lose your arm?"

"At Medash," he told her. "It was severed by Keelan's sword."

Zara absorbed the truth she had long suspected. "Is that why my husband hunts the rebels with such a vengeance?"

"Partially," Sherard admitted. "I would hunt Keelan just as keenly if it had been Logan's arm."

"I'm sure you would." She smiled a sad, sweet smile that made Sherard wish she didn't belong to his friend. He'd never seen a more lovely woman. "You no longer wear the artificial arm. Why?"

Sherard shrugged. "No one here seems to notice that I'm lacking a limb. It's cumbersome and heavy, so I don't bother. I'm not a vain man."

This time Zara laughed. "All men are vain."

"You're confusing vanity with pride."

"Aren't they one and the same?" Zara remarked candidly, then became serious. "I sense the hatred my husband holds for Keelan, and I sense your wounded pride when you think of yourself as half a man. You are no less whole than a man with all his limbs intact. It isn't our bodies that give us life, but our hearts."

"Logan said you weren't a subtle woman. Do you always confront things so directly?"

"Forgive me, Nubrians aren't used to keeping our thoughts closed. Or our hearts." She plucked a small flower from among a cluster of green leaves and held it to her nose. "Talk to me."

Sherard viewed his commander's wife through narrow eyes for a long, tense moment before he took a deep breath and relaxed. "I don't think a woman can understand," he began. "Being a soldier is more than fighting. It's knowing you've been trained to protect and defend those who can't protect and defend themselves. It's our code of honor. To serve those who cannot serve themselves."

"And you think you've betrayed that code of honor by losing your arm. Is that why you took off your uniform and lived on Rysor? The planet's desolation matched your own."

"Yes." The answer was short but true.

Sherard looked up to see Logan mere feet away, standing beside a towering tree whose branches seemed to reach up and touch the clouds. If Zara knew her husband was nearby, she didn't let on. When Logan nodded for his friend to stay put, Sherard continued his conversation with the Nubrian queen.

"I hate Pharmons more than I hate rebels. I chose Rysor because I knew I'd eventually have a fight with one of them. If I died, I wanted it to be with Pharmon blood on my sword."

Zara shivered at the harsh truth in Sherard's confession. Like her husband, he had a singular comprehension of life—honor and blood. One couldn't exist without the other. For a man to prove himself worthy of honor, he had to be willing to sacrifice his life. The concept was as foreign to her as Nubria's ancient rituals were to her husband. Two people, two worlds, opposites bound together by vows neither was willing to break.

"Is there nothing else you want?" Zara asked, knowing her husband was listening as intently as she. "Nothing that could bring joy into your heart?"

Sherard scoffed. "Once I thought about retiring. Finding a woman and having a son. But what woman would want a scarred, one-armed man?"

"A woman who isn't afraid of love."

Silence gripped the forest as Sherard looked at her, his eyes searching for the answer her softly spoken words had offered.

"I need to be alone," she finally said. "Go, Sherard. Enjoy the feast. Let down your defenses long enough to smile. One arm or two, your scars aren't as ugly as you think."

Chapter Fifteen

The sky was a deep amethyst, the exact color of Zara's eyes, as Logan cast his head back to look at the forest again. The air was crisp, laced with the scent of woodlands and ferns and wildflowers. The night's sweet fragrance reminded Logan of his wife. Zara's scent was one of the things he liked best about her. When he kissed her body, he could taste the sweetness.

One thought of his wife quickly brought another, and Logan looked to the small hut where she was changing into her prayer robe. Her conversation with Sherard still puzzled him. Was she planning on playing matchmaker to his men, teaming them up with pliable Nubrian women who would soften their hearts until they forgot how to be soldiers? Is that what she'd done with Keelan and his men? Were they farmers now, or artisans, living among the mountain folk, converted to the faith that didn't think swords and watchtowers were necessary forms of protection? Somehow Logan doubted it. Keelan had been one of the Guard's best.

"Must I stand here forever?" he grumbled as Tolman approached.

"Our lady will join you soon," the servant replied. "The ceremony demands your presence. Didn't Nessa explain?"

"She explained," Nessa spoke for herself. The old woman was dressed in the gray robe she'd been wearing the day she'd performed the ceremony that had joined Logan and Zara as husband and wife. "As king, you must honor Zara as high priestess. This corner is the northern point of the prayer mat. It is where Zara's father stood when her mother blessed this village many years ago. If you move from this point, it will dishonor his memory."

"I won't move," Logan assured her. "How long is this going to take?"

The padding beneath his feet was soft and subtle. The reeds had been soaked in a special oil, or so old Nessa had told him earlier. As befitted his rank, Logan was standing at one corner of the prayer circle. The large woven mat was several yards long and just as many yards across. Although the mat was square, the white emblem woven into it was a perfect circle. The four corners were marked with strange signs, symbols he couldn't identify that held some sacred meaning to the people who were waiting for Zara to join them.

"It will take as long as it takes, my lord," Nessa said patiently. "Relax." She stood next to him, her sandaled feet resting on the cool grass rather than the soft matting with its strange symbols. "Watch and listen, so you may learn. A man who thinks he knows everything is a man who knows little."

Logan almost rebuked the old woman for her disrespect, but he held his tongue. He was the outsider here, a king who ruled without knowing who and what he ruled. His wife had reminded him of it often enough.

He looked at the three circles woven into the mat. The smallest circle was woven with reeds that had been dyed red with the juices of some forest plant. Logan knew without being told that it was the spot upon which Zara would stand. His wife was the focal point of Nubrian religion, the priestess who directed their faith.

Suddenly the door of the hut opened and Zara stepped into the dim evening light. Her hair fanned out behind her as she walked toward the prayer mat. The village citizens began to gather around the reed carpet.

Zara looked at her husband as her bare feet slipped through the neatly cropped grass. She'd sat in the forest for several hours, trying to find the answer to her dilemma. None had come to her. Instead, she'd found the object upon which she intended to focus her prayers this evening. Not a village, but a man. Sherard. The guard her husband had sent to watch over her.

The core of her faith was its unselfish nature. Sherard's heart was more burdened than anyone she'd ever met. If she could open the link enough to touch him, there was hope that one day she could do the same with the man she'd married. But even more than her desire to find her husband's well-guarded heart was her need to prove that her faith was real. That it held powers neither soldier could dispute once they recognized it for what it was.

"My lady," Nessa said as Zara came to a stop at the northern corner of the mat. "May our faith bless you this evening."

Zara reached out and took Nessa's wrinkled hand. She cradled it within her own two hands and smiled. "There is no greater blessing than your devotion," she replied, then looked at her husband. "I know this must all seem strange. My father was born in this village. Having you take his place is an honor. Please accept it."

"I accept that I am their king, and as such, I owe them the same respect they show me," Logan replied, wondering what else his wife would have him say.

When she was dressed like this, in robes decorated

with symbols like those on the prayer mat, her hair hanging down her back like silver moonlight, her eyes alive with the faith she believed was the most powerful force in the universe, she ceased being his wife and became Nubria's queen. The familiar jealousy he always felt when she focused on her religion resurfaced, but Logan pushed it aside. This night belonged to the people of the village.

"Are you ready?" Nessa asked Zara.

"I'm ready," she replied.

Giving Logan one long, last glance, she stepped onto the mat, but instead of walking directly to the small inner circle, her feet began to trace the outer circle.

"The outer circle represents the never-ending cycle of life," Nessa told Logan in a soft whisper meant only for his ears. "It is day and night, life and death, hope and despair. It is everything that exists in the universe and everything that exists within us."

Logan looked at the old woman, but her eyes were on the young priestess walking the outer circle of the prayer mat. Zara's arms were lifted high and wide as she looked at the night sky. She began to recite words he couldn't understand, although he'd heard them dozens of times since their marriage. As always, they seemed to blend into a song, a musical chant that pleased the ear.

"The second circle is the thoughts that occupy our minds. Even when we sleep, our dreams talk to us. Our minds are never empty, never idle."

Logan kept his eyes focused on his wife as Nessa's explanation reached his ears. The people of the village began to recite the prayer with their queen. Dozens of voices added a magical quality to the chant, giving it a forcefulness that made it echo off the distant mountains.

Zara turned slowly as the rhythm of the chant changed, the words blending with the soft sounds of the night and the voices of the villagers.

Logan noticed that Zara's eyes were closed, yet her feet

didn't miss their mark by so much as an inch. How many times in her life had she walked these circles? Hundreds? Thousands? He knew she thought her faith was guiding her, but Logan was too practical to believe that her flawless performance was anything but years of practice.

A tingling sensation raced through his body as he listened to his wife's voice. The primal feeling was familiar. Zara's voice had always beckoned to him, promising things that seemed just beyond his reach. Even now, surrounded by people, with his guards watching as keenly as night hawks, Logan could feel his body yearning for what he couldn't have until he and Zara were alone.

His eyes scanned the village. His men were at their posts, but the forest remained dark and silent behind them, letting none of its secrets escape.

"The inner most circle is the home of our faith," the old woman said soberly. "It is the place where the universe combines with our minds, the place where our individuality is defined. Mind, body, and spirit, three never-ending circles. Physical and spiritual. That which can be touched, and that which can only be felt. Our faith makes them one."

When Zara finally stopped moving, she stood in the middle of the inner circle. Her arms raised high, her eyes closed, she began to slowly turn, the hem of her robe spiraling out around her slender legs. Logan watched the graceful dance and felt his body tighten with desire. He wondered what Nessa would think of a man who could watch a religious ceremony and grow hard with need. He'd never seen anything more beautiful than Zara dressed in shadows and moonlight, the way he'd found her on their wedding night, kneeling in front of a stone altar.

Finally, his wife stopped swirling. Another chant began, but this time the villagers didn't join her. Zara's voice possessed a different tone now, as if she was speaking to the stars, or some unknown god residing on one of Nubria's two silver moons.

"Put all the elements together in perfect balance and you have a world where birth doesn't lead to death, but to new life. Faith turns fear into hope. Hatred into love. All energy flows from the circle, spiraling outward in another never-ending circle that has no boundaries, no beginning and no end. Living within that circle, understanding it, gives you faith," she added. "Faith gives you wisdom and peace of heart. It is the final element, the thing that brings the tangible elements of the universe into balance with the intangible."

"You speak in more circles than my wife walks," Logan replied in a stiff whisper. "I know nothing more about your faith now than I did when I first stepped upon this mat."

"That's because you've been listening with your ears, not your heart," Nessa said, then moved away.

Logan watched her disappear into the shadows that surrounded the village. Thinking the old woman had set out to confuse him, he redirected his attention to his wife. He couldn't let himself be distracted from his real purpose, finding Keelan and the band of rebels who had survived the crash. Nessa and his wife might believe that their faith held all the answers, but Logan wasn't a believer. He'd fought too many battles, seen too many men maimed or killed, to believe that musical words spoken by a beautiful woman could change the future.

Nubria and the Union wouldn't be safe until he completed his mission. Until he found Keelan and built the tower that would act as a guardian against a Pharmon invasion, he couldn't afford to forget he was both soldier and king.

As Zara recited a prayer for the people of the village, she sensed her husband's thoughts. The power of his mind made the link vibrate. She could feel his power and silently willed it to combine with her own, to bring them both the strength and faith they would need to face the future, where no compromise would be made by either husband or wife.

She could love Logan with all her heart. She could explain their religion, teach him the ancient words, but only he could open his heart to the power his mind already possessed.

Knowing he was still beyond her reach, Zara turned her energy toward the people surrounding the ritual mat. Her thoughts blended with the men, women, and children of the Nubrian village. Her energy was rejuvenated as it moved among them, building in intensity, until she could reach beyond the circle, to the men standing in the shadows of the forest.

She sought out Sherard. In her mind's eye, she could see him, standing erect, his only hand resting on the handle of his sword, his eyes searching for anything that didn't belong to the warm night or the thick forest.

With only one purpose in mind, Zara willed her thoughts to touch his, to join the one-armed man, to become a small part of his complex character. At first, she couldn't find an opening. The scarred soldier didn't seem to have an unguarded gateway, a small sliver of space that would allow her thoughts to flow into his.

Then it was there.

Zara's mind pushed forward, flowing through the small crack in Sherard's personal armor, until she could feel his mind as surely as she felt the night air against the bare skin of her arms.

Cold images confronted her. Images splashed with blood and pain and death. Visions of cold indifference, forces she'd only encountered once before, when she'd reached for another man's mind—Keelan's.

Forcing herself to endure the pain that came with opening her mind to another person's memories, Zara kept pushing forward through the mental corridor until she found something that didn't have death and destruction clinging to it. She wanted to weep for the man who had felt the cold steel of battle. Her heart experienced searing pain when she relived, through his thoughts, the moment when Keelan's sword had cut his arm from his body. The memory was as fresh as if it happened only moments before, and Zara knew that Sherard had relived it a million times in his mind, keeping it alive, refusing to let his spirit heal along with his body.

She pushed past the pain, until she discovered memories of better times, recollections of friendship and laughter. She searched for a time when the soldier with one arm had looked to the future, instead of the past.

Unaware that her voice had softened to a bare whisper, that the ears of the village people and her husband strained to hear her chant, Zara kept her mind focused on Sherard.

His body shifted, and she knew that he felt her on the lowest level of his consciousness. Like her husband, Sherard had been trained to believe only what he could see with his own eyes and hear with his own ears. Because he wasn't a believer, he wasn't putting up mental walls. He had no idea what was happening on a greater plane, an invisible dimension where mind touched mind and heart touched heart.

The chant continued as she mentally searched for that one single thought that would allow her to plant a seed of hope in Sherard's heart and mind. Transfused into the tormented memories were flashes of good remembrances, moments of peace and tranquillity. Zara probed for one that didn't disappear the moment she found it.

Then, like a falling star streaking across the heavens, it appeared.

Zara felt the link tremble again as her mind strained to maintain the momentary connection. Sherard's mind opened, snatching the thought from the link like a hand plucked fruit from the branch that gave it life.

It was done.

Patricia Waddell

The ceremony came to an abrupt halt as Zara slumped to the mat.

Logan ran to her side, mindless of any breach in etiquette he made by trampling on the prayer mat. He drew Zara into his arms, his eyes wide with concern as he searched her pale face. Her breath was coming in short gasps, as if she'd been running. His fingers sought out her pulse, while he said her name over and over.

When violet eyes blinked at him, Logan let out the breath he'd been holding. "Are you all right?"

Zara smiled up at him. "Sometimes renewing the spirit weakens the body," she whispered. "It will pass."

Logan's expression was somber as he lifted her into his arms and marched toward the hut they would share that evening. A nod of his head told Maddock and Sherard to hold their positions. The guards came to attention, waiting for the command to attack whatever had brought Logan's wife to her knees.

The villagers watched, surprised that their new king didn't understand why his wife had collapsed, while Tolman hurried ahead to open the door of the hut.

Suddenly, Nessa blocked Logan's path. "There is no reason to be angry," she told him. "A good night's sleep will restore the energy our lady has given to others."

"Is it always like this?" Logan said, looking from the old woman's leathered face to his wife's pale one. Zara's body was limp in his arms, as if the very life had been drained out of her. "She's never fainted before."

"You've never seen her share her heart and mind with other people," Nessa explained. "It is a gift, not a burden. Worry not. What she does, she does freely, and with great love."

Love.

Logan let out a heavy breath as he stepped inside the modest hut one of the villagers had given to the royal couple so they could have some privacy. Love was as alien to him as his wife's unusual religion. What little he knew of the complex emotion was limited to friendship to a few carefully chosen men and his loyalty to the Guard. He wasn't sure if he was capable of the unlimited kind of love his wife showed for her people and her faith.

"I'm fine," Zara whispered as he laid her on the bed. "I just need to rest."

"Why?" Logan asked, desperately wanting to understand how praying could drain a woman's strength to the point of fainting. "What do your gods demand that is so taxing?"

"My faith demands nothing more than that I believe," Zara told him.

"Nessa said you shared your heart and mind. Solon told me almost the same thing." Logan's hand reached out and smoothed a strand of silver hair away from her pale face. "Explain this gift to me."

Zara turned her face away. The movement made her hair shimmer in the moonlight. She licked her lips while her husband waited for her explanation. "It's difficult to explain," she said in a low, trembling voice. How was she going to tell him where her energy had gone without revealing that the link was a two-way street; mental energy flowed both in and out when she opened her mind to others. Sensing that her husband was growing more impatient by the moment, she turned to find his dark eyes staring at her. He looked so serious. Zara offered him a weak smile. "Have you ever thought of someone, only to have them appear before you as if they'd been silently summoned to your side?"

Logan nodded. "Solon told me your talent wasn't telepathy. Are you saying it is?"

What else had her brother revealed? Zara wondered. She shook her head. "No. The gift isn't telepathy. I don't talk to someone with my mind. It's a different type of communication."

A black brow lifted with skepticism. Logan moved from the side of the bed to the serving table. He poured a glass of water, then carried it to Zara. With effortless strength, he helped her to sit upright, then held the glass to her lips. "Drink."

Zara sipped the cool water. She could feel the heat of Logan's body chasing away the last of the chill that had overtaken her when the prayer had ended. Although the door of the hut was closed, the windows were open, letting in a mild breeze. But the soft wind couldn't blow away the tension filling the room. Her husband wanted answers, and he wasn't going away until he got them.

When the glass was empty, Logan set it aside and studied his lovely wife, a young woman with powers she was finding hard to explain. "Tell me what's so special about this communication you have with others," he asked. Then asked in a clipped voice. "Have you used it on me? Do I have any secrets from you?"

"I can't take anything from your mind you aren't willing to give," Zara told him. It was the truth. "I can sense your moods."

"Even when I'm not near you?" He stood up, unbuckling his sword belt. Once it was draped over a nearby chair, he began removing his boots, then his uniform.

When he was as naked as the moonlight streaming in the window, he lifted Zara off the bed. A few seconds later, she wasn't wearing anything but her silvery hair and the wedding amulet old Goldwren had given her. Her dress landed on the floor, next to her husband's discarded uniform. A quick sweep of Logan's hand turned down the quilt covering the bed. He slid Zara under it, then joined her.

But instead of lying down, his back rested against the wooden headboard. Zara was cradled in his arms, her naked bottom resting on his muscular thighs. She could feel his arousal, and his self-control. He was going to make love to her, but not until she'd regained her energy and he'd gotten his answers.

"Well?" he asked impatiently. "Do I have any secrets,

or have you been probing my mind ever since we met?"

"Whatever secrets you had when you arrived on Nubria are still yours," she told him. A sensual shudder ran the length of her body as his hand began caressing her thighs.

"What of my moods? Must I be on guard whenever you're not at my side? Will you chastise me for grumbling at my men, even if they deserve the reprimand?"

Zara smiled. "I will not interfere in what you see as your duty."

"What do you call tricking me into this pilgrimage, if not interference?"

"Doing whatever I can do to help you see what you refuse to see," she told him candidly.

Silently Logan studied her face, searching the uncanny violet eyes of the woman whose naked body was making him hard with desire. As always, he sensed no falseness in Zara's words, no deception, yet he knew she was withholding the total truth from him. He knew it as well as he'd known the fear that had gripped him when she'd slumped to the ground.

"What about your mind?" he asked, as his hand moved from the silky perfection of her thigh to drift across her lower abdomen, then upward to cup one of her breasts. "Must I be a high priestess to know what's inside it, or does my gender forever deny me from knowing my wife as she knows me?"

Zara's eyes closed as sensations spiraled through her, pushing aside the mental weariness she'd felt since leaving the prayer mat. Without thinking, her hands went to Logan's chest and her fingers began to comb through the thick dark hair that covered hard male muscles.

He stayed her hand, pressing it palm down so she could feel his heartbeat. "Tell me," he demanded in a husky whisper as his hand molded her breast and his fingertip teased the rosy crown at its tip. "Am I married to a priestess or a witch?"

"You're married to a woman who wants you to open your mind to the treasure of Nubria," she admitted after a moment. "You need to understand the people before you can understand what I am."

Logan made a soft grumbling sound before his hand moved from his wife's flushed breast to the line of her jaw. He watched her with hungry eyes as he traced the line of her bottom lip. "You keep telling me that I need to understand. Yet you give me nothing in the way of an explanation. All I get from you and the old woman are riddles. Are you testing me?"

Zara opened her eyes and looked into dark ones that burned with desire and determination. It was so easy to forget that her husband was a soldier when he was touching her as gently as sunlight touched the petals of a forest flower. Wanting to see more of the man's heart and less of the warrior's determination, she smiled slowly. "I'm trying to understand you the same way you're trying to understand me," she confessed. "If we are to live in harmony, there can be no secrets between us."

"Then tell me where Keelan and his men are hiding," Logan demanded in a soft voice that belied his true feelings. "It is the only secret that lies between us."

Zara pulled away from the war-callused hand that was touching her mouth as lightly as the summer breeze touched the cloth draperies framing the windows. Despite the pleasure her husband's hand was giving her, she could sense the hatred in his heart. Hatred for the man who had betrayed the honor of the Galactic Guards and taken Sherard's arm.

The shifting of Zara's body brought a groan of sensual pain from her husband. When she tried to move off his lap, he held her firmly in place, his eyes glittering like black jewels in the dim light. His voice was soft but firm as he spoke. "You want understanding; then understand this, my beautiful, bewitching wife. No prayers can dissuade me. I can understand only what you clarify to me.

If you choose riddles instead of facts, my lack of understanding is your doing, not my own."

Zara's teeth gripped her bottom lip. Logan was right. He'd never be able to fully understand until she opened the link and solved the riddle. But she couldn't open it knowing he'd use what he found in her mind against those who had survived the crash of a rebel transport ship. Once again, she was caught between promises, a prisoner of her faith.

"I cannot break a promise. Understand that, if you understand nothing else."

For a moment she thought Logan was going to set her aside, but his anger vanished as his hands began exploring her unclothed body. His fingertips skimmed from her face to the valley between her breasts where her wedding amulet lay warm against even warmer skin.

"You are a witch," he whispered as his mouth came down to claim hers.

His mouth was hard and demanding, but Zara savored the feel of it. A breathless sound came from deep within his chest as she returned the kiss. Her mind was drained, but her body wanted the pleasure only her husband could give her. As clearly as she sensed his need for her, she felt the passion flowing through his body. Her hands became human sensors, feeling the beat of his heart, the texture of his skin, the urgency of his need, as she moved closer to the fire burning in his warrior heart.

Slowly, Logan told himself. *Too often I let my passionate wife take control. Tonight, she will tell me what I want to know. No matter how difficult the riddle, I will solve it.*

"Tell me what you feel," he said as his hands returned to the softness of her thighs and belly.

"Pleasure," she whispered, unable to hold back the word. "Your hands are like the sun. Warm and strong."

Logan smiled, then shifted his body until he was looking down at his wife's hair spread across the pillow. He could feel the heat rising up from her body, luring him closer to the flame, but he held his desire in check. He couldn't let himself be bewitched again.

"Does this please you?" he asked as his hand moved closer and closer to the small cluster of curls that shielded her femininity.

"Yes," she confessed with a soft rush of breath. "Your touch always pleases me."

Logan fought the desire Zara's sweet voice always aroused in him. "As you please me," he admitted when he could speak without his voice revealing how desperately he wanted to forgo the sensual torment and bury himself inside her warm, tight body. "Talk to me," he urged in a strong whisper as his mouth brushed against her temple, then moved down the curve of her face to find the hollow of her neck. "Tell me what I need to know to understand you."

The seductive question made a subtle shiver move through Zara's body. She longed to explain, yet she didn't know the words to make him understand. What she had to share with Logan couldn't be described in language. It was a feeling, a deep burning truth that had to be experienced to be realized.

The touch of Logan's mouth against her breast made Zara's breath catch. Her eyes opened, but he closed them with soft kisses. "Talk to me," he said again.

"I don't have the words," she told him. "The gift comes from my heart, not my body."

"Then open your heart to me," he whispered against her mouth.

Passion clawed at Zara's body as Logan continued tormenting her with soft kisses and sunlight caresses that had her twisting beneath him.

"You don't want my heart," she gasped as the tip of his tongue teased the tip of her breast.

"Yes, I do," Logan said, surprising himself as much as the woman in his arms. "I want everything you have to give. You pledged it to me on the day we married. It's mine by right."

Zara started to say that everything Logan was belonged to her as well, but a kiss kept the words from escaping her mouth. The last thing she wanted to do was talk, so she didn't protest when the kiss became more urgent, more demanding.

Her fingers speared through her husband's midnight hair as her hands savored the sheer delight of being with him. "Tomorrow," she whispered. "We can talk tomorrow."

As Logan eased her legs apart and cradled his weight between his wife's smooth thighs, he smiled to himself. He'd never been so passionately defeated. And he was defeated. His body was screaming for release, for that one moment when loss brings victory. All thought of outwitting his lovely wife vanished as he felt her body willingly accept his.

The special feeling he got whenever he slid into her tight channel never ceased to amaze him. He reveled in the warm, silky texture of her body as he began to move. Soon he was lost in that special place only Zara could take him, a place where everything he touched was her, everything he felt was her, everything he tasted was her. The way they fit together was unbelievably natural, as if she had been made just for him. The feel of her body, moving with his, mixed with the sound of her breathing and the scent of her arousal, took him outside himself. There was only the pleasure and the pride of knowing that she was *his* and his alone.

When the pleasure became a sweet pain, Logan did his best to prolong the sensual agony, but his control couldn't compete with his need. He groaned deep in his throat, then buried his face in the curve of Zara's neck and let the passion take over.

His body exploded like a nova, pouring his seed into her womb, while behind his closed eyelids colors flashed and he experienced the sensation of dying and being reborn at the exact same instant. He felt Zara's climax just as keenly. It was as if he'd somehow miraculously switched places with her. He could feel the small tremors that overtook her, the warmth of her blood rushing through her veins, the pleasure that made her body arch up one moment and slump back in sweet exhaustion the next. Her heartbeat was his heartbeat, her gasp for air, his gasp.

Zara flinched as she realized the link had opened without her knowing it. The same moment Logan was experiencing her climax, she was experiencing his. The pleasure was an avalanche, an explosion that had her writhing beneath him. She couldn't stop the feelings that poured from her body into his and from his into hers. It was life itself, flowing from his body into hers, life and the promise of life. What she had thought was only a physical need on her husband's part took on a new dimension as she felt his muscles clench and his satisfaction erupt in a tidal wave of pleasure that washed over and through her at the same time.

The entire universe seemed to vibrate for a brief, fragile instant. Zara forced her mind to close, shutting off the flow of mental energy that was feeding the physical pleasure, intensifying it until she thought she was going to faint, but she couldn't hold back the soft moan that was Logan's name.

As she felt Logan relax and his breathing return to normal, Zara experienced an unexpected yearning to return to that moment in time when they had been more one person than two, that moment in time when their individual identities had totally merged. That moment had been the true consummation of their Nubrian marriage, the total unity of their minds and spirits.

At the same time Zara wanted to return to that moment, she feared the next time it happened. Sooner or later, Logan would recognize that what he experienced with her went beyond the scope of physical pleasure. He was too smart not to question the uncharted depths to which their lovemaking had taken them.

Blaming the mental fatigue that had followed her prayers for Sherard, Zara knew she would have to keep her husband at a distance the next time she entered the prayer circle. Her mind was too vulnerable and the passion he sparked within her too strong to maintain control of the link.

Chapter Sixteen

Logan walked through the outer door of the hut, then stopped to let the warm morning sunshine finish awakening his body. His gaze swept the quiet hamlet of small homes and merchant shops, ending a few yards before the lush green forest began.

As he shifted his weight from one leg to another the soft grass under his feet gave with his weight, reminding him that the world he ruled was a generous one. Very much like his wife.

He'd never had a woman give herself as freely as Zara. There was no pretense in her pleasure, no deception, only pure sweet passion.

He glanced over his shoulder, back inside the hut where she still slept, her silver hair spread across the pillow, her face as tranquil as that of a child. Looking at that face, it was hard to imagine the swirling lights and dizzy blackness that had overtaken him when he'd found release in her arms. There was nothing about her sleeping serenity that signified how passion had ruled the night, nothing about her relaxed body to remind him how high he had flown in her arms.

Logan made his way to the well at the far end of the village, nodding good morning as he passed several of the village folk who were early risers like himself. Sherard was also up and about, his scarred face unusually bright as he greeted Logan.

"Good morning," he said much too cheerfully for his commanding officer to be anything but suspicious.

"How many bottles of Bervian whiskey are missing from the supply pouch?" Logan said as he dropped the wooden bucket into the well and began turning the antiquated crank that would bring it back up.

"None." Sherard beamed at him. "I slept like a babe." He shook his head, as if sleep was still lingering there, then smiled. "I can't remember the last time I closed my eyes so easily. It must be the fresh air."

"You've been breathing the freshest air in the galaxy for over three weeks now," Logan reminded him.

"So I have," his friend laughed. "So I have."

Logan dipped the wooden scoop into the bucket of water he'd just retrieved, then brought it to his mouth. The water was cool and refreshing. He frowned. Was there anything about Nubria he could criticize, except its stubborn queen?

"What's got you frowning?" Sherard inquired, leaning against the stone barricade that protected the well.

"Nothing," Logan grumbled, before turning and marching in the opposite direction. Maddock had been assigned the dawn watch, and he wanted to make sure the forest was as peaceful as it looked. Logan found his second in command talking to one of the villagers. Noticing the young woman, standing slightly behind the man, was just enough of a diversion for Logan to forget his wife for a moment or two. The girl was a year to two older than Zara, with dark brown hair and wide brown eyes. Her body wasn't as slender nor her face as beautiful, but she was pleasant enough for a man to look upon.

She smiled hesitantly as her king approached, but she didn't retreat.

"This is Frabra, my lord," Maddock introduced the man. "He was born in the mountains north of here."

Frabra was thickening around the middle, with stout arms and legs. The man's hair was thinning and more gray than brown. His forehead was high and his skin weathered from the elements, but his smile was respectful and his teeth white and even. "Lord Logan," he said, bowing from the waist as was the custom. "May I present my daughter, Ganece."

Logan gave both the man and his daughter a curt nod.

Sherard greeted them more enthusiastically. He stepped forward and took the young woman's hand, smiling all the while. "Good morning."

Maddock muffled a laugh while his commanding officer looked at the guard as if he'd lost his mind. It wasn't like Sherard to openly solicit a woman's attention, not since he'd lost his arm. Before the battle at Medash, he'd been as rowdy as any of Logan's men, but like most soldiers he'd limited his female companions to women who expected payment before any pleasure was given.

"Good morning, my lord," Ganece replied, smiling up at Sherard as if he was the most handsome man on the planet. "I hope you are enjoying the hospitality of our village."

"I am now," Sherard told her, seemingly unembarrassed that he was being watched by both the young woman's father and his two best friends. Whatever had come over Sherard had him acting like a raw recruit.

Logan didn't like it. He needed his men alert now that they were about to enter the mountains. He cleared his throat, breaking the romantic moment that had sprouted out of nowhere. "See to the men," he instructed Sherard.

"Yes, sir."

Ganece watched Sherard disappear into the forest.

Frabra watched his daughter.

Logan watched both of them, fully expecting the father to demand an apology as soon as he turned his head. Nubrian parents were very protective of their offspring. When Frabra politely asked if Sherard had a wife, Logan shook his head.

"Your friend is welcome to call upon my daughter," the man said before taking his leave.

All Logan and Maddock could do was stare as the villager and his daughter went about their business.

"What's going on?" Logan demanded, once he and Maddock were alone.

His second in command shrugged his shoulders.

Logan's frown grew more intense. If his lovely wife hadn't been sleeping the morning away, he'd have bet his sword that she had something to do with Sherard's strange behavior.

Maybe she was to blame?

She'd told Sherard that his missing arm and scarred face didn't make him ugly. Perhaps that was all he had needed to get his male assurance back. He'd never lost his confidence as a soldier. Even with one arm, the seasoned guard could bring a man of equal height and weight to his knees. But women weren't opponents, at least not the kind a man overpowered on the battlefield. Women required a more delicate approach.

"What did you find out about our destination?" Logan asked, putting the issue of his wife's gifted interference aside for the moment. If Zara was responsible for the change in Sherard's disposition, he wouldn't tolerate her continued machinations. He alone commanded the guards who served under him.

"The final altar is halfway up the summit of Mount Oberlin itself," Maddock informed him.

"The final altar?"

"There are at least two more on the way," he added as they walked toward the forest that had enveloped Sher-

233

ard moments before. "Frabra said your lady would be stopping at both of the sacred places. One is a crystal pool where legend states the first of Nubria's queens was gifted with the power of insight. The other is a less significant altar, in size but not in legend. According to Frabra, the second altar, a good four days' journey from here, is the place where Lady Zara was seen taming some kind of mountain cat. After several people watched her, they rolled one of their white stones onto the spot and declared it a sacred altar."

"Taming?" Logan went back to frowning.

Maddock stopped walking, a sure sign that what he had to say wasn't going to please his commanding officer. "The villager called it a . . ."

"A *juna*," Logan supplied the correct term.

"It's not a small cat," Maddock told him. "Frabra said *junas* have been known to outweigh a full-grown man."

When Logan didn't reply immediately, Maddock went on. "Frabra was one of the men who saw Lady Zara tame the cat. He said she spoke to it in the ancient language and the animal literally curled around her feet, rolled onto his back, and asked to have its belly rubbed."

Logan knew the feeling.

Unaware that his commander's thoughts had wandered back to the hut and the intense pleasure he always felt when his wife touched him, Maddock continued reciting the story Frabra had told him. "When twilight fell that evening, a whole pride of the cats showed up. He said Lady Zara stood in the meadow, praying and turning in circles while the cats moved around her. When she sought her bed, they went with her, lying at her feet. Come morning they were gone, but none of the pilgrims who walked with her that year ever forgot what they had seen."

"Would you expect them to?" Logan scoffed. "Do you know any women who can tame wild animals with nothing but whispered words?"

"Your lady has many talents," Maddock agreed, keeping his smile to himself. It hadn't taken Logan's men long to discover that he was as possessive of his new queen as he was of his Galactic sword.

"So it seems," Logan agreed halfheartedly.

By the time they joined Sherard and the other guards, sunlight was illuminating the forest floor. A small rut ran between two trees, marking the path they had used to reach the village. Logan still didn't know the name of the settlement; no one, not even his wife, had used its formal title.

The thin path widened where Sherard stood talking to the guards who had joined Maddock for the dawn watch. Vegetation grew all around them; tall spiky plants with small blue flowers bobbed their heads in the wind that danced through the trees. Lower bushes with squatty thick leaves glistened with dew, while tall, thin grass waved to and fro. The air was crisp and laced with the scent of pines. The sky was still tinged with pink when Logan dismissed the men, instructing them to eat and get some sleep. They wouldn't be leaving for another few hours.

"What else did the old man tell you about the mountains?" Logan inquired as a lone bird flew overhead. With its wings spread wide, it floated on the air currents that followed the natural slope of the mountains.

"The trail isn't a dangerous one," Maddock informed him. "Frabra said it's wide enough for two men to march side by side."

"And the mountains themselves?"

"Rugged but passable. On foot," he added. "The final altar is reached by a winding path that's followed for its scenery, not its swiftness."

"Keelan?" The name was both a question and a curse.

"Frabra denies knowing anything about the crash or the rebels. He was in the capital city when it happened. All he is willing to admit is that a transport came down

Patricia Waddell

in the mountains north of here. It's no secret. What happened to the survivors is. No one is going to break the promise Lady Zara gave with her own breath."

Neither Logan nor Sherard questioned the man's honesty. The short time they'd spent on Nubria had taught them that lies weren't common. In fact, not one of Logan's men had stumbled over a single falsehood during their endless questioning of the people in the city.

"Stay alert," Logan insisted. "Keelan may or may not have an ambush planned. Until we know more, assume the worst."

With his orders given, Logan turned toward the village. Once he was alone, surrounded by the thick greenery of the forest, his mind returned to his wife. Despite the knowledge that if Keelan was alive, he wouldn't be taken without a fight, it was hard to concentrate on matters of war when life flourished everywhere he looked. Taking a moment to compose his thoughts, Logan stopped and leaned against the thick trunk of a gum tree. The bark was grayish-brown and smooth. The coolness of the morning forest enveloped him, easing away the tension he always felt when Keelan's name was spoken.

How many years ago had it been? Twenty, at least. Twenty years of calling a man your friend, twenty years of trusting him to cover your back when the enemy swarmed like flies over a dead body. Twenty years of trust and faith and friendship that had ended in betrayal.

He should have known. Keelan was always ambitious. Always wanting a higher rank than the one he had earned with his sword. Always striving to be a notch higher on the ladder of power.

The rebellion he had spawned from within had been a mark of his military genius. His only weakness had been his greed. He had moved his rebels too fast, and his carelessness in not holding the land he had gained had finally been his undoing. Still, the war had lasted almost five years. It had cost thousands of lives—many of which

236

Logan had taken with the sword strapped to his side.

The forest's quiet promise of a life without war softened the last of Logan's regrets. He stared at a shaft of sunlight piercing through the trees. Tiny particles of dust danced in the untamed light, swirling and dancing the same way colors had swirled and danced in his mind the previous night.

What had he felt last night? The most shattering climax of his life, yes. But it had been more. Since their marriage, he hadn't abstained from enjoying Zara's body. If anything, the pleasure should have lost the glow that always came with a man's first conquest. It hadn't.

What had been cloaked in the pleasure he'd shared with his wife the previous night? Something unknown. Something mysterious. Something wonderful.

"Good morning."

The sound of Zara's voice broke the stillness of the forest. Logan came away from the tree, his dark eyes gleaming. "Good morning," he replied, realizing how much he'd missed her since leaving the hut. It was a fever in his blood, this need to have her constantly by his side. "Are you rested?"

Zara knew he was inquiring if her energy had returned, but before she could reply, his mouth covered hers and his tongue teased her lips into parting for an intimate kiss that left her hands clinging to his shoulders. She had never experienced anything like the dizzy pleasure she always felt whenever Logan kissed her. There was no ignoring it, no defending herself against it, and no denying it. It burned as bright within her as the sun burned overhead.

"I *was* rested," Zara teased, enjoying the feel of her husband's embrace.

"Have you eaten?" he asked, smiling at her response to his first question. He liked knowing that he had some power over her, even if it was only the power of passion.

But deeper down, in a place he hadn't known existed

until now, Logan knew he wanted more than Zara's body quickening to his touch. He wanted her smiles and her laughter. He wanted her to trust him with the same unwavering faith that she offered to her nameless gods.

Zara felt the link begin to vibrate with the power of Logan's thoughts. The invisible chain between them pulsed and ebbed like the unending currents that made white waves crest on a bottomless ocean. The changing textures of the link were as subtle as the shadows cast by clouds, but they were there, alive and moving, binding her mind to his as surely as he'd united their bodies during the night.

Pleasure gathered in her senses, making her body tremble.

Logan tightened his arms, holding her closer to his body, nearer to his heart.

Zara shut her eyes tight, forcing the doorway to close, pulling back her thoughts before they reached out to Logan's the same way her arms were reaching up to encircle his neck.

Every time she denied the link it was more difficult. Each time she called her thoughts back inside her own mind it demanded more and more energy. Keeping the passage closed would soon become impossible. One day Logan would be able to stroll into her thoughts as easily as he marched into a room.

When that day came, Zara prayed that she had captured his heart as surely as he had captured hers.

Logan held his wife close, enjoying the softness of her body pressed intimately against his. Her hair was pulled back and braided. The dress she was wearing was as soft as the sunlight streaming through the green canopy above them. The simplest touch of her hand on his neck made him want to sweep her into his arms and stomp through the forest until he found a glade like the one they'd encountered on the first day of their journey. He'd willingly give his kingdom for a blanket of grass where he could lay her down and make love to her until there was nothing but mindless ecstasy and her soft cries of pleasure.

Knowing Maddock or one of his men wasn't far, Logan reached for his self-control. He relaxed his arms and brushed a kiss against Zara's forehead before he let her go completely. When she was staring up at him with jeweled eyes that saw more of his soul than he liked, Logan frowned. "What have you done to Sherard?"

Zara laughed. The sound echoed off the trees, rousting the last of the nesting birds from their beds. "I have done nothing to Sherard."

"He's taken with one of the village girls," Logan told her. "I've often accused you of being a witch. Have you cast a spell over him?"

"No," she countered, more amused than insulted. "The girl is Ganece." Zara smiled. "I saw them at the well. They seemed engrossed in conversation."

"Sherard may have one arm, but he's too much of a man to be satisfied with conversation for long," Logan said flatly. "I don't want some outraged father demanding a marriage."

"Ganece isn't a child. If she likes Sherard, the outcome won't be outrageous."

Not as outrageous as a Galactic Guard wedding a queen, Logan thought. Had the Unity Council really known what they were about when they'd ordered him to Nubria? The queen they had hoped to chastise was standing before Logan now, looking perfectly content with herself, while the rebels he'd been sent to capture enjoyed the freedom of the mountains.

Two guards marched in front of the Queen of Nubria while six followed behind her. Each man was armed and each one had specific orders not to slacken their attention as they worked their way up the narrow path that led from the village to the first summit of the Oberlin

Mountains. The forest still grew thick around them, giving way occasionally to large boulders and rugged cliffs where vines draped downward like green curtains. Hidden by a morning mist, the peaks of the mountain range loomed above them. The long, rugged mountains jutted out of the northern continent like a granite spine, dividing it into two halves.

Zara walked alongside her husband, who shortened his normally long, impatient strides to accommodate those of his wife. The blush of their early kiss was still clinging to her cheeks as she turned at the crest of the hill and waved good-bye to the people of the village. A loud cheer went up from them, an offering of blessings yet to come.

Zara clung to the blessing as her bare feet made small imprints in the thick grass that covered the meandering path. Wildflowers bloomed on either side of the grassy walkway, their tiny petals open to the warmth of the sun, their colors vibrant against the browns and greens and grays of the earth.

Logan paused long enough to watch a wide-winged hawk with a cream-colored belly soar overhead. Its cry was a song of wild music, as untouched as the rocky peaks where it built its nest.

Ahead of the guards, Tolman pointed the way that led to a small mountain valley where the noon meal would be taken. The pilgrims would rest there, before beginning the second half of their day's journey.

Logan gave the winding path ahead of them a sweeping glance. His keen eyes memorized everything they saw before he looked at his wife. He glanced at her bare feet, already smudged with dirt, and smiled. "I never imagined a queen going barefoot."

Zara returned his smile, noting that the expression came more easily to him the longer he lived among her people. "And I never imagined Nubria having a king. It's a rarity for my people, but they're becoming accustomed to the idea."

"Are they?"

"Yes," she replied. "The weapons you and your guards insist on wearing make them ill at ease, but they understand that you haven't lived among us long enough to realize swords and laser pistols aren't needed here."

"They think time will cure our foolishness," Logan mused.

"Something like that," Zara retorted. She was about to skip ahead of him, but his hand stilled her.

"Stay by my side," he ordered.

"Why? The path isn't filled with peril. The grass is as smooth as a baby's skin and the day bright with sunlight. I won't fall."

"It isn't your agility that I'm worried about," Logan told her.

Zara refused to tell him there weren't any rebels waiting in ambush. If the stubborn man insisted on acting as if danger lurked behind every leaf, then let him. She fully intended to enjoy the day and the freedom that her yearly pilgrimage allowed her. Being Nubria's queen meant that most of her time was spent in the capital city, greeting planetary delegates, attending political meetings, and seeing to the religious needs of her people. When she walked the mountains she was free to enjoy the blessings of her world for herself.

The pilgrimage was a renewal of faith and purpose, but it was also a time meant to renew the body and spirit. The Oberlin Mountains were Nubria's most majestic setting. All around them the forest reached its lush fingers upward, as if it wanted to embrace the rocky peaks. Above them was a flawless sky, dotted with amethyst-colored clouds. There was a consecrated beauty about the mountains as the sun arced across the sky, revealing them by inches instead of miles, unveiling their beauty with slowly spreading light that filled the gorges and valleys that looked like small dents in a granite suit of armor. If she couldn't reach her husband's heart somewhere along this beautiful trail, it was hard as the granite cliffs they'd be climbing to reach the final altar.

Clinging to the hope that Logan would admit to feeling more than just physical pleasure in their marriage before they reached their final destination, Zara allowed herself to be restricted to his side.

Cautious and curious, Logan found himself as enthralled by the mountains as he was by his lovely wife. The mixture of sunlight, green forest, and rugged peaks made the memories of battle seem centuries old. Was the sun actually warmer on Nubria, or was it the feel of his wife's hand cradled casually in his that made the heat seen unusual for so early in the day? Were the tiny flowers pushing their way through clusters of rock more brightly colored than the blossoms he'd seen on other worlds? Or was it the way his wife stopped to touch them that made them seem unique?

She caressed the delicate petals the same way she had caressed his skin after they'd made love. Her touch was as light as air, barely bending the frail skin that blossomed out to cup the sunlight. When she knelt to inhale the fragrance of several plants, Logan remembered the way she'd whispered that he smelled good just before she drifted off to sleep. Then Zara smiled at him, and he felt as if the sun had exploded inside his chest.

They had gone several miles when she tugged at his hand. "Follow me," she said, glancing up at him.

The soldiers behind them slowed as Logan held up his hand. "Where? There's nothing here but the path we follow."

"It's just a few feet in front of us." Zara beckoned him forward. "There." She pointed at what seemed to be a large boulder resting against the sloping side of a hill.

Logan stared at the gray slab of rock for a long moment before he realized what he was looking at. The rock was covered with tangled vines woven together so tightly that the blanket of greenery seemed to be one large plant. Only the keenest of eyes would be able to see that the darkness of the granite changed beneath the twisted blanket of tiny vines. It was split down the center, creating a small cave.

"Don't step on it," Zara said, cautioning her husband to keep his booted feet firmly planted. "They're very small."

"What are they?" Logan asked, dropping his voice to match the softer tones his wife was using the closer she stepped to the slender fissure in the face of the slated rock.

"Limpkins," she told him. "They make their nests in places like this. It's dark enough to suit them but warm enough to keep their babies content."

Logan watched, along with eight curious Galactic Guards, as Zara reached out and lifted the thick drapery of green vines that covered the narrow opening between what had first appeared to be one rock but was actually two. A soft chirping sound was followed by a slight movement in the grass and moss that grew between the base of the two large rocks.

A smile tugged at Logan's face as he saw his first limpkin. The animal wasn't much bigger than his thumb. The tiny ball of fur stood on its hind legs, while stubby whispers twitched and a shiny black nose sniffed the air. The small rodent was as wide as it was tall, with a white belly and tiny paws. Miniature black eyes blinked at the encroaching sunlight as a thin, threadlike tail jerked back and forth, protesting Zara's intrusion.

When his wife leaned down and offered her hand, Logan's mouth opened in surprise. With only one twitch of its pointed nose, the tiny rodent leaped into Zara's palm. Logan clamped his mouth shut as his wife reached her hand high, looking the limpkin in the eye while she chanted to it in a soft whisper.

"They eat nuts and berries," she explained, still cradling the small animal in the curve of her palm. "And they like dark places. When we camp tonight, if you listen carefully, you'll hear them scampering around in the rocks."

Her other hand reached out to part the vine drapery wider. Inside, sleeping in a nest of twigs and grass, were more limpkins. The babies were small and snuggled closely together.

With a soft word that was as ageless as the mountains, Zara returned the mother limpkin to her nest. Once the vines covered the fissure in the rocks, she stepped to Logan's side.

"Your magic seems to have the same effect on all beasts, no matter their size," her husband said. "From the largest *malaro* to the smallest limpkin, you bewitch them all."

"It isn't magic," Zara told him. "It's acceptance. That's the true key to our faith, lord husband. Accepting that life flows to life, like water from a mountain stream seeks a path to the sea. Nothing exists alone, not man or animal or plant. Everything is linked to something else."

"A never-ending circle," Logan said, remembering the patterns woven into the prayer mat. "A path that has no beginning and no end."

"You're learning," Zara said. "The journey, not the destination."

"A destination we'll never reach if you don't get moving." Logan urged her ahead with a hand splayed across the small of her back.

Zara smiled to herself as she fell into step beside the man who was gradually learning to look toward the future instead of dwelling on the past.

Chapter Seventeen

It took four days to reach the crystal pool. As Logan stepped from the thickly wooded trail they had been following since leaving the village, he stopped in awe at what lay before him. The snakelike path opened into a wide mountain meadow. Rocky cliffs loomed on three sides, draped with richly colored vines heavy with colorful flowers. From his vantage point, Logan could see that the meadow was actually more a ledge than a valley. The mountainside dropped away directly in front of him, as if some celestial hand had reached down from the heavens and scooped out a large chunk of earth.

To his right, where two large cliffs met, water cascaded downward, sending a churning mist of vapor into the air. The water bubbled and swirled as it emptied into a large pool, rimmed by rocks beaten smooth by the constant friction. A small stream ran from the crystal pool, gliding effortlessly across the meadow to form another waterfall that emptied over the edge of the flat ledgelike valley and down the face of the mountain they had just climbed. The narrow creek slipped and curled around small rocks and clusters of tall, wispy trees with leaves as long as Logan's arm. The slender fronds swayed in the wind, while purple clouds glided across the sky.

Logan couldn't remember seeing anything quite like it before.

"We will rest here," Tolman said, laying his pouch on the ground next to a clump of plants with bright red blooms at the tips of their thorny stems. "Our lady will not enter the sanctuary until the moons have risen."

"What sanctuary?" Logan inquired.

"The sacred pool," Tolman told him, pointing toward the waterfall.

Ignoring his wife's brilliant smile, Logan marched toward the pool. The water falling from above was deposited into the large pond with enough force to keep it churning like a whirlpool. He looked down at the rippling currents of water, lapping at the moss-covered rocks. He couldn't see the bottom, but he could see bright flashes of sleek color as fish swam back and forth. He wondered if Zara was a good swimmer.

"You're going to pray in the water?" Logan asked skeptically when Zara joined him.

She'd been walking by his side since leaving the village and sleeping next to him every night on the mats Tolman and Nessa had woven. Her constant presence both pleased and annoyed him. The annoyance came from having too many people nearby. Logan longed for the privacy a closed door would provide. His body ached to be satisfied as only Zara could satisfy it.

More than once he'd been tempted to leave the narrow path and strike out into the forest with his wife in his arms, but he'd managed to keep his lust under control.

"There is another pool," Zara explained as the wind wrapped her silvery hair around her shoulders and plastered the soft fabric of her tunic to her body. "Behind the waterfall. The path is hidden, but it isn't dangerous."

"A cave."

"The mountains are full of them," his wife replied. "Caves and grottoes and hidden valleys. There's more here than rocks and trees. Or haven't you noticed?"

Logan had noticed. Nothing had escaped his wary eyes. He'd spent the last four days studying the plants and animals and the effect the mountains were having on his men. Instead of weariness from walking countless miles, his men seemed rejuvenated. Even Maddock was smiling. The stiffness of a military patrol had been replaced by something else. Their eyes still scanned the horizon for any sign of trouble, and they were still diligent about keeping watch during the night, but they were more relaxed at the same time. Logan wasn't sure what to call the change in attitude that had overtaken his men. It was a subtle difference, not one that deserved reprimand or punishment. His guards simply seemed content to be where they were, doing what they were doing.

But more importantly, Logan had noticed his wife. With every step up the mountain, he'd become more aware of her.

The awareness was more than knowing where she was every minute of the day or watching her every move as they continued their pilgrimage. It was . . . Logan searched his mind for the words to describe what he was feeling, had been feeling, since the night before they'd left the village in the foothills. There had been no more lovemaking; they were sleeping under the open sky, surrounded by armed men who had been ordered to watch over his wife. Yet Logan felt as if he was making love to Zara with each beat of his heart. The feeling was more arousing that anything he'd ever experienced, a sensual yearning that was satisfied each time he saw her smile, only to be reborn when their hands casually touched or her voice reached his ears. His breath caught at the sight of her now, standing by the pool, her image reflected in the crystal-clear water, her face brightened by the afternoon sun.

The feathery feeling shivered and expanded inside him, a silent explosion of emotion that made him want something invisible but so real he was certain it existed.

Zara felt the link quiver with Logan's private thoughts. The bond between them was growing so fast, it took all her energy to keep the door closed. She knew the time was fast approaching when her energy wouldn't be enough, when the strain of keeping her emotions and her feelings so tightly leashed would have to end. It wasn't her nature to hide things, yet she had to hide her mind, at least until Logan's pattern of thinking broadened enough to understand what her thoughts would eventually reveal.

"Caves," he mused aloud as Maddock and Sherard joined them. "Rebels have been known to hide in caves. It could explain why our sensors couldn't find them when we orbited the planet."

"No sensors can find what isn't there," Zara said in a tight voice.

Logan shrugged. "Perhaps not. But then again, perhaps your mountains are hiding more than waterfalls and crystal pools."

Maddock and Sherard avoided the argument that had been going on for several days. Whenever Zara pointed out something she saw as beautiful, Logan reminded her that the plant had thorns or the insect, no matter how brightly colored, had a stinger that could cause pain. The tension between the royal couple was stressful and amusing at the same time. The two soldiers suspected it had more to do with their commanding officer's lack of sexual activity than it did with rebels, but they kept their opinions to themselves.

Old Nessa wasn't as careful of her words. "It's time to stop worrying about rebels and start to prepare the evening meal," she announced as she gingerly leaned over the rim of the pool and washed her wrinkled hands in the cool water. "I'll need some strong arms to pull the roots I want to prepare for supper.

"Come along, Maddock," she said. "Let our king and his lady have a moment alone. I fear it is the only thing that will take the bite out of him."

Logan bristled under the old woman's remark, but he kept his temper in check. If he gave in to Nessa's teasing, he'd find himself the loser. The old woman's tongue was as sharp as his sword when it came to cutting a man down to size.

"Are my words biting?" Logan asked once the others were occupied with setting up camp.

"At times," Zara told him. "You've seemed preoccupied the last few days. Aren't you enjoying the mountains?"

"Am I breathing?" Logan chuckled. "I'm not so calloused that I can't appreciate the color of a flower or the freshness of air that hasn't been tainted by industrial waste. It's not the mountains that are on my mind, and well you know it."

"I know," Zara sighed.

Her heart ached to be able to tell Logan what he wanted to hear, but she was bound by a promise she couldn't break. It didn't matter that the words would sweep the tension between them away, as if it had never existed. What did matter was the fundamental quality of the pledge. Her faith demanded the promise be kept. If Logan couldn't accept that essential truth about her and her people, he could never accept anything about them, including her love.

His glance shifted away from his wife, moving across the grassy meadow to where the stream rushed over the mountain ledge. "This would be an excellent location for the watchtower."

"There will be no watchtower built here." Without another word, she stomped away from the pool.

It took her a long time to get her temper under control once she found a comfortable place to sit among the tall grass and wildflowers that carpeted the valley floor. Tolman spread out her sleeping mat, giving her a reassuring smile as he placed the small basket that held her personal items on the ground within her reach.

"Lord Logan is still new to our ways," the servant reminded her.

"Do you think he will get any less stubborn once he realizes he's looking for something that doesn't exist?" Zara asked hopefully.

Tolman grinned. "No. Do you?"

"No."

Logan turned abruptly when his wife's laughter echoed off the cliffs that surrounded them on three sides. He saw her, sitting on the sleeping mat. Tolman was standing by her side. The old servant was pleased with himself as his lady wiped humorous tears from her eyes.

By the stars, Logan wished he could understand his wife and her simple but complex people. On the outside, Nubria looked like an uncomplicated world that shunned technology. In reality, it was the most multifaceted society he'd ever encountered. There was no singular political system, no social hierarchy, except that of their queen, no military, and no rules, except those of common decency and courtesy. Their laws, both civil and religious, were simple enough for a child to understand: nothing harmful was to be done to anyone.

Chaos should rule this world, not a beautiful woman. Yet chaos was nowhere to be found. Nor was greed, ambition, or selfishness.

Nubria was indeed Utopia, if it could be judged by the same standards that measured the rest of the galaxy. But Utopia didn't exist. It was a figment of men's imagination, a fantasy that had led generations of people to explore the galaxy, searching for an excellence that was forever elusive.

Logan shook his head as he began walking the perimeter of the valley, gauging the distance between the vine-covered cliffs and the cascading waterfall, sorting out the complexities and simplicities of the world he now ruled as king. There was no comparing Nubria to the other worlds in the galaxy, no common ground that united them other than their allegiance to the Unity Council. Yet this world was part of a larger one, a federation of planets that had sworn to uphold one another in times of peace and war. He couldn't forget that elemental bond. It was the reason he'd been sent to Nubria in the first place, and it was the reason he would remain here, married to a woman who was both the mystery and the solution. The question and the answer.

Everything Logan knew and everything he had yet to learn were all contained in the woman he had married. She was the guiding force of her planet, yet she followed rather than led, her steps guided by an invisible faith that seemed as elusive as utopian perfection.

As the afternoon sun shone down on the rippling pool of water, Logan heard the call of one of his guards. Maddock waved his arm, calling his commanding officer to the place where the narrow path began winding back down the mountain.

"We have visitors," the second in command announced as Logan joined him.

"Who?"

"Nubrians," Maddock told him. "It looks like several dozen."

"Pilgrims," Logan suggested with suspicion in his voice.

Before the other soldier could render an opinion, the visitors came into view. Like the village people they'd left behind, these Nubrians were dressed in loose-flowing tunics and homespun leggings. With leather sandals and wide-brimmed hats to shield their faces from the heat of the sun, they climbed steadily upward, toward the crystal pool where their queen would offer a moonlight blessing.

Men, women, and children of assorted ages followed the path their beloved queen had taken earlier that morning. Some carried woven baskets, some small reed mats upon which they would kneel as their voices joined the voice of their faith's high priestess.

From the top of the path, Logan could see more visitors appearing out of the forest. They walked single file up the narrow trail, their faces alive with hope and the same contentment Logan had noticed on the faces of his own men.

His mind, always diligent of his duties, wondered how quickly that contentment would vanish when the soft-spoken Nubrians came face-to-face with an invading army of Pharmons. Logan realized just how important it was to protect these people, his people, from the dark forces that propelled the Pharmon Empire beyond its borders, even if his wife didn't.

Zara never spoke of what she'd seen on Rysor, but Logan knew she hadn't forgotten the young girl the Pharmon slave trader had put up for auction.

"Double the guards," Logan told Maddock. "I don't know where these people came from. Keelan could have one or more of his men mingled among them. Stay alert."

By the time darkness fell, the mountain valley was crowded with pilgrims. Nessa moved among the people, thanking them for their offerings of food and spiced wine, reassuring them that their lady was content with the husband who had been forced upon her by the Unity Council.

Logan stood in the shadows of the northernmost cliff, watching his wife as she brushed her hair and prepared for an evening of prayers. Unlike most religious ceremonies he'd witnessed, Zara's faith didn't require elaborate robes and precious artifacts. She walked to the rim of the crystal pool the same way she'd walked there earlier in the day. This time she was dressed in a soft gown of blue silk that shimmered in the moonlight. Her feet were still bare. She sat down on one of the smooth rocks that rimmed the pool, then put her feet into the cool churning water. Once they had been washed clean of dirt and grass, she held on to Nessa's hand until a prayer mat had been placed on the ground.

Zara stepped onto the mat and raised her arms toward the silver moons suspended in a starless sky. Behind her the pool reflected the moonlight like a liquid mirror. When his wife's voice broke the fragile silence of the night, Logan felt his chest muscles tighten around his heart.

The night was warm and balmy, the wind blowing with a gentle force that belied the strength of the mountains it caressed. Nubrians moved to surround their queen, forming a circle around the young woman who was offering a prayer to the silent heavens.

Logan's eyes searched the faces of the faithful, looking for anyone who didn't belong to the faith, but he saw nothing unusual. Slowly, as Zara's voice filled his ears, his gaze moved beyond the crowd to the shadows that circled the mountain valley, then to the left and right, scanning the granite cliffs.

He saw the animal perched on the top of the highest cliff, its sleek body almost as black as the night that provided natural camouflage for a stalking hunter.

Logan knew he was looking at a *juna*. The big cat was resting on its haunches, its wide, thick tail curled up behind it. But it was the animal's eyes that held Logan's attention. They burned like amber fire, deep and golden and as round as an owl's. Sharp, predatory eyes that saw through the darkness as easily as its razor-sharp white teeth could chew through a man's flesh.

A thick pink tongue came out, then disappeared, as the *juna* stretched out on its belly with its wide, padded paws in front of it. Raw power radiated from the animal as its powerful muscles relaxed and its sleek ebony coat soaked up the moonlight.

If this was the big cat his wife had scratched behind the ears, it was little wonder that the people had built an altar to honor her. The *juna* wasn't a domesticated animal; its wildness was easy to see and to respect. Teeth created to bite through bones, and muscular limbs designed to chase down prey, made it the perfect predator. But the animal didn't look hungry. It looked curious, as if Zara's words might hold some special blessing only the big cat could understand and appreciate.

Logan kept his hand near his laser pistol just in case the *juna* let its curiosity get the best of it. As his wife's prayer progressed, more cats joined the first, until the entire pride was perched at the edge of the cliff and a dozen amber eyes pierced the darkness.

Slowly Logan's attention was drawn away from the visiting *junas* and back to his wife. She was kneeling on the mat this time, her body wrapped in moonlight, her eyes closed, her mouth barely moving as she recited words that were too old for anyone to remember who had spoken them first.

Just as the moonlight enwrapped his wife, Logan felt her voice bathing his thoughts with images he knew wouldn't go away until he had sated his need for her. Tonight he wasn't going to be content to merely hold Nubria's queen in his arms.

Grass, dampened by the night air, made no sound under Tolman's feet as the servant came to stand beside Logan. No words were exchanged between the two men as they stood and listened to Zara's voice rising and falling on the gentle breeze like a bird floating through the sky. The ancient words seemed to hang weightlessly in the air as a young woman stepped out of the crowd.

Logan's eyes moved over the Nubrian female. She was pregnant, her abdomen swollen by the child growing inside her. He continued watching as Zara reached out her hands and placed them on the woman's enlarged belly.

A smile preceded his wife's announcement that the child would be a son.

"Solon told me she'd never been wrong," Logan said to the old man standing beside him.

"Our lady is gifted with a knowledge few can fully understand," Tolman replied. "The child will be male. His mother will smile while his father struts with pride."

Logan gave him a sideward glance.

"What more could a man want than a gentle woman and strong sons?"

What more could a man want?

Logan felt his body tighten in anticipation of the day when Zara's body would swell with his child. Would she be able to lay her hand upon her expanding abdomen and tell if a son or daughter was growing inside? Did her mystical powers apply to herself, or only to others?

His gaze was drawn to his wife as a renewed determination to keep her and her world safe flared within him. His children, sons or daughters, would know the peace of this world. He would make sure of it.

As Zara came to her feet, she turned her thoughts away from her prayers and onto the people circling the woven mat. On the outer rim of the mental spiral, she sensed her husband. As was his custom he was standing in the shadows, his mind filled with doubts and worry that would disappear as easily as a morning mist if he opened his heart to what was all around him.

Zara exchanged pleasantries with her people, accepting their blessings as genuinely as she gave hers in return. The women moved away from the pool to a flat place in the grass where Nessa had spread out a blanket. There under the dual moons that gleamed like silver eyes in the black face of the night, a meal was prepared. Bread and cheese and wine were handed out to the men and guards, while the children dined on sweet fruits and crunchy nuts harvested from the forest.

Patricia Waddell

Finally, when the hour was late and the pilgrims had all sought their sleeping mats, Logan found his wife sitting by the edge of the pool. She was alone, but instead of the fatigued face he'd expected to find, she looked rested and more lovely than he'd ever seen her before. Moonlight and shadows suited her almost as well as the sunlight of early morning.

"It is time to rest," he said, holding out his hand. "Come. Tolman has found a soft bed of grass where we can sleep, away from snoring guards."

As Zara accepted his assistance in coming to her feet, she knew her husband hadn't instructed the servant to place their sleeping mat in a distant corner of the valley because he feared Maddock's snores would keep her awake. Logan's dark eyes glowed with the desire he'd held in check for the last four days.

"I have a better idea," she whispered, placing a fingertip against his mouth to keep him from arguing. "Follow me, lord husband."

Logan let his wife lead him around the perimeter of the pool. Maddock gave the signal that all was clear as his commanding officer passed his post. Logan nodded in return, but his mind was on Zara, and what she had in mind. A few feet in front of them water poured down the face of the cliff like a silver storm. Placing her bare feet on the water-drenched rocks, Zara moved cautiously to the left of the waterfall.

"You might get wet," she said over her shoulder as she got closer to the thundering rush of water. "Be careful."

Logan had the natural balance of a cat. Holding on to his wife's hand he stepped up onto the rocky ledge that skirted the mountain pool. He held his breath as his wife moved behind the liquid curtain and into the stone grotto that nature had honed out of the mountain eons before.

The cave wasn't dark. A ring of candles burned around a small tranquil pool. The rock walls were as smooth as tile, with etchings of animals and exotic plants carved into the white granite. The candlelight gleamed off the water like gold. Logan saw the sleeping mat spread out on the packed earth at the far end of the grotto and smiled.

"This is my private retreat," Zara told him. "Nessa brought the candles and the mat when you weren't watching. She knows I enjoy the privacy of the grotto after being with my people."

"Are you fatigued from your prayers?" Logan asked, hoping his wife felt as energetic as she looked. He wasn't in the mood for sleep. The soft thunder of the waterfall masked any sounds that came from the meadow, just as it would hide any groans of pleasure that came from the candlelit grotto.

"A blessing isn't like a prayer circle," Zara said, slowly easing her hand free of his grasp. "My mind isn't weary."

"Nor your body?"

A soft smile came with his wife's answer. "No, lord husband. My body needs only the warmth of your arms."

Logan didn't waste any time reaching for the buttons on his uniform. He always wanted his wife, but tonight there was an urgency in his movements that said he was close to the point of completely losing his self-control.

"The water is pleasant," Zara said, moving away until she stood on the opposite side of the small oval-shaped pool. "And warm."

"Warm?" Logan queried as he unbuckled his sword belt and laid it aside but still within reach if he needed it. Next came his pistol harness. He was sitting down to take off his boots when he saw that Zara had shed the blue gown.

His breath lodged in his chest. She stood at the rim of the water wearing nothing but silver hair, a wedding amulet, and the most beguiling smile Logan had ever seen on a woman's face. Without a word, she stepped into the pool.

He watched as the water licked at her ankles, then her calves, then slowly moved upward, caressing her ivory thighs. She stopped and held out her hand, silently beckoning him to join her.

Logan cursed the eternity it took him to get his uniform off.

He felt his breathing quicken at the seductive expression in his wife's compelling violet eyes. His gaze dipped down to where the water lapped at her belly, teasing the underside of her breasts but not covering them. Logan felt the throbbing of his own body and the strength of his arousal as he stood tall and naked in front of her.

With deliberate slowness, because he wanted to make the sensual, silent foreplay between them last as long as possible, he stepped into the pool. Warm water circled his feet, and his mind briefly registered that this small swimming area was created by an underground spring. The water from the smaller pool mixed with the water of the larger outer pool to create the narrow stream that ribboned its way across the valley, then over the edge of the mountain.

The warm water heated his body, while the look on his wife's face heated his blood.

If Nubria's queen was set on seduction, Logan was her willing victim.

He was achingly aware of the perfection of his wife's body as she slowly moved through the water, staying just beyond his reach. Not being able to touch her was an exquisite form of torture, but one he could endure, knowing that the final reward was well worth the wait. What he didn't know was that Zara had more in mind than seduction.

When she was as far away from Logan as the small pool allowed, she stood still in the water, letting her hands caress its crystal surface. All around her the pale walls of the grotto reflected the flickering light coming from the dozen candles old Nessa had left behind. The only sound was the gentle rumble of rushing water in the outer pool as she looked at the man she loved. Naked, Logan was a formidable sight. His body was hard and muscular, the body of a warrior. His facial expression was almost fierce, and Zara realized that if she wasn't careful her well-laid plan would go awry. Her husband wasn't a patient man.

The pilgrimage wasn't over, and the crystal pool was the last place where they could escape the prying eyes of her husband's guards. Once they left the mountain valley, they would be passing through several small villages. If she dared to reach for her husband's heart, it would be here, where there was nothing to disturb the link but their private thoughts and the gentle movement of bubbling water as it escaped through the rocky surface beneath their feet.

Nessa had told her that this grotto had been her mother's favorite place. Here, she had ceased being Nubria's queen and high priestess and been just a woman, just a wife. This was the spot, according to old Nessa, where Zara had been conceived. She prayed she would receive the same blessing. She wanted Logan's child.

"What are you thinking?" Zara asked softly.

Logan grimaced at the sensual pain that was gripping his body. The water deepened as he moved to the center of the pool. "What do you think I'm thinking?"

Zara gracefully dodged his outstretched hand and began circling the pool. Her body, gliding gracefully through the water, created tiny waves that licked at Logan's bare middle. The water caressed them both, the way they longed to caress each other.

"I've never been one for sensual games. But I'm enjoying this one," Logan said, delighted that his wife wasn't content to merely lay under him. Still, the anticipation of sealing their bodies together was making him ache.

"It isn't a game," Zara said "It's a lesson."

"A lesson," Logan said through gritted teeth. He stared

at his wife, his eyes as dark as the night that enveloped the mountain valley just beyond the waterfall. "Do I need lessons to please you?"

"No." She smiled another bewitching smile. "The lesson isn't one of lovemaking. It's one of trust."

"Trust?"

"You asked me to trust you when it came to the watchtower," Zara said, still moving through the water, staying just beyond the reach of her husband's hands.

She knew Logan had the speed and strength to catch her if she tried to leave the pool, but she also knew he wanted her enough to have his patience tested to the limit. For once in her life, Zara was willing to use her female powers to her own advantage. She wanted to open Logan's mind a little at a time, to teach him to trust her womanly instincts the way he expected her to trust his male ones.

"I'm a soldier," Logan reminded her. "Defending this planet is my responsibility."

"And your right."

Her words surprised him, but not as much as what she said next. "I'm willing to trust you and your ability to protect my world if you're willing to trust me until the sunlight chases the moonlight from the sky."

Hesitation showed in her husband's eyes as he watched her. Trust wasn't something he gave easily. Finally, he gave in. "I'll trust you until sunlight calls us from our bed," he told her. "Now stop running away from me. Come here."

"Not yet," Zara said teasingly, then sat down in the water.

It took Logan a moment to realize that she was sitting on a rock ledge beneath the water. Her breasts were hidden from his view. All he could see was her naked shoulders and silver hair floating on the water around her. When she licked her lips, he gritted his teeth again.

"Sit down," she said. "The ledge circles the pool."

"Here," Logan asked, disgruntled. "Too far away to touch you."

Zara nodded. Logan's lack of patience was her biggest obstacle at the moment. When he wanted her, he was used to reaching for her and having her come willingly into his arms. He wouldn't be content to sit idle for long.

"Close your eyes," she instructed him, once he was submerged in the crystal pool. The water licked at the round male nipples on his chest and Zara smiled. "Please."

"This is going to put you in my debt for a very long time," Logan warned her. He shuddered heavily as the water moved over his body, its warmth and liquid movement heightening his arousal until he thought he'd come then and there. He wasn't sure how long he could endure his wife's bewitching idea of foreplay.

"I'll pay the price," Zara replied, wondering if her husband had any idea just how high the price would be if she couldn't convince him to trust her. "Now close your eyes. And no peeking."

"I don't peek," Logan grumbled.

"Relax," she said. "Take a deep breath and feel the water."

Logan remained as quiet as the stone walls of the grotto.

"The water's warm and liquid and soothing," Zara said. "I can feel it moving over my body like your hands, touching me everywhere."

Logan said a swear word he'd learned on Rysor. "If this is supposed to prepare me for lovemaking, then I'm as prepared as I've ever been in my life."

"It's supposed to relax you," she explained.

Logan opened his eyes and gave her a fierce glare that said she'd lost her mind.

"You're peeking."

His eyes closed as tightly as his clenched jaw. His arms were raised and extended outward, over the rim of the pool. Zara could see that his fists were clenched as well.

Patricia Waddell

"Forget about making love to me," she said, then paused, expecting a roar of outrage. When none came, she spoke again. Her voice was as soft as the candlelight dancing on the water. "Think of the water, its fluid motion, its warmth. Take a deep breath, and as you breathe, let your thoughts run out of your mind and into your body. Let the water ease away everything but the sound of the waterfall and my voice."

She watched her husband to see if he began to relax. Slowly his fisted hands came undone and his fingers stretched out. It was a start.

"I've got my eyes closed, too," she told him. "I can hear the water pouring off the cliff. I can hear it bubbling as it meets the outer pool. I can feel the rhythm of it soothing my senses. Can you hear the same thing? Do you feel the same thing?"

"Yes."

The gruff answer brought another smile to Zara's face.

"Are you trying to hypnotize me? Is that how you tamed the *juna*? I warn you, I'm not a big cat who wants to curl up at your feet. I'm a man who's hungry for his wife."

"And I'm a wife who's hungry for her husband."

They opened their eyes at the same time. They stared at each other from across the expanse of the grotto pool.

"Make love to me with your mind," Zara challenged him. "Tell me what you're feeling, how you're feeling it. Then make me feel what you're feeling."

Chapter Eighteen

"What!" It was the only thing Logan could think to say.

Zara dared to tell him what she could. "You've been told I have a gift," she began. "I do. But it isn't my gift alone. Everyone has the same ability I do. It's there, inside your mind. Most people don't use it because they aren't aware that it exists."

"Are you saying I can read your mind?"

"No." Zara smiled. "I'm saying that if you open your mind to me, and I open my mind to you, we can communicate in a way that doesn't require us to touch."

Logan gave the idea some thought before replying. "Your brother told me that your gift wasn't telepathic."

"It isn't. Not exactly." She searched for a way to explain something that was second nature to her and almost incomprehensible to Logan, who she sensed was growing more skeptical by the moment. "Telepathy is mentally talking to another person. I don't talk. I sense things. I feel them."

When her husband didn't say anything, she knew he

wasn't satisfied with what she'd told him so far. "Remember the day you arrived on Nubria?"

"I remember," Logan told her. The warm water bubbling up from the bottom of the grotto's pool wasn't making it easy for him to sit still and listen, but he told himself patience was more important than sexual gratification. Especially now that Zara was willing to reveal some of her secrets.

"I looked out the window without knowing who you were, but when I opened my mind to the thoughts stirring about the courtyard, I found you. My mind *touched* your mind."

Logan remembered the moment. He'd felt as if someone had mentally tapped him on the shoulder. "You've touched me several times since then, haven't you?"

Zara nodded.

"That night in the village," Logan said in a low voice. "When we were making love. Something happened then, too."

"Yes," she replied hesitantly, knowing she didn't dare reveal everything. Not yet. Logan wasn't ready. But if she could make him understand the link that existed between them, he might be more willing to understand the link that existed between herself and the people of Nubria. That link was the key to everything he had sworn to protect and defend. "When I open a prayer circle," she went on, "I open my mind to the needs of the people around me. It's a very draining experience. That's why I need to rest afterwards."

"Are you saying that you were too weak to stop what happened between us."

"Something like that," she replied. She needed to choose her words carefully. "My mind was still open. That's why the link between us formed so easily."

"I wasn't trying to get inside your mind," Logan said with a glint of humor. The smile on his face faded when he realized that if he had felt Zara's climax, she must have felt his in return. It was an unsettling idea. Could he have no secrets from this woman, not even the pleasure felt within his own body?

"Yes, I felt you," she told him, sensing the direction of his thoughts. "Just as you felt me."

"We were touching then," Logan reminded her. "I was as deep inside you as I could get."

Zara blushed in spite of herself. "Imagine a world where things that are felt and things that are thought merge. Thought and feeling become one and the same."

Logan wasn't sure he could imagine it. "I feel the water, but I'm not thinking about it," he complained. "They're two different things."

"Try to imagine they aren't," Zara urged. "Close your eyes and try to imagine a place deep within yourself where whatever you think can be felt, and whatever you feel can be thought. Your mind and body become one; your mind and spirit become one."

"I'll try," Logan said, closing his eyes.

Zara took a deep breath, then opened her mind. Like so many times, she mentally reached out with her thoughts, searching for Logan's mind, then finding it. It was just beyond her grasp, but it was there. All she had to do was coax him a little closer.

"Think about the water flowing around your body. It's warm. It's wet."

"Like you when I'm inside you," Logan whispered.

"Yes," Zara said, so softly the word could barely be heard. "I can feel the rock ledge under me and behind me. I can feel its texture, its strength. Like when you're inside me."

Logan flinched, then forced himself to relax.

Zara's voice became a sensual song as she continued talking. "I can feel the water moving around me, licking at my breasts, caressing my thighs. I can feel its pulsing energy. It's soothing but stimulating. Can you feel it?"

"Yes." Logan's reply was a low groan.

"You said you would trust me." Her voice was as gentle as the spring water that surrounded Logan's naked body. "Trust me enough to believe what I'm saying. Trust yourself enough to open your mind. I can't take your thoughts from you. They have to be given freely."

Logan remembered what old Nessa had told him the night Zara had collapsed on the prayer mat. *"What she does, she does freely, and with great love."*

Did he dare think that she might love him? Did he dare trust any woman enough to open his mind and invite her inside?

Zara felt Logan's hesitation. The doubt was hovering in his mind. Saying he trusted her was as difficult as admitting that he might feel more than physical desire. As much as she wanted to reach his heart, Zara knew she'd have to be satisfied with his mind, at least for tonight.

"Until the sun chases the moon from the sky," Logan finally said.

For a long time there was only the soft thunder of the waterfall and the soothing warmth of the grotto pool, teasing Logan's flesh like liquid fingers. The pool was a warm, wet blanket around him as he began to relax. The soothing current eased the tension from his body. The temptation to open his eyes and look at his wife was great, but he resisted it.

Zara had asked for his trust. How could he expect to gain hers if he wasn't willing to give his in return?

"Clear your mind. Listen to my voice," Zara said softly. "My voice. The warmth of the pool. The rhythm of the waterfall. Each different, but you hear them as one. Feel them as one."

The soothing sound of his wife's voice mixed with the soothing currents of the crystal pool and the liquid rhythm of the waterfall. Little by little, Logan emptied his mind of everything but those sounds and sensations.

Zara felt Logan relaxing, giving as much of himself as he could. The power of his mind was overwhelming and he wasn't completely committed to the link. If and when that commitment ever happened, she knew their spiritual communion would be the strongest she'd ever felt.

"I'm the water," Zara finally said in a soft whisper. "I'm moving around your body. My hands are liquid. They're touching your chest, your legs, your belly."

Logan's breath came in swiftly, then lodged in his throat. Pleasure rippled through his body as he felt his wife's voice as much as he heard it. He could sense the power of what was happening between them, the way he'd sensed it that night in the village.

Could he make her feel his voice in return? *"Make love to me with your mind,"* she had asked of him. Could he?

"No." Logan said huskily. "I'm the water. I'm moving around you. My hands are touching your breasts. My mouth is warm and wet and it's kissing your breasts, suckling them. My hands are touching your thighs, opening them slowly, teasing the soft curls between your legs. Feeling your silky heat."

"Do I feel like silk?" Zara had to swallow hard before she could ask the question. Her husband was a quick learner.

"You feel like silk to me. You're tight and smooth and—"

"And you're hard and hot," she said, interrupting him. "I feel stretched and full and yet I feel empty. I can't take more of you physically, but I want to. Oh, how I want to. I want to hold you inside me forever. I want to melt into you, until there's nothing between us. Until we're so close together, I'm you, and you are me."

Logan gritted his teeth. His self-control was vanishing. He'd never had a woman tell him how she felt when he was inside her body. His wife's honesty was pushing him to the edge. "When I'm inside you, I want to keep pushing to get even closer. I want to . . ."

"Shhh," Zara whispered. "Enough words."

Logan wanted to open his eyes. He wanted to see the

expression on Zara's face. He wanted . . . *I want to touch you right now,* he thought. *I want to feel your skin under my hand, feel it growing warmer with each touch, each caress. I want to . . .*

He stopped in mid-thought. Something was happening to him. The air around them was sweet with the scent of herbal candles. When he took another deep breath he could smell the metallic quality of the water pooling up from the ground. In his mind, he focused on the tiny bubbles that were escaping from the minuscule scratch in Nubria's outer crust. He could see them in his mind; then he pictured them floating toward the surface, twisting up and away from the smooth rock floor of the grotto pool. He imagined himself being that water, floating upward until he touched Zara's calf.

When Logan heard her moan softly, he knew she had joined his thoughts, and he slowed his breathing. *I'm touching you now,* he said without speaking. *You can feel my fingers moving up your calf, the back of your knee. You can feel my hands slipping slowly upward. Your thighs are warm on the inside, warmer than the water that's caressing them. But my hand is even warmer. I'm touching you. You're wet and slick. So hot. So soft. So giving.*

His body shuddered with the effort to keep his own pleasure contained.

I'm touching you Zara said without speaking. *My hands are against your back, holding you close. I can feel your heart beating as your chest presses against my breasts. Your body is hot. Hotter than the water in the pool. Harder. Stronger. It's pushing the sensation of the liquid away. All I can feel is you.*

As much as Logan wanted to open his eyes, he dared not for fear that the magic between himself and his wife would disappear. It felt like magic to him. He was touching her, feeling the silky texture of her response as his fingers teased and tantalized her. It was the most incredible sensation. Zara was across the pool, but she wasn't across the pool. She was with him, or was he with her?

Neither one had moved, yet they were together. Touching without touching.

The feelings inside Logan intensified as his thoughts intensified. He envisioned himself holding Zara against his body, his manhood cradled in the soft wetness between her thighs, his hands molding her breasts, as he kissed her. He tasted the sweetness of her mouth.

She moaned.

Was the sound inside his mind, or had it actually come from her? Was the sensation of sliding inside her real or imaginary?

He pulled her closer to him, raising her from the ledge. The water turned to liquid fire as he began to move within her, in and out in a slow rhythm that made her nails dig into his wet shoulders. Her knees buckled, but he held her upright. One arm circled her waist to keep her within his embrace while his other hand moved to the curve of her bottom, pressing her more intimately against him.

His face was buried in the hollow of her neck. His teeth bit her gently. She shivered in his arms. Another moan. No, a purr. The female sound made him push deeper, harder.

Her fingers combed through his hair. Her mouth was hot against his chest. He couldn't stop the rhythm his body demanded, pushing deeper, harder, with each thrust of his hips. Tiny convulsions gripped, then released him, as Zara's body demanded what his had to give. Her legs shifted, letting him go deeper. Her heat bathed him more intimately than the crystal pool. The heat moved through his body, curling tighter and tighter, until it exploded. Everything spiraled away from him. The sensation was electric, primal, reality, illusion. Colors and blackness occupied the same space. He was dying, but he was more alive than he'd ever been before. He couldn't separate his thoughts from his feelings.

The pleasure burst inside him, inside Zara.

His pleasure.

Her pleasure.

He couldn't tell the difference. They were one and the same.

Finally, Logan opened his eyes.

Candlelight was still flickering off the pale rock. Water still swirled upward from the bottom of the grotto pool. The gentle thunder of the waterfall still echoed in the air. And Zara was still sitting several yards away from him. Her eyes were open, their violet depths soft and velvety. Her face was flushed with satisfaction. When she smiled, Logan smiled back at her.

"Now you know," Zara said, her voice breaking as she regained her breath.

Logan fought for the control that had eluded him moments before. He'd had sexual fantasies before. All men did. This had been different. What had just happened between himself and his wife had been . . . he didn't know how to describe it. No language in the galaxy had the right words. The knowledge that he'd found satisfaction without actually touching her was embarrassing, yet he had made love to her. Reality or illusion, their joining had been as fierce and sweet as any they had ever shared.

"Why?" He asked a dozen questions with one word.

Zara's hand moved through the water, creating small waves that rippled across the pool to crest against his upper body. "I want you to understand me," she confessed. "This is what I am. It's a part of me. I don't put my gift on, then take it off, like a ceremonial robe. It's what I am. It's inside my mind and my body and my heart."

Logan felt the magic slipping away as he wondered if Zara had ever shared herself so intimately with any other man. Mystical lovemaking didn't take a woman's virginity. Had other men shared his wife's mind? He knew she could sense the change in his mood, but he couldn't stop the thought from taking shape.

"You still don't understand, do you?" A stinging pain pierced Zara's heart. She tried to hide it, but she couldn't. Her senses were too open, too vulnerable.

Logan watched as the pleasure faded from his wife's eyes. "I'm trying to understand," he said. "It's another riddle to me. Never-ending circles. Making love to a woman I'm not even touching. Feeling things I shouldn't be able to feel, because someone else is thinking them."

Her husband was right. She was giving him riddles, pieces to a puzzle he couldn't solve with only a few small clues. She wasn't being fair to him, or to herself.

"I'm sorry," she said. "I don't know how else to explain it." She frantically searched her mind for a better description. She disliked having to weigh her words, choosing each one as carefully as Nessa chose spices for her stew. Above all, she wanted to be honest.

Slowly her eyelashes lowered, blocking herself from her husband's icy stare. She licked her lips and tried once again to make him understand without telling him too much. "Your mind sensed what I was thinking and turned those thoughts into physical feelings."

"I suppose it did," Logan admitted.

"My mind sensed what you were thinking and turned those thoughts into physical feelings, but I didn't have to work to do it. I don't have to concentrate. It's an automatic reflex with me. If I open my mind, it happens as naturally as breathing."

"I see," Logan said stiffly. "You've been taught since birth to accept this gift. To sharpen it until it's second nature."

"I suppose so." Zara shrugged. The elemental sound of water rushing from the overhead rocks into the outer pool filled the silence. Thoughts and images swirled inside her mind. Her ability to concentrate had been weakened by their mental lovemaking, but she wasn't immune to the power of her husband's thoughts. They circled her as effortlessly as the warm water that was bathing her body.

Logan sat silently across from her. His body was sated, but his mind was full of questions. She could feel them bombarding the link, making it tremble.

"Come here," he finally said.

Zara moved toward him, the water parting, then flowing gently around her body, caressing all the places Logan had touched with his mind. Candlelight gleamed and flickered, the flames too weak to do more than cast the grotto in a soft amber light that made her damp skin glow like warm sunshine. Her waist-length hair was a pale shadow on the water, floating out around her as she walked slowly into her husband's waiting arms.

"I want to hold you," he said. "Really hold you."

Zara couldn't be more pleased. Logan might not understand what had happened between them, but he wasn't angry over it. The gentle flow of the water eased the tension in both their bodies, and they began to relax again. Her husband's sigh told Zara that he was still trying to solve the puzzle.

"I'm not sure I like the idea of having someone else inside my mind," he said as his hand brushed over her damp hair and down the length of her body.

The heat of his open palm joined with the warmth of the grotto pool as Zara pressed a kiss in the hollow of his throat. His arms tightened, then relaxed. "You're distracting me again," he rebuked her in a husky whisper that had no sting. "I'm trying to think."

"Are you?" she teased. With an almost painful slowness her hands went from his waist to his chest, then on to his shoulders. "About what?"

"As if you don't know." Logan chuckled. His body was fully aroused. Although it had enjoyed their mental love-making, it wanted more. He wanted more. "You are a witch," he whispered against her moist lips. "But you're *my* witch. And tonight is the last night that will offer us any privacy. I don't plan on wasting it."

For once they were in total agreement.

Logan's arms came out of the water in a graceful, powerful motion that lifted Zara until she was looking down at his handsome face. She stared into his compelling dark eyes at the same time she sensed the wariness in his thoughts. He was holding them back, trying to keep them under lock and key. Respecting his privacy, she focused on other things. The strength of his arms as they held her high above him and the gleam of mischief in his ebony eyes as he slowly drew her back down, letting her damp skin feel every inch of his damp skin.

For a moment there was only the sound of the waterfall and their own breathing. Zara let her hands follow their natural inclination as she traced the thick muscles that covered her husband's ribs, enjoying the mat of damp hair as she drew invisible lines from one flat male nipple to the other, then slowly downward until her hand dipped beneath the crystal surface of the pool.

Logan smiled down at his wife, then grimaced as her hand found and teased the part of him that yearned to be buried in her silky body. He surged up out of the water, holding her cradled in his arms as he walked to where Nessa had spread their sleeping mat. He lowered her onto it, then stood over her, admiring the way the water droplets gleamed on her body like liquid jewels. Her eyes were closed, as if she was savoring the moment, and he wondered how much of his thoughts she could read. Did she know that every time he looked at her, he wanted to touch her? Could she tell that his desire was mixed with the pride of knowing that she belonged to him? Could she decipher the thoughts he couldn't understand himself?

As Zara slowly opened her eyes and looked up at him, Logan put his questions aside. Tonight wouldn't last forever, and he wanted to spend every moment of it with his wife, not with questions that could be answered once they'd left the privacy of the grotto.

Zara smiled as her eyes traced the muscular planes of her husband's wet body. His strength was more than raw, naked power. It was as elemental as the universe. Wild and untamed. As primal as the stars that glowed like untouchable tongues of light. She realized that he was perfectly suited to the profession he'd embraced as a young man. There was a savage quality to him, yet that savageness was tempered by intelligence.

Shivering in reaction to his wife's admiring gaze, Logan lowered himself until he was stretched out beside her, their bodies touching in all the right places. When he pulled her into his arms, she came willingly. Their lovemaking was gentle but intense, and once again he felt her mind pulling at his, her thoughts invading his head.

Nothing in his life had ever felt as right as it felt when she shuddered in his arms, her body holding his tightly inside her. Sensual images flickered like candlelight in his mind, and like candlelight brushed by a gentle wind, they were impossible to control. He saw points of light and valleys of darkness, he felt the mysteries of life as deeply as he felt its certainties, then all he could feel was pure satisfaction. A pleasure so deep it robbed him of his breath.

A short time later, Zara was content to lay in her husband's arms and listen to the rush of the waterfall and sounds that came only with the night. She yawned, snuggled closer to her husband's warmth and said, "I'm sleepy."

"I'm exhausted."

He had every right to be. They'd entered the grotto more than two hours earlier and they'd been making love, mentally or physically, ever since.

"Then put your thoughts aside and sleep," Zara whispered.

"Gladly," Logan said lazily. "But not until I've had one questioned answered."

"What?"

"The unborn child," Logan said. "Do you know its sex because you touched its mind?"

"Yes," Zara told him. "Thoughts are as male and female as bodies."

"Incredible," Logan mumbled just before he closed his eyes and drifted into the most peaceful sleep he'd had in years.

Chapter Nineteen

Over the next few days the party wound their way through the mountain passages and lush greenery that led to Mount Oberlin itself. Logan found himself constantly amazed by his wife's compassion and her ability to make the most casual experience something to be remembered.

By the time they reached the last village on their journey, he was still trying to understand the people he ruled and the world they lived in. All along their pilgrim's path, Nubrians had gathered to wish them well. Their food was provided to them on a daily basis, presented in artfully woven baskets, along with the fruit wine that was quickly replacing the whiskey Sherard had drunk daily since the battle at Medash.

As they traveled Logan had continued to notice the change that was slowly overtaking himself and his men. The Galactic Guards still remained cautious, alert to any sign of trouble, but the tranquillity of the mountains was difficult to ignore. Sleeping under the stars and awakening to the soft pink rays of sunlight that heralded each morning had a soothing effect on their war-weary nerves. As for their commanding officer, Logan found himself content to open his eyes and hold his wife's warm body even closer than he'd held her in sleep. Every night since the grotto, their mental link had grown stronger. He could sense that Zara enjoyed his touch, and because she enjoyed it, Logan found himself touching her at every opportunity.

Even now, walking toward the village elders who had gathered to greet them, he was holding his wife's hand. The memory of the thoughts they had shared the previous night, and again that morning, echoed in Logan's head as they entered the village. He peered down at his wife, dressed in a soft knee-length tunic and green leggings. With her silver hair flowing freely in the wind, she looked more like a woman enjoying an afternoon stroll than the reigning monarch of a planet.

Once the introductions were made, Maddock positioned his men around the village. Their final destination, a large stone altar near the summit of the mountain, was another day's walk to the north. The pilgrims would rest for the night. The King and Queen of Nubria would have the comfort of a farmer's hut, generously forfeited by its owner, while the guards and servants would be housed by various families.

A feast would be held that night in honor of the pilgrims, and once again Zara would conduct a prayer circle.

"What will you pray for?" Logan asked as he shut the door of the hut. The floor was made of grayish-white stones that had been chiseled, ground, and polished until they were as smooth as skin. The furnishings were simple, as were all things Nubrian. A large bed was covered by a colorful quilt, hand-stitched by the farmer's wife. Wooden platters of fruit, bread, and cheese had been left on the table for the queen's enjoyment. A bottle of wine sat nearby. "There is nothing lacking in this village."

"It depends on the people," Zara told him. "There are always needs. Disobedient children who have their parents concerned. Discord among the village elders. Nubria isn't perfect."

"It's as perfect as any place can get," Logan remarked. "And the most peaceful world in the galaxy. Which is what makes it a perfect target for the Pharmons. Don't forget that, lady wife. I haven't."

Zara didn't need to be told that her husband's thoughts rarely wandered far from the Pharmon threat he'd been sent to Nubria to deter. Silently, she wished it was different. But she couldn't deny what she'd seen and felt on Rysor. She was forced to agree with Logan. On a physical level, her people couldn't defend Nubria against the heartless greed of the Pharmon Empire. On a spiritual level, their faith could withstand much more than Logan gave them credit for, but even the most faithful of people needed a peaceful land in which to reside.

"What, no argument?" Logan teased her as he helped himself to a succulent piece of yellow fruit.

"There is nothing to argue," Zara replied. "One Pharmon merchant was enough to open my eyes to the threat thousands of them present. I haven't argued against the watchtower since returning from Rysor."

"No," he said simply. "But you've postponed it."

Zara shrugged, then opened the pouch that held her brush and personal items. The nearer they came to the last altar of their pilgrimage, the stronger the link between herself and the man she had married grew. Yet the more Logan shared with her, the stronger she felt his need to find Keelan. It was as if discovering the rebel was the final step in another journey, the last act in a long drama that had to be played out before the curtain could be drawn.

Reluctantly, Logan found himself wishing there was no

one on the top of Mount Oberlin but himself and his lovely wife. The more time he spent in her company, the more hours he craved to be with her.

He was too practical to think it was all physical. His wife was a woman who enjoyed physical pleasure, but she was also a woman with mental abilities that went beyond anything he'd encountered on other worlds. Knowing the effect she had on his own mind, Logan couldn't rule out the possibility that she could cloak the rebels and their whereabouts as easily as she reached out to touch his most private thoughts. Did her mental powers enable her to disguise the very things he wanted to see?

He had to be on guard around her if he expected to put an end to Keelan's rebellion. Unlike his wife, Logan knew that as long as there was breath in the rebel's body, the war would continue. Clandestinely at first; Keelan wasn't a fool. But one day the danger would surface anew, and war would touch the serene soil of Nubria for the first time in its history.

As much as Logan wanted the tranquillity and beauty of his wife's world to chase all thoughts of death and war from his memory, he couldn't forget the lessons his long years as a warrior had taught him. The watchtower had to be built before Keelan could establish a dialogue with the Pharmon Empire and its spies. The Pharmons weren't fools, either. If they had aid from within, conquering Nubria would be almost effortless on their part. Logan had no doubt that Keelan would sell his very soul if it meant breaking the unity of the galaxy council that had labeled him a traitor.

"What are you doing?" Zara asked as her husband flipped down the quilt on the bed.

"You need to rest," he said matter-of-factly. "I don't want you fainting again tonight."

The velvety tone of his voice didn't disguise the firmness of the order he was giving her. Zara walked to the bed, smiling all the way. Her husband wasn't going to be satisfied until she'd slept, so she slipped out of her tunic and leggings and crawled between the cool sheets. "Thank you," she said, feigning sleepiness as he looked down at her.

"You're welcome," Logan replied as he headed for the door. He wanted to talk with Maddock and Sherard before the feast. Despite his wife's soothing charm and beguiling violet eyes, his instincts told him something was amiss. Trusting them more than Zara's magical, mystical ability to confuse him at every turn, Logan exited the hut and went in search of his men.

Zara lay on the bed, her mind racing behind the defensive walls she'd had to build since divulging her true abilities to her husband. She hated being secretive, but Logan left her no choice. She couldn't let him discover the worry that had her guarding her thoughts and her words now that they'd reached the village. Soon he was going to discover that the rebel cruiser had crashed not a day's walk from the very bed upon which she was resting. When that happened, her husband would turn back into the grim, hard soldier who had marched into the throne room of Nubria's palace. The tenderness she'd nurtured in him would be replaced once again by doubt and determination.

She dreaded that moment as she'd dreaded none other.

"Where is my wife?" Logan asked of Tolman several hours later. He'd returned to the hut to find the bed empty and Zara nowhere to be found.

"I believe our lady is walking in the woods," the old servant told him as he hurried by. The village was a whirlwind of energy as it prepared for the feast. Tolman was directing the women and men who were setting the table and fetching bottles of aged wine from the underground cellar that kept it cool during the summer months. Tolman stopped long enough to give his lord a reassuring smile. "It is her custom to clear her mind before entering the prayer circle. Worry not. Nessa is with her."

Logan wasn't worried. He was angry that Zara had disobeyed him by leaving the safety of the village. He'd left specific orders that she was to stay inside the hut until it was time for the feast. Would the woman never learn to listen to him?

The village prayer bells rang out, reminding the people who occupied the steep mountainside hamlet that it was time for the evening meal to begin. Going in search of his wife, Logan was too busy controlling his temper to notice the fragile blossoms his boots crushed as he made his way from the soft meadow that surrounded the village into the thick wooded area that sheltered it from the winter winds. The sun was sinking rapidly behind Mount Oberlin, casting shadows among the dense trees and dappling the ground with tiny rays of pale sunlight that would soon disappear completely. By midnight, when Nubria's twin moons were full, the forest floor would be carpeted with a silvery mist that floated inches above the decaying leaves and thick undergrowth. The chirping of curious birds would be replaced with the haunting howls of the *juna* cats and the keen eyes of the nocturnal owls that slept in the treetops during the day.

Logan found Maddock first. The stout soldier was standing near a tree that was several centuries' old. The rugged bark was scarred in places, marked by the wild cats that roamed the mountains as freely as birds explored the amethyst skies overhead.

"Where?" Logan asked, keeping his voice low because Zara was nearby.

Maddock pointed slightly ahead and to the right. "Your wife and the old woman are talking. Mostly in whispers. I can hear them, but I can't tell you what's been said."

A quick motion of Logan's hand sent his second in command back to the village. He made his way silently toward the spot where old Nessa was conversing with her lady. With the instincts of a man who was no stranger to silently stalking his prey, Logan slipped close to the small opening in the crowded forest where branches entwined like lovers and it was impossible to tell which leaves belonged to which tree.

"Keelan wants to see you," old Nessa said to his wife.

Logan's back went stiff at the same time Zara turned tearful eyes toward the setting sun.

"I cannot," Zara whispered. "It's too risky."

Logan stood as motionless as the mountain under his feet. The thought of Zara betraying their marriage vows went through him as quickly as water through a sieve. Realizing that she might sense his thoughts, he pushed everything from his mind and concentrated on the sounds of the forest, animal and human.

"I have tried to explain to him that it isn't a prudent request, my lady, but he longs to see your face again. His body is strong, but his heart still bears the scars of what happened."

Logan felt something inside him turn to brittle ice, then break in half. So he wasn't the only man to fall prey to his wife's enticing charms. She held a special place in Keelan's heart as well. There was no consolation in learning that the other man was his enemy, a rebel he'd sworn to bring to justice.

The coldness inside Logan's chest chased the warmth of the setting sun from his body. The beauty of the forest was lost to him as he strained to hear every word that passed his wife's beautiful, betraying lips.

"You must make him understand," Zara said. "It is too dangerous for Keelan and the others to attend the blessing at the altar. They must stay hidden."

Her voice was as gentle as the wind that brushed the leaves aside, and just as treacherous to the man who was listening. Like the wind, betrayal couldn't be seen. It was an invisible deed that once committed left forgiveness

282

impossible. His wife's confusing faith couldn't explain or excuse her behavior. Zara had kept the rebel's location from him, denying him the answer no matter how gently he presented the question. Even now, minutes before they were to attend a feast to honor Nubria's new king and queen, Zara's thoughts were on the rebel leader. Her face was solemn, while tears were being shed for the danger her husband presented to her lover.

Logan no longer thought himself the first man to enjoy his wife's mystical lovemaking. He was certain that the same mental trap that had been set to snare a husband had been cast at least once before. He'd been a fool to think his wife's gift more than a well-skilled magic act. Her faith was a disguise for her own selfishness. She wanted no part of the Unity Council and its plans for the future, and she'd do anything within her substantial power to keep Nubria free of outside influences.

While Nessa and his wife talked about the dangers to Keelan and his band of surviving rebels, Logan felt the danger of Zara's action to his own heart. He'd come closer to trusting her than he'd come to trusting anyone since Keelan had misused their friendship. He'd been a fool to let down his defenses. He had no one to blame but himself for the disaster that was about to occur. And occur it would. If Logan had his way, there would be no more survivors, no men of tainted spirit to be brought to justice. At that moment, he hated Keelan with every fiber of his body. Whatever favorable feelings he had for his wife were pushed aside, along with the ferny branch that yielded to the pressure of his hand as he moved it and stepped into the clearing.

Zara closed her eyes at her husband's appearance and prayed for the strength she would need now that he'd heard Keelan's name. With a grace that belied the tension making her stomach clench, she stood up to greet him.

"My lord," she said as calmly as if she was greeting him in the palace courtyard.

Nessa stood by her side as solidly as the trees rooted in the forest floor, but Logan barely gave the old woman a glance. His dark eyes were focused on the young, beautiful woman who had betrayed him.

"Where is Keelan?" Logan demanded.

His voice sounded through the otherwise silent forest, rousting birds from their nests and echoing off the distant summit where a holy altar had been erected to commemorate a faith that held no truth for him.

Zara's breath wedged in her throat for a brief moment as her heart went wild with a storm of emotions. Every muscle in her body tightened as she opened her mind to Logan's thoughts. They were dark thoughts. Fearful thoughts. Bitter with the hatred he'd carried inside for the last five years, they put a sourness in her mind that she'd never before tasted. For the first time since seeing him march into the throne room of the palace, Zara came face-to-face with the soldier, the Galactic Guard who was capable of killing a man with his bare hands.

Nothing about Logan's voice or stance, or the angry glint of his ebony eyes, gave her hope that he'd be willing to listen to the words her heart longed to speak. Nothing about the anger racing in his thoughts gave her any hope at all.

"I asked where the rebels are hiding," Logan said with a cold calmness that made his wife grimace on the inside. "Tell me and I might be able to forget that an old woman and her Nubrian queen are traitors to everything I hold dear."

"There's no forgetfulness or forgiveness in your heart," Zara replied softly. "Think what you will, Lord Logan. A promise given by Nubria's queen is a promise kept."

Logan clenched his fists to keep from lashing out at the beautiful woman who had tricked his mind and his body into believing that love might exist.

"Look inside your own heart for the answers you seek," Nessa told him. "Whatever secrets you desire lie there waiting to be discovered."

"Enough!" Logan held up a fisted hand. "I've had more than enough of your riddles, old woman. Keep quiet if you don't want to find yourself chained to one of my guards."

Nessa's expression didn't change, nor did she waiver in her defense of the young woman standing silently before the fierce soldier. "My lady is right. Your journey has been only a few short steps. You have much to learn."

"I've learned that women can be as treacherous as men," Logan replied in a dangerous voice. "Come, ladies. Your feast awaits."

Zara didn't have to ask what Logan was thinking. He was too angry to shield his mind from her. She could feel the darkness. It reached out and wrapped around her like a cloak stitched from the blackest of fabrics. There was no light to be found as the sun sank behind the mountain, leaving the forest a mass of shadows and eerie shapes that changed with each fluttering of a tree branch. And there was no comfort in the painful thoughts that held her husband hostage, just as there could be no yielding of her mind.

Her promise must be kept. To betray it would be an even greater sin than the one her husband had accused her of committing.

The short walk to the village was a silent one. Nessa walked beside her. The old woman's thoughts were the only spark of life Zara could feel. Her husband had turned his heart to stone. There was no softening it now that he thought her a traitor.

What had she expected? Zara asked herself as Tolman hurried to join them when the dense trees gave way to damp meadow grass and a sky that was as starless as the deepest void of space. One look at her face and the servant knew trouble was brewing.

"Are you ill?" Tolman asked.

"No," Zara told him. "Only hungry."

If her husband thought to deny her the pleasure of taking food with the villagers, he didn't say so. Instead he motioned for Maddock and Sherard. When the two guards were standing by his side, he spoke to them in a language learned on a faraway world, words that Zara didn't understand. But she knew their meaning. Her husband was telling the two men that she wasn't to be trusted, nor were her servants. She was to be watched at every turn, lest she be given the opportunity to betray him a second time.

Zara felt the bitterness of Logan's thoughts grow darker with each alien word he spoke. A shiver of fear ran the length of her body. Not fear for herself or the people who served her, but fear for the man she had come to love. And love Logan she did. The emotion had stolen into her heart and mind alongside the passion until it was as much a part of her as the gift that had been with her since birth.

As if Logan could read her mind, his hand closed around her wrist and pulled her close. His mouth covered hers in a hard kiss that sent a breathless longing through Zara's body, but there was no love in the public affection he gave her. His mouth lifted and his voice lowered to the slightest of whispers as he warned her to stay at his side.

Since she had no defense against his distrust except a truth she had promised not to reveal, Zara gathered her composure and looked toward the feasting tables. Her people were waiting.

Telling herself that her faith was the only companion she needed, Zara moved toward the tables laden with food. Logan moved like her shadow. During the course of the next few hours, Zara began to understand how the small animals the wild *junas* hunted in the darkness must feel. She couldn't take a breath without her husband's watchful, distrustful eyes seeing the rise and fall of her breasts. Not a single word she spoke passed her lips without him hearing it. By the time midnight approached and the prayer mat was rolled out, Zara wasn't sure she could pray.

Her body was as tense as her mind, a jumbled, tangled web of muscles and nerves that wanted nothing more than to relax. But easing her burden wasn't something that was going to happen easily. Logan was intent on discovering the whereabouts of the rebels and he was convinced that she was hiding them.

Twin moons bathed Nubria's most sacred mountain in pale light. Nearby, the forest seemed to reach out dark fingers, as if it wanted to grab the open meadow where the people formed a circle around the mat where their queen stood with her back straight and her eyes closed against the constant hum of her husband's dark thoughts.

Slowly Zara began to turn, facing the northernmost part of the circle. Logan stood just beyond the mat, his feet firmly planted on the ground, his mind locked into thoughts of revenge. Like a diver balanced on the edge of a cliff, Zara lifted her arms high and wide in a gesture meant to embrace the silent truth of the universe. Here, standing in the middle of a prayer circle, she should be able to feel that truth.

But it evaded her, the same way it was evading Logan. No matter how hard she concentrated or how deeply she searched the darkness of the warm summer night, there was no truth to be found. The only thing she could feel was the bitter fact that Logan thought her a liar and a cheat. A woman who used others to her own advantage. A magical whore who had given her body but withheld her love.

Stop reaching outside yourself. The truth lies within.

Zara heard the unspoken words of her mentor the way she'd heard them countless times before. Nessa could feel her despair and she was offering what comfort she could with Maddock standing so close that his boots all but caught on the hem of her robe.

Taking a deep breath, Zara turned her attention inward, hunting for the faith that had always been a part of her. When she found it, a serene smiled crossed her face. With her eyes closed, she had no way of knowing that dozens of villagers smiled with her, or that one cold-hearted soldier yearned to put out his arms and draw her close.

Totally absorbed in the inner peace that existed within her own heart, Zara let the healing powers of her faith slowly erase the tension from her body. Logan had asked her what she would pray for when evening graced the meadow. Zara had planned to search the mind of her people, as she always did on a pilgrimage, but she knew if she let go of the inner peace she'd found, there would be no retrieving it. Instead of praying for the village and its inhabitants, Zara prayed for herself. For the courage to do what had to be done, for the strength to keep her mind from joining her broken heart as she realized Logan had stepped beyond her reach.

She couldn't touch a closed mind, a mind that refused to believe that love and faith and hope and trust existed so closely together that they were one and the same thing.

Chapter Twenty

Maddock started to speak, but a curt gesture from Logan cut off his words. It was just morning, that colorless time between darkness and dawn that the second in command had come to enjoy the most. The sun had yet to show its face above the horizon and the mountains were blanketed in a grayish mist that kept the light at bay. The night had been a long one, what with Logan pacing the village like a caged animal and his queen locked inside the farmer's hut.

Not a single sound had penetrated the locked door to tell him if Logan's captives were content or disturbed by the latch that had kept them prisoners during the night. The only thing that assured Maddock that they were still indeed prisoners were his frequent glances through the small windows that framed the doorway. Every time he looked inside the hut, he saw the same thing: Lady Zara kneeling on her prayer mat, while her faithful servants slept on mats near the far wall. Not once during the long night had the woman moved. Not so much as a finger of her graceful hand had twitched. She looked like a pale statue.

"Open the door," Logan commanded in a fierce whisper. Like his wife he hadn't slept during the night, and it showed. His temper wasn't to be tested.

The latch gave way under Maddock's agile hand and the door creaked open. Logan stepped inside and waited for his wife to stop praying and look at him. It wasn't a long wait.

Slowly but gracefully, Zara came to her feet. Her hair was unbound and Logan did his best to forget how it felt when it caressed his skin. A single look at her beautiful face said she was as stubborn now as she'd been when he'd ordered her and her faithful servants to be locked away until morning.

Barely able to contain his temper, Logan moved to where his wife was standing in the center of the room. Her feet were still bare, her eyes as clear now as they had been when she'd awakened by his side the previous morning, yet he knew she hadn't slept. He'd sensed her during the night, but he hadn't been able to let down his defenses long enough to reach out for the thoughts she had sent in his direction.

He didn't dare. There was no way he could be sure that her thoughts wouldn't somehow persuade him to forgo the justice he'd been sent to Nubria to serve.

"How far is the altar?" Logan asked.

Behind his wife, Tolman and Nessa were coming awake. There was no warmth in the eyes they cast Logan's way, but neither was there coldness. Like so many times in the past, the two servants simply watched as the drama between their queen and king began to unfold, each confident that Zara would be the victor.

But even the faithful servants could sense the difference in this confrontation. Their queen stood regally before them, her violet eyes staring at the man who could label her a traitor and steal her throne, turning Nubria's peace into chaos.

"You will walk by my side," Logan said stiffly. "Your servants will be guarded each step of the way. If you or those loyal to you speak a word or perform an act that alerts the rebels, it will not go unpunished."

"Those who serve me, serve only me," Zara told him calmly. "As for walking by your side, I have not moved away from you, but you from me. Know the difference, husband, if you know nothing else."

Logan gritted his teeth to keep from shouting the roof off the modest hut that had sheltered his wife. He gave the small cottage a surreptitious glance, then motioned toward the door. The village was waking up with the morning sun and he wanted the last segment of their journey completed as quickly as possible. Before Nubria's sun rose again, the rebel Keelan would be his prisoner. Logan could sense the victory as surely as he could sense his wife's displeasure at having her cunning little secret finally discovered.

Galactic Guards watched with wary eyes as their commanding officer and his queen stepped into the morning sunlight. Neither the armed men nor the villagers knew the turmoil that was brewing in their hearts, but they could sense it. In that moment there was no distinction between soldier and Nubrian farmer. Their differences were put aside as the regal couple walked to where a modest breakfast of fresh fruit and bread waited to be consumed.

In spite of the tension, the day broke over the mountains with its usual brightness, bringing Nubria's customary joy into full light. Children began to play in the meadow while their parents went about the daily work of coaxing their livelihood from the furrowed fields at the south end of the mountain valley.

It was a normal day, but unlike any day Logan had ever lived. Keelan was within his reach, yet he felt as if some-

thing much more precious was slipping away. The feeling
was an uneasy one that made his temper even more vol-
atile as they left the village behind them.

Ahead was a narrow mountain pass, lined with lush
greenery that concealed the purplish texture of the
mountains as sunlight streamed over them. The thick forest also disguised hidden trails and a honeycomb of caves
where rebels could shelter themselves against prying
eyes.

If Keelan planned an ambush, Logan was almost certain it would be on their return from the holy rock where
Zara would offer more prayers. While the people re-
joiced, the rebel would attack.

But Logan was too good a tactician to be that easily
outfoxed. He knew little of the mountains—that advantage belonged to Keelan, who had been hiding there for
months—but he was a soldier. The best the Guard had
to offer. And as a soldier he knew that an ambush could
be ambushed in return. By the time Nubria's queen
ended her prayers, Logan would know where the rebels
were hiding. He'd search every inch of the mountainside
himself if necessary.

Zara noticed the departure of Maddock and six of the
guards with total indifference. As they left the narrow
mountain pass lined with wildflowers and scented by
pines, she knew they wouldn't find what they sought. Neither would her husband.

The peacefulness that she'd finally achieved during
the long night was still with her. Sensing that her need
was greater than ever before, the nameless god of creation had answered her prayers by allowing her faith to
renew itself. As she walked, she moved with the genuine
knowledge that what she believed was right and true. She
also knew that Logan's heart would remain closed until
he opened it himself.

Until then, she couldn't allow her mind to be poi-
soned by the bitter thoughts that had taken control of

his. There were no words to undo the leash of hatred that was holding Logan's heart and mind captive. He had to set himself free.

"Were you Keelan's lover?"

The question was spoken in a low whisper meant only for her ears, and Zara heard it like crystal bells calling the faithful to pray. She stopped as the trail twisted and turned, constantly upward, leading them to the highest place on her world.

"Did you enchant his mind and seduce his body the same way you did mine?"

Zara looked at her husband with violet eyes that hid her innermost thoughts and pain. So Logan thought her more than a traitor. He'd labeled her a sinner of the worst kind, a woman who would set aside her husband for another man. The crime was almost unheard of on Nubria, but it was a rampant sickness throughout the galaxy, and one of the many reasons her people kept themselves segregated from the outer worlds.

"Whatever I shared with Keelan was given openly and honestly," she told him. "Think what you will of my answer."

"Then you don't deny it," Logan said in a voice so cold that it sent chills up and down his wife's spine.

"I deny nothing," Zara replied with a calmness that raised her husband's temper to the boiling point. "I have nothing to deny. Or defend," she added. "I am a Nubrian priestess. I cannot lie, nor can I nullify a pledge. Words from my heart fall on deaf ears. You don't want to hear them, so why ask them to be spoken?"

Logan clenched his fists, then motioned for her to begin walking again. The next few hours were consumed by a tense silence that left the beauty of the mountain gateway unnoticed as the pilgrims approached their final destination.

The valley that sheltered the sacred altar was narrow, ledged with high cliffs and dressed in wildflowers that were so fragile, the slightest rainstorm would shred the petals from their stems. The sky was clear above them, burning brightly through the purple clouds that drifted aimlessly across the summer sky.

As always, Nubrians had seemed to sprout out of the ground, swelling the number of people who trekked slowly up the narrow path that led to the altar. Logan's men were on full alert, studying each face, hoping to recognize one of the traitors who had followed Keelan into exile.

Zara noticed the diligence in Sherard's gaze. It was the same attentiveness that had been with him on Rysor, as if he expected to be attacked within the moment. Her husband was the same, his eyes scanning the horizon, his body tense with a soldier's readiness.

Zara heard the jests and teasing of the children as they ran behind their parents. She looked at a dark-haired little boy, then flashed him a smile. The boy waved at her, but before he could run to where she was standing at the edge of the mountain meadow, a man reached out and took him by the hand. The parent told him it wasn't polite to interrupt the queen on her pilgrimage and the little boy accepted the reprimand with a sad nod of his head as he was led away to where a group of children were waiting for their noonday meal.

Zara watched the children, wondering if Logan noticed them. Was he aware that they represented the future? Could the hardened heart of a Galactic Guard give guidance to the young or, like his own father, would he offer only military instruction and inflexible rules that required unquestioned obedience?

"Do you have any orders for the men?" Sherard asked as he joined Logan.

"Stay alert. If anyone acts suspiciously, separate them from the crowd as quickly as possible. Keelan is nearby. I can feel him."

The one-armed soldier didn't question Logan's instincts. It wasn't unusual for a warrior to sense the enemy before he saw him.

The moons rose above the mountain summit like two glowing dancers, floating on the wind. The illumination of the twin moons cast silver shadows all around the huge rock that stood silently in the middle of the high meadow. Logan's penetrating gaze moved over the large slab of stone. There was nothing unusual about the white rock. He'd seen hundreds like it during their trek up the mountain.

Another riddle, he mumbled under his breath. But his wife was still the greatest riddle of all. She'd walked silently by his side during the day, saying little unless spoken to, and when she did speak it was with words that did nothing to clear the confusion between them.

Logan refused to dwell on the discord that had existed since he'd heard Zara say Keelan's name with tearful concern. If she loved the rebel, there would be more tears to come. And years of regret as she found herself tied to a husband who had chosen for his loyalty to the Unity Council.

All around him Nubrians chatted leisurely while they gathered to watch their queen and the high priestess of their faith deliver the final prayer of her yearly pilgrimage. Faces looked anxiously in his direction, filled with doubts as to whether the stern-faced soldier could bring happiness to their beloved queen. Logan could sense their distrust, the same way he could sense the distance between himself and his wife widening with each passing moment.

From across the valley Maddock waved his sword. Moonlight reflected off the wide blade, telling Logan that nothing unusual had been seen or found during the day's search of the mountainside. Sherard signaled the same from the opposite end of the narrow meadow. Men had been placed along the trail to guard the only path a rebel and his followers could use to gain access to the holy gathering.

Logan himself had walked each inch of ground, his eyes surveying the cliffs for any sign of a cave or hidden passage that would allow an ambush to be launched or escape to be gained by men who no longer wore a Galactic uniform. He'd found nothing but the solid face of a rock mountain.

Since arriving at the altar, Logan had kept Zara at a distance. She was being watched by Maddock and Sherard, so no one could get too close to her. Not even the man who wished she would offer one word of explanation, an apology for her actions. As moonlight covered the mountain, Logan knew he was hoping in vain. Zara was too proud, too sure of her faith and what it demanded of her, to ask for his forgiveness. *A promise given is a promise kept.* The words echoed in his head, honoring her courage and dishonoring her vows to him at the same time. At least that was the way he saw it. As his wife, Zara owed him her loyalty above any pledge she'd made to the rebel leader, but she saw things differently.

The difference was enough to keep husband and wife apart for a very long time.

"The heavens offer their own blessing," Tolman said as he approached Logan. "Two moons in alignment. It only happens on this night. The night our lady gives thanks for her people."

Logan looked up. Tolman had spoken truthfully. Nubria's twin moons were drenching the mountain in a single stream of light that seemed to be focused on the large flat rock in the center of the narrow meadow. His attention returned to the crowd, then the young woman who began to move through it. Dressed in a white flowing robe, with her feet bare and her hair falling down her back, Zara walked toward the holy shrine.

Nessa walked behind her, carrying the pouch of prayer stones. The people in the meadow went silent as the pouch was opened and the first stone passed into Zara's waiting hand. Slowly, with a gracefulness that made Logan's body tighten with desire, his wife moved around the sacred rock altar, placing the smaller white stones in a perfect circle. As each stone touched the ground a prayer was offered to the gods that protected her world.

While her husband watched, Zara reached inside herself for the strength she needed to do what had to be done. Unless she could touch Logan's mind, they would leave the valley more like strangers than husband and wife. The fragile trust that had been forming between them was in danger of being totally shattered. She couldn't let that happen.

Hours of thinking, and praying, and sorting through her thoughts and feelings had ended with only one truth: She loved Logan. Realizing that truth, she also realized that he had joined the circle that was a love for all things Nubrian, a love for her people and their simple ways. Her love for life was now undeniably entwined with him. Her heart was his heart. Her mind was his mind. Her spirit was his spirit.

As the last prayer stone was placed on the ground, Zara turned to face her husband. He stood in the shadows, his body as straight and tall as the mountain, his strength of purpose just as strong.

Taking a deep breath, Zara opened her mind. Slowly she yielded her body to the mental powers that had always been stronger than the womanly form that contained them. She felt the power building within her, fueled by a need that was greater than herself and her people combined. The need came from generations past and generations yet to be born, centuries of time and millions of souls. Spirits of the universe that held no form filled the night sky over her head, whispering her name, and with each whispered breath giving her more and more power, enough power to reach out and touch another person's mind.

Her husband's mind.

Logan felt Zara calling to him. In the hushed silence of the meadow her silent call was like a scream for help. Dare he heed it? Thinking that it might be a trick, Logan fought the power of the link forming between them, but his greater physical strength was nothing compared to the power his wife was summoning against him.

Zara felt the power swelling inside her body, filling her mind slowly, until the power became a warm tingling beam of energy. Her voice lifted in the chants of her people, ancient words that called to gods long forgotten, yet at the same time she called to the man she loved.

Open your mind and see what I am, Zara called to him. *Open your heart to the words I cannot speak aloud. Look inside my heart and feel what I'm feeling. The sorrow of losing you, the warmth of the love that binds me to you, the fire of our passion. Look inside me and see all these things, my beloved.*

Logan shut his eyes against the visions that began to swim inside his head. Images of Zara's body yielding to his, flashing bursts of light and color, swirling pictures of laughter and love. But he couldn't keep the images from forming. He could hear his wife's voice, chanting the sweet music of her prayer at the same time she was whispering to him. *I love you. I love you. Love me in return. Trust me in return. Give to me what I am finally willing to give to you. My heart, my mind, my very soul. There are no walls inside me. No secrets.*

Logan forced his eyes to open, hoping that if he saw reality the mystical visions would cease, but they didn't. Instead he saw the meadow, glowing with moonlight, and the ancient rock altar. Just beyond it he saw Nessa, standing at the edge of the prayer mat, holding a young boy's hand. The boy had dark hair and wide round eyes. His face was as innocent as any child's face, yet it seemed strangely familiar. But while Logan's eyes saw the reality of the night, his mind saw something else.

The smoldering remains of a transport ship. Twisted

metal and burnt bodies. Smoke hovering over the mountainside. And voices. *"Promise me."*

The voice belonged to the past. It was a friend's voice. The voice of a traitor.

"Promise me."

"I promise."

Logan's body clenched with the pain that accompanied the words. It ripped through his gut as the falling transport had torn through Nubria's atmosphere. He could see Keelan's bloody body. And Zara's face streaked with tears. He could hear a little boy calling for his father not to leave him. He felt the despair of the dying man. Too late Keelan had realized that by destroying the present, he had ruined the future for his son. Visions of battles fought, images of regret. And love. The love of a father for his son.

"Keep him safe," was the rebel's final plea.

With a strength born of desperation and love, Zara kept the images flowing from her mind into Logan's. As her husband felt the pain of Keelan's last mortal hours, she felt them as well, reliving them as if they were just happening.

Her strength was almost gone; she could feel it leaving her with each breath that Keelan drew in her memories. Even as Zara crumpled to the ground, her mind forced one last thought into the link that had formed between her mind and her husband. *I love you!*

Logan sprang forward with the speed of the wild cats that inhabited the mountains. He held his wife against his chest, while his trembling hands gently wiped the tears from her face. His voice was shaky as he whispered her name over and over, calling her back to him.

But Logan wasn't the only one heralding Zara back from the mental fatigue that had caused her to faint. A small boy with tears flowing from dark brown eyes held on to her left hand, begging her to open her eyes, begging her to keep her promise.

"Keelan," Zara breathed out the name as the little boy's hands gripped hers.

Logan looked from his wife's pale face to the child. "What did she promise you?"

The little boy sniffled, then wiped his eyes with the sleeve of his tunic. "That she would take care of us."

Zara opened her eyes to see her husband smiling at the son of a traitor.

"I couldn't tell you," she whispered. Her body felt as weightless as the clouds drifting across the night sky. Sleep was calling to her as strongly as her husband's heart. Zara welcomed both of them with a smile.

"You didn't tell me," Logan assured her. "Not with words. You didn't break your promise. Not to Keelan, nor to me. A promise given on Nubria is still a promise kept."

Zara looked from the boy to the man who had finally learned to open his heart. *There are more children,* she thought weakly. *And wives who no longer have husbands.*

We'll take care of them, Logan said through the link that was still vibrating with emotion.

Things weren't so puzzling now.

Nubria's queen hadn't risked her throne to protect rebels. She was protecting children who carried their fathers' names. Women and children who had inherited a legacy of death and rebellion. Women and children who would be outcasts on any world but the one she had given them.

The size of Zara's heart, of her generosity, humbled Logan beyond words. What was even more amazing was that her heart still had room for him. Holding her, he felt at peace for the first time in his life. Loving her made him whole.

As he stood, cradling Zara in his arms, Logan's smile was there for everyone in the meadow to see. Nessa smiled back at him, while Tolman grinned, then hurried to prepare a place for his lady to rest.

Logan's face was concerned as he lowered his wife onto the woven mat. She looked so tired, yet he didn't want her to sleep. He wanted to share what he was feeling with her. Feelings that had been caged for too long.

Gently he covered her with a blanket, then fitted his body against her, content for the moment to feel the warmth of her resting against him. While moonlight covered the meadow and the people who had gathered for the blessing sought their own beds, Logan held his wife close.

"I love you," he said, feeling the freedom of the words spiral through him.

"I love you," Zara said. She took his hand, moving it slowly down her body until it rested on her lower stomach. "Can you feel what I feel?"

Logan wasn't sure what he was supposed to feel, but he forced his mind to relax. Gradually the link came back to life. With it came the realization that peace was more complicated than war and much harder to obtain. Faith was believing in things unseen. It was hope in its purest form.

As the link intensified, he was engulfed by soft colors and gentle sounds, a universal harmony that surpassed anything he'd ever felt before. He felt surrounded by love, totally immersed in its giving power. Then he felt what Zara was feeling.

A spark of life.

A child.

Dark warrior eyes filled with tears as his hand pressed gently against the tiny pulse of life he felt beneath his hand. His talents couldn't compare to those of the woman smiling up at him, so he had to ask. "A son?"

"Not yet," Zara whispered. "The House of Queens will have a new daughter to cherish."

Logan's kiss was as tender as the love he felt for his wife. "Then a son."

301

"Lots of sons," Zara told him. "With dark eyes and stubborn hearts just like their father."

"My heart isn't stubborn anymore," Logan told her. "It's too full of love."

Epilogue

"It doesn't look like a watchtower," Maddock said.

"It's not suppose to," Zara countered, smiling at her husband as his second in command studied the highest peak of the Oberlin Mountains. "Goldwren is an artist, not an engineer."

Logan laughed, then looked around him. The valley was growing green from the first rains of summer. Old Nessa was holding the newest addition to the House of Queens. At times, Logan feared that his daughter, Myresa, would never learn to stand on her own two feet. The slightest whimper brought every servant in the palace to her crib. Maddock was the worst. He'd taken to sleeping across the hall from the royal nursery the night of Myresa's birth. If any man had ever been wrapped around a female finger, it was this gruff old soldier.

As if she could sense her father's thoughts, Myresa chose that moment to stretch out her chubby hands toward Maddock. Once the transfer from Nessa to the Galactic Guard had happened, Logan's daughter wiggled her bare toes and smiled. Her eyes were the same violet color as her mother's, but she had inherited her father's impatient nature, along with his ebony hair.

Logan loved his daughter with the same unwavering love he felt for her mother.

"What do you think, Sherard?"

Nubria's king waited for Sherard to pass final judgment on the watchtower that had been constructed to protect the Union's easternmost border.

"It's different," Sherard concluded, wrapping his only arm around the thickening waist of his Nubrian wife, Ganece. The village girl smiled up at him, distracting her husband for a moment before he remembered he'd been passing judgment on the watchtower. When he turned to Logan, Sherard was smiling. "As long as the sensors give the alarm, who cares what they look like?"

Logan laughed. "It was either Goldwren's creative talents or my wife's constant bickering," he announced.

Zara slapped at the arm that was slipping around her, but her eyes were bright with love. "There's no law that says a watchtower has to be ugly," she told him. "Besides, the carvings are beautiful. You said so yourself."

They were beautiful. The artist who had designed their wedding amulets had cast his spell over the mountain as surely as Nubria's queen had cast her spell over the heart of a warrior. Instead of metal beams and ugly grid work, the mountain itself had become the watchtower. Goldwren had used the caves that naturally honeycombed the mountain to conceal the electronic equipment that could detect an invasion into Unity space. The summit had been skillfully carved and etched with ancient patterns, turning it into a shrine at the same time it concealed the sensitive instruments that would keep the Pharmon Empire on a leash.

Nubria was still a world of beauty and simplicity. The

Unity Council felt secure. There was harmony in the universe and in the hearts of Nubria's queen and king. Together they ruled a world that believed in love and honor and promises kept.

THE SHADOW PRINCE

JAN ZIMLICH

Adrik should be an honored prince of the Median Empire. Instead, he is sacrificed at birth to his father's lust for power. He becomes the property of a great demon, and is taught the ways of sorcery. Someday he will enter the Shadow Realm, trade places with his master, and be damned for eternity.

His black fate keeps Adrik from others. There is no solace for a man like himself. Then he meets a woman who streaks into his life like a dying star. The Arizanti priestess is everything he's ever dreamed of, and she sparks in Adrik a terrible desire for freedom. For the first time, he dares to hope that their love might overcome the darkness.

Mine To Take

DARA JOY

He is full-blooded and untamable. A uniquely beautiful creature who can make himself irresistible to women. With his glittering green and gold eyes, silken hair, and purring voice, the stunning captive chained to the wall is exactly what Jenise needs. And he is hers to take . . . or so she believes.

___4446-3 $5.99 US/$6.99 CAN

RAVYN'S FLIGHT
PATTI O'SHEA

Ravyn Verdier is on a mission to test the habitability of Jarved Nine. Damon Brody is sent to rescue her when the rest of her team is mysteriously killed. Trapped on a planet that harbors an unimaginable evil, they have only each other.

An abandoned city holds the key to their survival, but what they find behind its ancient walls defies all their preconceived notions and tests the limits of the bond that has formed between them. To succeed, they will have to cast aside their doubts and listen to their hearts. For only when they are linked body and soul—when they realize love is their greatest weapon—will they be able to defeat the force bent on destroying all life.

LORD
OF THE
DARK SUN
STOBIE PIEL

Ariana awakens a captive. Her ship has been disabled and her friends hurt, and she is to blame. She cajoled them into braving the outskirts of space. And now they are to be transported to a non-Intersystem planet where they will be slaves.

The world is bleak and shadowy, as are its inhabitants. And though these men are slaves as well, that hardly makes them less dangerous. Yet one rises above the others, and Ariana sees in him nobility. This is a prince in a barbarian's body, one who can teach her how to be wild. On this planet with its dark sun, Ariana knows he will help her survive. And she will show him a love that will last through whatever follows.

CONTACT
SUSAN GRANT

A BEAUTIFUL CO-PILOT WITH A TERRIBLE CHOICE.

"After only three novels, Susan Grant has proven herself
to be the best hope for the survival of the futuristic/
fantasy romance genre." —*The Romance Reader*

A DARK STRANGER WHO HAS KNOWN NOTHING BUT DUTY.

"I am in awe of Susan Grant. She's one
of the few authors who get it." —*Everything Romantic*

A LATE-NIGHT FLIGHT, HIJACKED OVER THE PACIFIC.

SUSAN SQUIRES
BODY ELECTRIC

Victoria Barnhardt sets out to create something brilliant; she succeeds beyond her wildest dreams. With one keystroke her program spirals out of control . . . and something is born that defies possibility: a being who calls to her.

He speaks from within a prison—seeking escape, seeking *her*. He is a miracle that Vic never intended. More than a scientific discovery, or a brilliant coup by an infamous hacker, he is life. He is beauty. And he needs to be released. Just as Victoria does. Though the shadows of the past might rise against them, on one starry Los Angeles night, in each other's arms, the pair will find a way to have each other and freedom both.
